"ELLIOTT'S SURE-HANDED AND SEDUCTIVE BLEND OF EXOTIC LOCALES, complex interstellar politics, intriguing cultures, realistic romance, and wonderfully realized characters is addictive. I want my next fix!"
—Jennifer Roberson,
author of *The Chronicles of the Cheysuli* and *The Novels of Tiger and Del*

"JARAN is an impressive first novel of interstellar empires and primitive cultures . . . a very strong debut."   —*Locus*

"Sweeps the reader along like a wild wind across the steppes. Tell Kate to write faster—I want to read the whole saga NOW!"
—Melanie Rawn,
author of the *Dragon Prince* and *Dragon Star* trilogies

"A new author of considerable talent . . . a rich tapestry of a vibrant society on the brink of epic change."   —*Rave Reviews*

"A bright new talent . . . complex politics . . . a wonderful, sweeping setting . . . reminds me of C. J. Cherryh."   —Judith Tarr

"Well-written and gripping. After all, with a solidly drawn alien race, galactic-scale politics, intrigue, warfare, even a crackling love story, all set in a fascinating world that opens out onto a vast view of interstellar history, how could anyone resist?"   —Katharine Kerr

HIS CONQUERING SWORD

KATE ELLIOTT

**THE SWORD OF HEAVEN:
BOOK TWO**

DAW BOOKS, INC.
DONALD A. WOLLHEIM, FOUNDER
375 Hudson Street, New York, NY 10014

ELIZABETH R. WOLLHEIM
SHEILA E. GILBERT
PUBLISHERS

"He, who the sword of heaven will bear
Should be as holy as severe . . ."

—SHAKESPEARE,
Measure for Measure

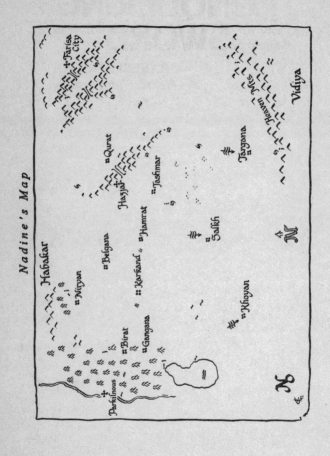

Nadine's Map

HIS
CONQUERING
SWORD

CHAPTER ONE

Aleksi could no longer look at the sky without wondering. On clear nights the vast expanse of Mother Sun's encampment could be seen, countless campfires and torches and lanterns lit against the broad black flank of Brother Sky. Uncle Moon rose and set, following his herds, and Aunt Cloud and Cousin Rain came and went on their own erratic schedule.

But what if these were only stories? What if Tess's home, Erthe, lay not across the seas but up there, in the heavens? How could land lie there at all? Who held it up? Yet who held up the very land he stood on now? It was not a question that had ever bothered him before.

He prowled the perimeter of the Orzhekov camp in the darkness of a clear, mild night. Beyond this perimeter, the jaran army existed as might any great creature, awake and unquiet when it ought to have been resting; but the army celebrated another victory over yet another khaja city. And in truth, the camp still rejoiced over the return of Bakhtiian from a terrible and dangerous journey. The journey had changed him from the dyan whom they all followed in their great war against the khaja into a gods-touched Singer through whom Mother Sun and Father Wind themselves spoke.

And yet, if it was true that Tess and Dr. Hierakis and Tess's brother the prince and all his party came from a place beyond the wind and the clouds, beyond the moon and the sun, then to what land had Bakhtiian traveled? To whom had he spoken? By whom was he touched? And how could a land as large as the plains lie up there in the sky, and Aleksi not be able to see it?

The stars winked at him, mute. They offered no answers, just as Tess had offered no answers before he had discovered that there was a question to be asked.

From here he could see the hulking shadow of Tess's tent at the very center of the camp—not just at the center of the Orzhekov tribe but at the heart of the entire army. Another, smaller shadow moved and he paused and waited for Sonia to catch up to him.

She rested a hand on his sleeve and he could tell at once—although he could not see her face clearly—that she was worried. "Aleksi," she said, whispering although they were already private. "Have you seen Veselov?" She hesitated, and he heard more than saw her wince away from continuing. But she went on. "Vasil Veselov. He came through camp earlier. He *said* he came to ask Niko about one of his rider's injuries, but I don't believe—" She faltered.

Aleksi was shocked at her irresolution.

"No one has seen him leave," Sonia continued. "And Ilya just came back. . . ." She trailed off and flashed a look around to make sure no one was close enough to hear, despite the fact that they both knew that they were well out of earshot, and that no one walked this way in any case. This part of camp, unlike the rest of the huge sprawl of tents extending far out into the darkness, was quiet and subdued. "The guards didn't see him, but you never miss anything, Aleksi." She waited.

A discreet distance beyond the awning of Tess's tent stood the ever-present guards, these a trio who had ridden in with Ilya. Aleksi had seen him arrive with a larger train and then dismiss most of them. Bakhtiian had gone into his tent alone.

"Oh, I saw Veselov leave camp," Aleksi lied in a casual voice. It wasn't true, of course. But Aleksi knew when to trust his instincts. Better that no one else realize where Veselov actually was.

"Thank the gods," murmured Sonia on a heartfelt sigh, and she gave Aleksi a sisterly kiss on the cheek and returned, presumably lighter in spirit, to her own tent.

It made Aleksi feel sick at heart, to lie to her like that, but he had learned long ago that orphans, outcasts, and all outsiders could not always live by the truth, though they might wish to. He trusted Tess to know what she was doing, just as she trusted him to protect her. No greater bond existed than love sealed by trust.

Aleksi touched his saber hilt and glanced up at the stars again. He wondered if Tess had not become like a weaver whose threads grow tangled: If the damage is not straightened and repaired soon enough, the cloth is ruined. Wind brushed him, sighing through camp. Songs drifted to him on the breeze, a distant campfire flared and, closer, a horse neighed, calling out a challenge. Above, in the night sky, the campfires of Mother Sun's tribe burned on, too numerous to count, too distant to smell even the faintest aroma of smoke or flame from their burning.

"We come from a world like this world," Dr. Hierakis had said, "except its sun is one of those stars." Could there possibly be another Mother Sun out there, giving her light to an altogether different tribe of children? He shook his head impatiently. How could it be true? How could it not be true? And what, by the gods, did Tess think she was doing, anyway? Did she truly understand what trouble there would be if it was discovered that Bakhtiian and Veselov had met together, secretly, even with her serving as an intermediary?

He cast one last glance at the silent tent and then began to walk the edge of camp again.

CHAPTER TWO

Ilya lay in elegant disarray beside her, breathing deeply, even in sleep marked by a harmonious attitude that drew the eye to him. A soft gloom suffused the tent. The lantern burned steadily, but its light did little more than blur the edges of every object in the chamber.

Vasil was one such object: the light burnished his hair and accentuated the planes of his handsome face. He lay on his side with his eyes shut, but Tess knew he was only pretending to be asleep. Somehow, not surprisingly, she had ended up between the two men. She traced her fingers up his bare arm to his shoulder.

"Vasil," she whispered, so as not to wake Ilya, "you have to leave."

He did not open his eyes. "If you were a jaran woman," he said, no louder than her, "you would have repudiated him, and never ever done such a thing as this. What is it like in the land where you come from?"

"In the land where I come from, there are marriages like this."

His eyes snapped open. He looked at her suspiciously. "Two men and a woman?"

"Yes, and sometimes two women and a man, sometimes two of each. It's not common, but it exists."

"Gods," said Vasil. He smiled. "Ilya must conquer this country."

"No," said Tess, musing. "It's a long way away."

"I never heard of such a thing in Jeds," said Ilya.

"I thought you were asleep! It isn't Jeds, anyway. It's Erthe."

"Ah," said Ilya. He shifted. She turned to look over her shoulder at him, but he was only moving to pull the blankets up over his chest. "Tess is right. You have to go, Vasil."

Lying between them, Tess was too warm to need blankets. Vasil reached out to draw a hand over her belly, casual with her now that they had been intimate.

"Not much here. You must be early still, like Karolla."

Tess chuckled. "Dr. Hierakis says I'm not quite halfway through. She says with my build that I carry well."

"*Dokhtor Hierhakis?* Ah, the healer. She came from Jeds."

"From Erthe, originally, but she lives in Jeds now."

"How can she know, Tess?" asked Ilya suddenly.

For once, there was a simple, expedient answer, and she didn't have to lie to him. "Because you got me pregnant after you came back from the coast with Charles. I know I wasn't pregnant before that. Ilya, if you think back, you know as well as I when it happened."

"I'm sorry I—" began Vasil, and then stopped. He withdrew his hand from her abdomen and sat up abruptly.

"You're sorry about what?" Tess asked.

"Nothing." He shook his head. Tess watched, curious. She had never seen Vasil at a loss for words before.

"You're sorry you weren't there," said Ilya in a low voice, "and you're sorry to think that I might have a life with my own wife that doesn't include you."

Vasil did not reply. He rose and dressed without saying anything at all. Tess could tell that he was troubled. She watched him dress, unable not to admire his body and the way he moved and stood with full awareness that someone—in this case she—was watching him. She could feel that Ilya watched him, too, but she knew it was prudent not to turn to look. Vasil did not look at either of them. He pulled on his boots and bent to kiss her. Then he stood and skirted the pillows, only to pause on the other side, beside Ilya. Tess rolled over.

The light shone full on Vasil's face. "Are you sorry I came here tonight?" he asked, his attention so wholly on Ilya that Tess wondered if Vasil had forgotten she was there.

Ilya regarded him steadily. "No." His gaze flicked toward Tess and away. His voice dropped to a whisper.

"No, I'm not sorry." Vasil knelt abruptly and leaned forward and kissed him. Lingered, kissing him, because Ilya made no move, neither encouraging him nor rejecting him, just accepted it.

Simple, ugly jealousy stabbed through Tess. And like salt in the wound, the brush of arousal.

Ilya shifted and suddenly he changed. All this night he had been astonishingly passive, going along with the choice Tess and Vasil had made as if he followed some long-set pattern, pursued acquiescing to his pursuer. As if that was how it had been before, between him and Vasil. Now he placed a hand on Vasil's chest and gently, with finality, pushed him away. "But it can't happen again," he said quietly. "You know that."

Startled, Vasil glared at him. "Why not? She said there were marriages like this, in that khaja land." He reached out to Ilya's face and splayed his fingers along the line of Ilya's jaw. With his thumb, he traced the diagonal scar up Ilya's cheek. "You are the only man marked for marriage in all the tribes."

"Oh, God," said Tess, recalling that moment vividly now. "And I was wearing your clothes and using your saber when I did it."

"So it is true," said Vasil triumphantly. "Can you deny it?"

Ilya closed a hand over Vasil's wrist and drew Vasil's hand away from his face, then released it. "It is also true that not twelve days ago a rider named Yevgeni Usova was banished from the army for lying with another man, with one of the actors. Shall I judge myself less severely than he was judged?"

"I was sorry to hear about Yevgeni," said Vasil carelessly. "But he was stupid enough to get caught."

"So we are to be allowed to continue as long as we are not caught? I think not, Vasil. I must be more holy than the riders I command, not less. Nothing else is just."

Vasil looked annoyed, as if he had not expected this turn of events. "So that is why after your family was killed, after the tribes agreed to follow you, you threw me out? That is why you stopped getting drunk? I remember after you came back from Jeds, how many women used to ask you to their beds and how very often you went. It is true, what I heard later, that you rarely lay with women afterward? After your family was killed? After I was banished? Were you punishing yourself? Is there a single piece of gold in this tent from any of the khaja cities your army has conquered? Once you questioned everything, you demanded to know why the jaran had to live as our grandmothers and grandfathers and their grandparents had lived, as the First Tribes had lived. Now you are the most conservative of all. Do you know who you remind me of? You remind me of the man who killed your mother and sister. You remind me of Khara Roskhel."

For an instant Ilya's anger blazed off him so strongly that he seemed to add light to the room. Then, as suddenly, he jerked his head to one side, to stare at the curtained wall that separated the inner from the outer chamber. "He was pure," he said in a low voice.

"And you are not? Because of me?" Vasil's tone was scathing.

Ilya hesitated. Tess had a sudden instinct that Ilya wanted to say "Yes, because of you," but that because he did not believe it himself, he could not bring himself to lie.

"Roskhel always supported you, Ilya," said Vasil, his voice dropping. "When we got to the great gathering of tribes, that summer eleven years ago, when we rode in to the encampment, he supported you. And then, the day you stood up in front of the elders of the tribes to tell them of your vision, he was gone. What happened there to turn him against you? Did he and your mother quarrel?"

The silence following this question became so profound that Tess heard, from outside, the bleating of startled goats. Tess realized that she was cold, and she wrapped a blanket around her torso. Vasil did not move, staring at Ilya.

"Yes," said Ilya in a clipped tone. He would not look at either of them. "Go, Vasil. You must go."

"Ilya." Vasil extended a hand toward Ilya, tentatively, like a supplicant. The gesture seemed odd in him, and yet, seeing it, Tess felt heartened. "You have always had such great visions, ever since you were a boy. What I want seems so small beside it."

"Yet what you want is impossible."

"It is because I'm dyan? I'll give it back to Anton. I never wanted it except to get close to you."

"You know that's not the reason."

"But I have children, and a wife. You have a wife, and soon you'll have children as well. What is to stop us continuing on like this?"

"You will never understand, Vasil. Only what I granted to the gods and to the jaran, that I lead us to the ends of the earth if need be, if that is our destiny. You aren't part of that vision. You can't be, by our own laws. I banished you once. I've already made that choice. Don't force me to do it again. Because I will."

"Damn you." Vasil rose abruptly, anger hot in his face. "I would have made a different choice."

Ilya's weight of authority lent him dignity and a sheer magnitude of presence that so eclipsed Vasil's beauty and charisma that Tess suddenly understood the desperate quality in Vasil's love for Ilya. "You are not me. The gods have touched me. Through my father and my mother, the gods chose to bring me here, so that I might act as their instrument. My first duty will always be to their calling."

"What about her?" Vasil asked bitterly, gesturing with a jerk of his head toward Tess.

"Tess knows the worth of my love for her."

"Yes," said Tess in a quiet voice, seeing how Ilya's shoulders trembled with emotion, and fatigue. "I do know the worth of his love for me. Vasil, you know what the answer is. You must have always known it. Why couldn't you have taken this night as a gift and let it go?"

She could not tell if Vasil heard her. But then, whenever Ilya was near him, the greatest part of his attention had always been reserved for Bakhtiian, no matter how much he might seem to be playing to others. "Let it be my curse to you, then," said Vasil, "that you always know that I have always and will always love you more than anything." He spun on his heel and strode out, thrusting the curtain aside so roughly that it tumbled back into place behind him.

"Oh, gods," said Ilya, not moving. He watched the curtain sway.

"You don't think he'll try to get caught on purpose—?"

"No. He knows I'll have to kill him. Whatever he may say, he loves his own life more than he loves me."

"Ilya." She reached for him. He flinched away from her. She stopped dead, and then pulled back her hand. He had never rejected her before, not like this. God, what if he really did love Vasil more than he loved her? What if she had misinterpreted the brief scene played out between them? But watching him as he sat there strung as tight as a bow, edged as sharp as any saber, she knew beyond anything else that he hurt. His pain distressed her more than the knowledge—which could no longer be denied—that he did in fact love Vasil and had for many years. Ilya was not rejecting *her;* he was rejecting himself, and thus anything that loved him and might yet scorn him for what he had revealed himself to be.

"I'm a damned hypocrite," he said in Rhuian. The curtain had ceased swaying, but he still stared at it.

Tess made a brief laugh in her throat. "Ah, Bakhtiian returns to the lands of the mortals. How unique you are. I'm sure you're the only person afflicted with hypocrisy."

He twisted around to glare at her. "You don't understand what that means!"

"What? That you're not perfect? But I've known that for a long time." She could see by his expression that she was offending him, so she continued gleefully. "Of course! Why didn't I ever see it before? Yuri always said so, that you thought you had to be the best. Kirill said it, too: that you always had to win. I didn't see then that it also meant that you had to be the purest one, the one with no flaws, no stain on your spirit, the one who never committed the slightest offense or the least impolite exchange. Do you know how boring that kind of person is? Why, I'm relieved to see that you're flawed like the rest of us. Even if it's only with so common a sin as hypocrisy."

"How dare you laugh at me!" He looked livid with anger.

"Because you won't laugh at yourself. Someone must. Since I'm your wife, I've been granted that dubious honor."

"The gods do not grant their gifts lightly, Tess," he said stiffly, "and with that gift comes a burden."

"Yes, a burden greater than that any other person has to bear. I'm well aware of it. I'm aware of it constantly, and it's beginning to weary me. It may even be true, but that still doesn't mean that you're any different than the rest of us. That you're any better."

"No," he said softly, still not looking at her, "I am worse."

"Oh, Ilya." This time when she leaned across to touch him, he sat motionless under her hands, neither responding to her nor retreating from her. As he had with Vasil. "You must know that I don't think it's wrong for you to love him. Only that I—" She hesitated. Their bed was a wild landscape of rumpled blankets, stripes and patterns muted in the lantern light, of furs thrown into topographical relief, mountains and valleys and long ridges and the far mound of her toes, of pillows, one shoved up against the far wall, two flung together at the head of the bed, more scattered beyond Ilya, and of his clothing, littering the carpet beyond. One boot listed against a stray pillow. His belt curled around the other boot, snaring it.

He said nothing, but his silence was expectant, and courageous, too; how easily he might think it would be natural for her to repudiate him, based on the morals of his culture, faced with what she now knew of him.

"He's just so damned beautiful," she said at last, afraid to say it, "that I can't help but think that—that anyone would love him more than . . . me. . . ." She faltered.

"Tess!" He spun back to her, upsetting her balance. She tumbled over and landed on her back, half laughing, half shocked, in the middle of the bed. "You're *jealous* of him!"

"Why shouldn't I be?" she demanded, rolling up onto her side. He rested on his elbows a handbreadth from her, staring astonished at her. "You've known him a long time, much longer than you've known me. It's obvious you still love him. All that keeps you apart is that the jaran don't recognize, don't accept, that kind of love."

"That is not all that keeps us apart, my heart," he replied gravely, but humor glinted in his eyes as well. "I loved him with a boy's awkward, headlong passion. But you," his gaze had the intensity of fire on a bitter cold night. "You I love like. . . ." He shook his head, impatient with words. When he spoke again, he spoke in his autocratic tone, one that brooked no disagreement. "You, I love." As if daring her to take issue with the statement or the nakedly clear emotion that burned off of him.

Tess was wise enough simply to warm herself in the blaze, and vain enough to be gratified by it. She had heard what she had hoped to hear, and she knew him well enough by now to know he spoke the truth. Vasil was certainly more beautiful than she was, or could hope to be, but he was also the most self-centered person she had ever met. And she suspected that Vasil's attraction to Ilya was likely not so much to Ilya as a person, as Ilya, but to Ilya as the gods-touched child, to Bakhtiian, the man with fire in his heart and a vision at the heart of his spirit.

"Still," she asked suddenly, "if it was possible, would that tempt you? A triad marriage?"

He rolled his eyes and sat up, sighing with exasperation. "All you women ever think about is lying with men." He surveyed the remains of the bed with disgust and rose and set to work straightening out the blankets and placing the pillows back in their appointed spots.

"But would it?"

His lips twitched. "I don't know," he said at last, flinging the last stray pillow at her, which she caught. He picked up his boots and his belt and folded his clothes in exactly the same order and with the same precise corners that he always folded them. She admired him from this angle, the clean lines of his body, the length of thigh, his flat belly and what lay below, the curve of his shoulders, his lips, the dark shadow of his luxuriant hair, tipped with sweat. He was a little thin yet, from the sickness, but that would pass. He sank down beside her, cross-legged, and considered her with a frown. "Does it tempt you?"

She sat up as well and shrugged. "Not really. I wonder if there's anything there, in him, past his undoubted beauty. Tell me about him."

He considered her. After a moment he slid in under the blankets and covered them both up. She lay on her right side, angling one leg up over his legs. But her belly, not yet large enough to need a pillow for support, still needed something. She shifted and grimaced; he turned by degrees until she found a comfortable position. She sighed and slid her shoulder in under his arm and rested her head on his warm shoulder. He lay on his back, with one hand tucked under his head and the other curled up around her back, fingers delicate on her skin.

"I was a singularly unattractive boy," he said at last, musing. "I was awkward. I was a dreamer, and I had strange ideas and stranger curiosities. I was also afflicted with—" He sighed. She had one hand tucked down under her belly, knuckles brushing his hip; her other hand rested on his chest, so she felt the force of the sigh under her fingers. "—very sudden and very strong desires, that winter, and no girl in any tribe we met that season had the least interest in me. Why should they? I was odd, and ugly. Then Vasil arrived. We were both passionate in our youthful desires."

"What was yours? Or was it only—"

He chuckled. "No, no, it was both. The physical craving was strong enough, but never as strong the other: I wanted to know everything."

"Then what was Vasil's?"

"I suppose I was. Vasil was radiant. He was beautiful. Girls followed him. They asked him everything they never asked me. They paid him as much attention as they paid the young men who had made a name for themselves riding with the jahar. I don't know why he chose me."

"Perhaps he saw what you would become."

Silence shuttered them. Tess felt as if she could hear the sound of the blankets settling in around them, caving in with excruciating slowness to fill the empty space left by the curves and angles of their intertwined bodies.

"He believed in me when no one else did," said Ilya, almost wonderingly, as if that moment of revelation, of the adolescent boy revealing with reckless daring his wild vision only to find that his listener did not scorn or laugh but rather embraced him, had set its mark so fast and deep upon his spirit that it had branded him forever.

"Not even your father?"

"My father rode out a lot in those days. He was a Singer. The gods called him at strange times, on strange journeys."

"Your sister?"

"Natalia's first husband had just been killed in a feud with the Boradin tribe, while she was still pregnant with her first child."

"Was that Nadine?"

"Yes. Oh, Natalia was fond enough of me, and kind to me, considering what an embarrassment I must have been to her, but she was busy and preoccupied. Riders were already beginning to come round, to see what they could see of her, to ask if she was ready to marry again."

"But, Ilya, women have no choice in marriage."

He tilted his head to look directly at her. His lips quirked up. "Nor should they," he said, and grinned. Then he yelped, because she pinched him.

"*That* for you, and don't think I'll ever forgive you for taking me down the avenue without me knowing what it meant, either."

"Perhaps it was rash—"

"Perhaps!"

"But, by the gods, I'd do it again. Tess." He pressed her against him, as close as he might, and kissed her long and searchingly.

There came a cough. There stood Vasil, framed in the entrance by curtain and striped wall. "If you will talk about me, then I wish you'd do so in a language I can understand. And, Ilya, my love, I don't know how you can expect me to leave here unseen if you post guards at the entrance to your tent."

Ilya swore.

"Wait," said Tess in khush. "Ilya, it's true he can't get out by the front entrance without being seen. They all saw you come in here. You'll have to go out front and distract them with something, and he can sneak out the back."

"You have a back entrance?" Vasil asked, looking interested.

"Go on," said Tess, forestalling what Ilya was about to say, which she guessed would be ill-considered and rude. Vasil stared at him as he dressed, but he dressed quickly and pushed past the other man without the slightest sign of the affection he had shown earlier. A moment later, Tess heard voices outside, engaged in some kind of lively conversation. "Here," she said, standing up with a blanket pulled around her. She went to the back wall of the tent and twitched the woven inner wall aside to reveal the felt outer wall. Here, low along the ground, the felt wall overlapped itself and, drawing the extra layer aside, Tess revealed a gap in the fabric just large enough to crawl through. She knelt and peered out.

Vasil laid a hand on her bare shoulder. His fingers caressed the line of her neck. "Here, I'll look. I've done this before."

Tess made a noise in her throat and stood up, and away. "I have no doubt of it."

He hesitated, and bent to kiss her. Then he knelt and swayed forward. Paused, surveying his ground. A moment later he slid outside. Tess knelt and looked out after him, but he had already vanished into the gloom. She twitched the fabric back, let the inner wall fall into place, and called for Ilya. After a little bit, he came back in, swearing under his breath.

"Well, you can hardly blame him," she began.

"I can do what I like," he said peevishly. "He's so damned charming that it's easy to forget how much trouble he causes."

"I think I'd better sew that back entrance shut."

He cocked his head at her. "Probably." He stripped and snuggled in beside her. And sighed. "It was a stupid thing to do."

"What? Letting him get out of here unseen?"

"No." By the constraint in his voice, she could tell he was embarrassed. "What—we did—tonight."

"No, it was the right thing to do. It never does any

good to run away from what you're afraid of. I should know. I've done it often enough."

"What was I afraid of?"

"I don't know. But I don't think you're afraid of Vasil anymore."

His face rested against her hair. He stroked her along the line of her torso and down along her hips, and up again, and down, while he considered. "No," he replied, sounding surprised, "I don't think I am."

"So. Is there anything else you haven't told me?"

His hand stopped. "I've kept no more hidden from you," he said indignantly, "than you've kept hidden from me."

Shame overwhelmed Tess. Gods, he didn't know the tenth of it. Yet what could she say? There was nothing she could say.

"It wasn't Natalia they were asking, anyway," said Ilya, "it was my mother and my aunt. It's decent to observe a period of mourning before marrying again"

It took Tess a moment to recall where they had left off their other conversation: with his sister, Natalia. "But she did marry again?"

"Yes." Although she wasn't looking at him, she felt him tense. "That's when I left for Jeds. I hated him."

"Why?"

Ilya let go of a shuddering breath, and he clutched her tighter to him. "He mocked me. He scorned me. Gods, he tried to rape me once. He knew about Vasil; he caught us together, one time, and he held the knowledge of it over me like a saber. He used to fence with the boys, those of us who aspired to be riders, and he'd torment me. He'd cut me up, fine cuts all along my arms and my chest."

"But, Ilya, how could your sister ever have married someone like that?"

"Oh, no one else knew. He made sure of that. He was charming to everyone else, a good rider, a fine fighter, good with horses and the herds. No one believed me. They all thought I was just jealous. They said I was too attached to Natalia. They said—" He broke off. "Anyway, I left."

"And you went to Jeds. It's strange, now that I think of

it, how much I know about your journey to Jeds, and how
little I knew of the reasons you left the tribes to go there.
But, Ilya." She laughed a little, into his shoulder. "Does
that mean that the courtesan Mayana was the first woman
you ever slept with?"

"Yes." He didn't sound amused; defensive, perhaps.

"She's so famous, though. I remember that she used to
come have tea with Cara once a week. She must have
been young, even though she seemed old to me. I was
only—what?—ten. She'd just recently bought her freedom from the brothel she was indentured to, so it
couldn't have been long after you left Jeds that I arrived
there from Erthe. So it wasn't only a university education
you got at Jeds."

"Are you complaining about the education I got at
Jeds?"

She canted her head back to grin at him. "Not at all.
Then you came back to the tribes. Was Vasil still with
your tribe?"

"No. He appeared about two winters later. He'd heard
that I had returned. My mother had already made me
dyan, so no one wondered at first when I took him into
my jahar. Josef left his tribe at about the same time, to
ride with me. The Roskhel tribe traveled alongside of us
many seasons during that time."

"Why did Khara Roskhel turn against you? Gods, what
brought him to murder your whole family?"

But the question evoked only silence. His left hand ran
a pattern, up and down, along her lower back. She felt as
if the gesture, repeated obsessively, was itself the answer,
but in a language she did not speak.

"Ilya?"

"No." He lay the index and middle fingers of his right
hand on her lips, gently. "No more, Tess. There's been
enough today, and tonight. I'm exhausted."

As well he might be. She sighed, knowing that if he
would not confide in her now, as vulnerable as he was because of all that he had laid bare this night, he probably
never would confess the truth of the troubling mystery of
Roskhel's defection and subsequent horrible revenge.

She shifted until she was comfortable. His breathing

slowed and gentled, and he slept. From outside, she heard the night guards conversing, the murmur of their words but not their meaning. Or perhaps it was just one of them, reciting an old story to keep them company on a dark night.

CHAPTER THREE

Boredom afflicted Jiroannes. He had nothing better to do than to interest himself in the goings-on in his guardmen's encampment. At dawn each day, he sent Syrannus to request an audience with Bakhtiian. Each day Syrannus returned with a polite refusal. In the mornings Jiroannes inspected the camp, ostensibly to make sure the women and children were being treated well by their keepers but in fact because the simple human contact with people other than Syrannus and the two slave-boys was as salve to him, who was otherwise alone.

There was something pathetic about how gratefully the women greeted him, eyes cast down, knowing as they did that it was on his sufferance they were allowed to be there. Sleeping with men of another race, soon to be pregnant with their children; and yet, most of them would otherwise have starved to death, or met a worse fate. They knew they were the lucky ones. The little children sucked on their fingers and stared at him. The older ones attempted to help out around the guards' camp. A few bold children even assisted Lal and Samae and the other slave-boy—whose name was Jat—in hauling water and beating carpets and collecting fuel for the benefit of Jiroannes himself. The guardsmen's camp tripled in size in ten short days. By the time Bakhtiian made his triumphal entry into camp, Jiroannes felt that he was master of an entire little tribe of his own.

When the citadel fell, his men went out searching for refugees. This time they brought back a princess. Waiting women and peasant women had been sheltering her, but the delicacy of her complexion and hands and the fine gold-braided shift she wore underneath the filthy gown her protectors had given her to camouflage herself in betrayed her high station. The captain brought her directly to Jiroannes as dusk lowered around them. Trembling, the woman knelt before him, hands crossed on her chest, head bent so that it almost touched the carpet, and begged him for mercy.

He took her to his bed. She was a virgin, which proved how great a prize she was. She wept a little afterward, silently; he was annoyed to discover that her grief made him uncomfortable. She was a handsome woman, insofar as any of the Habakar women could be called handsome, and she had a pleasingly full figure and soft, yielding flesh. A few drops of blood stained her inner thighs, but he had been gentle—as gentle as he could be, considering how long it had been since he had lain with a woman.

But now that he had satisfied his craving, he wondered if the jaran women, if Mother Sakhalin, would consider this night's work as any different from a rape. Still, the woman had begged him for mercy, and she had given herself into his hands of her own free will. This was war, after all, and in war, the conquered must expect to become servants. Yet his captain had remarked that he had yet to see jaran riders carrying off any khaja women.

Jiroannes tried to talk with her, but they spoke no language in common and she seemed either stupid or so frightened as to be stupid, so he soon grew bored with the effort. She called herself Javani, but whether that was her name, or a title, or a word describing her feelings he could not tell. He called Lal to him and had the boy lead her away to the women's tent, which now she would share with Samae.

In the morning, a rider came by to say that all ambassadors were required to attend court at midday.

"Eminence," said Syrannus as he and Lal helped Jiroannes dress in his most formal sash and blouse and turban, "what would you have me do with the woman?"

"She will remain in seclusion, as befits her station," said Jiroannes. "I will send for her again tonight. Make sure she is comfortable, Lal, and see that she is allowed to wash."

Lal accepted these orders with his usual gratitude.

Jiroannes wondered if the boy was ambitious. After all, since Lal was a eunuch, he might aspire to the honor of tending to Jiroannes' wives and the other women in the women's quarter. Not that Jiroannes had wives yet, but in time he intended to marry often and well.

"Lal, treat her as you would any woman of high station in your care, and see what you can discover about who and what she is. I would be—most—grateful for such information."

Lal dropped to his knees and touched his forehead to the carpet. "Your eminence, you honor me with this responsibility." Then he jumped to his feet and hurried off to his tasks.

Definitely ambitious. With Syrannus and four guardsmen attending him, Jiroannes walked through camp. As usual, the guardsmen stayed behind at the first circle of jaran guards while jaran men escorted Jiroannes to the flat triangle of ground where Bakhtiian sat invested in all his authority on a carpeted and silk-hung dais. His chief wife and a blinded man sat on pillows to his right. To his left sat Mother Sakhalin, an older man dressed as a rider whom Jiroannes did not recognize, and, surprisingly, Mitya.

Jiroannes was brought forward. He made his bows; he was recognized. As he backed up, he caught Mitya staring at him. The boy flushed and averted his gaze, looking ashamed and uncomfortable. His aunt Sonia came forward from her station to one side and spoke to the boy for a few moments in a low voice. Mitya straightened his shoulders and drew himself up. What was he doing up there? Was it possible that Mitya was one of Bakhtiian's heirs? Was Bakhtiian showing him off, or showing him preference? Jiroannes realized that he had not the slightest idea of who might or might not succeed Bakhtiian if Bakhtiian died, and this irritated him. But at least Bakhtiian looked hale, if a little pale about the lips. If Bakhtiian had indeed been ill, he looked no worse for the experience. Other ambassadors came forward in their turn and were recognized and dismissed to the audience.

The afternoon dragged on as one embassy after the next appeared to entreat Bakhtiian for clemency: Habakar city-elders and Habakar governors and one furtive-looking Habakar prince with two wives and nine children surrendered one by one, begging nothing more than that they and what they offered into Bakhtiian's hands be spared the destruction being visited on Habakar lands by Bakhtiian's ruthless general Yaroslav Sakhalin. They pledged undying loyalty to his person; the Habakar prince offered him his eldest daughter—who looked all of twelve years old—to wife.

The offer prompted a long exchange between Bakhtiian and his chief wife which Jiroannes was too far away to follow. Partway through it, Mitya's head jerked up as if his name had been mentioned, and the boy wrung his hands in his lap and gazed sidelong at the Habakar girl and then away.

It was hot and dusty. The sun burned through the silk of Jiroannes's emerald green blouse and baked his back. Syrannus fanned him, but the tiny breeze gave no relief. Sweat trickled down in rivulets and streams on Habakar faces, on other foreign faces, dampening backs and arms, staining the rich fabric of their clothing. Awnings shielded all of the jaran sitting or standing in attendance, except for the guards. Of the foreigners, only the four interpreters stood under cover.

The Habakar prince knelt in the dirt with his wives and children huddled behind him and the girl in question standing on display to one side with her gaze cast down. They did not veil their women here, so her face was plain for all to see. Her clothes were breathtakingly rich, and she was laden with jewelry that Jiroannes would have been proud to see his own wife wear. How had her father managed to get his family through the lines with his wealth intact? The girl kept glancing to one side, not at her father, but at the boy who knelt at his father's right hand, the eldest of the brood, who looked to be about Mitya's age.

Mother Sakhalin had joined in the discussion up on the dais, and some agreement was reached.

"To seal our promise," said Bakhtiian, addressing the Habakar prince, "we will agree to take both the girl and the eldest boy."

The prince went white, as well he might: to have one's heir and beloved eldest son wrenched from you ... even Jiroannes, who had no legitimate children yet, knew how hurtful a blow that must be. But what could he do? The man had other sons, that much was evident. The girl maintained her composure; the boy took it bravely enough, rising to stand protectively next to his sister.

"May I beg of you," said the prince in a low voice, "that you treat them well?"

Bakhtiian regarded him with bemusement. "We are honoring you by this alliance. You are the cousin of the Habakar king, are you not, by your inheritance laws? Thus will your children marry into the noble families of the jaran and be exalted for this reason. For this reason as well, you will remain in our heart." Clearly, it was a promise. The prince's face cleared and he looked thoughtful more than anything, now. "You may return to your lands, which will be spared," finished Bakhtiian.

The dismissal allowed for no reply. The prince bowed deeply and led his entourage away. One of his wives wept copiously. The other looked slyly pleased. Mitya's Aunt Sonia came forward and herded the two Habakar children away into the jaran camp. Jiroannes felt a sudden and surprising sympathy for the brother and sister, abandoned among the barbarians, hardly knowing whether they might ever see their family or any familiar Habakar faces again. He had glimpsed the ruins of the Habakar cities on the march, and although certainly they did not compare in size or evident scope with Vidiyan cities, still, he could see that these Habakar were civilized people, unlike the jaran.

Another embassy came forward, elders begging clemency for their city, which Sakhalin had invested with some small part of his army before riding on. The afternoon wore on. Jiroannes began to feel faint from heat and sun and thirst. His eyes drooped. Syrannus prodded him awake. After a time, his eyes drooped again. His chin nodded down, and down.

Bells shook him awake. He started up, heart racing. He recognized the sound, the one made by jaran messengers as they raced on their way down the line. A rider appeared at the inner ring of guards. The messenger dismounted, throwing the reins of his blown horse to a guard, and strode forward, bells chiming. Except it wasn't a man.

Bakhtiian stood up out of sheer surprise. "Nadine!" He got right down off the dais to go and greet her. He embraced her, kissed her on each cheek, and then pushed her back to stare at her. A recent scar disfigured her left cheek. He brushed the line of the scar with his right hand. His eyebrows arched up. "What is this?"

She had a fulminant look about her. "I am married, Uncle. He told me you were dying, and that it was my duty."

"Is that so? I suppose it was Feodor Grekov. Are you sorry?" He regarded her with a pained expression that might have been amusement or distress.

Her eyes burned. She looked furious and yet well aware that she was the focus of everyone's attention. Jiroannes enjoyed watching her helpless rage. "That you're not dead?" Her voice rasped with anger. "If I had to sacrifice myself, then I think you might have been polite enough to die and make it worth my while." To Jiroannes's amazement, she flung her arms around her uncle and hugged him tightly.

She let go of him and stalked past him to the dais. She greeted his wife warmly, the blind man warmly, Mitya warmly, and the old crone with distinct reserve. Mother Sakhalin looked smug. Bakhtiian followed her back, not at all offended by her rudeness. Jiroannes was not sure whether to disdain her for her ill-mannered greeting or admire her for having the courage to speak so disrespectfully to her uncle.

"What news from Morava?" Bakhtiian asked of her in a perfectly friendly voice. Then he glanced up, as if recalling that the entire court watched the proceedings eagerly. He gestured. The audience ended.

Soldiers herded the ambassadors away with their usual ruthless efficiency. Jiroannes was glad to retreat to the cool shelter of his awning, to have Jat bathe his feet in lukewarm water and Syrannus recite poetry to him. Lal had done wonders making dinner with the provisions available to him, but then he always did. Just as the boy served him dinner on the three traditional silver trays, Syrannus rose and signaled to the slave to pause. Jiroannes turned.

Mitya had halted at the edge of the Vidiyan encampment, looking uncertain as to what his reception might be if he tried to venture any farther in.

"Go and ask him to share dinner with me," said Jiroannes sharply, afraid the boy would leave.

Syrannus hurried out and returned with Mitya. The boy glanced around the camp and relaxed when he saw no sign of Samae.

Jiroannes stood up. "I am honored by your presence," he said, and realized that he was smiling with pleasure. "I have missed your company." There, it was said. Let the boy scorn him if he chose.

"I'm sorry," said Mitya hesitantly. "My aunt said—" Samae came out from inside the women's tent, saw Mitya, and ducked back inside. The boy went crimson.

"I beg your pardon for whatever insult I may have unwittingly offered you," said Jiroannes hastily. "Please, sit and eat with me. Syrannus, the other chair."

Syrannus brought the other chair. Mitya sat. Lal retreated, only to return quickly with a full set of dishes for two diners and the food cunningly set out for both men. They ate in polite silence.

Lal cleared the dishes away and brought hot tea, spiced to perfection. Mitya sipped cautiously at the aromatic liquid. "Are you married?" he asked suddenly.

"Not yet, but I hope to marry once I return to my country."

"Whom will you marry?"

Jiroannes shrugged. "There are several women I have in mind. They must all be of good birth, of course. The Great King's fourth cousin has a daughter, and with my uncle's influence to favor my suit, I may be able to marry her."

"But she is a Vidiyan woman. Of your own kind."

Jiroannes thought now that he knew why Mitya had come to him, this evening. "Yes. But if an advantageous match with a woman of high birth from another kingdom presented itself, I would certainly accept it."

"Even if it meant you couldn't have the—the fourth cousin's daughter?"

"Why should it prevent me from marrying her as well?"

They stared at each other in mutual incomprehension. Light dawned on Mitya's face. "You mean it's true, what Tess says, that you marry more than one woman? At the same time? Gods!"

"So did the Everlasting God ordain, that each man may marry as many women as he can support. Thus also may he guarantee that he has heirs to carry on after he dies."

"Gods," echoed Mitya. Then he flushed and stared down at his hands.

"You're young to think of marrying."

Mitya's hands moved restlessly in his lap, twisting and wringing and lacing his fingers together and then pulling them apart. "Ilya wants me to marry the Habakar princess. Not now, of course, but when I'm old enough. In four winters it will be the Year of the Wolf, and I'll be twenty years old and of age to ride in jahar. But then he wants me to become the dyan, the *governor*, of these lands, Habakar lands, with her as my—my etsana, I suppose."

"Ah," said Jiroannes, seeing that Bakhtiian had more than simple plunder on his mind. "Well, you must know, Mitya, that the Great King of Vidiya has a wife who is the daughter of the Elenti king, so it's common enough for nobles to marry women of other races."

Mitya looked skeptical. "Galina said she won't marry the boy no matter what, even if they all agree to it."

"The boy?"

"The prince. He'll have to marry an etsana, of course, or an etsana's daughter. They mean him to stay with the camp. They're going to send both the sister and the brother out to the plains for a few years and then decide. Do you think I should marry her?"

"I'm flattered that you desire my opinion, Mitya," said Jiroannes, thrilled that the boy had come to him in such a confiding mood.

"But you're not jaran. You must think about these things differently than we do."

"A prince rarely marries to suit himself. Is that not also so with the jaran?"

"My cousin married to suit himself," muttered Mitya.

"Your cousin? Oh, you mean Bakhtiian. But he married the sister of the Prince of Jeds. That was surely a wise match for him to make."

Mitya laughed. "You don't know Ilya at all. That isn't why he married her."

Well, Mitya was still young, and Jiroannes too delighted by his presence here to want to ruin the mood by disabusing the boy of his fantastical notions about Bakhtiian. Of course a king like Bakhtiian married where he found the most benefit for himself and his ambitions. Certainly for this upstart barbarian to marry the sister of the Prince of Jeds was a tactical victory of the highest order.

"Do you want to marry the girl?" Jiroannes asked instead.

Mitya shrugged. "I don't know. I want to please Ilya. I want to do my duty to the jaran. He told me that until Nadine has a child, I'm his heir." He made a face of comical relief. "Gods, I'm happy Dina got married. I don't think I want to inherit, or at least, not everything."

"You don't want to be Bakhtiian in your turn?" Jiroannes was astonished.

"Of course I will do what Ilya asks of me." Lal came by and refilled their cups with steaming hot tea, fresh-brewed and piquant. "But because my mother will become etsana in time, I never thought as a boy to dream about becoming dyan."

"Now you must think again."

"Yes," replied Mitya, seeming as struck by Jiroannes's simple comment as if it were the most profound revelation. He lapsed into a silence which Jiroannes nourished with a companionable silence of his own.

"You have many khaja women in your camp now," said Mitya finally.

"Yes. My guardsmen have—married them."

"Mitya considered this statement. "Do they have wives at home as well, then?"

"Well. Yes. Some of them do. Not all."

"Ah." Mitya lapsed into silence again. Lal brought more tea. It was dark by now. A cool breeze sprang up, rustling through the dagged fringe of the awning. The moon was up and near full, and its light spread a soft glow over the endless sprawl of tents. The boy looked up at Jiroannes and down again as swiftly. "What does it mean," he asked softly, "when they say Samae is a *slave?*" He pronounced the Rhuian word awkwardly.

Jiroannes flushed, glad of the covering darkness. "I don't know your language well enough to explain it. Perhaps Bakhtiian's khaja wife can."

"She did. Is what she said true?"

Jiroannes wondered if he had been cursed in a former life. "Perhaps. Probably."

"But that's barbaric," said Mitya. "Only savages would hold to such a custom."

"There are strict laws—" Jiroannes began.

"But if a woman or man of the jaran violates the gods' laws, then they are put to death. That is just."

"Don't you have other laws as well? That a man or woman might break?"

"Yes." Mitya frowned. "It's true that Vera Veselov betrayed the sanctity of her tribe and was cast down from her high position to act as a servant to the Telyegin family, for so long as she may live. Although now she's riding with the army, and is a good commander, they say. But still—"

"A slave is a servant," said Jiroannes, grasping at this explanation. He so desperately did not want Mitya to leave with a disgust of him. "Many people in my country become slaves because they have violated our laws."

Mitya appeared mollified. "That's not so different." He rose and handed the delicate cup carefully back to Lal. "I must go. Perhaps—I may visit another time?"

Jiroannes leapt to his feet and escorted Mitya out to the edge of the encampment. "Assuredly. I would welcome it." And followed with other effusions, until the boy took his leave and walked out into the night, away into the jaran camp. Jiroannes returned to his chair and sank down into it with a sigh of contentment. Perhaps there was hope for this friendship after all.

"Eminence." Lal touched his head to the carpet and waited for Jiroannes to notice him.

"You may speak."

"Eminence, I beg your pardon for this indecent request, but the girl insisted I bring it to your attention."

"The girl?" He thought for an instant the Habakar captive had importuned Lal. "Did you discover anything more about her?"

Lal was quick. "About the Javani? Nothing, eminence, except that it is a title, not her name. It is Samae who demanded I ask of you if you wish her to go to the young prince tonight."

The young prince. Jiroannes could not for an instant imagine what Samae meant by this puzzling request. Then, of course, he knew exactly what she meant. The damned whore wanted to go to Mitya. In the four years he had owned her, she had never once come to him without being commanded to. Never. And now she begged for permission—no, for an order—to go to a damned barbarian. He felt a red rage building in him. How dare she make her first request of him now, she who had refused her freedom in order to stay his slave, and make it this? She mocked him. She preferred a half-grown boy to him, who had proven his manhood many times over, with her, with all his concubines, with the quickness of his intellect in the palace school, with his prowess on the hunt and even, once, in battle.

"Tell Samae that the women who run this camp have decreed that she may do what she wishes," he snarled. He got to his feet in one sharp movement and stalked over to the entrance to his tent. "Send the Javani to me."

Lal bowed with his hands crossed over his chest and scurried away. Jiroannes thrust the curtained entrance aside and strode into the seclusion of his tent. There he paced up and down, up and down, along the thick carpets that cushioned the interior. When the Javani came at last, she was still afraid of him, but her fear only whetted his appetite.

CHAPTER FOUR

Depression hung over the Company's camp like a miasmal fog. Each day they traveled with the wagon train farther on through the devastated Habakar lands. Each evening Owen drove them through rehearsals, rearranging parts to cover for Hyacinth's absence, doubling lines, changing bits of stage direction, but there was no spark. Each day took them that much farther from the place where Hyacinth had left them and that much farther from any hope of seeing Hyacinth alive again.

Gwyn flung a tangle of ropes and stakes down onto the ground in disgust. "Who packed these?" he demanded of Diana as she unrolled the Company tent.

She glanced incuriously at the shapeless mass. "Phillippe."

Gwyn shook his head, frowning. "At least he remains a professional with his music."

"Oh, he'd never be that sloppy with music, Gwyn. You know that. There is a point beyond which one *can't* go, as an artist." She managed to draw a smile from him, which was astonishing, considering the mood everyone had been in since Hyacinth had fled over twenty days ago.

"Anahita is sick again." He crouched and began the laborious task of unraveling the tangled skein. "She spent all day throwing up over the side of the wagon. Yomi took her to see Dr. Hierakis. Diana." Hearing an odd note in his voice, she looked up at him. His gaze measured her. "You ought to ask Owen if you can take over the leading roles."

"But—"

"Don't protest that you don't want them."

"Of course I want them! But—"

"But—?"

"I'm too young. I'm not experienced enough."

"You're still young to the craft, it's true, but you're good enough, and you have more than enough room to grow. You have to make the leap. Otherwise you'll never be anything but a supporting player. Is that what you want?"

She dropped her eyes away from his gaze, unwilling to let him see the extent of the sheer driven ambition in them. "No. You know it isn't."

"That's why you must take advantage when the opportunity presents itself."

"But it just seems—unethical, somehow."

"This isn't politics, Diana, it's art."

"Does that mean that simple standards of human decency don't count for us, because we're artists? That we're beyond ethical considerations because art is a higher form of discourse? I don't think so. Quite the reverse, I'd say."

He laughed. "That's not what I meant. I meant that in politics there may be times when it's expedient to leave someone in power who's become incompetent, because in a web like that, there are ways to circumvent the damage that person might do. But not on stage. Her work is suffering."

It was true. Anahita's work *was* suffering. Diana felt it impolite, as a junior member, to agree with Gwyn.

Gwyn added, "And that impacts on all of our work."

"But to be fair, Gwyn, it's not just her. We're all suffering. I never imagined what a catastrophe it would be to lose an actor like this. Not to mention what a catastrophe it must be for Hyacinth, if he's even still alive."

"I can't imagine anyone less suited to wilderness survival than Hyacinth. But he made the choice. Here, I've got this all in order now."

While they raised the tent, Owen came by. "Diana." He blinked owlishly at her as she struggled to lift the canvas up over the pole. "You'll be taking over the leading roles starting tonight. We'll have our first performance with you in that capacity as soon as the army halts for longer than a single night."

If Diana had not been so well-trained, she would have let the entire edifice, balanced precariously between her and Gwyn, collapse on top of her. "Of course, Owen," she said, her voice muffled by fabric. She wanted to ask about Anahita, but felt it impolite to do so. It might seem too much like crowing.

"How is Anahita?" Gwyn asked.

"Doctor says she has an ulcer, and some other unspecified complaints. She's agreed to take supporting roles until her health is better."

"She *agreed* to it?" Gwyn asked.

Owen wore his vague look. "She understands professional necessity. Rehearsal in thirty minutes, then, and I'll need extra time with you afterward, Diana." He left.

"I wish I'd been able to eavesdrop on *that* conversation," said Gwyn. "I wonder what he threatened her with? Hyacinth's fate?"

"Owen wouldn't threaten anyone—" Diana trailed off, seeing that Gwyn was laughing at her.

"Di, the man is as ruthless as Bakhtiian when it comes to his domain. You're being sentimental."

"Goddess," she swore. "The leading roles." She fell silent. He honored her silence, and they finished setting up the tent without another word.

That evening, at their rehearsal on the flat square of ground in between the company tents—there not being time enough to set up the platform and screens—they walked through *King Lear,* which necessitated few changes except those Ginny wrote in as they worked. Ginny had already recast the play so that Seshat played Lear as an etsana, rather than Dejhuti playing him as the old king. Ginny had as well conflated the parts of the half brothers Edgar and Edmund with those of Goneril's and Regan's husbands. Diana played both Cordelia and the Fool. For whatever reason, rehearsal went well; Owen was pleased. For the first time since Hyacinth's disappearance, the mood in camp felt optimistic.

Thirty days after Hyacinth's disappearance, which was also twenty days after Bakhtiian's return to the army, they came to a great river that wound through the land. There, like a vision on the other side of the river, Diana saw a city with gleaming white walls and silver towers and goats grazing peaceably outside the walls amid the sprawl of huts and hovels where, presumably, the poorest people lived. The city astonished her, all marble and colored tile, a romantic's dream. Beyond the city, grain ripened in the sun, and farther still, orchards blanketed the gentle slopes of surrounding hills. This was a beautiful countryside, rich, fertile, and handsome. And yet, on this side of the river, the army arranged its camp on fields long since trampled and withered by the summer's heat. She felt a sudden, sharp sympathy for the Habakar people and for their lands. What a horrible thing it was, to destroy such beauty. How had this piece survived? Had the jaran army been unable to cross the river?

But even as she thought it, she saw a troop of red-shirted, armored horsemen riding out from around the city: jaran riders. What if one of them was Anatoly? She had an hour before her call for rehearsal, so she ran to the Veselov camp, hoping to get news from Arina.

The Veselov camp was settling in for what Diana could now recognize was a long stay—at least two days. Girls beat carpets and laid them out to air in the sun. Three boys dug out a huge fire pit in the center of the camp, in front of Arina's great tent. Mira, running around with a pack of children, caught sight of Diana and ran over to greet her with a kiss. Diana hoisted her up and went in search of her mother. She found Arina at the other edge of camp, saying good-bye to her husband. Kirill rode off with a handful of other men, including the gorgeous cousin Vasil, and Arina turned and saw Diana.

"I'm so pleased to see you." Arina kissed her on each cheek and regarded her with pleasure. They exchanged more commonplaces as they walked back into camp.

"Will the camp be staying here for long?" Diana asked.

"Yes. There's forage and supplies to be had here. Yaroslav Sakhalin has returned."

"With his whole army?"

"Oh, no. Evidently they've laid in a siege at the king's royal city, but Sakhalin returned to see if it was true that Bakhtiian did not die. Then he'll return. Kirill went to attend Bakhtiian." She said it proudly. Diana thought it sweet how proud Arina was of her husband, who had done so well despite his debilitating injury. "He can use his hand again, although it's very weak."

"He can? How did that happen?"

"The gods graced him, I suppose. I think he's suffered enough." Arina paused to survey her domain and to direct some girls in the placement of an awning, two tents, and a bronze stove. "Do you think," Arina added in a lower voice, "that I'm selfish to hope that, even if his arm does heal, Kirill won't be able to ride with the army again?"

Which, like all of these men, was probably his greatest desire. "No," said Diana softly, touching Arina's hand, "I don't think so. Is there any news of Anatoly? Did he come back with his uncle?" A surge of hope shook through her.

"I don't know. But Kirill will know, surely, when he returns."

Diana lingered there until it was time for rehearsal, but Kirill did not return. That night, Anatoly did not come to her tent. In the morning Owen appeared in high good humor, having managed a coup of sorts. He had convinced Bakhtiian to let the troupe ride with a jaran escort into the Habakar city and there put on a performance. He chose *The Caucasian Chalk Circle* in its untranslated, unexpurgated form, since these Habakar people could not understand them anyway and would presumably have no problem accepting a male as judge. Diana already played the leading role, and Owen and Ginny, as understudies, could cover Hyacinth's parts.

They rode out in the wagons about noon. Members of the Veselov jahar had been assigned as their escort. Arina agreed to come along, and the excursion along a winding road past a bend in the river and to the long pontoon bridge laid out over the waters proved marvelous. It was hot, but not too hot. Trees lined the riverside, shading the road. Rushes carpeted the shore. Out on the water, with the huge inflated skins and wooden road rocking beneath them, a breeze sprang up and curled in Diana's hair and cooled her cheeks. The muddy water flowed on, oblivious to their passing. If only Anatoly were here, this day would be perfect, but Arina had not seen Kirill since he went to council with Bakhtiian. Vasil had come back to lead the little expedition, but he had no news. However, Arina had heard from Mother Sakhalin that Anatoly was not with his uncle and that, indeed, Yaroslav Sakhalin had already ridden out at dawn, to go back to his army.

On the other side of the river, Diana felt like she had come to some fairy country. Farmers stared at them from fields turning gold in the stark, clean light of the summer sun. The people looked cautious and frightened, but their clothes were sturdy and their faces hale. Grain trembled in the wind, flowing in waves across lush acreage, bordered by dry ditches out of which green shoots and scarlet lilies poked ragged heads. The city loomed before them. With their escort around them, the company passed through the open gates without the least trouble and trundled into a city for the first time in what seemed years.

Diana stared, enchanted by the scene. Gardens flowered between orderly groups of stone and mudbrick houses. Trees overhung the streets. A marble fountain graced a courtyard, glimpsed through a latticework doorway. A white citadel rose in the center of the city; off to one side soared the delicate minarets of what she presumed was either a palace or a temple. Down side streets she saw Habakar natives dressed in bright clothing, hurrying about their business. This main thoroughfare along which they rode sat deserted, as if the populace had been warned to stay out of their way. Pale brick paved the avenue, so smooth and cunningly fitted together that the wagons did not jolt at all as they made their way in to the central marketplace. Would it, too, be deserted?

But the market colonnade bustled with activity, even when they reached it with their escort of dread jaran riders. Streamers of variegated silk hung from the sexpartite vaults that made up the colonnade, which were otherwise open to the air on all sides. Diana could see that it was gloomy underneath the vaulted colonnades, but all around on the outskirts old women in embroidered black shawls sold fruit and vegetables from the backs of painted carts and men with frogged, knee-length brocaded jackets and dyed leather shoes hawked bolts of silk and utensils of bronze and iron. The intense bustle of the marketplace slowed to a halt as Habakar merchants and buyers froze and stared. Many melted away. Others, more brazen or perhaps simply resigned, returned to their business. Veselov fanned his riders out, and they sat with their horses on a tight rein and watched this activity with perplexed expressions. Owen herded the actors out of the wagons and, in record time, they set up the platform and placed the screens for their makeshift stage.

They drew an odd sort of audience while they set up. People stared but did not linger, as if they did not want to draw attention to themselves. Children edged close to watch and were dragged away by their elders.

Owen strode up to Diana as she adjusted a screen to Joseph's precise specifications: a 38-degree angle exactly, no more, no less. "Diana. Who is that?" He gestured. She turned.

He was looking straight at Vasil Veselov, who sat astride his horse not fifty paces from them, watching the stage assembly with interest. With that absolute instinct for an audience that he possessed, Vasil shifted his gaze to look toward Owen and Diana.

"That's Vasil Veselov. He's Arina Veselov's cousin, and he's also dyan—warleader—of their tribe."

"Perfect." Owen examined Veselov. "Look at the angle of the shoulders, and the tilt of the chin. He's canted just off center, too, in his seat on the horse, which draws attention without seeming to and without imperiling his stability in the saddle. And that face. Goddess, if I'd had that face, I would have stayed an actor."

"A good thing you didn't have it, then," retorted Diana, stung by his praise. It wasn't as if Veselov was acting; he was just being himself. She had never heard Owen praise anyone so extravagantly, not even Gwyn. "Everyone says your genius is for directing."

"So it is," agreed Owen without a trace of arrogance. "He's acting without knowing he's doing it, and he's doing it right, by and large. I've been watching him for the whole ride over here. He's taught himself the art of listening and the art of connecting. Do you know how many competent actors I've worked with who took years to get where he is now?"

Diana wondered ungraciously if Owen counted her among their number, but then Yomi came over to chase her back to the tent set up as a dressing room behind the platform.

The performance was a disaster and yet absolutely wonderful. The setting itself could not be improved upon. Coming onstage for her first entrance, Diana felt transported to some ancient scene. They could have been any group of itinerant actors out making their way along the Silk Road, the famous Earth trade route that ran across the mountains and deserts and steppes of Asia, stopping in this medieval oriental city made glorious by its marble colonnades and gentle silk banners. Even the play, in its own way, seemed ironically appropriate: During a revolt in feudal Georgia, Grusha, a servant girl, flees to the mountains with the Governor's small son, who has been abandoned in the panic by his mother; in the second act, a drunken village clerk named Azdak is made a judge by the rebel soldiers and tries the case to determine which of the women is the child's true mother.

From the beginning, they attracted a hard-core audience off to the left who stayed in place for the entire play. But other than that group, and the jaran riders who patrolled the square with half an eye on the Habakar natives and half on the play, the audience shifted and grew and shrank according to some tidal schedule that Diana could not interpret. It was frustrating, and yet, it was in part for this experiment that she had come, to see what would play, what could communicate, across such a gulf of space and culture, to touch those who were open to being touched. And, inspired by the setting, by the city, by the bright colored silks or the clear blue of the afternoon sky, the acting fell into place and they worked off each other in that seamless fiction that can never be achieved except by grace, fortune, and sheer, hard repetitious work brought by a fortuitous combination of events to its fruition in transcendent art.

It worked. Diana knew it worked. They all knew it had worked. At the end, sweating and exhausted and for once sated, she took Gwyn's hand—he had played the soldier and lover Simon—and, with the lifelike doll that represented the child tucked in the crook of her other arm, she, and he, and the others, took a single bow, which was all that they needed to take, or that the audience understood. Straightening, she flashed a grin at Gwyn and he smiled back, wiping sweat from his forehead. She turned to look toward Arina, who had watched it all from a wagon over to one side, and discovered that Vasil had dismounted to stand next to his cousin and was regarding Diana, and the stage, with uncomfortably intent interest.

"You've made a conquest, Di," said Gwyn in an undertone as he turned to go back to the dressing room and strip his makeup off.

"I hope not. Wait for me." Veselov bothered her. One of the things she so liked about Gwyn was that when he was offstage, he was off; he did not drag the one world into the other. She knew she emoted offstage, at times, but it wasn't a habit she wanted to foster in herself, and she usually only did it when the person she was with seemed to expect it of her. A professional knew how to separate work and life. But Veselov was always on, always aware, always projecting. The Goddess knew, it ought to be tiring, going on like that all day and presumably all night. She went with Gwyn back to the awning and wiped her face clean. They took down the stage. By the time they got the wagons loaded, the afternoon had mostly passed, and the marketplace lay quiet and almost empty. They started back.

"I liked that story," said Arina. "It was true, what the judge did, knowing which woman was the true mother. But I can tell it's a khaja story."

"How?"

"Well, it isn't a man's part to make such a judgment. That is women's business."

"But we changed it," protested Diana, "when we did it at the camp. We made Azdak into an etsana."

"I didn't see that." Arina smiled, looking ahead, and lifted a hand to greet a rider. "Here is Vasil."

Vasil reined his horse in beside them, on Diana's side of the wagon. "Why is it I've seen none of these songs of yours before?" he asked.

"I don't know. We've—sung—them many times, and we—practice—every night, in our encampment." She could think of no words for "perform" and "rehearse" in khush.

Veselov did not look at her directly, and yet Diana felt his attention on her as much as if he had been staring soulfully into her eyes like a besotted lover. She shifted on the hard wooden seat. He sat a horse well, and his hands were light and casual and yet masterful on the reins. For an instant, she wondered what he would be like in bed. His lips twitched up into a bare, confiding smile, as if he had read her thoughts and promised as much as she could wish for, and more.

"I would like to see more," he said, but did he mean more plays or more of her? "You become the woman in the song, yet you remain yourself."

"Yes," said Diana, surprised, because Anatoly had yet to grasp the concept of acting.

A rider called to Vasil from farther down the line, and Veselov excused himself and rode away.

Arina coughed into one hand. "Although he is my cousin," she said, "and I love him dearly, I would recommend to you, Diana, that you be wary of him."

"I'm married, after all!"

"What has that to do with anything?"

Diana changed the subject, and they discussed other things until they got back to camp at dusk. Where Kirill waited. He came up to them immediately, Lavrenti nestled on his good arm, his other arm hanging free for once. Diana could see the fingers on his withered hand twitching and curling, but without much force or coordination.

"I beg your pardon," said Diana to Kirill as Arina climbed down, "I must return to our camp and I just wanted to know . . . is there any word of my husband?"

"He wasn't with his uncle," Kirill assured her.

"Oh, then he's at the beseiged city?" Karkand, it was called, the seat of the Habakar kings.

Kirill shook his head. "No. Bakhtiian sent him to capture the Habakar king, who fled on beyond his city."

"I don't understand. Anatoly went after him?"

"Yes, with a picked troop of five thousand riders."

"But where did the king flee to?"

Kirill shrugged. He glanced at his wife, as if for help. "To the lands beyond, I suppose."

"Out ahead of his uncle's army?" Diana demanded. "All by himself?"

"Well," replied Kirill apologetically, "he did promise Bakhtiian to bring back the king's crown, coat, and head, for the offense the king gave to Bakhtiian's personal envoys."

"Thank you." Diana stuttered over the words and started the oxen up as quickly as she could, to get away. She felt sick. The wagon jolted over the uneven ground toward the Company's encampment, and all she wanted to do was to throw up. The day's triumph turned to ashes in her mouth. Anatoly had ridden out into hostile enemy territory in pursuit of a king. Was he mad? Was he suicidal? Had he had the slightest thought for her before driving forward into unknown lands without his uncle and his uncle's army in order to avenge Bakhtiian's honor? Already she pictured Hyacinth lying twisted and dead on the ground, slain by arrows or knives, lying alone, left to rot. Now a second image rose unbidden to meld with Hyacinth's, that of Anatoly tumbled from his horse, lying half-dead with a spear through his left breast, swarmed by rank upon rank of enemy soldiers rabid for jaran blood.

Would she ever see him again? She would have cried, but she had already wept enough tears to bring life to the trampled, parched fields over which she now drove her wagon. She had a horrible, wrenching premonition that she had done crying for him. Like a little shield, the first layer of bricks had gone up, sheltering her. She couldn't go on, hurting and hurting, never knowing, always wondering: would he come back? when? would he still love her? and when would he leave her again?

The Company encampment loomed before her, sturdy, plain, with its practical square tents and the little canvas cubicle that housed the necessary off to one side. Entrance flaps lay askew, revealing the friendly beacons of lights burning inside the tents. A single fire smoldered into ashes between the tents, but the actors had left it and gone inside to spend their time with the comforts of the technological luxuries they had smuggled along on this barbarian year.

CHAPTER FIVE

After Yaroslav Sakhalin left at dawn, to return to his siege of the royal city of Karkand, the council dragged on for the rest of the day. In the morning, they all sat out under the open sky. By noon, with the sun overhead, they moved onto carpets rolled out under a vast awning. Bakhtiian sat on a pillow at one end, and the council fanned out in a rough semicircle in front of him.

Aleksi swallowed a yawn. The talk had been going on since yesterday and, as usual, the discussion had reached that point where the councillors were talking at each other, not to Bakhtiian. Ilya often ran his councils this way: The councillors talked for so long over the greatest and least choice at issue that in the end they reached a consensus without him having to demand obedience.

The longest council Aleksi recalled was the one soon after the assembly on the *khayan-sarmiia*, which had lasted six days and included three days of vicious argument between Yaroslav Sakhalin and Mikhail Suvorin and their respective supporters. In the end, Bakhtiian's patience had worn them all down. Now that he had what he wanted—the loyalty of the jaran—he no longer had to be so impulsive. Before that long council had begun, Tess had told Aleksi in confidence what Ilya's hopes were for the council; and so it had fallen out—with a few changes wrought by good advice or prudent compromise—exactly as he wished, and it was the councillors themselves who agreed upon the issue, among themselves and not as a mere passive instrument to Bakhtiian's voice.

So Bakhtiian sat now, listening more than he spoke.

Tess sat at Bakhtiian's right hand, and Aleksi sat to Tess's right and back a bit, close to Josef Raevsky, whose lips moved soundlessly as he memorized the proceedings. The blind man canted his head from one side to the other, to catch a sentence here, a tone there, as the women and men seated in attendance on Bakhtiian spoke in their turn.

Now and again during the exhausting session, Tess rose and walked away—sometimes to relieve herself, sometimes just to stretch her legs, once to sleep for several hours—and returned to sink back down beside her husband. No one minded; she was half gone in pregnancy. The children of the Orzhekov tribe brought drink and food at intervals. Sonia sat in on the council, as her mother's representative.

Aleksi leaned forward and found an angle at which he could peer between Tess and Ilya and catch a good glimpse of the two parchment maps spread out flat in front of Nadine, who sat on her uncle's left. Mitya sat next to her, stifling a yawn with a hand. The poor boy had fallen asleep three times now, and Aleksi supposed he would probably be allowed to nap this time. Since the shock of Ilya's illness had forced everyone to realize that it was remotely possible that Bakhtiian might actually someday die, poor Mitya had been displayed prominently at every gathering and forced into a passive role, listening and learning about the duties and burdens of adulthood. Not that he hadn't been involved in such things before, but now it seemed he was at Ilya's side at every council, every assembly, and riding out with him to inspect jahars each morning. Often Galina went with them, since she would most likely become etsana of the Orzhekov tribe in time. Today Sonia had left Galina in charge of making sure that drink and food flowed freely.

"Twenty days ride to the south," Nadine was saying, shifting the maps she had so laboriously drawn over the last fifteen days, "according to the merchants and caravan masters Tess and I interviewed, there lies a great trading city called Salkh. From there the road leads to two more great cities, Targana and Khoyan, Targana about fifty days ride southeast and Khoyan about sixty days ride southwest. The caravan masters say that if you go along past Targana in the summer, there is a high narrow pass over the Heaven Mountains beyond which lies Vidiya, although there is another safer route to Vidiya lying much farther to the east. I imagine, Uncle, that Khoyan lies along the road that would eventually lead all the way down through southern lands to Jeds and the cities of the Rhuian peninsula. But I don't know."

Bakhtiian's tent lay pitched on a grassy knoll overlooking the river and the gleaming city beyond, called Hamrat by the Habakar and *sarrod-nikaiia,* Her Voice Is Merciful, by the jaran. Sakhalin had spared the city because it was here that he and his army had been encamped when the first messenger had ridden in with the news that Bakhtiian had woken from his sorcery-induced trance.

"Karkand lies about fifteen days ride to the west, and there is a city ten days ride to the northwest called Belgana which Sakhalin took before he rode on to Karkand. North beyond Belgana on the edge of a great forest stands another city, Niryan, which has already surrendered to us. West of Karkand lie two more cities, neither as great as Karkand, and a range of mountains, a forest, a great lake, and a river, and on that river a city called Margana by the Habakar merchants but *Parkilnous* by the people who live there."

Aleksi admired Nadine's maps. She admired them as well; she had worked diligently enough on them since her unexpected arrival about fifteen days ago. She said that one of the Prince of Jeds's men had taught her a great deal about maps and mapmaking. David ben Unbutu, that was it; the one who had been so hasty with Tess the day the prince and his entourage arrived at the jaran camp in the spring. Aleksi suspected that Nadine had taken him as a lover, but, of course, she never said as much.

Bakhtiian leaned forward and touched the map nearest him reverently. "And beyond this city called both Margana and Parkilnous?"

"They don't know. That's as far as they trade. At Parkilnous, other merchants take the goods and travel on with them, and trade goods from the south in return."

"So." Bakhtiian removed his hand from the map.

The discussion erupted again. Send the entire army to Karkand. No, that's stupid; the broader the net, the more

game could be drawn in. Send ten thousand men to each
city, then. That's doubly idiotic; if you only knew a tenth
again as much as Yaroslav Sakhalin about strategy; many
small forces are weak against a single large army, and it
isn't impossible that the Habakar king might be drawing
together an army for a final strike. The Habakar king is
running like any damned coward into the west, with
Anatoly Sakhalin at his heels—no longer a threat. How
can the honored dyan possibly know that? Why, because
only a beaten coward would abandon his own tent and
family, of course. How else explain that he had deserted
his own royal city? All this talk of fighting is all very
well, but what about the camp? What are the water
sources between here and the southern cities? How much
forage? How bad are the winters here, and farther south?
When do the caravans stop running? Can a large detach-
ment winter off forage from the countryside, in the south?
Will there be food enough for the wagon train? And so
on.

Nadine had made many cunning little marks on her
maps, each indicating information about water sources
and forage and towns—insofar as the caravan masters and
merchants knew or were willing to part with such information, insofar as any of it could be trusted. Of course, it
was all hearsay. Still, Aleksi did not doubt that in the
short time Nadine had been back with them, she and Tess
between them had tripled jaran intelligence of the lay of
the land. Aleksi wondered about Tess's sources of information, too, because now and again, during the intermi-
nable translation sessions between Tess and the
interpreters and the Habakar merchants, Tess would make
a sudden correction to something Nadine mapped in. Had
Tess had access to maps in Jeds that were more accurate
than the merchants' recollections? But why would they
have such maps in Jeds? Jedan merchants never came
here, as far as Aleksi knew.

Or perhaps, perhaps if that had not been Bakhtiian's
actual spirit that Aleksi had seen hovering in the air, the
night Bakhtiian had been witched away to the gods'
lands—or to the heavens from which Dr. Hierakis
claimed she and Tess had come—if it really had been an

image of his spirit, of his body, then perhaps Tess knew how to make an image of the land that was equally accurate. Everyone knew that the land remained constant, that seen once, and remembered, you could ride that way again twelve years later and find your way. That was how the jaran navigated the endless plains. That, and by the stars and the winds. Along the Golden Road that ran east to the riches of Empire of Yarial there was said to be a country where the land did shift, where no traveler might walk without becoming lost, where mountains moved at night and rivers changed their course between the seasons. But Aleksi knew that such a place could only exist because every khaja in it, child, woman, and man, was a sorcerer born and bred, or else because the gods had put a curse on it.

The afternoon wore on. Fifty disagreements dwindled to ten, and ten to two. "But if we are agreed," said Venedikt Grekov, dyan of the Grekov tribe, "that Bakhtiian must direct the siege of Karkand personally, because of the insult given him by the king, then wouldn't it be wisest to send Sakhalin south to Salkh? If that city is so valuable?"

Heads nodded all around. Fifteen days ago, Venedikt Grekov would never had been so bold as to speak with this much authority this late in the council. Now, however, his nephew was going to be the father of Bakhtiian's heirs. The Grekov tribe, important as one of the Ten Elder Tribes, had just taken a sudden and impressive leap in status—though with Mother Sakhalin's blessing, of course. Nadine had a frown on her face. She did not look up at the speaker, which was impolite. Everyone knew she wasn't happy about the marriage.

"Surely," added Kirill Zvertkov, "we should secure the two cities west of Karkand, so no Habakar army can march from their protection on Karkand."

"Will it take so long for Karkand to surrender to us?" asked another dyan.

Mother Sakhalin cleared her throat. All fell silent. "My nephew assures me," she said, "that the stone tents of Karkand are built in such a fashion that simple force, even using the archers, cannot overcome the walls."

"Had we been forced to storm the walls of Qurat," said Kirill, "we would have suffered severe losses. Sakhalin said that Karkand is better placed."

"Then, as Zvertkov says," replied Grekov, "we had better ride a ring around Karkand and cut it off from the rest of the country. Then the khaja can starve or surrender."

Everyone nodded.

"If we take prisoners," said Vershinin, "then when we do attack, we can drive them before us as we did at Tashmar—you weren't there, Bakhtiian—up to the walls as the first wave."

"There are other ways," said Nadine suddenly, "to break a siege. The Prince of Jeds has an engineer with him who knows many tricks. I expect the prince's woman soldier Ursula el Kawakami does as well."

"What kind of tricks?" asked Bakhtiian.

"Well, if we can make the walls collapse, then they can't protect the khaja army, can they?"

"I will think on this," said Ilya. "Meanwhile," he glanced up to survey the council, "as you say, Sakhalin ought to ride south to Salkh, once I arrive at Karkand, and Grekov, Vershinin, you will double your jahars in numbers and ride on west, to the cities beyond Karkand. Nadine." He tapped a finger on her maps, but northward, now, at the edge where the Farisa city lay, the one the Habakar general had himself burned, at the northeastern boundary of Habakar lands where they bordered the plains. "You will return to Morava, to escort the Prince of Jeds back to me."

"Uncle!" Ah, but she looked angry.

"That would be best," said Mother Sakhalin smoothly, "since her husband is there." Everyone knew what she meant: that it was long past time for Nadine to start having babies.

Nadine rarely sat still. She did so now, but it was a stillness brought on by fury, not by peace. "Uncle, what if the prince has already left Morava?"

"You rode the same route, there and back, both you and Feodor Grekov. You will go." He set his hands, palms down and open, on his knees, and surveyed the council. "So will it be."

Rather than reply, Nadine made a great business of rolling up her maps. She was angry, but what could she do? Bakhtiian had spoken. She rose, excused herself, and left. Bakhtiian rose to follow her. The council, dismissed, broke up into a dozen disparate groups to gossip and stretch their legs. Kirill came by to speak for a few moments in a low voice to Tess; then he strode away into the lowering twilight.

Tess leaned back. "Aleksi, Cara wanted to see you."

"To see me?"

"About—don't you remember?" She dropped her voice to a whisper. "As you watched her do with me. She wants to look into your body with her machines. To—to map it."

Aleksi remembered. He wasn't sure whether to feel honored or nervous, but Tess wished him to do this, so he would. "I'll go," he said, not one to hesitate once he had made a decision. He kissed her on the cheek, bade farewell to Josef Raevsky, and went on his way. Passing between his tent and Tess's on his way to the hospital encampment, he heard Bakhtiian and Nadine arguing in Rhuian just out of sight behind Tess's great tent. He paused to listen.

"What right has she to interfere?" Nadine demanded, sounding quite intemperate. "I know she convinced Feodor to mark me. He would never have done it otherwise. He would never have had the nerve."

"Yes, and faced with the prospect of being married to you in this temper, Dina, can you blame him? In any case, you know very well what right she has to interfere. She is Mother of all the tribes."

"Yes, but we've been to Jeds. We're not bound by useless jaran customs. You and I should know better—"

"Listen to me, young woman. I know better, and I know that for all that I learned in Jeds, for all the knowledge that lies in these khaja universities, we jaran are stronger because of what we are and because of how we live. The khaja can't stand against us. They will never be able to. So the gods have gifted us. Would you like to have married in Jeds, instead?"

A fulminating silence. "You know very well how they treat women in khaja lands."

"Yes, I do."

"I don't want to marry at all. I want to ride."

"Then ride. You are already married, Dina. The nine days have passed."

"I wasn't in seclusion."

"That's true. If you wish to go through the ceremony—"

"I don't!"

"Then accept what you must. And you must have children. You know it as well as I do." There was another silence, but this one had more of a despairing edge to it. "Dina, I have already been advised to remove you from command of your jahar."

"Who—!"

"None of your business. Listen to me, damn you. You're worse than I was at your age." That brought a reluctant chuckle from her. "I won't do it. You're a good commander, and even if you weren't my niece, you would deserve such a command. You will remain a dyan. But there will be times when you can't ride."

"When I'm pregnant."

"Yes. Don't you see, Dina? The gods never give out unmixed blessings. They gifted women with the knowledge that is also a mystery, that of bringing children into the world, but knowledge is also a burden."

"A heavy one, in this case."

"If you only had a sister to bear children while you rode, then that would be well. But you have none."

"I want to explore, like the prince's man, Marco Burckhardt, does." Said stubbornly.

Bakhtiian sighed. "You have no choice, my niece. You will have children. I order you to. Do you understand?"

"I understand."

"During such time as you can't leave camp, you will work with Tess. Her work is every bit as important as Yaroslav Sakhalin's." His voice dropped into a coaxing tone. "Those maps you made together are very fine."

"Thank you." Was there a slightly warmer edge to her voice? Was she melting. "Praise from Bakhtiian is as a blessing from the gods themselves—"

"Stop that! Don't mock me!"

"Uncle. . . . I didn't mean. . . . I only meant. . . ." She faltered. Aleksi was amazed to hear her sound chastened.

"Never show such disrespect for the gods. You should know better, you who only by the gods' grace are alive today, when everyone else in our family died."

"My father didn't die. You didn't die."

"Go," said Bakhtiian.

Aleksi heard Nadine take in a breath to say something. Instead, she said nothing, and a moment later he saw her emerge from behind the tent and stride away out into camp, which he thought showed great wisdom on her part.

"Aleksi," said Bakhtiian, sounding no less curt. Aleksi started, and then walked around the corner to face Bakhtiian. Ilya turned from looking out after his niece to glare at Aleksi, and Aleksi wondered abruptly how many times he had been saved from a lecture—or worse—from Bakhtiian because of Tess's implicit protection. "I don't like it," Ilya said, and Aleksi knew that he meant Aleksi's habit of listening in. "Do it to others if you will. Don't do it to me."

"I beg your pardon," said Aleksi. "An incurable habit from my youth. It saved my life more than once."

"No doubt," replied Bakhtiian. Aleksi could not tell whether he meant the comment to express sympathy or censure. "Nevertheless, not to me."

"I understand and obey, Bakhtiian." He bowed, as they did in Jeds; Tess had taught him how to do it.

"Go," said Bakhtiian, but the word wasn't as terse as it had been when he had ordered Nadine to leave. He might even have been amused.

Aleksi escaped and, whistling under his breath, he considered the world while he made his way to the doctor's tent. He decided that the world was a strange place, stranger than any one person ever might suspect, knowing only what she knew from the narrow path she rode through it. Aleksi felt sometimes that he himself rode

more than one path, that there were two, or three or four
of him, each scouting a different path, each in constant
communication, as though belled messengers raced between the routes carrying intelligence from one to the
next. And once you saw the world from three, or five,
different roads, the view was never the same. The map
changed and altered, and its details became more accurate. The landmarks receded or grew, depending on
the angle from which you observed them, and at once,
there might be an escarpment from which the astonished
traveler would rendezvous with her selves and could suddenly comprehend the land as it truly was.

"Ah, Aleksi." Dr. Hierakis emerged from her tent, wiping her hands on a rag. "Come in. Come in." He followed
her back inside. She had sewn tiny bells all along the entrance flap, and they tinkled as the flap fell down behind
them. Aleksi understood the bells, now; just as the messengers wore bells to alert the next garrison or tribe to
their coming, the doctor positioned bells around her tent
so that no person might enter unannounced and surprise
her at her machines. A lantern sat placed in the center of
a table, but Aleksi knew this trick. Tentatively, he put out
a hand toward it, touched it, and his finger passed right
through it. It was only an image of a lantern, not a lantern
at all, although it looked so true that he would never have
known if Tess had not told him.

"Sit down." The doctor indicated first a chair and then
a pillow, so that he might choose whatever was most
comfortable. "Will you have some *tea?*"

Aleksi didn't like *tea*, but he was far too polite to refuse any drink offered him in a woman's tent. He sank
down onto the pillow and received the hot tea from Dr.
Hierakis. He sipped at the spicy drink cautiously and regarded the doctor from under lowered lids. She reached
under the table with one hand and did something there
with her fingers. The lantern grew a little brighter; otherwise he saw no change.

"Recording," she said into the air. Then to him: "Do
you have a second name, Aleksi?"

"Soerensen," he said promptly.

"I meant, a jaran name, or a tribal name."

"Not one I remember."

"How old are you?" She stared at him with that gaze he recognized as impartial, measuring him against some pattern only she knew, not for any personal reason.

"I don't know."

"I mean, in which year were you born? Eagle? Rat? Lion? Horse, perhaps?"

"I don't know."

"But everyone knows that, here."

"I beg your pardon. I don't know. My tribe was massacred by khaja raiders when I was very young."

"Tess mentioned that. How did you escape?"

Aleksi shut his eyes and struggled to recall anything from that time. He shrugged. "All I remember is the dew on the grass, and lying half sunk in water in a little hollow of swamp. I lay there so still for so long that a frog crawled right up onto my right hand. It was a blessing, you see. The gods took pity on me, because the khaja had taken my family, so they sent the frog to gift me with speed for fighting."

"Why a frog?"

"Haven't you ever seen how fast a frog jumps? He sits perfectly still, and then he's gone."

She chuckled. "Yes, I suppose that's a fair analogy. But Aleksi, were they all killed?"

"Yes," he repeated patiently, "all but myself and—" Here he faltered. Always he faltered. "—my sister Anastasia." Her name came out hoarsely.

"No, I meant, is it possible that it was a slave raid? Or was everyone killed?"

Her question, like a blessing, allowed him to recover. His memories of the rest of his tribe were so dim that they had long since ceased to trouble him. "What is a *slave* raid? Oh, that they would take the people away to sell in other lands, to serve a khaja master. I don't know. I don't remember seeing any bodies except that of my father."

"Oh, Goddess. I'm sorry, Aleksi."

Aleksi found her sympathy interesting. He never told jaran as much as this; any respectable jaran listener would have been appalled that a child could lose his entire tribe and still go on living. The gods had cursed people for less. "It was a long time ago," he said, to reassure her.

"Then what happened?"

This was harder. He managed it by breaking each word off from the next. "Then Anastasia took us away from there. She took care of me for as long as she could. Three or four years, I think."

"What happened to her?"

Aleksi set the cup down and bowed his head. This one memory, he could not bear to look upon, but it flooded over him nevertheless. Anastasia had grown steadily weaker over that third—or was it fourth?—winter and then, with spring, she became feverish and unable to eat. The gods had spoken strange words through her mouth, and she had seen visions of creatures terrible to behold and creatures as sweet as flowers, and she had wept for fear of leaving him when he was still too young to take care of himself. Not that she had been so much older than he was, but her first course of woman's blood had come on her that past autumn, so she was no longer a girl, although of course she had never received any of the rites investing her with her womanhood.

The doctor waited patiently. Aleksi's throat was thick with emotion, too choked to speak. Hands shaking, he lifted the cup to his lips and sipped at the tea. The gesture soothed him enough that he could force out a sentence. "The gods took her on a spirit journey, but she never came back."

"Ah," said the doctor. She poured more hot tea into his cup, and by that gesture Aleksi knew he had her friendship. "You love Tess very much, don't you?"

He glanced up at her, astonished. She smiled warmly at him; he did not need to reply, because she already knew the answer and the reason for it. With her, he was safe. How strange to know that. How strange to be safe at all. He felt dizzy.

"Goddess," she said, "you must have been—what?— eight or ten years old? Well, what did you do then?"

"I wandered. I got by. Eventually I came to the Mirsky tribe late one summer. Old Vyacheslav Mirsky's wife was very ill, but they had no children or grandchildren to help them. It was a terrible disgrace, how the tribe treated him. Everyone knew what a great rider he was, but they thought Stalia Mirksy ought to know that her time was through and simply remain behind on the grass so that she wouldn't slow the tribe down. Stalia kept telling Vyacheslav she ought to, but she was all he had, and he wouldn't let her do it. So I saw—well—I saw that if a small orphan boy helped bring in fuel and water and beat carpets and built fires and gathered food and went to get their share of the meat at slaughtering time, they might let that boy sleep on the ground next to their tent without driving him away."

"And did they?"

But while the memory of Anastasia always filled him with a horrible dread, a painful, dizzying fear that his heart had been torn out and dropped into a black abyss from which he could never retrieve it, the memory of Vyacheslav and Stalia always brought tears to his eyes. "No, they took me into their tent and treated me as their own grandchild. Stalia got better. They said I was their luck. Eight years I lived with them. Vyacheslav trained me in the saber. You've heard of him, of course." By her expression, he saw that she hadn't heard of Vyacheslav Mirsky. "You haven't! Well, everyone knows he had the finest hand for the saber in all the tribes, before he grew too old to ride in jahar. The Mirskys still brag about him, though they treated him badly once they had no more use for him."

"And then?"

"Then one winter they both died of lung fever. They were ancient by then. Stalia told me they both would have died far sooner if it wasn't for me. Perhaps it's true. But as soon as they died the Mirskys drove me out."

"Isn't there something about horse-stealing in here?"

Aleksi considered his cup. It was metal, but the heat of the tea did not burn his hands where he cupped the round surface between his palms. An etching of fronds edged the rim and the base. Steam rose from the tea, caressing his face. But he had already trusted her with so much, and Tess, with everything. "Stalia and Vyacheslav had given me things: his saber, a beautiful blanket she had woven, the tent that belonged to her only daughter, who had long since died, their *komis* cups and flask, some other things. I overheard the etsana—their own cousin's daughter!— speaking to her sons and daughters, saying that if they didn't throw me out of camp immediately I'd try to steal everything in the tent and run off with it. So that night I took what I could carry, and stole a horse, and rode away. Oh," here he glanced up at her, "I knew it was wrong. The penalty for stealing a horse is death, of course. But I couldn't bear to lose every little thing they'd given me, because everyone else in the Mirsky tribe was so petty and small-minded."

"Where did you ride to, then?"

"There was one jahar that would take men who didn't belong anywhere else. The *arenabekh*."

"The arenabekh. They were outlaws, weren't they?"

"Men who had left their tribes for one reason or another—for some crime, because they loved men more than women, because they no longer wanted to live with the tribes."

"Did you like it there?"

"Not at all. How can any person love a tribe where there are no children?"

"Wouldn't someone like that boy who was exiled— with the actor—wouldn't he seek out the arenabekh?"

"He would, if he could find them. Keregin, their last dyan, led the arenabekh into a hopeless battle in order to save Bakhtiian's life. But Tess would know about that. She was there."

"Was she, now? I haven't heard this story yet."

"Well, but with the arenabekh gone, Yevgeni Usova has nowhere to go, if he's even still alive."

"So there you were with the arenabekh."

"I stayed with them for almost two years, because there was nowhere else to go. Keregin was hard but fair, and he never treated me any differently from the others because I was an orphan—or a horse stealer. Then I heard about these training schools, where young men might go to train for jahar, and I thought I'd go and see if Kerchaniia Bakhalo, the man who ran one, would accept orphans. He did. When he discovered that Vyacheslav

Mirsky himself had trained me—well—he never said as much, but I knew I was his favorite pupil. But then, I was a better fighter than the rest. It was the frog, you know. And after that, Bakhalo brought us to the great camp that was growing up around Bakhtiian."

"Where you met Tess."

At the mention of Tess's name, he could not help but smile. "Yes. She trained with us. Although she was Bakhtiian's wife, she never treated those of us who were orphans any different from the rest. Of course, she is khaja, which accounts for it."

"How did she come to adopt you as her brother?"

"Every woman needs a brother, and hers had died— that was Yuri Orzhekov, Sonia's younger brother. She and I always got along well, and we liked each other right away. We felt—" He thought about it, two outsiders working and training together, both with quick minds and ready laughter, detached and yet involved in the jaran camp. "—linked, somehow. But then the Mirskys rode into camp. They were well within their rights to kill me, of course. In fact, they were in the process of doing just that—"

"How, in the Lady's Name, were they doing that?"

"Well, there were five of them, and they caught me in the dark coming out of a woman's tent, and then they beat me with sticks. But Tess happened to walk by and she stopped them."

"You're casual about it."

Aleksi laughed, recalling what Bakhtiian had said to his niece. "The gods never give out unmixed blessings. So who am I to complain about bruises and a broken arm and collarbone when it brought me Tess as a sister?"

One of the things Aleksi liked about Dr. Hierakis was that she could laugh compassionately. "Who, indeed?"

"You see, they demanded to know what right she had to stop them meting out the justice I did, after all, deserve, for stealing one of their horses, and she said, 'the right of a sister.' And so she adopted me."

"Did she consult Bakhtiian?"

"Why would she consult Bakhtiian? She brought me back to her tent and nursed me back to health and I became her brother and have been ever since, and always will be. Bakhtiian did take me into his jahar, then, but he might well have done so anyway—although, if Tess hadn't adopted me the Mirskys would have killed me sooner or later, so I suppose I'll never know if Bakhtiian took me into his jahar to give me his protection or because he admired my fighting."

"Perhaps both."

"Perhaps."

"Well, you've led a harrowing life, Aleksi."

He sipped at his tea. "I'm content." And he was.

"End recording," said the doctor to the air. "Will you come with me?" she asked. She passed through into the inner chamber. Respectfully, he followed after her.

In this miraculous den, many strange and wondrous machines cluttered the long narrow table and crowded into each other on the carpets. An image shimmered in the air. Aleksi recognized it immediately: the shrine of Morava, with its great shining dome and its twin towers framing the curved expanse of roof.

"That's where the prince is," he said in surprise.

Cara glanced at the shrine. The image was so lifelike that Aleksi could not believe that he himself was not standing some distance from the actual shrine, seeing it with his own eyes. Had she witched it and brought it here, making it small enough to fit in her tent? But no, Tess said that the machines called modelers made images of things, not the things themselves.

"Lie down there." The doctor patted a low couch with one hand. On this couch, Bakhtiian had slept through his *coma.* "I'm going to scan you. You saw when I did the same thing to Tess. Take off your saber first, and any gold or metal—yes, your belt buckle."

Aleksi did as he was told and gingerly lay down on the pallet. Tess had lain here without the slightest sign of nervousness. Now, the doctor spoke a few Anglais words he did not recognize and he felt the air hum around him. Then she took a little box, lit with jewels of light, into her right hand and, starting at his head, passed it down over his body. The humming air moved as well, like an invisible ring of pressure, down along his torso and his hips, down his legs, dissipating at last by his feet. It took a long time. Torn between awe and fear and curiosity, he watched his spirit drawn into the air at the foot of the couch. His spirit shone as brightly as Bakhtiian's and Tess's did, which surprised him a little, and yet, hadn't the gods gifted him with many blessings?

"Lady in Heaven. This is astonishing. You're a perfect specimen, Aleksi. No wonder you survived your hell of a childhood. I think you may well be one of the keys I need to crack the code. I think whatever tinkering those damned chameleons did to the humans they transplanted here bred true in you. Have you ever been sick, a day in your life?

Aleksi thought about this, since it was the only thing in her entire speech that he understood. "No, not that I remember."

"And your reflexes—I must find a way to test them. I'll just bet that they're part of the package. Aleksi, have you ever thought about having children?"

There were definitely times when Aleksi thought the doctor was a little mad. "Every man thinks of it at some time. But if I marry, I'll have to leave Tess, and I don't want to do that."

"Of course. The jaran are matrifocal. Still, I'd love to try a little selective breeding—" She broke off and coughed into one hand. "In any case, this is a needle. I'm going to take blood. You saw me do that to Tess as well."

"Yes." He watched with interest as she pricked his skin with the tiny blade. The viscous scarlet of his blood filled a tiny chamber of glass, a red as rich as the red of his silk shirt. She removed the needle and gave him a piece of fluff to press onto his skin, though the point of entry scarcely qualified as an injury. At the long table, she busied herself with some of the machines, but he could not see what she was doing because her back covered his view of the table. Instead, he regarded his spirit, turning in the air before him.

"Oh, you can sit up now," she said over her shoulder.

He sat up. His spirit still turned. He rose and walked closer to examine it. It seemed to emanate from the very base of the couch, like a rainbow emerging from the

ground and arching up into the heavens to scatter its color
across the rain-drenched sky. But it was him, clearly so.
He reached to touch it, but just as his fingers met its surface, it sparked and vanished into a thousand flickering
lights and then to nothing. He jumped back. The image
appeared again: there, his narrow chin and thin face, in
gold and white and blue; the curve of his throat a glitter-
ing, soft green; the relaxed slope of his shoulders in green
and blue, with a hint of violet; his chest and hips, his
legs, his feet fading into a cloud of deepest violet at their
base, the exact curve of his kneecap, the knob in his left
little finger, gold with a tracery of red, where it had never
healed straight when it was broken many many years ago.
He was crowned by a bright silver formless light, just as
Bakhtiian's spirit had been, just as Tess's had been.

"It's beautiful, isn't it?" asked the doctor from her table. He felt her move, without seeing her. He caught a
movement in his peripheral vision; an instant later he shot
his left hand up and caught a little ball she'd thrown at
him. "Good reflexes," she said. "Squeeze that as hard as
you can." He complied, then transferred it to his other
hand and squeezed it again. The ball was made of some
strange substance he did not recognize: not wood or
metal, not ceramic or cloth. Little bumps nobbled its surface, and when he squeezed hard enough it gave slightly
beneath his hand, and he felt warmth from inside of it.

The doctor came over to him and squinted at his eyes.
She held up a black stick with a light nestled in its tip.
"Look at me. Straight at me. Don't mind this. They say
the actor Gwyn Jones is a martial artist."

"What is that? *Martial artist?*"

"Someone who has studied the art of fighting, not just
the craft of it. I'd like to see the two of you spar together.
He won a number of tournaments, of—well—contests,
say when you race a horse. Surely you fence together and
see who comes out the winner?"

"I always did," Aleksi admitted humbly. "Come out the
winner. That's what Vyacheslav often said to me, that
most men are blind to the saber, that they only use it to
cut with and kill with, but that the saber is like a Singer's
lute, that it could itself sing. He said I was a Singer, that

I had made a long journey, but that my instrument wasn't tales and song but the saber itself, just as the saber had been his instrument in his time. So he taught me."

"You are a Singer? A shaman?"

He shrugged. "I never went to the gods' lands, if that is what you mean. But I learned from him as much as there was time to learn, about the—*art*—of saber." He grinned. "I like this word, *martial artist*. You khaja are always surprising me. I thought you weren't civilized."

Dr. Hierakis laughed and withdrew her light from his face. "That's all. What news from the council?"

Aleksi also liked her brusqueness and the way she came straight to the point and never hemmed and hawed about the least detail. "The main army, with Bakhtiian, rides to Karkand. Sakhalin rides south. Grekov and Vershinin ride west past Karkand. Nadine will ride north to escort the prince back here."

"Oh," said the doctor.

"Will he know this before she arrives?" Aleksi asked.

Dr. Hierakis laughed. "Yes. We have a way of talking that can send a message faster than the fastest horseman can ride. You see the image of Morava, there?" He nodded. "That isn't an image modeled out of the memory, but a real image, sent to us by Marco Burckhardt from half a kilometer away from the palace. He sent it this morning."

Aleksi regarded the image of Morava. The view looked down the long avenue that led to the front of the shrine. He could just make out the sweep of white stairs framed by thin black pillars that led to the huge doors embroidered with tracery and fine patterns. "But, Doctor," he said, "if you can send messages so quickly, why not show Bakhtiian how to do this thing as well? If his generals could speak together like this, then imagine what they could do."

"Oh, I can imagine it," said the doctor. "But we've done too much already. Casualties are high, of course, but deaths are low. We're saving and healing a much higher percentage of the wounded than would have survived without my training. And yet, and yet, I can't just stand by and watch them die, knowing that with a little knowledge they could be saved. What of the khaja living in the army's path? But I can't reach them. I can't reach everyone. Not yet."

The doctor often talked to herself like this, to him and yet to herself and to some unnamed audience which Aleksi supposed was both her conscience and the absent prince, with whom she shared more than simple friendship and loyalty. He knew some vital issue troubled her, but he had not yet puzzled out what it was. And if she and the prince did not want to share this swift messenger they hoarded between them, after all, why should they? They owed Bakhtiian nothing. Aleksi did not think they were Bakhtiian's enemies, but neither did he think they were Bakhtiian's friends. Allies, perhaps, because of Tess, but it was an uneasy truce. They were only here because Tess was here. Even Bakhtiian knew that. They needed no alliance with Bakhtiian, and certainly with such machines, they had nothing to fear from him, however powerful and vast his army might be. Jeds was a long ride away, according to both Tess and Nadine, according to Bakhtiian himself.

But if Tess left, if the prince and Dr. Hierakis convinced her to go, Aleksi had long since promised himself that by one means or another, whatever he must do, he would go with her.

CHAPTER SIX

At first the color gray, like a fog, sank in around them. Fog lifted to become mist, and through the mist towers appeared, rising up toward the sky in such profusion that they might have been the uplifted lances of the jaran army, one hundred thousand strong.

But to call them towers did them no justice. Not one tower looked like any other tower. Each possessed such striking individuality that even from this distance—from this relative distance, seated on the floor and staring into the three-dimensional field of Hon Echido's *ke*'s representation of the palace of the Chapalii Emperor—David could distinguish some characteristic in each tower his eye had time to light on that set it apart from the others. Why had they chosen to do that? So many and yet each unique? David thought of the Chapalii as so bound by the hierarchy of their social order that he would never have guessed that they valued diversity.

"The Yaochalii reigns forever."

Was that Echido talking, or a voice encoded through the image building in front of them? David couldn't tell. The image itself wore such depth and reality that he could easily imagine himself actually transported there, staring at the city from high above. He recalled the emperor's visit to Charles and Tai Naroshi—or their visit to the emperor. Maybe he *was* there. The thought made him giddy.

"For time uncounted, years beyond years, has the Yaochalii reigned, and so will he reign, for time uncounted, years beyond years."

It was hard for David to judge distance because of the scale and the slowly turning field of the image, but in any case, the city was huge. Of course, it wasn't actually a city; it was the palace of the emperor, a megalopolis by human standards and yet devoted entirely to the emperor and his business. Had it once been a real city? As the Chapalii Empire had expanded out into space, had it been abandoned bit by bit, or had the emperor decreed it so and forced the evacuation? The Chapalii home world of Chapal was the emperor's world alone now. Or at least, so the Protocol Office said. No other cities existed there, although this one was itself the size of a small continent.

"The Yaochalii holds his gentle hand over vast territories. The docks of Paladia Minor flow with ships. Merchants spin the heavens with their web of commerce. Lords preside with wisdom over their houses. Dukes administer justly. The princes are at peace. Each lord, each duke, each prince, sends a woman of his house to build a tower for the Yaochalii's pleasure, so that the emperor may rise in the evening and see a thousand thousand lights set upon his earth to rival the thousand thousand lights that are the markers of his domain in the heavens."

Beside him, Maggie covered her mouth with a hand and muffled a cough. Night descended on the field. The towers burned in brilliance, each one a star, reflecting the stars above. Great tiers of darkness blanketed the interstices between the blazing towers, and as the field lightened into day again, David recognized these as concourses and avenues and colonnades and gardens and labyrinths and ornamental terraces and every kind of engineering marvel, laid out in breathtaking extravagance and detail, more than he had modeled or imitated or—perhaps, just perhaps—dreamt of in his extensive studies.

"In these days comes the Tai-en Mushai to Sorrowing Tower. Thus does he choose to walk on his own feet into Reckless Tower, and so by his actions does he bring himself to Shame Tower. Thus does his name pass through the rite of extinction, and his house is obliterated forever."

"Under which emperor did this happen?" asked Charles out of the darkness on the other side of the brightening field.

"All things happen under the eye of the Yaochalii, Tai-en," replied Echido.

"What was the emperor's name? Was he related to the Yaochalii-en who now graces the throne? What princely house did the emperor of that time come from?"

"I beg your pardon, Tai-en. Once a prince becomes emperor, then he becomes the Yaochalii-en. He has no other name. What he was before is lost to him. All he had before is lost to him. He brings nothing with him, nor does he leave the throne with anything but his shroud. Thus is each emperor the same, and thus is the line of the Yaochalii unbroken."

"What about his family?" Maggie asked.

"The Yaochalii has no family. He is the Empire. All of us are his house."

"But—what if he was married? Had children? Siblings? A favored steward?"

"All that he had before," repeated Echido, as if it were catechism, "is lost to him."

Marco whistled under his breath. "That'll teach you to have ambition," he said softly. "There's not much advantage in it, is there, if you have to give up everything to become emperor?"

Maggie gestured with her right hand toward the glorious city shifting before them in the field, although the movement was lost to everyone but David and Marco, who sat on either side of her. "Everything but that."

"Still," said David, much struck by this revelation, "I'll bet it's a lonely life, Mags."

"Very human of you, David, but how do you know they have the same motivations and emotions that we do?"

"Sorry. My stock in trade is anthropomorphism. What about the names for the towers? Sorrowing. Reckless."

"It's a translation. Who knows what they really mean in Chapalii?"

"Spoilsport. Though it would be nice to have Tess—" But he broke off.

The scene changed. The city melted away into spinning fractals which then formed themselves into the heartachingly beautiful blue and white and muddied continental brown of a carbon-oxygen-nitrogen world: Rhui, rotating in the heavens.

"Though no male may know," contined Echido, "still, some say that it is here on this planet that the Tai-en Mushai meets his fate, dying before his years unroll into their fullness, holding to himself his secrets, and his shame, and his reckless heart."

"So we can't get a date?" asked Charles.

"A *date.* I beg pardon, Tai-en, but this term *date* is one whose meaning I am unfamiliar with. Perhaps you mean the sweet, oblong, edible fruit of the date palm, a tree named *phoenix dactylifera* in your scientific lexicon. It grows in tropical regions and bears clusters of *dates* as its fruit."

"Never mind. *Ke,* perhaps you understand my question."

The female had a peculiarly reedy voice with distinct tones whose cadences David found difficult to follow. "Tai-en, this low one does perceive the meaning you grasp for. This low one has assisted the craftsman Rajiv Caer Linn in reconstructing the data banks of the Tai-en Mushai's network, but as you are both males, this low one can proceed no further in the particular matter you explore now." On a whistling breath, her voice ceased. After a moment, it started up again. "If one of the females of your party wishes to discuss this particular matter with this low one, then this low one will broach with her subjects fit only for a female's constitution."

"What in hell is she talking about?" murmured Marco.

"Maggie?" said Charles.

"Yes." Maggie jumped to her feet and slipped away into the darkness. A breath of air brushed by David's face. Evidently Maggie and the ke had gone beyond the long chamber they all sat in now, back between the pillars into the white room that concealed the entrance to the control room. Above and around them hovered the field, projected out above and surrounding the two rectangular countertops that none of the humans had understood until now. They were field generators for the huge imaging three-dimensional field at which humans and Chapalii stared, watching Rhui turn and implode and reemerge as the palace of Morava, the Tai-en Mushai's secret retreat.

As if they walked themselves, they came up the avenue

bounded on the sides by precise gardens of translucent statues and flowering vines and above by four jeweled arches. The great doors glided open—David ached to know the mechanism by which their massive bulk swung so smoothly outward—to reveal the grand concourse. Along the upper half of the walls, a procession of creatures tangled with plants drew the eye along with it to the distant end. These reliefs seemed grown of some living crystal; they grew and changed as David walked down the concourse. A lion grew wings and a snake's tail and transmuted into a gryphon. A sinuous, tentacular alien *Spai-lin* curled in on itself and became a multifaceted snail wreathed in vervain. Through grand corridors and intimate salons they passed. All was alive as it must surely have been during the Mushai's residence. The dome lit when they entered, drowning them in the depths of a nameless sea populated with grotesque amphibious creatures. In a vast hall, a stellar map spread out along the floor in a mosaic of intricate tiling, and the map rose as light into the empty air. It was as if he walked as a god into the vast depths of space, as into an ocean as black, splintered with light and chasms of shadow, as the other had been sea-green. He strode through the spinning universe, and the music of the spheres hummed like a chorus of drowned bells in his ears.

With great relief, David came to a room where he could sit down and rest. Except, of course, he already sat cross-legged on the floor, next to Marco. Dizziness swept him as the movement and the stillness collided and merged. He let out all his breath and felt Marco slump at the same time, two sighs in concert. Glorious.

"Thank you," said Charles. His voice shook with emotion. Charles showed emotion so rarely in his voice, these days, that each time it startled David anew, to recall that Charles still lived in there; he had simply given up most of himself in order to assume the role he had to play.

"Rather like the emperor," said David softly.

"What?" whispered Marco.

David shook his head. The field shrank in until it encompassed only the boundaries of the innermost ring of counter. Rajiv spoke, and a bewildering array of charts and graphs and figures emerged in three dimensions and multiple blocks in the field.

"He keeps coming back to this," said Marco in a low voice, "all these figures, timetables. I think the Mushai must have stolen the contents of every data bank in the empire and compressed them into here. Why?"

"Knowledge is power."

"Easy answer. Why does Charles keep coming back to this?"

"Easy question. Same answer."

"It's time," said Rajiv suddenly.

"End program," said Charles. The field broke into a thousand bright pinpricks and sparkled and faded and vanished. Charles rose. Echido hurried over to stand beside him, the Keinaba house steward at his heels. A moment later, the door between the two black megaliths that led into the buffer room opened to admit Maggie and the ke.

"Hon Echido." Charles acknowledged the Chapalii merchant with a nod of his head. "Marco Burckhardt will escort you and your party back to your ship. Tonight is the new moon. It will be necessary for you to leave the planet during this window."

"Tai-en." Echido bowed, hands folded at his chest. "May I be allowed to inquire about the other errand we spoke of?"

"Oh, yes. Indeed, I shall require your services in this other matter. You will retrieve the equipment Dr. Hierakis has requested and stay in touch. We will arrange a rendezvous at some point along our journey south."

"Keinaba House would be honored, Tai-en, to transport you to these southern latitudes on our shuttle, thus sparing you the arduous physical journey."

"I hear your offer, Hon Echido, but you know that as this planet is interdicted, by my own order, we must travel in as unobtrusive a manner as possible."

"As you command, Tai-en. I await your word." He bowed, precise and low. His steward bowed. The ke was not of sufficient rank to be allowed to bow to a member of the nobility, but Charles glanced her way and acknowledged her with a nod. Marco led them away to the stables, where their horses waited.

"Well?" Charles asked, turning to look at Maggie in the now quiet room.

"I think I've just discovered something amazing," said Maggie. "Rajiv, can you call up that image of the Imperial palace? Not that big. Yes, that's a manageable size."

The field remained within the confines of the inner counter, and the five people loitering in the chamber walked forward to stand leaning at the outer counter, staring in. The sight was less overwhelming, confined in a sphere of pale blue light.

"Li an sai," said Maggie, the code that instructed the banks to respond to her voice commands. "Show the Imperial palace as it existed in the days of the Tai-en Mushai." The image did not change. "Show the Imperial palace as it exists in the days of Tai-en Charles Soerensen."

The image did not change.

"Is this a trick question?" demanded David. "Is there some time paradox here? Jo says that her dating indicates that the Mushai must have lived a good ten thousand years ago, Earth standard."

"No time paradox." Maggie looked smug. "There's an essential point missing. The Chapalii always say, 'time uncounted, years beyond years.' "

"A phrase Tess once told me applies equally to past, present, and future," said Charles suddenly. "She said that the Chapalii live in the present. That they have no concept of past or future, in the sense that we do. No strong concept of history. The Mushai's revolt is more of a legend than a historical event."

"The Imperial city is the same as it always has been," agreed Maggie. "As it is now, so must it have always been. The same with the emperor. He's the same emperor now as he was ten thousand years ago, even though he's a different individual. But we thought that was the Chapalii psyche, or mind-set."

"Based on the language study Tess did, yes." Charles nodded.

"Did Tess ever have access to Chapalii females?"

"Not that I know of. We never see Chapalii females on Earth. Or on Odys, for that matter."

"We never see them anywhere."

"I thought," said Rajiv, "that they were inferior citizens. Put in seclusion, purdah. You know. It's one of those primitive ancient Earth customs that human culture finally outgrew. You still see it in places here on Rhui. That's one thing I'll grant the jaran, however barbaric they might otherwise be. There's a kind of shared authority between the women and the men. But anyway—"

"Damn it, Mags!" David laughed out of impatience and amusement at Maggie stringing them all along. "What did the ke tell you?"

"I think it's just the males. The Chapalii males. That live in the present. They don't deal with the concept of history, or past, or future. Because they're the face we see, the face we've always seen, of the Chapalii, we assumed it was the only one they had. The ke gave me a date for the Mushai. An imperial date. Rajiv, you'll have to run it through the computer. I can't calculate these things. I'm just a damned journalist. I deal in image and word, not in mathematics." She shut her eyes, concentrated, and then reeled off a string of numbers and strange sounding words.

Rajiv pulled out his slate and began some feverish work.

"Why not do it through the field?" Charles asked.

Rajiv glanced up. "If what Maggie says is true, then perhaps this field won't even acknowledge this kind of data. Anyway, I'd prefer to do the initial calcs on my own equipment."

Charles began to pace, looking thoughtful. "So there might be a whole strata of Chapalii life that we've missed? You know, I made Tess my heir because I thought with her language skills that she would then be allowed access to all levels of their culture, and thus she could penetrate deeper than we had yet managed into an understanding of their psyche. But now I wonder if by doing so, if by making her an honorary male, as it were, I limited her instead. History!" He lapsed into silence.

"A whole other strata?" Maggie asked. "I don't know.

All I got were the dates of the Mushai's rise and fall. The rest—" She shrugged.

David leaned on his elbows on the counter and stared into the tiny image of the palace. The image shifted and rotated, highlighting first this cluster of slender pagodalike towers, then that tiered garden, then that ten-kilometer-long concourse of seamless diamond roadway. "But they keep referring to the women who build the towers. And the Tai-en Naroshi offered his *sister* to design and oversee a mausoleum for Tess."

"Artists and craftsmen," said Jo suddenly. "There is a difference."

They all contemplated the difference for long minutes of silence while Rajiv's fingers brushed the keys of his hemi-slate and he muttered under his breath in a singsong voice.

Charles tapped his ear suddenly. "Incoming from Cara," he said. "Who has a—?"

David drew his slate out of its loop on his belt, unfolded it, and set it on the floor. He stepped back. "Receive," he said into the air.

Cara's face materialized above the slate. Her image looked gritty and flat after the Chapalii display. "Charles," she said. She smiled. He smiled back. "You're well?"

"I'm well," he acknowledged.

"Any news?"

He lifted both hands. "Much news. You'll hear about it when I get there."

"Ah. I'll look forward to it. Bakhtiian is sending his niece back to escort you. She's leaving tomorrow."

"As are we. We'll look for her on our way."

"Goddess," muttered Maggie, "how are we supposed to meet without any tracking equipment, over such a distance?"

"We'll have to trust that they know their way around," said David softly. "Anyway, I've been teaching her to make decent maps."

Maggie snorted, but said nothing more.

"I'll pay no mind to the peanut gallery," said Cara's

image, but she looked amused. "Have you ordered my shipment?"

"Yes. Suzanne requisitioned it. Delivery downside is being arranged. I still think that given the potential for serious complications, Tess must at least return to Jeds for the remainder of her pregnancy."

"Charles, leaving aside questions of transport at this late date, I remind you that to remove her forcibly at this point would probably alienate her from you completely. You must trust to my judgment. With the additional equipment, with the antigen solution, and with the studies I've done on Bakhtiian's chemistry and blood, I feel certain of a positive outcome even with complications."

David knew well what Cara's promises were worth. She had never been a person to offer what she could not deliver.

Charles frowned. "Perhaps if the experience is difficult and painful, then she won't be so sanguine about remaining in these conditions."

"Charles!" David was appalled.

Cara snorted. "I can't imagine why you keep underestimating her stubbornness, Charles, since she inherited it from the same two people you did."

"You don't understand, Cara. Maggie's overturned the boulder and we've found a whole new ecology lurking underneath. I need Tess."

"You're talking in riddles, my love. I'll wait for the report. Have you gotten that fix on Hyacinth yet? Is it possible he's still alive?"

"Yes, in fact, Rajiv has the fix. It's moving steadily, if slowly, northeast. They'll make the plains soon."

A silence. "Well," said Cara at last, her expression a mask of relief, "bless the Goddess for that, at least. May I tell the actors?"

"Yes. Why do you ask?"

"You're rather close with information sometimes."

"Only when it's vital. I'll do my best to swing our route south so that we can pick him up. Anything else?"

"Tess is fine. We're heading west tomorrow toward the royal city of Karkand. If we have to besiege it, then doubtless that's where you'll find us when you get here in—what—I don't know how fast you can travel."

"Not as fast as the messengers, but I'll encourage our escorts to push the pace. Out, here, then."

"Out, here." The image flickered and dissipated.

"I wonder why Bakhtiian decided to send his niece back?" asked David.

"She's married now," said Maggie. "And her husband is with us. That sounds like a reason. Doubtless he trusts her in a way he doesn't necessarily trust a captain not of his own family. You're a valuable hostage, Charles. Too valuable to lose."

"Am I a hostage?" Charles looked amused.

"Don't you think so? A hostage to force Tess's cooperation."

Charles quirked a smile at her and paced back to stand next to Rajiv. "I rather thought it was the other way around. That Tess was a hostage for *my* cooperation."

"Are we really going to pick up the actor?" asked David.

"If we can."

They all fell silent, waiting for Rajiv to finish.

"Wow!" exclaimed Rajiv suddenly, Rajiv, who was not wont to indulge in vulgar or antiquated expressions of astonishment. "According to this, he flourished for five hundred years. Do you suppose they live that long?"

"How should we know?" asked Jo. "We don't know a damned thing about their physiology. They are clearly built for efficiency, though, or perhaps have engineered themselves to be so. Cara's studies of the Rhuian population indicate that the humans transported here were engineered as well, to make them disease resistant and to adapt them to the planet. So why shouldn't they live that long?"

"It might explain," said Charles slowly, "why their social structure is so static. Longevity might encourage stability, or even stagnation."

"Like the old folk stories of elves and the fairy kingdom?" asked Maggie. "Isn't that the analogy Cara used? Their world is static because it can't change."

"Yes," said David, breaking in, "but we don't know if

five hundred years is a short life span or a long one, then, even if it's true. What if it refers to the amount of time the Mushai dukedom flourished? Not the individual?"

"No," said Rajiv. "I'm certain it's the individual. The famous. *Our* rebel Mushai. Hold on." He mumbled under his breath, talking to himself as he manipulated a three-dimensional matrix that floated above the surface of his slate.

David stared at the Imperial palace and wondered what it had really looked like in the Tai-en Mushai's time. Or had it looked the same? Was the empire so old and so unchanging? They did not know. And indeed, why should they, humanity, minor subjects of powerful alien masters, be granted access to such information?

Rajiv sighed. "All right. As far as I can calculate, the transportations from Earth to Rhui of human populations took place over a two hundred year period approximately fourteen thousand four hundred years ago. I've got three calendrical dates. Chapalii *yaotiwaganishi-chichanpa-oten-li.* Before League Concordance 14,185 to approximately 13,985. Let me see, or, archaeologically speaking, you could use the old Common Era dates of approximately 12,135 B.C.E. to 11,935 B.C.E. I'll get exact figures in a moment."

"It jibes with Jo's dating." Charles nodded. "Remarkable, and that's from a Chapalii source."

"If she was telling the truth," said Maggie.

"If." Charles walked over to stand next to David, examining the glories of the imperial palace. "But I have no evidence to suggest that she is lying. Rajiv. Bring up the tables again. Everything."

Rajiv had ordered the sequence in some wildly confusing web, with spheres and cubes and flat tables displaying scrolling data bases. David found the spray of color and shifting symbols nauseating.

"Rajiv, what is your analysis of the material contained here?" asked Charles, seemingly unaffected by this dynamic.

Rajiv considered before he answered the question, because he preferred accuracy to speed. "The easiest analogy would be to imagine we had contained here all economic, political, transportation, and commercial schedules and statistics and timetables and—well, you get the idea—for all the planets contained within the League. Except it's far more complex than that, and not only because it contains this vast amount of information on the inner workings and structure of the Chapalii Empire. Timetables, calendrical dates within the year although not of the years themselves, economic indices, shipping charts and cargo information, freight schedules, census of house affiliations and house wealth, an atlas of all inhabited and uninhabited regions with reference to population, movement, available resources and potential resource exploitation—" He paused only to take in a breath.

"Complete and extensive."

"Encyclopedic and precise. Cross-referenced. Triple cross-referenced. Their referencing system is nothing like ours. It's neither linear nor hyper, but both, and something else as well. But extremely efficient."

"Of course. What do the Chapalii prize above everything else? Efficiency. Peace. Those two things. So, what if we put a spoke into the smooth turning of their wheel? What if we disrupt their efficiency? What if we disturb their peace? As the Tai-en Mushai did, fourteen thousand years ago."

"I record his death as 10,382 B.C.E," said Rajiv.

David felt a shudder of misgiving—no, more a premonition, a feeling that they stood on the edge of a momentous step, that once the word was spoken, once that first step was taken, once the reckless hand turned over the first card, that there was no going back. That their road would be chosen, for good or for ill. To the death, or to freedom.

"Sabotage," said Charles. "It's an old Earth strategy. Constant, unending, unexpected, disruptive. A campaign of sabotage."

"You mean terrorism," said David.

"No, I think that's a later accretion to the term. But use terrorism if you want to. These timetables, these charts, these merchant houses—have they changed significantly since the Mushai's time? Do we have reason to think the Empire is static enough, the Chapalii so addicted to stability, that they might still be—" Charles paused and abruptly grinned. "Still good?"

David and Maggie and Jo all laughed. "Does the eight twenty-nine still leave Rigel for Betelgeuse?" said Maggie.

"That could take years to research," objected Rajiv. "We don't know enough about the Empire. But certainly many of the structural systems could have remained parallel, even pertinent to our situation now."

"We have years. We have eternity, if our heirs keep the torch burning. But I'm convinced of it. I'm convinced that this is why the Mushai accumulated this knowledge here. I'm convinced that this is how he broke the empire that he lived in. There is proof here that the borders of the Chapalii Empire were once larger than they are now. Rhui is proof. Before they absorbed the League, before they absorbed human space, Rhui and this system were not part of the Empire just as human space was not part of the Empire. But the Mushai's movements prove that they were once part of the Empire, long ago. How could they lose track of them? Of what they once had?"

"What if they had no history?" asked Maggie. "Or no access to historical records, at least. Or—I don't know. Given this lead to go on, and time to work, Tess could probably make some sense of it."

Charles bore that fixed expression on his face that meant he was absorbed in the genesis of a new idea. David was not even sure that he had heard Maggie. "For the sake of argument, let's say that those who administered did so as if every day was the present day. So they lost track, somehow. If we fix in our minds that they don't operate like we operate, that they don't think like we think, then it's possible. If all is in the present, and they are otherwise stable, why shouldn't the information in these banks be reliable? Why shouldn't we be able to use it in the same way he did?"

"You want to bring down the Empire?"

"I want to free humanity. I sincerely doubt we have a chance against them, main force against main force. But if we're persistent enough gadflies, perhaps they'll consider us too much trouble and let us go."

"Or crush us entire."

"There's always that chance. Every risk we take in life risks, as one of its consequences, oblivion. But the hand of the Yaochalii is gentle. I've never seen the least sign that they're as ruthless in war as, say, Bakhtiian is."

"Well," said David, encouraged by Charles responding to Maggie's comments, "and we've certainly seen more of the Chapalii in war than any other humans have. I don't know."

Charles shook his head impatiently. "We don't need to know, yet. We've got a lot of work to do, just to see if it's even feasible. We'll have to use the Keinaba house to spread out a gathering net. We'll need to apprentice more humans into that house, to give them wider access to Chapalii space. And to get the Chapalii used to humans running around Chapalii space. We'll need excuses for humans to travel extensively. Merchants. I doubt if they'll let linguists and xenospecialists move so freely—"

Maggie laughed. "Repertory companies."

"What!" David rolled his eyes, but he could not help but laugh with her. "Can't you just see Anahita playing Mata Hari?"

A light sparked in Charles's eyes. "Yes! Repertory companies. Musicians. Artists and craftsmen. They can gather information and have a perfectly legitimate excuse to be wandering around the Chapalii Empire."

"But, Charles," said Rajiv in his usual cautious manner, "all of this would have to proceed in utter secrecy. Where can we possibly find a secure base of operations?"

"Rhui," Charles said casually, and the dizzying array of the data banks hazed and melded to become the blue globe of Rhui, dazzling against the black veil surrounding her. For a moment, David thought that Charles had simply wanted to see the planet. It was a beautiful enough sight.

"What better base than Rhui?" Charles continued. His face was quiet, but David still knew him well enough to know that Charles was concealing a perfectly violent sense of triumph. "Rhui is interdicted already. It's off-limits to casual Chapalii observation, and any official delegations must come through me."

"What about covert operations?" David asked. "Like the one that brought Tess here in the first place?"

Rajiv lifted a hand from his slate. "We covered that. There won't be any more of those."

"Yes," Charles murmured, watching the rich globe turn. His globe, by the emperor's decree, to do with as he willed. "All the more reason to maintain the interdiction, to keep it in force for years, for decades, for as long as it takes us. Cara's been doing her research in Jeds all along for that reason. Why not this as well?"

Rhui. It made sense. It made perfect sense. The Mushai had planned and implemented his rebellion from here. Why not the Tai-en Charles Soerensen as well? Would the Chapalii expect it? And yet, how could they predict what the Chapalii would or would not expect? What other planet did humans control so completely? No other planet. There was no other choice, not really. And there was a certain pleasing symmetry to this resolution as well. As it was, so will it be.

Rhui spun in her halo of space, unaware of the destiny being visited upon her.

ACT FOUR

"The gates of mercy shall be all shut up. . . ."
—SHAKESPEARE,
The Life of King Henry V

CHAPTER SEVEN

Hyacinth was soggy, cold, and miserable. He shivered while he hammered a tent stake into the damnably hard ground with the butt of his knife. How stupid could he possibly be? he wondered for the thousandth time. He had neglected to take a mallet, or a hammer, or even a hatchet, so every night this farce had to be played out, and it took five times as long to set up his tent as it should have. At first they hadn't set up the tents at all, but with this awful rain, he couldn't endure sleeping out in the open in just a blanket, no matter what Yevgeni and Valye might say, no matter how tough they might be.

Rain fell. He was already soaked to the skin, although by now the precipitation had slackened enough that it didn't really qualify as rain. More of a mizzle, perhaps, a pathetic reminder of the storm that had blown through yesterday. Yevgeni sneezed and coughed, off to the left where he desperately tried to get a fire started with dry twigs and some dung he had scavenged. Valye was out hunting.

Four days ago they had eaten meat; since then, they had subsisted on berries and the tasteless tubers that they gathered when they paused to rest the horses. They saw no game, and certainly, in the ruined land they rode through, no stray livestock. It was as if the jaran army, sweeping through, had obliterated every living creature in its path: humans, livestock, wild animals, and all the grain that had once grown in the fields. Orchards still surrounded the occasional wreck of a village or town they passed, but Yevgeni refused point-blank to ride close in to khaja habitations, even the ones that looked deserted. It was hard enough avoiding the jaran patrols.

Hyacinth sighed and rested his forehead on a palm. He stared at the knife in his right hand. The single jewel buried in the hilt was not, as Yevgeni and Valye thought, a true jewel; it was a laser crystal, gleaming red to show that the emergency transmitter and stun pack disguised within the knife's shell was still powered. It would be so easy to trigger the transmitter and bring—something—some kind of help. He still ached from the constant riding, but the intense pain of the first ten days had passed. Blisters covered his fingers and his palms, some worn at last to calluses. They had bled at first, and Yevgeni had bound them with a tenderness incongruous in a young man who could slaughter khaja with no sign of remorse.

He felt Yevgeni behind him a moment before the rider touched him on the neck. Yevgeni knelt beside him and leaned his dark head against Hyacinth's fair one. They just crouched there awhile, saying nothing. Hyacinth took comfort in Yevgeni's closeness and in his silence. A bird warbled in the twilit gloom, but otherwise only the rain sounded, muted, dying, and an occasional drip or shower of water from leaf-burdened branches.

"I'm sorry," said Yevgeni finally, in a soft voice, "that I have nothing better to give you, in return for what you gave up for me."

Hyacinth stared at the sodden ground. A trail of cold rain seeped under the collar of his tunic and raced down his spine. He shuddered. Yevgeni started back, and Hyacinth grabbed for him, staggering to his feet. "No. No, it's just the rain. Please." His heel turned in a sink of mud and he slipped on the slick ground.

Yevgeni had better footing. Catching Hyacinth, he pulled the actor close and buried his face in Hyacinth's neck. He was perfectly still.

Hyacinth held him. Yevgeni was shorter, and seemed slight, but he had broad shoulders and was, in fact, quite strong. Neither he nor his sister was particularly striking, but they were handsome in a proud way, resembling each other in their broad cheekbones and brown eyes and coarse, dark hair. They never complained, and they good-naturedly put up with Hyacinth's complaining in a way that made him ashamed of himself. He could, after all, be rescued at any time. They had nothing now but each other, and him, and he was an embarrassment to them. He was a constant reminder of why Yevgeni had been banished, and Hyacinth knew damn well that it was his own fault that he had been caught in Yevgeni's tent to begin with. If he hadn't been so careless, because, of course, *he* found nothing wrong with what he and Yevgeni shared together, and it was so easy to forget that for Yevgeni, with the jaran, it was an entirely different matter.

"It's I who should be sorry," said Hyacinth. Yevgeni's hair smelled of smoke. Behind, the fire smoked more than burned. "It's my fault. I should have left sooner. I—"

Yevgeni laid a finger over Hyacinth's lips. "It's done. We were outlaws anyway and only there on sufferance. If we can make it back to the plains . . ."

"Then?"

Yevgeni sighed and embraced Hyacinth more tightly. Out here, quit of the tribe—and when his sister wasn't around—he had become freer with signs of affection. "Then we'll find my aunt's tribe and throw ourselves on her mercy, and perhaps she'll take us in. Or at least Valye. We must convince Valye to go with her." He cocked his head back suddenly. "If you married Valye, then it might be perfectly respectable."

"If I *married* Valye!"

Yevgeni chuckled. That he could still find humor in anything, out in this rain, in this horrible situation, amazed Hyacinth. "I thought you didn't mind women."

"I don't, but—" Faced with the prospect of living out his days among these savages, married to one of their women, carrying on discreetly with her brother, and enduring, year after year after year, the rain and the dirt and the filthy tasks they engaged in—none of which he was suited for—Hyacinth found himself appalled. And trapped. He felt trapped. He had a pretty good idea that if they left him, he would die. Even in the time it would take for the transmitter to recall help, he could die. He was a drag on them; he knew it, and they knew it, and yet they had never once taxed him for it, and Yevgeni apologized to him for what he, Hyacinth, had given up for Yevgeni. Their generosity so eclipsed his that it shamed him.

"I love you," said Hyacinth, because in its own way it was true. Yevgeni made a strangled noise in his throat and no other response, only stood there, holding on. One of his hands clenched and relaxed. The rain ceased, finally. A wind came up.

"Oh, gods," said Yevgeni at last in a muffled voice, talking into the collar of Hyacinth's tunic, "I want to go there so badly, to this place where you come from, this *Erthe,* where there's no shame for a man to tell another man that he loves him."

"Of course there's no shame! Why should there be?" Hyacinth stroked Yevgeni's hair.

The sound of a horse crashing through brush stirred them. Yevgeni spun away and drew his saber. But it was only Valye, returning empty-handed from her hunt. She swung down and kissed her brother on the cheek and nodded to Hyacinth. Yevgeni went back to the fire, to try to spark it to life, but it smoldered and refused to give either flame or heat. Valye unsaddled her horse and rubbed it down and hobbled it with the others, under the shelter of a grove of scrub trees that ringed a little pond. Birds skittered across the water on the far side. Birds. But perhaps Valye wasn't a good enough shot to kill birds for dinner.

Valye cast a practiced eye up at the lowering sky. Darkness swept down on them. "I think it's going to rain again tonight," she said to her brother. "I'd better set up my tent."

Again. She kept setting up her tent, and Yevgeni always had to sleep there. Yevgeni didn't want to offend her sensibilities, even though she knew damn well what he had been banished for. "It's stupid," said Hyacinth suddenly, surprising even himself, "for you to set up your tent. Mine is warmer."

Valye flushed and drew up her chin. "It isn't proper."

"Hyacinth," said Yevgeni softly, "she's right, of course."

Of course he did anything his sister said. They went to bed that night on empty stomachs. Valye had first watch.

Hyacinth crawled alone into his own tent and set the perimeter alert. He took off his clothes and slid them into the drying pouch slung at the base of the tent. Then he dozed, until Valye woke him for his half of the watch.

At dawn, while the others still slept, Hyacinth walked down to the water. In the quiet, he watched birds swarming over the pond and along the shore. Such abundance, and he was so hungry. Yevgeni and Valye weren't around to see. He circled around to the far side of the pond, staying out at a safe distance, and then aimed his knife and fired.

It was like fishing for trout in a barrel—that was an old phrase his great-grandmother Nguyen always used. Within moments two dozen birds lay dead or stunned, some on the ground, some along the shore in and out of the reeds, most floating in the lake. He left the ones in the water and, with a great sense of pride and a fair measure of squeamishness, hoisted the others by their feet and carried them back to camp.

At camp, Valye and Yevgeni had woken up. Valye tended to the fire while Yevgeni tied Valye's rolled-up tent onto a packhorse. Yevgeni flung up his head and saw Hyacinth. A look of such overwhelming relief passed over his features that Hyacinth was embarrassed.

"Look what I got!" he said instead, displaying the half-dozen birds he had salvaged from the massacre. "Now we can eat for the next day or two."

Valye flung herself down on the damp ground and began to wail. Yevgeni simply stared. He looked as if he were in shock. He looked horrified.

Hyacinth actually turned around to see if some loathsome monster followed in his wake, but there was nothing there. A flight of birds erupted from the pond, driving up into the cloud-laden sky. A single hawk circled above, and abruptly, it folded its wings and dropped like a stone toward the ground.

"Build the fire," said Yevgeni suddenly in a hoarse voice. "Valye, build the fire, quickly. We'll give them back to her and beg her forgiveness. We'll release them into her hands."

"What about him?" Valye wailed. "Who will kill him?"

What, in the Lady's Name, were they talking about?

"No one, damn it!" snapped Yevgeni. "It's obvious he doesn't know. Go on."

"But she'll demand retribution!" Valye cried.

"Just do as I say!"

"What's going on?" demanded Hyacinth.

Yevgeni took in a deep breath, as if by main force of will he controlled himself, and strode over to Hyacinth. "Birds are sacred to us. Perhaps they aren't to you khaja." He put out his hand. "Give them to me."

Relieved to be free of the limp birds, Hyacinth handed them over. Only to watch in shock as Yevgeni carried them across to the fire and, once its flames had gathered force and heat, simply laid them over the pit.

"Aren't you supposed to pull the feathers off first, and maybe get rid of the heads and the feet?" Hyacinth asked, utterly confused.

"Take down your tent unless you want us to leave it here," said Yevgeni in a voice so cold that Hyacinth abruptly knew that if he didn't obey, he would be left behind as well. He obeyed. As he worked, Yevgeni and Valye stoked the fire, feeding it, nursing it, encouraging it to consume the birds. They chanted in singsong voices, sometimes together, sometimes separately, sometimes overlapping.

"Grandmother Night, forgive us for drawing ourselves to your attention. We beg your pardon. We draw back. It was a child's error, that your messengers, your holy ones, were taken from life this day. Even you yourself did not blame your children when, all ignorant, they transgressed your laws. Spare us from your just retribution. Allow us to beg for your mercy. Look not upon us with your dreadful sight. We are not strong enough to endure the terrible glance of your eye. We send these messengers back to you, in the old way, to grace your lands once more. Grant us mercy for our transgression."

They were praying. They were just going to burn the birds and leave them.

"How can you waste them like that?" demanded Hyacinth, stopping in the middle of his task and staring. "I'm hungry!"

"Valye." Yevgeni dropped out of the singsong chant and motioned with a turn of his head toward the horses. "Saddle and pack up. Go. Quickly." She glanced toward Hyacinth, but she obeyed her brother. Yevgeni looked back over his shoulder at Hyacinth and then away. Hyacinth felt that *he* himself had somehow taken on the aspect of a loathsome monster, but he didn't understand what had happened. Drawing a knife, Yevgeni opened his palm out flat over the fire and before Hyacinth realized what he meant to do, he cut his own skin. Blood welled up. Yevgeni turned over his hand and let the blood drip into the fire.

"Take this offering, Grandmother Night, whose name is terrible to hear, whose glance is terrible to suffer, and grant us mercy, grant us forgiveness, for the death of these, your holy messengers."

Blood scattered into the fire. Singed feathers poured an acrid odor into the air. Yevgeni rocked back on his heels and stood, clenching his hand tight to stop the bleeding.

"Get your tent down," Yevgeni said to Hyacinth, so harshly that Hyacinth felt his courage and his heart melt within him. But he obeyed.

They packed up and rode on. The clouds scudded away. It did not rain. A low range of mountains loomed before them, the next obstacle.

Valye would not talk to him. Yevgeni answered his comments, his questions, in curt monosyllables, and finally Hyacinth gave up talking. He had never felt more alone in his life.

They climbed by winding paths up into the hills. A packhorse went lame around midday, picking up a stone in its hoof. They halted in the lee of a copse of trees that straggled along the steep slope that bounded the north wall of the valley up which they rode. Hills loomed around them. The sun burned bright overhead. Here between the rocks, it grew warm. It was a gloomy countryside. A few green shoots sprouted up, encouraged by the recent rains, but otherwise the land lay rocky and barren. Their trail wound up into the heights, and Yevgeni seemed sure that it would lead them over the hills and into Farisa country, past which lay the plains and freedom.

Hyacinth stood beside the horses under the shade of a clump of trees. Yevgeni and Valye argued over whether to kill the injured horse for food or to nurse it along.

"We have little enough now to carry," said Valye.

"But if we get more, we'll need it. We need remounts, in any case." Yevgeni knelt and ran his hand along the horse's leg. The animal was a kind, patient beast and submitted to this care equably enough. Yevgeni found the stone and drew it out, but the cut bled. He shook his head. "I've nothing to put on it for a compress."

"I've got a *medical* kit," said Hyacinth, tentatively, "but I don't know if it works for horses. I don't know—" He faltered, because Valye had turned her back on him. Yevgeni hung his head. "Oh, Goddess! You won't even tell me what I've done, and it's just plain stupid not to see if what I've got can help!"

Yevgeni had one pretension to beauty. He had a mobile, prettily-shaped mouth. His lips twitched now, and Hyacinth could tell he was struggling inwardly. Finally he flung his head back. "Let me see."

Hyacinth rummaged in his saddlebags and brought out the med kit. He fingered through its riches and brought out the things that he thought would be most recognizable to Yevgeni; and in the end, they worked out a rough compress and some salve and decided to nurse the horse along.

Valye watched with disapproval. "Do you think you should accept his khaja medicine? It was his khaja ways that brought down *her* enmity on us."

"We don't know if she's angry, yet," retorted Yevgeni.

"You're a fool if you think we won't pay for it, Yevgeni."

"I'm a fool four times over, then," he snapped, "once for leaving the tribe to ride with Dmitri Mikhailov, once for agreeing to bring you with me, once for riding away with Vasil Veselov when I should have stayed and begged for mercy."

"What about *him?*" Valye jerked her chin toward Hyacinth. "Five times, then, for taking up with him."

"No," said Yevgeni in a low voice, not looking toward Hyacinth though he must know that Hyacinth could hear every word they were saying. "Not for him. You don't understand what it's like to feel shame every time you look at a man with desire, to know you can never speak of your feelings to him. Oh, I thought for a while that Vasil might—but he needed a second in command, he needed men for a jahar, he used his beauty to make me think he might love me, but he never did, and then I felt ashamed for being a fool, for not knowing better. But *he* never made me feel ashamed. Because he never felt ashamed. That was a gift, Valye, but perhaps you can't understand that."

Her throat worked. She wiped her nose with the back of her hand. She had pulled back her hair into a long braid, but the sunlight betrayed how dirty it was. Dirt encrusted the cuffs and hem of her tunic and caked the knees of her trousers and the palms of her hands. Not that Hyacinth was any cleaner. "I'm sorry," she said in a low voice. She offered a hand to Yevgeni and he accepted it, and she lifted him up and hugged him. "You're all that I have, Yevgeni. I won't judge you."

He smiled tremulously. "You're the best sister any man ever had, even if you are wild, and won't listen when you ought to." He kissed her on the cheek. A pang gripped Hyacinth's heart, seeing their true feeling for each other, seeing their bond. Like the one he had once had with the actors in the Company. Was this how Yevgeni felt, riding in the army, as if he was always on the outside looking in?

Yevgeni pushed her away. "We'd better go. It's never wise to stay in any place too long."

Except that they already had stayed too long. Or perhaps their fate had been tracking them all along and simply chosen this moment to strike.

One moment, the scene was all silence. It was bleak, true enough, but there was hope in the way the path wound up into the heights, suggesting freedom in the distance, and hope in the way Yevgeni turned and with a shy smile glanced toward Hyacinth and away, as if he flirted with him. Then he stopped in mid-stride. His expression shifted abruptly. He canted his head to one side, listening. Hyacinth heard something, a gentle ring, the echo of a sound like a voice's echo. Yevgeni drew his saber. Valye pulled her bow from its quiver. It was already strung; it was always strung. Hyacinth stared.

"Mount." Yevgeni sprinted toward him.

Hyacinth heard a *whoof,* like air being expelled; heard the ring of bridle; heard the shout. Yevgeni called a warning. It all took place in a vast sink of time, drawn out so excruciatingly slowly that to experience it was painful. Valye staggered forward in the act of fitting an arrow to her bowstring. She half turned to raise and aim at the sudden clot of khaja riders on the ridge above them, but a strange shadow cut across her.

Two arrows stuck out of her back. She shot anyway. She shot again as the riders charged down toward them, and a man toppled from his horse. Yevgeni scrambled onto his horse and swung round to go back to her. His horse stumbled and staggered and crumpled to the ground, pierced through the neck with a mass of arrows. Thrown, Yevgeni tumbled down, landing at Valye's feet. She shot again. An arrow skewered her in the thigh. Still she did not go down. A trio of arrows pinned Yevgeni to the ground, but he tore free of them and struggled up to stand next to her.

They were going to die.

Then Hyacinth remembered his knife. What did he care what prohibitions he broke? He drew it and raised it and fired. He saw nothing but a shimmering in the air. But the effect was stunning, and immediate. Twelve riders closed in on them, a thirteenth left back on the ground with an arrow in his chest. Twelve khaja men fell like stones from their saddles. That fast. The horses faltered. One went down. The other horses pulled up short not six paces in front of Yevgeni, riderless, confused, and probably half stunned themselves by the concussion.

"Gods!" cried Valye, whether from her wounds or from astonishment Hyacinth could not know. She collapsed to the ground at Yevgeni's feet.

"Hyacinth, look after her!" Yevgeni cried. He ran forward, drawing his knife in his other hand, and knelt by the foremost khaja bandit. "Gods, he's still breathing. So is he!" He glanced back toward Hyacinth, looking suspicious, looking apprehensive. Then, methodically, grue-somely, he slit each man's throat.

Hyacinth roused himself out of his stupor and dropped the reins and ran over to Valye. Mercifully, she was un-conscious. Blood bubbled out of her mouth, welling in and out in time to her labored breathing. Hyacinth fumbled in the med kit and brought out the scanner and ran it over her. Then he flipped over his slate and read the re-sults into it. They flashed RED RED RED: condition crit-ical; advise moving subject to urgent care facility immediately; wounds to deep tissue in thigh; damage to internal organs; right lung has been pierced; do you wish a more detailed diagnosis?

"No," said Hyacinth.

"She's going to die, isn't she?" said Yevgeni. Hyacinth jumped, startled, and turned. Yevgeni limped up to him. He bled from his leg, from his arm, and from a gash to his head. "What is that?" He pointed with his blood-stained knife to the open slate.

"It's a *hemi-modeler.* Maybe you'd know it as a *com-puter.* Never mind. It doesn't matter what it is. Do you know how to get those arrows out?"

Yevgeni shrugged, staring at his young sister. "Yes, but it doesn't matter. I've seen wounds. She's breathing blood. It's got her in the lungs. She won't live."

"She can, if I can get help."

Yevgeni gave him a look of complete incomprehension and then knelt beside Valye and began the slow process of turning the arrows out of her wounds. Blood gushed. Hyacinth had to turn away before he threw up. He grabbed his slate and went and crouched beside the horses. He lifted the knife, and held it up so that it could read his retinal print, and then he released its code. For five minutes, he knew, it would pulse silently, broadcast-ing the distress signal. He tried to gauge how long it would take for them to get a ship here. Could they get one here soon enough to save Valye?

"The horses," said Yevgeni.

Hyacinth hobbled their horses, caught the strays and as many of the others as he could, and hobbled them as well.

Yevgeni's horse—well, it was suffering, that much was apparent.

"Kill it," said Yevgeni.

What choice did he have? Force Yevgeni to leave his sister? The rider had two of the arrows out, by now, but the third came slowly, spiraling out along its tracks on the silk undershirt she wore, driven into the wound. Hyacinth hadn't a clue how to kill a horse. He used his knife to stun it into oblivion and hoped it would bleed to death before it woke up. Then he went back to Yevgeni and ran the scan over him. He set the med kit out and queried the modeler about first aid, and the slate began a stream of directions to him in clear Anglais.

Yevgeni started so badly that he almost twitched the arrow still lodged in Valye's side. He swore, and then again, seeing that Hyacinth wasn't speaking. He went white. "What is that?" He was terrified. "Who is that speaking?"

"Trust me," said Hyacinth. "Just trust me. Take that arrow out." Listening to the directions, Hyacinth did as well as he could with the equipment in the med kit. He used a sonic cleaner to sterilize the various wounds and an antibiotic spray to prevent infection. The seamer stitched up Yevgeni's head wound, sealing it, and his leg wound as well, and Valye's thigh wound, but there was nothing he could do about the internal damage. He ran the emergency pulse again, or so he hoped; he could not hear anything. Yevgeni was in shock by this time. He stumbled away from Hyacinth and began to gather wood for a fire, refusing to be deflected from this task, so Hyacinth set up his tent by himself. They carried Valye into it and laid her on the floor. She did not regain consciousness. Her breath bubbled and subsided. Night fell. No one came.

All that long night Yevgeni sat beside her. Hyacinth set up the lantern, not caring now if its constant, fireless glow amazed Yevgeni, but Yevgeni sat so sunk in grief that he did not seem to care. Valye breathed. Night passed. No one came.

She died at dawn, slipping peacefully out of herself and away. Yevgeni readied the fire, evidently not caring that it would provide a beacon for any other khaja bandits passing by. He dressed her carefully and folded her hands over her chest; he laid her on the fire, and lit it. It blazed up. Soon smoke and flames concealed her from their view. Yevgeni flung himself on the ground and keened. He threw off his shirt and slashed himself with his knife, over and over, along his arms and on his chest. Blood, like tears, washed him.

Hyacinth stared at his transmitter. No one had come. They had abandoned him.

Morning passed. The pyre burned. The sun rose to its zenith, reminding Hyacinth bitterly that exactly one day had passed since they had halted here before. The bodies of the dead khaja still lay on the ground, ravaged by night stalkers. Insects swarmed them. A bird circled down and settled with lazy grace on the corpse farthest from the horses. It began to feed. Soon another bird joined it.

Hyacinth walked forward and touched Yevgeni on the neck. "Yevgeni," he said softly, not trusting the other man not to jump up and threaten him with that knife. At least Yevgeni had stopped mutilating himself, though blood still seeped from the cuts scored all over his skin. "Shouldn't we move on? What if they come back? If someone else comes?"

"Ah, gods," said Yevgeni, his voice hoarse with rage and sorrow, "she trusted me. When did I bring her anything but grief?"

Hyacinth winced. Yevgeni's desolation was a palpable thing, like a blow. Yevgeni stared at the fire that consumed his sister's body. If he even noticed Hyacinth's hand on his neck, he gave no sign of it. "Yevgeni, we should ride on. What if there are others around here?"

"What does it matter? Grandmother Night will have her revenge on us in the end." His voice sounded hollow and lifeless. "We killed her holy messengers, and the only punishment for that crime is death. It has already begun. Valye is dead. What does it matter if we die, too?"

Yevgeni had given up. Hyacinth shut his eyes. "Yevgeni, listen to me. I don't believe in grandmother night. I'm not going to die, not for grandmother night, not for you, and not for them!" He opened his eyes, shocked at his own vehemence. But it was true; now that they had lost everything, now that he had been abandoned by his own people, now he refused to give up.

Yevgeni lifted his head. His eyes were glazed, but a sudden gleam of fear lit them. "You mustn't speak of her with such disrespect," he said, but with no force behind the comment.

"And risk what? Valye is already dead. What else is there but our own lives? I'm going on, and you're coming with me." Hyacinth did not know what else to do, except to keep moving. Yevgeni rose, stiff with pain and drying cuts, but he would not let Hyacinth clean his wounds. Face drawn, he pulled his shirt on over the raw cuts. He hesitated. The pyre burned steadily now, but Hyacinth was not sure how much of Valye's body would actually be consumed by the time it went out. He didn't intend to wait around to see what khaja locals the fire attracted.

"Yevgeni, come on."

Yevgeni obeyed numbly. They strung the khaja horses on with the rest and set off northeast, up the valley.

That night, Hyacinth downed two birds with his knife and brought them back to camp. Yevgeni sat slumped over his knees, apathetic now in his grief. Hyacinth sighed and stared at the two birds. He steeled himself, going off a few paces away from the safety of the hobbled horses, and he began the disgusting, messy work of preparing them for supper. He hadn't a clue what to do with them. He plucked at the feathers, but they wouldn't come out cleanly. He had to hack and tear at the skin and peel it off entirely. It was horrible. He cut off their heads and feet, swore copiously, gutted them, and threw up once at the smell and sticky texture of the fluids that gushed out of them. But he did it.

Yevgeni just sat there. Hyacinth got out the little solar powered oven he had stolen from the Company's camp and roasted the two birds in it. That wasn't so bad, since the oven had all kinds of timing devices built into it according to weight and type of meat. He also heated water to boiling and while the meat cooked, he took a cloth and dabbed the cuts on Yevgeni's back with hot water. Yevgeni let him do it. He was otherwise listless. He shivered, and Hyacinth hoped that he wasn't going to get some kind of infection. He brought out the scanner again and ran it over Yevgeni, and the med program on his slate advised him to use the antiseptic mist.

"What are you doing?" Yevgeni asked at last, roused out of his stupor by the stinging of the mist.

"Keeping you well. Roasting some meat."

But Yevgeni wouldn't eat when Hyacinth brought him the roasted fowl.

Hyacinth crouched beside him and took Yevgeni's chin in his hand. "They've all abandoned you, Yevgeni, don't you see that? So what does it matter what you do?"

"It matters to the gods."

"Well, I don't believe in your gods. How did those twelve men fall off their horses?"

For the first time since Valye's death, Yevgeni lifted his gaze to look directly at Hyacinth. "I don't know," he whispered.

"I did that, and you know I'm no fighter."

"You're a Singer. A shaman. Perhaps you know sorcery."

"It's not sorcery either. Listen, Yevgeni. Maybe we have a way out of this. Do you know where the shrine of Morava is? Maybe Soerensen is still there."

The glaze of dullness that stiffened Yevgeni's expression lightened slightly. "Who is Soerensen?"

"The Prince of Jeds. If we can find him—"

"He would help us?" Yevgeni shook his head. "He can't help us. No woman or man can, now that Grandmother Night has settled her terrible gaze on us."

"Yes, he can. He's more powerful than grandmother night."

"Don't say that!" Yevgeni shrank away from him.

"But it's true. I made those men fall down, with this knife. I can heal your wounds with these simple instruments. That box is an oven that baked this meat without fire. I'm more powerful than grandmother night. Let me show you something."

He brought out his slate and unfolded it, so that it lay flat on the ground. In silence, Yevgeni watched. "Do you remember the jaran tale we sang? The one about Mekhala, the woman who brought horses to the jaran?"

Yevgeni lowered his eyes. "Yes." He said it as if something shamed him about the memory. "I was with Valye. She liked to see your people's singing."

"Run Mekhala folktale, scene two. Meter field."

In scene two, Hyacinth played the khaja prince who had come to demand tribute from the rhan, as the jaran tribes had called themselves before they had gotten horses and become ja-rhan, the people of the wind. Above the slate, about a meter cubed, the play unfolded: Anahita as Mekhala and Diana as her sister, Hyacinth entering as the prince with his retinue of Quinn and Oriana.

Yevgeni stared openmouthed at the image, moving, playing out. He reached out and snatched his hand back before he touched it. "Sorcery," he murmured.

"No, it's not sorcery. It's a—oh, hell, there's no way to explain it to you. Run image of Morava."

The image melted away and re-formed into the gorgeous dome and towers of the Chapalii palace the jaran called Morava. Hyacinth had not seen Morava except through this program, and he was delighted to be able to pace around it and see the complex from all angles. He envied the duke's party for experiencing it firsthand.

"But how did it get so small?" Yevgeni demanded. "How did you capture it and bring it here?"

"It's just an image, Yevgeni, not the shrine itself. Look, do you know what a map is? Let me see. Maybe I can reconstruct where we left the army, and where we are now. It's been thirty-five days since we left camp and if we've ridden northeast. . . . Goddess. I should have paid more attention in cartography tutorial."

"But no one is more powerful than Grandmother Night," said Yevgeni suddenly. "Even seeing these things and what you did to those khaja bandits, still. . . . She attends us at our birth and grants us a measure of days in which to live. She is the One with whom we may bargain for gifts, if we're willing to risk the bargaining, if we're desperate enough. She is death, Hyacinth. No person can escape death."

"How old do you think the Prince of Jeds is?"

Yevgeni shrugged. "Of an age with Bakhtiian, I suppose."

"He isn't. He's older than Mother Sakhalin."

"He can't be."

"He is. Why would I lie to you? Dr. Hierakis is older than he is. Owen is in his seventies, too, and Ginny is at least as old as that. Yet they are still young. My great-grandmother Nguyen is one hundred and sixteen years old, and I can expect to live at least as long as she has and stay young until I'm ninety or so. Grandmother night doesn't scare us. You've got to believe me, Yevgeni. You've got to *want* to believe me, you've got to want to live. If we can make it to the shrine, if we can find the duke—"

Yevgeni reached up abruptly and touched Hyacinth's cheek. "That's when I fell in love with you," he said in a low voice. "When I saw that song, the song you did about Mekhala. Valye said you were really the khaja prince and that it was a wind demon truly drawn down to walk among us, but I knew you were just a person singing two different songs. You were so beautiful."

Hyacinth shut his eyes. How Owen would have loved this scene: Yevgeni's voice blended grief and wonder and a shy yearning so perfectly, and the way he held his body reflected his longing and his sorrow and his actual physical pain. But this was real. Hyacinth knelt and put his arms around the other man. Yevgeni gasped, from the pain of the embrace, but he did not draw away.

"Oh, damn," murmured Hyacinth, "it must hurt."

"No, no," said Yevgeni into his hair, "never mind it. I gave it for her, who followed me to her death."

"We won't die. That way you can remember her. That way part of her will always live, with you."

Yevgeni sighed against him but said nothing. There was nothing he needed to say, not at that moment. Hyacinth stroked his hair and held him carefully, tenderly.

After a little while, Hyacinth warmed up the meat in the oven and Yevgeni ate a sliver of it, though it was the flesh of the gods' sacred messengers. Not much, but by that small gesture, Hyacinth knew that Yevgeni had cast his lot with his khaja lover and abandoned his own people once and for all.

CHAPTER EIGHT

In the middle of the night, Tess woke to the sound of footsteps in the outer chamber. She heaved herself up and slipped on a silk robe, tying it closed just under her breasts and above her pregnant belly. She pushed the curtain aside and walked into her husband.

He had been pacing. She could tell by the way his shoulders were drawn forward and one hand clenched up by his beard. He opened the hand and splayed it over one side of her belly. "The child is growing," he said. "And all of a sudden, it seems. I think you're twice the size you were at Hamrat, and it's only been sixteen days since we left there."

"Oh, gods, and it's all pressing on my bladder."

"Do you want me to walk with you?"

"No." She slipped on a pair of sandals, threw a cloak over her silk robe, and walked out to the freshly-dug pits sited at the edge of the Orzhekov encampment. At night, it was quiet and peaceful here, but she knew that about a kilometer away lay the royal city of Karkand, settled in for a long siege. She greeted guards, and they greeted her in return. They were used to her nightly peregrinations. The guards looked a little chilled, but she was never cold now, even in the middle of the night.

When she got back to the tent, Ilya was pacing again. "Here," she said, "stop that. It's moving again. Sit down." She settled down cross-legged beside him and opened her robe. He rested both of his hands on her belly. "What's bothering you?"

He did not reply. He concentrated on her, on her belly, on his hands.

"There, did you feel that?" she asked. He shook his

head. "It's mostly like a fluttering, now, like butterflies. When I get bigger, you'll feel it."

He sighed and withdrew his hands, and stood, and walked to the entrance of the tent and then back to her. "How does Ursula know so much?" he demanded. "Although she is always respectful, she speaks with the authority of Sakhalin himself. We rode a circuit of the city today and she pointed out where siege engines might be used to the greatest effect, and how the river might be dammed so that it could flood the walls and the citadel. She speaks as if she has seen and done all these things before, as if she has already ridden with an army like ours."

"She's read many books." Tess rose and poured two cups of water, and offered one to him. He ignored her. He went to the table and unrolled two pieces of parchment on the tabletop. One was Nadine's map of Habakar lands and beyond. The other was a rough map of Karkand and the surrounding countryside.

Karkand, like Jeds, was a walled city, but here the resemblance ended. Hovels and houses and palaces, poor and rich alike, lay crammed within the protecting walls of Jeds, and only the prince's palace and the university lay outside within their own ring of walls. Huts and shanties had sprouted up immediately outside the walls and along the road that led to the palace, but only the poorest people who could find no foothold inside the city lived out there.

In Karkand, the rich lived outside the inner city. They lived in a vast sprawl of villas along avenues spread out on the fertile plain that surrounded the two hills on which lay the citadel and the king's palace and the innermost city, which was itself as large as Jeds. The outer city was also protected by a wall, not as formidable as the walls ringing the twin hills but impressive for its sheer vast circumference. It took half a day to ride around the suburbs of Karkand.

"Sakhalin has ridden south," said Ilya, staring at the maps. "Reports have come in that the king's nephew has raised an army there. He is said to be courageous and an able leader."

"What news from Anatoly Sakhalin?"

"None. Grekov and Vershinin have reached the two cities west of here, by forced march—"

"Gods, that was fast."

"—and a courier just came in to say that one of the cities, Gangana, has already surrendered. Should I take the main army south?"

"What do your commanders advise? Has Sakhalin asked for your help?"

"Sakhalin has not asked. Yet. The council is divided. If it's true, and the main threat lies in the south. . . . The nephew could easily drive north and east and cut off our supply route back to the plains. We're losing forage here. And yet, and yet, Karkand is the king's city, and it is the king I must be seen to punish."

"Unless it is the nephew who has the people's hearts, and not the king."

Ilya turned and folded his arms over his chest, examining her with a frown on his face. "That's just what Ursula said. I thought—for an instant I thought it was as if she knew what was going to happen next. As if she'd heard this tale before." He shook the thought away with an impatient shrug of his shoulders. "No. I must stay here until the city is taken. I intend to sit in the king's throne, so that the Habakar people will know who rules here now."

He bent back over the table, poring over the two maps. Tess watched him. She could see that he was too agitated to sleep. His lips moved, sounding out names, but he did not speak aloud. With a finger, he traced lines of advance: Grekov's command driving west; Sakhalin riding south, and the army led by Tadheus Yensky swinging in a wide loop south and east. His hand found the cup she had set beside him. He raised it to his lips and took a deep draught, then made a face, as if he had been expecting something else, not plain water.

"Ilya, come lie down with me."

He shrugged, as if to say: not now, I'm too busy.

Tess loved to just watch him. She thought he looked, if anything, a little younger these days. He glowed with health, or perhaps it was only the restless energy radiating off him. She had finally come to an understanding of how different he and Vasil were. They were both self-absorbed, but Vasil was absorbed in knowing how he appeared to others while Ilya was absorbed in the vision that led him. Vasil always knew where he stood in relation to others. Ilya simply *was,* and he drew his thousand thousand followers along with him as does any juggernaut. And she, one of them. She smiled wryly and settled her hands on the curve of her abdomen.

"I know it's none of my business, but have you lain with any other women since we got married?"

His fingers halted midway down the map. His chin lifted. She could tell by the angle of his shoulders and the way his mouth twitched once, and then was still, that he was embarrassed. "It's none of your business."

Tess laughed and pushed up to stand. She went over and slid an arm around him. "You haven't, have you?"

"I've been busy. Very busy. And preoccupied."

"Yes, my love. Come lie down with me." He followed her in to their bed meekly enough. He might even have slept, but she woke later to find him gone.

In the morning, she woke to find him sleeping in his clothes next to her. She rose quietly and dressed and went outside. Konstans greeted her with a yawn.

"You look tired," she said.

"Gods. In the middle of the night, Bakhtiian made us ride out along the northwest prospect, to look over the walls, not that we could see them, but he was more interested in the orchards, anyway. Doesn't he ever sleep?"

Tess grinned. "As I hear it, he sleeps more now than he ever used to."

"That's true enough," agreed Konstans. "It's a good thing he married, for the rest of us, at least." He smiled at her, remembered that she was Bakhtiian's wife and not his old comrade-in-arms, and looked away.

"Oh, don't be shy with me, Konstans. We've known each other too long. Is there any word about the embassy from Parkilnous yet? Hello, Aleksi. Can you ride down to the ambassadors' camp and see if they've arrived?" Aleski nodded and left. Tess went over to greet Sonia and to send Kolia with hot tea to wake Ilya.

Karkand lay beyond, its vast sprawl of suburbs fortified by walls and its inner city grown up in rings around a hill that rose out of the flat land. On a second hill, a twin to the first, lay the acres of white and gleaming stone, festooned with pennants and banners, of the royal palace. Here on the flat, they saw the city mostly as two distant heights thrusting into the sky, the gray citadel crowning the first hill and a shining pair of towers crowning the second. The citizens of Karkand had not elected to defend the outer city, but Ilya had decreed that the fields and orchards and suburbs remain untouched except to feed the camp, and what farmers had not fled within the inner walls or away into the countryside were ordered to work their lands on pain of death. Sonia offered Tess some fresh melon, and Tess ate the sweet fruit gratefully.

"I rode through the outskirts of the city yesterday," said Sonia. "It's very handsome, and it's certainly bigger than any city I've ever seen. Why, there must be as many people living there as there are riders in Ilya's army. No, there must be far more."

Josef Raevsky came around the side of the tent, his left hand touching Vania's shoulder so that the boy could lead him in under the awning. Ivan led him to a pillow next to Tess and Katerina brought him a tray laden with meat and melon and sweet cakes.

"Do you think the embassy from Parkilnous has arrived yet?" Tess asked him.

Josef shook his head. "We've met only the merchant, who says one was sent. They won't understand yet what a threat we are to them. Like all the khaja, they believe that mountains and rivers can protect them."

"And desert. There's a desert called the Al Dinn Kun, the Wailing Death, to the south. That's the one Tasha is riding through."

"No one will expect him on the other side. Well," Josef ate a bit of cake and considered, "I don't think the khaja princes are trustworthy in any case. If they'll cast off their loyalty to their own king, then who says they won't do the same to Bakhtiian?"

"Are you suggesting that there's no use in us receiving an embassy from Parkilnous, if one comes?"

"No, simply that I trust the word of a merchant better. Their first wish is for safe roads, so that they can continue to trade. They will serve us out of expediency, but serve us nevertheless."

"Here is Ilya," said Tess, but Josef only smiled. He already knew. Ilya ducked under the awning.

Ilya greeted Sonia, greeted Tess, greeted Josef and the children. He ate sparingly and paced off with Konstans and Vladimir and Mitya in attendance to oversee the first line of earthworks being built along the river. Cara stopped by to assure herself that Tess was well, and then she left. A while later Mitya returned.

"Aunt Tess," he said, "Bakhtiian is riding out, and he wishes to know if you'd like to ride with him."

Tess laughed. "No, certainly I'd prefer to sit in camp all day. I'm sure the countryside is very pretty." Eventually, they left Katerina in charge of camp, and Sonia rode out with Tess and Mitya and Aleksi. When they met up with Ilya's party, they found Arina Veselov in attendance with her husband, as well.

Kirill chuckled when he greeted Tess. "That's very handy, how you've slung your saber over your back. Don't you trust us?"

"Kirill, I learned long ago never to ride out without being armed. Let me see your hand."

With a grin, he lifted his left arm up as high as his shoulder and then lowered it again. He opened the hand, stretching it wide. Sweat broke on his brow, and he let the hand relax back into a loose curl. "It aches," he said. "It aches constantly. I never thought that pain could feel so sweet."

Tess glanced toward Arina, to share Kirill's triumph with her, but Arina had clenched her hands tightly on her reins and her mouth drew into a thin line.

"Do you think I'll be able to ride in the army again?" Kirill asked, and Tess saw Arina whiten about the mouth.

"You *are* riding with the army, Kirill. I notice that Ilya keeps you as one of his closest advisers."

"Many of whom are too old to ride to battle. I'm still young, Tess. I could have led the army down through the Al Dinn Kun with Tasha."

He could have, had he possessed two good arms. "You must be patient, Kirill, and remember, there are other ways to serve Bakhtiian besides fighting. Look at what Dr. Hierakis has done."

He studied his hand. It had color, and he could open and close it at will now. "It's true that she by herself serves Bakthiian as well as any general. But she's a healer, Tess. That's how she serves the gods. All I've ever been was a rider."

"And a teacher." He shrugged, acknowledging the title but not embracing it, not now, when he could dream again of riding with the army. It was strange to see him shrug with both shoulders after growing used to the way he had moved before, one side lifeless and stiff. She sighed and did not know what else to say. Arina cast her a grateful glance and moved forward along the line to ride beside Sonia. The two women talked easily together. Tess trailed behind, falling back with Aleksi.

The party broke away from the fringe of camp and rode beside acres of lush fields. It was warm, and the air smelled fragrant and rich. Peace lay on the scene. A score of farmers toiled out in a field, harvesting. They started up, staring at the hundred riders picking their way along the edge of the field, and froze. After a bit one, then a second, then four more, then the rest, bent back to their task.

Farther out, the city growing pale against the sky behind them, another group of laborers sowed seeds, some kind of winter grain, Tess supposed. Ilya lifted a hand and the entire party came to a halt while he watched the farmers. His face was still. The sunlight cast its bright glow on his face, illuminating him. Tess wondered what he was thinking as he watched the khaja farmers scattering their seed.

But stillness never lasted long, with him. All at once riders appeared, coming toward them at a breakneck pace. Immediately every rider drew his saber, and the guards shifted to form a ring around Bakhtiian. Aleksi drove Tess into the center and stationed himself beside her. Arina and Sonia drew their bows and nocked arrows to the strings. Behind them, Mitya calmed his restive mare.

"It's Veselov," said Kirill. But no man sheathed his saber. Neither did Tess.

The laborers had rushed together into a clump in the center of their field, but the troop of horsemen rode past without noticing them and drew up before Bakhtiian. Vasil rode forward. The guards parted to let him through. His hair was windblown and his face flushed with sun and air.

"There's been a sortie," he called, pulling his mount around next to Ilya. "At least two thousand men. Heading southeast."

"This way?"

"Possibly. We can't tell if it's an attack or if they're trying to escape south. They carry the colors of the governor of the city, blue and white."

"If they're simply trying to escape, then why not ride out at night?" asked Ilya. "Well, we'll go back to camp." He addressed Vasil calmly, as if the blond man was just any of his commanders: loyal, trusted, true.

Vasil obeyed—how should he not?—but Tess thought he looked a little puzzled, as if expecting Ilya to be angry that *he* had come with this message. They started back at a fast clip.

A cloud of dust alerted them to the battle headed their way. Ilya reined his horse back beside Tess, so that she rode with him on her left and Aleksi on her right. Arina and Sonia rode behind them, and at their back, Kirill and Mitya. Ahead, she saw the blur of arrows. A troop of jaran archers rode parallel to the khaja fighters, firing into their ranks, but like an arrow sped forward from a strong bow, the blue and white governor's banner flew high and the army of men it heralded pressed south with determination.

Ilya swore under his breath. A rider broke away from the jaran unit harrying the khaja left flank and raced over to Bakhtiian's party. It was Anton Veselov.

"We left the one gate unguarded, as you ordered, Bakhtiian," he shouted as he pulled up beside them, flashing a glance back at his sister Arina and then returning his attention to Bakhtiian. "Sakhalin faced sorties before, by that gate, and a troop of one thousand horsemen escaped out of it one night, but this—! We never expected an attack like this."

"Do you think they knew I rode out today?"

"How could they have known?" asked Anton.

How, indeed? What drove the governor to take flight in the afternoon? As the khaja troop closed, Tess could see that they were all heavily armored, presumably the pick of the garrison. Ilya spurred his horse to a gallop and the entire party raced to one side, to avoid the fray.

Somehow, a column of heavy horse coiled free of the khaja ranks and smashed into them. As if she stood at the eye of the storm, Tess watched the chaos from her still eddy in the very center. There rode Vladimir, parrying, cutting. A khaja horseman fell, dragging down a jaran rider with him. Vasil pressed forward into a gap with his riders ranged alongside him. Then, like a whip's snap, the trailing end of the column hit the center. At once, Tess knocked a thrown spear aside with her saber and saw it spin harmlessly to the ground. Three armored riders bore down on her and Ilya, and she set herself in the saddle, bracing for the impact; Ilya swore. All at once Aleksi drove through the riders; he forced one off his horse and grappled with the second from the saddle and then knifed him through the faceplate, and then Vladimir appeared and stuck the third through from behind before he could cut down Aleksi. Grim-faced and silent again, Ilya stuck next to Tess, shielding her, though twice at least the tide of the battle tried to tear him off to the left, and once he took a cut meant for her.

Then, as abruptly as it had struck them, the column was shorn off by the combined weight of the Veselov jahar and a reinforcement of men from the Raevsky command. The governor's flag receded southward, fighting its way away from the city.

Ilya wore a mask of fury. His hands shook. He looked at Tess. She nodded curtly, so he would know she was unhurt. Blood seeped from his left arm, but she could tell by the way he moved the arm that it wasn't a serious wound. She turned to look behind her. Sonia swore and ripped a swath of fabric from her fine tunic to bind Arina's ribs while Mitya held Arina upright on her horse. Kirill, white with anguish, could only watch. His lips moved, but

whether he cursed the khaja or his own helplessness, Tess
could not be sure.

Aleksi pulled in beside her. "Thank you," Tess said to
him. "That was very impressive." She felt like a fool,
saying it, but her heart was pumping and her breath was
ragged and she had to say something, no matter how foolish.

Vasil cantered up, flushed, looking terrified. "You're
wounded!" he exclaimed, gaping at Ilya.

"Collect your men, Veselov, and go after them!" ordered Ilya. "Bring me their heads. If one man from that
troop of riders escapes, I'll demote every commander of
these units back into the ranks. How dare they threaten
my wife!" He was pale with rage.

Without another word, Vasil rode away.

There were wounded in plenty. Tess took Vladi up behind her; others walked. Arina fainted halfway back to
camp, and they had to stop. Ilya took her himself, on his
horse; she was so slight a thing that she was no burden to
him. Kirill looked not just afraid for her life but ashamed
of having to watch while another man cared for his wife.

Cara came out to meet them, having already heard of
the engagement. She took Arina immediately. Niko
tended to Ilya's arm. Tess sat in the shade of Cara's tent
and sipped at juice brought to her by Galina and watched
Kirill pace.

It took two days before Vasil came in at last, bearing
the governor's head on his spear. The rest of the heads the
jahar riders carried in, in baskets and bags. The jaran riders had taken heavy casualties, women and men both, and
in the end it was the archers under Vera Veselov's command who had brought down the final two hundred fleeing soldiers. The collected commanders swore that not
one khaja from the governor's party had escaped, and
they begged for Bakhtiian's pardon that the entire episode
had happened at all.

Working with captured engineers, Ursula had already
made up a catapult as a model to demonstrate siege tech-
niques to the commanders. Bakhtiian gave her all the
heads to fling back into Karkand. Ursula was enchanted.

For only the second time in her pregnancy, Tess threw up. But she could see by the set expression on Ilya's face that this was one of those times when it was useless to argue with him.

CHAPTER NINE

Nadine loved the breakneck pace of a courier's life. Through Habakar lands she raced, stopping at the staging posts set up along the northeast road that led back to the plains. Some nights she rode straight through, dozing in the saddle, her way lit by men bearing lanterns on either side. Some nights she slept in the comfort of a tent and went on at dawn. She loved the music of the bells that accompanied her at every instant, whether riding or walking, that chimed her awake in the morning and serenaded her to sleep at night with each slight movement of her shoulders or her chest.

In eight days, she crossed out of Habakar lands and onto the farthest southern edge of the plains. Five days later, she rode into a tribe at midday to receive the information that the Prince of Jeds and his party had passed by the morning before, headed south. Out here, on the grass, the wind raked over the tents and already the people wore heavy outer tunics against the chill. Women and children greeted her cheerfully; there were a few young men, so few that the old men seemed numerous in proportion. But Nadine enjoyed just walking through camp. She felt at home, at her ease, here in a tribe going about its life out on the plains. The etsana hurried up, advised of her arrival, and led her to the great tent at the center of camp. The elderly woman sat her down and fed her and offered her milk while the etsana's own grandson saddled a new horse for her.

"Ah, you are Bakhtiian's niece," said Mother Kireyevsky. "Natalia Orzhekov's daughter."

"I am." Nadine accepted a second cup of fermented milk from a dark-haired boy about Katerina's age.

"Your mother was a fine weaver. She had few rivals among all the tribes, although she was young to be so accomplished."

"Thank you," said Nadine politely but coolly. She didn't like to talk about her mother because the memory of her death was still too painful, and the ache of her loss had never dulled.

"We have sixty-eight men riding under Vershinin's command," continued Mother Kireyevsky, sliding easily off the subject of Nadine's mother. "Perhaps you have news of them."

Nadine was happy to indulge Mother Kireyevsky with such news of Vershinin's movements as she had. The Kireyevsky tribe was a granddaughter tribe and thus neither particularly important nor very large, but Nadine remembered them from her childhood, back from the golden days when her mother had still been alive. In any case, it was only common courtesy, and wise strategy, to give her a firsthand account of Bakhtiian and the army. Relatives filtered in and settled down to hear the news. The grandson brought a new horse, but Nadine felt she could spare a little time, since she was only turning to go back the way she came. Since Feodor Grekov was less than a day's ride away from her, now. She had no desire to hasten their meeting and what must inevitably come of their marriage.

"So, Vershinin and Grekov were sent to the khaja cities off to the west, to pull a circle all around the royal tent."

Mother Kireyevsky nodded. "Very wise of them. Like a *birbas,* where we circle the game and drive it in to the center. Vasha, bring more sweet cakes."

The boy shot a glance at Nadine before he trotted off. He had dark hair, as dark as her own, and deep brown eyes, and there was something familiar about him that nagged at her. "Is he also one of your grandchildren?" she asked. "He's a nice looking boy."

There was a silence. Mother Kireyevsky gestured, and the knot of relatives hurried away, leaving the etsana alone with Nadine. "You don't know who that is?" she asked.

"Should I?"

"That is Inessa Kireyevsky's only child."

Nadine shook her head. "I don't know her."

"Oh, but you do. Although I suppose you were only about Vasha's age the year that we rode beside your tribe for many months, so you might not recall. Certainly Bakhtiian would recall her."

"Would he?" Nadine felt suddenly that she was on the verge of an important discovery, rather like a mapmaker cresting a ridge to see virgin country beyond.

"Inessa Kireyevsky was my grandmother's sister's great-granddaughter. Inessa's mother was etsana before me, but when she died three years past, the elders refused to elect Inessa etsana and the position passed into our line of the family."

"Was she too young? Was there some other problem?"

"She was young, it is true, but youth alone will not necessarily bar a woman from becoming etsana."

"No, Arina Veselov was very young when she became etsana. There was never any question with her."

The boy appeared, bearing a golden tray laden with sweet cakes. "Was Arina Veselov married?" asked Mother Kireyevsky. "Ah, well, married soon after; it comes to the same thing. Vasha, set those there. Then you will sit beside me." The boy obeyed. He sank down beside the etsana and folded his hands in his lap. He had a quiet, muted air about him, which he utterly spoiled an instant later by looking up at Nadine. His gaze was scorching in its intensity. "Vasha." He dropped his gaze and stared at his hands. "Inessa Kireyevsky was not married when her mother died, although by this time she had an eight-year-old child."

"Ah. Her first husband had died, then."

"She had no first husband. She never married."

"But then how—" Nadine faltered. The boy's cheeks burned red, but he kept his gaze fastened on his hands. Well, she knew how; it was just astonishing for a jaran woman to bear a child without being married. The unmarried girls were so careful with the herbs that stopped them from conceiving, because, of course, it was shameful for a child not to have a father and a child's father was the man who was married to its mother.

"Yes," agreed Mother Kireyevsky. "You can see that Inessa was too stubborn and too impulsive to be given the authority of etsana. The man she wanted to marry did not marry her. The rest, she avoided or insulted or drove off in one fashion or the other until in the end they all shunned her. Luckily, she died the winter after her mother died."

The boy sat perfectly still through this recital, but his hands betrayed his distress, one clenched in a fist, one wrapped around it, like a shield.

"Leaving her son." Nadine pitied the boy, his mother torn from him, leaving him among relatives who clearly thought him a shameful reminder of his mother's disgraceful behavior.

"Leaving a boy with no father, dead or otherwise, and no closer relatives than distant cousins. That line was not strong."

"Why are you telling me this?" asked Nadine suddenly.

"Will you have another sweet cake?" Mother Kireyevsky asked. Nadine accepted, and the etsana placed the tray back on the carpet beside her pillow. "Inessa claimed to know who the child's father was. It was her last wish, as she lay dying of a fever, that the boy be sent to his father. The truth is, if it is at all possible that the child would be accepted as a servant, as a cousin, even, we would prefer to send him away. We would never have presumed ... but when you came, today, I can only believe that it is a sign from the gods, that what Inessa wished ought indeed to happen."

Nadine knew what was coming. Now, when she looked at the boy, she understood why he seemed familiar to her, why his features struck such a deep chord.

Mother Kireyevsky cleared her throat, coughed, and spoke. "She claimed that his father was Ilyakoria Orzhekov."

"My uncle. Bakhtiian." The resemblance was striking, once you looked for it. The boy had Ilya's eyes and forehead and stubborn mouth, and the same sharp chin that she—his cousin!—had. Nadine stifled an urge to laugh. Gods, not just laugh, but crow. After what Ilya had done to her, forcing her to accept the marriage to Feodor

Grekov, ordering her to have children, well, by the gods, she would bring this little bit of mischief home for him to face. What a scandal! Nadine was delighted. "Of course he must return with me. I'm riding back to the army now, as you know. I will take responsibility for his well-being myself."

The boy's head jerked up and he stared at her. Nadine saw light spark in his eyes. Evidently he wished to be rid of his relatives as much as they wished to be rid of him.

Mother Kireyevsky eyed Nadine's clothing and her saber, and then her keen gaze came to rest on Nadine's cheek. "You are recently married yourself."

"Yes. I also command a jahar. You may be assured that the child is safe with me. What is his name? Vasha is short for—?"

"Vassily."

"Vassily!" Nadine was shocked right down to the core of her being. "How did he come by *that* name?"

To her surprise, the boy spoke in a gruff little voice. "My mama told me that that is the name *he* said to give me."

At once, Mother Kireyevsky cuffed Vasha across the cheek. "Don't mind him," she said hastily. "It's a story Inessa told the boy, that she told Bakhtiian that she was pregnant with a child by him, and he said that if it was a boy, to name it Vasil. As if any woman, even her, would do something so unseemly, and any man—especially not your uncle, of course—speak of such things so casually, even in jest. She told the boy many things, I'm afraid, and he's always been full of himself, thinking that he's the son of a great man. You needn't mind it. Of course Bakhtiian can't recognize him as his son—it's all quite ridiculous, of course, that an unmarried woman—of course he has no father, but we're grateful to you for taking him—"

"He looks like him," said Nadine, cutting across Mother Kireyevsky's comments, "as I'm sure you must know." She was beginning to dislike the woman. She was beginning to dislike Inessa Kireyevsky, too, and wondered if she would dislike the boy just as much. Although it was rather late for that, now that she had already agreed to take him. "But in any case, I must go. I'll need a horse for him and whatever things are his, or that he got from his mother."

Mother Kireyevsky stood and shook out her skirts briskly. "Oh, he'll travel very light. He's got nothing, really, just her tent and a few trinkets."

"*He* gave my mother a necklace," said the boy. "It's gold with round white stones. He brought it from over the seas. From a khaja city called Jeds." He said the word as if it was a talisman, a mark identifying him as the true prince, the heir, because what common boy of the tribes, of a granddaughter tribe like this one, would have any reason to know of Jeds?

"Go get your things, Vasha," said Mother Kireyevsky curtly. Now that she had what she wanted, she sped Nadine's leave-taking along as swiftly as if she feared that Nadine would change her mind and leave her with the unwanted child.

They rode out in silence. After a while, seeing that his seat on his horse was sturdy and that he was minded to be quiet and obedient, Nadine spoke to him.

"How old are you, Vasha?"

"I was born in the Year of the Hawk."

"Oh, gods," she murmured under her breath. The Year of the Hawk. The year her mother died; the year her brother and her grandparents died; the year Bakhtiian killed the man who had murdered them. The year Bakhtiian stood up before the assembled elders of the tribes—most of the tribes, in any case—and persuaded them that the vision the gods had given him was the vision the tribes ought to follow. Eleven years ago all this had taken place. In eleven years, much had changed. Everything had changed. Nadine felt a sudden misgiving, wondering how Ilya might treat a child who reminded him so bitterly of those days. Eleven years ago Ilya had banished Vasil from his jahar; he had seen his mother's younger sister invested as etsana of the Orzhekov tribe and had himself become the most powerful dyan in the jaran. Perhaps he didn't want to be reminded of what he had paid to bring his dreams to fruition.

"Is it true?" asked the boy suddenly. Nadine looked

at him and saw the aching vulnerability of his expression. "Is he really my father? My mama always said so, but ..." His face twisted with pain. "... but she lied, sometimes, when it suited her. She said it was true. She said he would have married her, but she never said why he didn't, so I don't think he ever would have. Only that she wanted him to. And then she always told me that he was going to come back for her. Every tribe we came to, she asked if they'd news, if he'd married. He never had, so she said he still meant to come back for her. Then after my grandmother died, the next summer we heard that he'd married a khaja princess. Mama fell sick and died. Both the healer and a Singer said she'd poisoned herself in her heart and the gods had been angry and made her die of it. No one wanted me after that."

Nadine stared amazed at him, until she realized that the stoic expression on his face as he recited this confession was his way of bracing to receive her disgust. Either he wanted it, or he was so used to being rejected that he wanted to get it out of the way early and go on from there.

"I think you're his son." Gods, what if she got his hopes up, only to have Ilya deny the connection? And yet, how could he deny it?

"How can I be?" demanded Vasha. "He wasn't married to my mother."

Nadine sighed. "I'll let him explain that," she said, calling herself coward as she did so. Gods, what was Tess going to say? Well, who knew with the khaja; they had different notions of propriety than the jaran did. Maybe Tess would want to have the boy strangled; maybe she would welcome him. Who could tell? But Nadine had promised that he would be safe, and she'd hold to that promise, no matter what. She rather liked his brusque cynicism, although it was sad to see it in a child. And anyway, Vassily Kireyevsky's presence made no difference to her problems. Bakhtiian still needed an heir, and he still expected Nadine to provide him with one.

So it was with a troubled heart that she and the boy rode into the prince's camp at dusk the next day. A scout from her jahar greeted her enthusiastically and directed her to a copse of trees around a spring, where the prince and his party had pitched their tents.

She saw David first. His face lit up. He had a charming smile, made more so by the interesting contrast of white teeth against his odd black skin. He lifted a hand and called a greeting to her. Others turned, the other members of the party. David strode over toward her, grinning with undisguised happiness—and then stopped. Pulled up like a horse brought up tight against the end of its rope. His smile vanished.

Feodor appeared from around the screen of trees, mounted. He reined his horse aside and waited for her. Once he would have flushed to see her; he would have turned his gaze away and cast sidelong glances at her in a way she found provocative and enchanting. Now he stared straight at her in a way that annoyed her, knowing that he had a perfect right to look her straight in the eye in so public a place, now that he was her husband.

She dismounted and walked first to greet the prince. Soerensen came to meet her, looking pleased to see her. She gave him the news of Bakhtiian's recovery, and he took it calmly enough. Nadine found him impossible to read. She would almost have thought that he already knew, though she couldn't imagine how he would have found out so quickly. Perhaps he'd had the news at the Kireyevsky tribe.

"Oh, and this is Vassily Kireyevsky," she said. "Vasha, please, you can dismount now. Come to me." The boy obeyed meekly enough. He stared at David's skin, recalled his manners, looked away only to glance at David again, and then turned his attention to the khaja prince. "This is the Prince of Jeds, Vasha. Make your greetings."

The boy made a creditable bow. "Well met," he said shyly. "I've heard of Jeds. It's a great khaja city, and it has a—" He faltered over the foreign word. "—a *uyniversite*. And craftsmen who make fine jewelry." The boy had good manners, Nadine was relieved to see. Ilya did not tolerate bad manners, so perhaps there was hope.

"Well met," replied the prince, looking amused. Nadine watched, impressed, as he asked the boy a few neutral questions about his age and the horse he'd ridden in on

and managed not to ask anything the least controversial—
like who his parents were, or why a child his age was riding with Nadine. Then, as neatly, the prince dismissed
him into the care of his assistant, Maggie O'Neill. Vasha
stared openmouthed at her red hair and followed her
away as if mesmerized by her height and strange freckled
coloring.

The prince regarded Nadine with interest and said not
one more word on the matter. "You came back to us," he
said instead, and mercifully did not glance toward her
husband, who had dismounted and given his horse to one
of her men to take away.

"Bakhtiian sent me to escort you back to the army,"
she said. "Tess is fine. She looked quite healthy when I
left her." She shot a glance at David, who had inched forward next to Marco Burckhardt to listen in. "We've been
making maps together."

Marco coughed into a hand. Nadine could tell he was
hiding a smile, but she wasn't sure what he found amusing in the statement. David looked troubled.

"I'm pleased to hear about Tess, of course," said the
prince without a flicker of emotion. "I hope you will let
us offer you some tea and some supper."

Before she could reply, she felt Feodor come up beside
her, right up next to her. "That would be most gracious of
you," Feodor replied, "especially since we haven't had
our wedding feast yet."

Every now and then, Nadine got so mad that she went
blind with fury. Usually she had a strong enough rein on
her self-control. Not now.

The shock of her anger, the sheer force of it, froze her
for an instant. The world had gone dark, though a moment before she could see trees in the twilight and clouds
roiling above, covering and uncovering stars. She felt the
cool wind pull at her hair. She heard the prince murmur
words and she felt more than knew that they had all retreated, leaving her alone with Feodor out beyond the
trees. She heard a man ask a question, and a voice answering, but these were distant, distant from her.

Feodor's hand closed on her elbow.

She jerked away from the touch and swung wildly. Her

palm connected with his cheek, the blow so hard across the cheek that he gasped with pain. He grabbed her arms. "Not out here in the open, by the gods," he hissed under his breath. "You won't shame our marriage by acting like this in public."

"How dare you speak for me!"

"I am your husband."

"Not by my choice."

"You have no choice in the matter, or did you think your journey to khaja lands made you different?"

Like light poured into a pitch-black room, her vision came back. She staggered, overwhelmed by the sudden shift, and he steadied her. This close, she saw the cleft in his chin, and the scar at the corner of his mouth, and the slight bump in his nose where it had been broken in a battle three years ago. She pulled back from him, but like all jaran men, his slightness disguised his true strength.

"Dina," he said more softly, "why are you fighting me? I never tried to mark you before, not as long as I thought you meant to stay in the army."

"I do mean to stay in the army. Bakhtiian promised me that he wouldn't take my command away from me." She could not keep the triumph from her voice. "And you know what Bakhtiian's promises are worth."

Feodor looked stunned by this information. Nadine rocked back, forward, broke out of his grip and took five swift steps away from him. Then halted. She was panting with anger, and her head pounded. Stars flashed in her eyes and she was afraid that she was going to go blind again.

"But Mother Sakhalin said—" he began.

"Mother Sakhalin does not rule me!"

Gods, he had a mulish streak in him. She recognized it now for what it was, masked under that sweet, modest exterior she had mistaken for his true self. His mouth turned down. His fine eyes glinted with anger. "Perhaps she doesn't," he said softly, "but I am now your husband. Keep your command if you will. I'd be a fool twice over to contest Bakhtiian if he's already given his word. But nevertheless, I remain your husband. You may wish to be rid of me, Dina, but even if I die, you won't be free. You

must have a child. You know it's true. If not with me,
then with another man."

"Is that what Mother Sakhalin told you?" she asked
scathingly.

"You may think as little of me as you wish," he replied, still speaking in a low voice, "you may think me a
fool, as it pleases you. Mother Sakhalin came to my uncle
and my aunt and pointed out that Bakhtiian must have an
heir, more than one, to be safe, and that you are his sister's daughter and thus by right the woman who should be
mother to his heirs. That much she said, within my hearing. The rest I managed to work out for myself."

Nadine had never suspected that Feodor Grekov, quiet,
mild, shy Feodor Grekov, was capable of sarcasm. The
revelation so amazed her that the shadow growing over
her sight receded, and she watched him straighten his
shirtsleeve self-consciously and wipe a bead of moisture
from the corner of his right eye. She shivered in the wind.
She wasn't dressed for the plains, for the night and the
chill wind that tore across the endless horizon. In
Habakar lands, heat still smothered the day and lingered
far into the night.

"I beg pardon for insulting you," she said, though it
pained her to say it.

"That was hard won," he said, with a toss of his fair
hair. "Does your head hurt you?"

The reversal confused her, not least because her head
did indeed pound furiously. She pressed fingers against
her left eye, wondering if it was possible that an invisible
knife was being driven into the flesh there.

"You need to rest." He did not move any closer to her,
but the tone with which he addressed her irritated her.
"You know very well," he added before she could respond, "that I've seen this happen to you before. I've already set up your tent. You should go lie down."

"You set up my tent!"

He shrugged. "Well, you left it with me."

"I left it with the jahar. That's not the same."

"But it's our tent now, or at least, I have every right to
share it with you. Say what you will, Dina, but I know

what obligations you have toward me, now that you're my wife."

"I had no idea that you were such an officious, stubborn, stiff-necked bastard, Feodor Grekov. I'd never have taken you for a lover if I'd known." He smiled. He usually had a surprisingly winsome smile; this wasn't it. This smile was smug and cocksure, and Nadine didn't like it one bit. "The boy needs a place to sleep tonight. I'll have to take him into my tent. I'm the only one he knows here."

"I'll make sure he has a place to sleep, but it won't be in your tent. Who is he, anyway?"

"None of your business."

He shrugged, not deigning to argue with her over so trivial a matter. "Do you want to eat first, or go straight to bed?"

The throbbing in her head had subsided to a steady, agonizing pulse. She did not want to go straight to her tent, but she knew she could not manage conversation with so illustrious a personage as the Prince of Jeds, and she did not want to face David and the others in this condition. She was ashamed.

"I'll take you to the tent," he said when she did not reply. What choice did she have? He knew what his rights were, and her obligations. But to her surprise, he left her outside the tent. She crawled in and flung herself down on the floor and just lay there in the darkness. After a while, the pounding in her head diminished to a dull, roaring throb. After a while, Feodor returned with hot tea, and Vasha, and a lantern to light them. The boy thanked her and begged leave to spend the night in the tent of the khaja lady with hair the color of fire. The entire speech had a rehearsed sound to it. Nadine didn't know the child well enough to know whether he was happy with the arrangement or resigned to his fate.

"You'll ride with me tomorrow," she insisted. Vasha agreed. Feodor sent him away. After a moment, Feodor crawled into the tent, hooked the lantern along the center pole, and took off his boots.

"Drink your tea," he said. He turned. He had long, pale eyelashes that never showed unless the light struck him just right, and lantern light usually struck him so as to bring out his most attractive features. "Gods, Dina, don't refuse it just to spite me. It ought to make you feel better." He began to pull off his shirt, hesitated, and then shifted to pull off her boots instead. She let him. Then she sipped at her tea and he watched her, just watched her, until she had emptied the cup. She was not used to him watching her so closely, so openly. The sensation made her skin crawl. He moved, and she tensed, but he reached away from her and extinguished the lantern.

Darkness. She sighed and shut her eyes. "You will have children. I order you to." She could still hear Ilya's voice. Ilya was all that was left to her of her mother. Nataliia Orzhekov would have had many more children, and gladly, to help her beloved younger brother. Was her daughter going to do any less than she would have? Nadine knew her duty.

Feodor's hand came to rest on her brow. He stroked her forehead and the circle of bone around her left eye, and the pounding in her head faded to an ache. He was gentle, and patient, and tender. She ought to have guessed long ago, though, about that other side of his personality, the determined, brash side. He was bold enough once he got between her blankets. She would never have kept him for a lover for as long as she had if he hadn't been.

She sighed and her right hand strayed onto his thigh. He made a noise in his throat and all at once—well, all at once. The change was so sudden that she only realized then how firmly he had clamped down on his feelings before. He shook with emotion, and she could not get him to take his hands off of her for even a moment, so she had a damned hard time getting him out of his clothes and he was a little rough with hers.

She was still angry, afterward, but much calmer. "Feodor," she began in a low voice, and then: "Oh, here, move over, will you? My back is up against the tent wall."

He shifted, and she shifted, and he traced her earlobe and the line of her jaw and her lips. "Hmm?"

"Feodor, you can't speak like that to me, like you did

out there, before. It just makes me furious. And it isn't right."

"I can speak to you however I wish. I'm your husband."

"Yes, as you're forever reminding me."

There was silence. "No," he said finally, so low that she had to strain to hear, "perhaps it's myself I'm reminding. Gods, I dreamed, but I never thought—" He broke off. He turned his face into her cheek and just breathed. She felt like she didn't know him at all. "Anyway," he said, his lips moving against her skin, "I'll bet your head doesn't hurt anymore."

"Oh, gods," said Nadine to the air. She settled in against him. He began to hum under his breath: He was happy. Nadine sighed and resigned herself to her fate.

CHAPTER TEN

Arina had died once already by the time Diana got to Dr. Hierakis's tent. A boy from the Veselov tribe brought Diana the news—garbled, she prayed—at the Company encampment, and she ran all the way to the hospital grounds and into the doctor's tent, pitched in the center. She stopped at the edge of the carpet. Her ribs were in agony; she gulped air.

Tess sat cross-legged on a pillow, mending the torn hem of a tunic. Her eyes lifted once to watch Kirill, pacing in the distance, and then shifted to Diana. Her face lit. "Ah, thank goodness," she said in Anglais.

"What happened?" Diana fairly shrieked the words. Beyond the tent, Kirill opened and closed his good hand to the rhythm of his pacing. His face was white. Once a man paused to speak to him, but the exchange was brief and the man shook his head sadly and walked away.

"We got caught in a skirmish. Arina was wounded."

"But—she's dead—?"

Tess pinned the needle into the fabric, bound up the loose thread, and set down the torn tunic. "Her heart stopped. At that point, Cara threw every jaran out of the surgery and began—well, she's operating now."

"Operating!"

Kirill halted stock-still and looked their way, caught by the sound of Diana's voice. He strode over to them and flung himself down on the carpet, next to Tess. Tess embraced him. He accepted it. More than that—he buried himself against her as if he sought his comfort from her. Diana knew body language. When acquaintances embrace, one can read the gap between them. When friends, when siblings embrace, no matter how close, there is still an infinitesimal distance, like a layer of molecules, separating them. When a mother hugs her child, they meet. But when lovers embrace, they don't just meet but join. Tess held Kirill against her as if he was her lover.

At this inopportune moment, Bakhtiian appeared. A bandage swathed his left arm. Tess's gaze lifted and met his. Diana watched an entire conversation pass between them, wordless and within seconds. A lifted eyebrow. A grimace. Eyes slanting toward the tent. The movement of a chin, signifying a nod. To Diana's astonishment, Bakhtiian grabbed a pillow, threw it down on the other side of Kirill, and settled down beside the other man. At once, Kirill broke away from Tess and sat up. He flushed.

"Here is something to drink." Bakhtiian offered the other man a cup of komis. Trapped between Tess and Bakhtiian, Kirill had to accept. He sipped once, twice, and then gulped the rest down like a man who has only just discovered that he is desperately thirsty. Then he sat, breathing hard, gaze fixed on his withered hand. He closed it into a fist, and opened it again. Closed it. Opened it.

"Do you want a command?" asked Bakhtiian, refilling Kirill's cup.

"Ilya—" began Tess.

Kirill flung his head back. "A command!"

"A general doesn't have to fight in every engagement. He only has to lead. I know your worth, Kirill. And I know the worth of your loyalty to me. You and Josef and Niko are the three men I trust most in the whole world. You'll never be the fighter you were, but you've some use in that arm now. Enough to lead your own command, I think."

Diana was appalled. Was this how Bakhtiian consoled him for the death of his wife?

Kirill's expression underwent so many swift changes from one emotion to another that Diana could not read them all: anguish, exhilaration, hope, fear, ambition—Goddess! He was going to accept.

"You honor me, Bakhtiian," he said softly.

Bakhtiian snorted. "It's only to keep you away from my wife."

Kirill grinned. Yes, he was a distinctly attractive man, and he knew it. "I suppose it's unlikely that she won't succumb to my greater charms sooner or later."

"Perhaps," said Bakhtiian. His lips quirked.

"I find this conversation offensive, considering the circumstances." said Tess in a voice thick with emotion. "If you can't talk about something decent, then stop talking."

Immediately both men looked chastened. Into their silence, bells sang softly and Ursula emerged from the doctor's tent. Kirill jumped to his feet.

"Arina?"

"She'll live," said Ursula curtly. "Tess, Cara needs you—Ah, Diana. You'd be much better. Can you come in?"

"Can I—?" Kirill faltered. "May I see her?"

"No. Diana?"

"Yes," said Diana hurriedly. "I'll come." She nodded at the others and escaped inside.

In the inner chamber, Dr. Hierakis leaned over the foot of the scan-bed and stared at a pulsing graph configured on a flat screen. "Tess," she said without looking up, "I want to look over the other wounded. Can you sit by—?" She glanced up. "Oh, hello, Diana. If you can spare the time, I'd be pleased to have you sit here and monitor her."

"Of course I can spare the time!" Diana hesitated, not sure how awful a scene she would discover. She edged closer, but Arina simply appeared to be deeply asleep. A slick transparent cap covered her hair, and her mouth gaped slightly open. A sheet draped her; warmth emanated from the bed on which she lay.

"Oh, there're no gaping wounds to see." Dr. Hierakis's attention had snapped back to the screen, but as usual she seemed able to read unvoiced thoughts. "All right and tight, and no scars except the ones they'd expect to see."

"What happened to her?"

"Spear or sword thrust shattered her rib cage and she got a bone chip in her heart. For one. Died twice on me, she did, but she'll be fine."

Diana crept forward and covered Arina's limp hand

with her own. "Why did you bring her in here? If she'd been a man, you'd have let her die, wouldn't you?"

The doctor glanced up, surprised. She blinked. Without its frame of black curls, her face showed stark and strong in the soft light. "Why I suppose I would have. Probably ten men less badly wounded than her have died already, while I've been in here."

"Not to mention the Habakar soldiers."

The doctor snorted. "Don't mention them, please. I have enough on my conscience as it is. Though the jaran healers are saving ten times the number of wounded they would have before I came. Still." She pushed off from the bed and pulled off her surgery cap. Though her hair was bound back in a twist at the nape of her neck, stray wisps had escaped here and there, giving her an untidy appearance. "Goddess. Maybe I'm biased. It just tore at me, though, when they brought her in that way. That, and Kirill's face."

"Doctor! You'd let a man's looks sway you?"

The doctor laughed. "I meant his fear and grief. But, yes, frankly, I would. Why not? There's little enough joy, and far too much pain, in a world like this not to appreciate the beauty that comes your way. He has a kind heart, and kind hearts count for a great deal in my book." She peeled off gloves so sheer that Diana hadn't known she was wearing them. "She'll be out for eight more hours at least. I've got her under deep recovery. I'd like to keep her with me for another two days, and then I think she can be moved back to her camp. How long can you stay here?"

Diana hesitated. "I don't know. Rehearsals. . . . Can Kirill come in and just look at her, at least?"

"Not today." The doctor ran a cool towel over her face and then scrubbed her hands under the sonic decontaminant shelf. "I don't have time to disguise the equipment, and I understand there're mobs of wounded and more expected. I'll tell Kirill to see to his children." She swept out.

Diana stood in silence, holding onto Arina's cool hand. At the foot of the couch, projecting up, a faint three-dimensional image of Arina's body rotated slowly in the air. Angry red pulsed around the heart and scored a half-dozen other places around her midsection. She did not stir, only breathed. Diana found a stool and sat down to watch over her.

After a long while, bells chimed and Tess entered. "Do you want anything?" Tess asked, regarding Arina pensively. "I can send Aleksi to keep watch—oh, hell—no, I can't. It wouldn't be proper. There's no one but the actors, you, and Ursula, and myself."

"Can you send Owen a message?"

"Better yet, I'll go myself and ask him to release you for two days. Will that be—?"

"No." Diana winced, thinking of rehearsals, thinking of the parts she had yet to master. Quinn and Oriana had divided her old parts between them, leaving an odd combination of secondary roles for Anahita to fill in, but Anahita had collapsed once onstage already so she could no longer be relied on. But this was Arina. "Yes. But could you bring my slate back, so I can study my parts? And a change of clothes?"

"Yes."

"What happened?"

Tess explained about a sortie and how the trailing edge of the battle had slammed against their surveying party and then charged on.

"Dr. Hierakis said there were lots of casualties."

"Many," said Tess grimly. "And many more to come." She left.

Diana did not understand what Tess had meant by that final comment until three days later, when the hospital was full of jaran injured, many of them from the Veselov tribe. The Veselov jahar had been hit hard by the battle and the pursuit. The doctor designated a stretcher for Arina that morning, and Kirill arrived breathless to walk beside his wife as they carried her back to her own camp. Arina was conscious but pale and weak. Diana walked on Arina's other side.

They walked in silence for awhile. At last, Kirill spoke. "Arina, Bakhtiian is going to give me my own command."

Diana winced. Arina had already expressed her fear that Kirill would want to ride in the army; this wasn't going to help her get better.

But Arina got a sudden spark of light in her eyes. Her voice, when she spoke, was faint but clear. "Your own command? Not just to ride in the army?

"My own command. My own army. We talked about it. There's much reconnaissance yet to be done. There's the Golden Road that runs east to be scouted, and the lands southwest from here, past the city the khaja call Parkilnous." He had warmed to his topic, but now he faltered and looked down at his wife in concern.

In the distance, Diana heard a rhythmic thump and whistle, thump and whistle, over and over and over and going on endlessly.

"What is that noise?" Diana asked when it became apparent to her that Arina had nothing to say about Kirill's good fortune—which, of course, must seem the worst of fortunes to Arina.

Kirill answered without looking up from his wife's face. He held her hand in his withered one, but Diana could see that the hand looked fleshier and the arm actually had some substance to it now, as if by constant exercise he meant to restore it to its former strength. "It's a *catapult*."

"Oh. What are they doing? Lobbing stones into the city for practice?"

"No. Heads. For a lesson."

It took Diana a full thirty strides to realize that he wasn't joking. She turned her face away and shuddered. Of course, she thought of Anatoly, sent out to bring the king's head to Bakhtiian. How did you separate a head from its shoulders? How difficult was it? Did it cause a terrible mess? Was there a lot of blood, or only if the victim was still alive? Or if the blade wasn't sharp enough?

"Diana, are you well? You're looking pale."

She started. "No, Kirill, I'm fine. Just worried about Arina."

Arina, on her pallet, smiled weakly. "I'll be well," she said. Her voice was breathless and wheezy, but determined. "Bakhtiian has honored you, Kirill," she said finally.

"You're content?"

"Your own command? Yes, I'm content."

She lapsed into silence. But her words shocked Diana. It hadn't been fear for Kirill's life that had caused Arina to speak so before, but only fear that he'd be just another rider. But make him a general in his own right, and then all was well. Goddess, she would never understand these people.

The whole tribe came out to meet them as the little party entered the Veselov encampment. They kept a respectful distance, but they wanted a glimpse of their etsana. At times like this, Diana was wrenched away from her view of Arina as a sweet girlfriend about her own age and forced to realize that Arina had considerable authority and extremely high status. It reminded her of Mother Sakhalin's disappointment in the common woman—a mere entertainer with a pretty face—whom her grandson had married. Anatoly should have married someone important, someone like Galina Orzhekov or a foreign princess, someone who wanted him to ride in the army, who was proud that he commanded his own jahar and was sent by Bakhtiian to perform important and dangerous deeds. She put a hand to her face, touching the scar that branded her left cheek. What was it Sonia had said, that a woman and a man are married as long as the scar marks the woman's face, or the man lives? And yet, on Earth, it would be a simple procedure to erase the scar forever.

At Arina's tent, Arina's young sister and Karolla Arkhanov waited to place her on pillows inside the great tent. They settled her in. Diana felt superfluous. Mira shrieked, to see her mother, but knelt a handbreadth away from her as she had evidently been instructed not to disturb her. Lavrenti bawled and arched his back in anger because his uncle Anton wouldn't put him down on his mother. At last Kirill took Lavrenti and the boy calmed, his thin face caught in a baby's sullen pout.

Vasil came to pay his respects. He looked battered and bruised, and he limped, but the injuries merely gave him an interesting air of nobility in the face of dangers seen and conquered. Diana edged away and backed out through the throng. It was time to go home.

At the outskirts of the Veselov encampment, Vasil appeared suddenly, mounted, leading a saddled horse. "Oh, I beg your pardon," he said, greeting her with a sidelong glance. He smiled that brilliant smile of his. "It's a long walk back across camp, and I have to deliver these horses. . . . Would you prefer to ride?"

"Oh, I . . ." His presence flustered her. He was so intensely good-looking and so determined to make an impression on her. And it was a long walk. "That's very kind of you. I'd be honored."

"Not at all. The honor is mine." He waited while she mounted. He did not once look at her straight on, and yet she felt that he looked at her constantly. They rode, and she knew that this was all somehow improper, but she wasn't sure she cared. "Five nights ago you sang the story of the etsana who judged her daughters poorly. Who has written this story? Or did you write it yourselves? Is it an old story of your people? And how—well, when a Singer of the jaran sings, she tells a story in music and with her words. How did it happen that with your people you tell these stories by—by becoming the stories?"

All the rest of the way to the Company encampment Diana explained to Vasil, as well as she could, about acting and theater. Vasil drank in every word. He asked a hundred more questions.

At the camp, she thanked him and dismounted. He turned the horses away and paused. "You have only to ask," he murmured, looking down at her from under lowered lids, demure and yet completely assured. He hesitated one instant longer. When she only gaped at him and did not reply, he rode away.

Quinn jogged out. "Well. Well, well. He's a stunner. That your latest lover, Di?"

"No." Diana stared at his retreating back. And a fine back it was, too, straight and even, with his golden hair lapping the collar of his scarlet shirt. "But I think he just told me that he was available to audition for the part. And

I don't think he was delivering those horses anywhere but here."

"What?"

"Never mind." She shook her head impatiently, as if sloughing off the last three days. "I'm back. What did I miss?"

Quinn launched into a long explication of how Ginny and Owen were disputing over whether translation hurt the text more than it helped the process of understanding, and what progress Ginny had made on crafting a telling of the jaran story about the Daughter of the Sun who came from the heavens to visit the earth and ended up falling in love with a dyan of the tribes.

"They're going to risk that?"

"Oh, Di, the jaran will never suspect. How should they? It's a wonderful story. Yomi said that Dr. Hierakis thinks that it's Bakhtiian's favorite story. Now they're talking about actually doing *Tamburlaine*."

"Oh, I hope not," said Diana with feeling. "I've had enough of war. What about *The Tempest*? Aren't we going to do that? And the folktale about Mekhala. What about Ginny's *Cyclopean Walls*?"

"Ah, absence does make the heart grow fonder. We've had to listen to Anahita complain on and on about how sick she is. We've been working like dogs while you've been away."

"I didn't enjoy it!"

"I'm sorry." Quinn backed down immediately.

"No, I'm sorry. I just—I don't know. Never mind. I'm glad to be back. 'I like this place, and willingly could waste my time in it.' Is there anything interesting to eat? Something—not what I could get in the camp?"

"You *are* out of sorts," said Quinn thoughtfully.

" 'How weary are my spirits.' "

Quinn rested a hand on Diana's arm. "Poor Di. Come home."

"Gladly," said Diana, and went with her into camp. Gladly she fell back into the routine. She went once a day to see Arina, who slowly grew stronger, but Arina's own people took care of her. As the days wore on, Diana noticed Vasil frequently, here and there, running across her path now and again as if by accident, usually at the Veselov camp. And often, now, she saw him loitering in the background, at the outskirts of the audience that always gathered to watch them practice, watching their rehearsals with a look of hungry intensity on his face.

CHAPTER ELEVEN

Despite himself, Jiroannes found the city of Karkand impressive. In its own foreign way, the city rivaled the Great King's capital of Flowering Mountain in southern Vidiya. Two walls enclosed Karkand. The outermost wall ringed a huge expanse of land, fields, gardens, orchards, and suburbs watered by canals, but the Habakar had given these flats up for lost and most of the population had retreated inside the massive inner walls that fortified the twin hills of the main city.

Eight days after the army had besieged the city, Jiroannes rode with Mitya through these environs. Peasants from the lands surrounding Hamrat and from farther south had filtered in behind the army and taken the fields and the houses and now worked them for their jaran masters. Still, the place was half deserted, and the season was turning.

The triple arched gateway through the outer wall opened onto a broad square paved with stone. Beyond the square three tree-lined avenues thrust into the suburbs. To the right, a marketplace sprawled along the inner wall, farmers and merchants selling vegetables and grain. They stared at the fifty jaran riders, Mitya's escort, but went about their business nonetheless. Traffic passed through the smaller of the three gateways, men trundling carts or leading donkeys laden with goods.

To the left, a marble fountain spilled water down a series of ledges. To Jiroannes's surprise, a woman dressed in white sat alone and unveiled and unmolested by the pool at the foot of the fountain. She sat with her hands in her lap and a ceramic beaker at her right hand. Now and again a man halted before her, and she dipped the beaker into the pool and offered him water to drink. When the jaran riders paced by, she watched them apprehensively, but she did not move from her station beside the splashing fountain. Jiroannes noted that the skin of her hands was very fine, the mark of a woman who has not been forced to engage in any heavier labor than dipping water from a font. Her complexion was not as fine, sitting out in the sun as she was, but she looked far less suncoarsened than did the jaran women, who without exception of rank or age worked at tasks fit only for a slave.

"She might as well be a jaran woman," said Jiroannes. "I had not noticed that Habakar women were so immodest. But perhaps she is a prostitute."

Bakhtiian had elevated the Habakar general's son up from his status as prisoner and allowed him freedom as Mitya's interpreter, because the boy had learned khush, and because the boy was about Mitya's age. Qushid hid a look of horror behind one hand and after a moment uncovered his face again. He was tall, taller than Mitya, dark-complexioned with close-cropped black hair, but reserved to the point of seeming stupid. Bakhtiian's chief wife conducted a school for those so favored by her husband, and this boy attended it by Bakhtiian's order, learning khush and the ways of the jaran.

Mitya threw a glance back at Jiroannes. "You must learn not to speak so disrespectfully of women, Jiroannes," he said mildly. "My Aunt Sonia still counsels Bakhtiian that you ought to be sent home in disgrace. He listens to her as closely as he would to my grandmother, who is Mother Orzhekov of our tribe."

"I beg your pardon," replied Jiroannes, not wanting to offend his friend. Mitya was too much a savage to understand how civilized women behaved. The Habakar boy doubtless possessed a finer education.

"She is a holy woman," said Qushid haltingly. "The priests choose girls each year to serve as the Almighty God's handmaidens. They are God's brides and are not meant for men."

"Ah." Jiroannes nodded. "I see. Such holy women may not be touched by men."

"Nor would any man touch one. To violate a holy

woman is the worst crime any man might commit, except to forswear Almighty God Himself. They are sworn to serve Him, not man."

Mitya looked mystified. "Do you mean to say those poor women aren't allowed to get married? Or even to—?" He broke off, flushing. "That's barbaric!"

"Don't you have priests?" Qushid asked.

"Of course we have priests, a few, and Singers. Both women and men. But just as the gods granted death to us, so did they also grant us love. It's not just foolish but dangerous to turn away from that with which the gods have gifted us."

"It is true," said Jiroannes thoughtfully, thinking of the captain of his guards and how he had pleaded with his master for permission to bring women into the camp, "that the Everlasting God enjoins a man not to go without a woman for more than ten days. But, of course, it is different for women."

"It is?" Mitya looked dumbfounded. "How can it be different for women?"

Jiroannes felt unable to answer this question. Instead, he glanced at Qushid and had the pleasure of seeing that the Habakar boy bore a sympathetic look on his face— one sympathetic to Jiroannes. It was, quite simply, impossible to explain some things to the jaran, because they were too uncivilized to understand such sophisticated philosophical and spiritual concepts.

Mitya pulled his horse aside to admire a cart stacked with ripe melons that gleamed a pale rich green in the noonday sun. At once, the old man tending the cart leapt to his feet and presented the boy with the pick of the melons.

"Here," said Mitya, turning to Qushid, "pay the man whatever is a fair price for these melons and tell him to deliver them to the Orzhekov camp. Aunt Tess loves melons. These look very fine."

"Surely, your highness," said Qushid, "you don't need to pay for the melons. If you wish them, they are yours."

Mitya blinked. The harsh summer sun of this climate had bleached his fair hair out to a coarse pale blond and tanned his skin until he was almost as dark as the

Habakar natives. Over the summer, he had begun to grow a light down of hair along his chin, the first sign of his manhood. Unlike the young riders in the army, he did not follow the fashion and shave off this suggestion of a beard; doubtless, thought Jiroannes, he was hoping enough would grow that it would become noticeable from more than an arm's length away.

"But if we mean to rule this country fairly, and if this man has already paid his tribute—his taxes—to our army, then we must act according to the law. By that law, it is robbery to take goods without paying for them. So you will pay him."

At times like these, Jiroannes recalled quite clearly that Mitya was not his friend but a prince, and heir to the most powerful man in this kingdom. He was a sweet boy, charming and unspoiled, especially compared to the princes at the palace school in Vidiya, who had been uniformly conceited, hedonistic, and cruel. But he was also arrogant, as all the jaran were, and well aware of the extent of his power.

Qushid obeyed. How could he not? Jiroannes knew that the Habakar boy held a rank equal to Jiroannes's own and that it was only cruel fate—or the Hand of the Everlasting God Himself—that had thrown him into the hands of the enemy and forced him to act as Mitya's servant and chamberlain. It must gall him, to handle money like any steward; to translate words as Syrannus—Jiroannes's own bond servant—had once done for Jiroannes before the Vidiyan ambassador had learned to speak khush himself. Jiroannes suspected that Mitya knew the rudiments of the Habakar language, but he would never stoop to using it in public. Why should the jaran speak the language of their subjects? It was fitting that their subjects learn to speak the language of their masters.

The transaction completed, their party rode on. Marble columns alternated with poplars and almond trees along the broad avenue they followed into the northwestern district. Here, villas sprawled, airy houses ringed with trees and manicured gardens, fronted by statues and elaborate fountains. Jiroannes noted that about half of the houses lay empty, stripped of their movable wealth. A few brave merchants had remained, casting their lot in with the jaran. Squatters had invaded some of the other houses, men dressed in homespun, rough clothing who looked quite out of place in these elegant homes. Or perhaps they were only slaves, left to tend their master's possessions until such time as it was safe to return.

Jiroannes doubted it would ever be safe for them to return if they thought that safety consisted of the absence of the jaran. He believed firmly, by now, that Bakhtiian would succeed in conquering the Habakar kingdom utterly. Clearly Bakhtiian intended Mitya to rule the Habakar lands once Mitya came of age. Why else give the boy a general's son as his interpreter? Why else betroth him to a Habakar princess?

Mitya pulled up his horse at a crossroads and stared down a broad avenue lined with great columns that led like an arrow's shot to the far distant gate to the heart of the city. Behind those inner walls, Karkand's population waited out the siege. Did they think their king was coming to relieve them? Or was it rumors of the king's nephew riding north that comforted them as they waited, day by day, gazing from their highest towers out over the suburbs to the surrounding plain, where the jaran army invested their city?

"Do you like this country?" Jiroannes asked, watching Mitya as the boy rode up next to a column and traced its carved surface with his right hand.

Mitya did not answer immediately. He regarded the avenue and the distant city with a musing expression on his face. Then he reined his mount around and pulled in beside Jiroannes. "When I become king here, will you ask your king to send you as the ambassador to my court?"

Jiroannes didn't know what to think. At first, he felt a thrill of elation, that he should be invited to serve as an ambassador, and not just as a common ambassador but as a personal one to a powerful king. But it might mean years and years spent in exile from his own land, and even if his success as an ambassador here won him the white Companion's Sash, and admittance to the Companion's Circle, what use was such influence if he did not live at court in order to exercise it?

"Well," said Mitya, turning his horse around and starting back the way they had come, "it was just a thought. It'll be four years yet before I'm of age. Bakhtiian won't let any man, not even me, ride in the army before the age of twenty. It doesn't seem fair, though, that girls can ride with the archers at sixteen. Anatoly Sakhalin's sister Shura is only seventeen, and she's fought in three skirmishes and one battle already. Then again, she'll be married soon and having babies, so perhaps this is the only chance she'll have to fight." He considered this in silence.

Jiroannes considered the suburbs of Karkand. What if he did return to Mitya's court? He would receive preference, certainly. Jiroannes reflected on the struggles his own uncle went through, balancing the cutthroat politics of the imperial court with his efforts to live in a comfortable style. Living in Habakar lands, Jiroannes would be well placed to benefit from opening up greater trade between Habakar and Vidiya. These rich villas had ample space and amenities for a man to live in style. Even a Vidiyan noblewoman might live here without disgust, and the homes seemed spacious enough that the women would have ample quarters for their seclusion. Perhaps he could even benefit by several advantageous marriages.

They passed out of the suburbs by a different gate, double-arched. The marketplace along the square here was dedicated to ironworks and blacksmiths, repairing wagons, shoeing horses. A white-clad woman sat in silence, head bowed, in the shade on a wooden bench next to a terraced fountain. A ceramic beaker painted with fantastic birds along the base and lip rested next to her.

"She is another holy woman?" Jiroannes asked. "If I ask for water, then must she give me a drink?"

Qushid nodded. "The Almighty God is served by these handmaidens, the *Vani,* who by offering each and every man water, remind us that God alone can slake our thirst."

"Did you say they are called Vani?" Hadn't his concubine been wearing fine white silk when she was brought to him? A sudden foreboding seized Jiroannes. His throat grew thick with dread. "Are any of these women called Javani?"

Qushid's eyes widened, giving him the look of a startled hare. He sketched a warding sign in the air with his left hand. "It is ill luck to speak so of the Javani, she who is now dead and not yet at rest in our Lord's bosom."

"Dead?" Jiroannes managed to choke out the word.

"When the citadel in Hazjan burned, thrown down by Bakhtiian, who does not honor the Almighty God and his Holy Book, so did the holy temple burn. Just as common women are marked by the priests to serve the Almighty God, so is one woman of the royal house honored as the Javani, the holiest of these maidens. Usually she is a distant cousin of the king. He sanctifies her and gives her into God's Hands, to serve Him all her days at the heart of the holy temple." He paused. "And, of course, a princess of the royal house also then can serve as the king's ear and mouthpiece to the priests. But it is God she serves first."

They crossed under the arch and came out between fields of hay drying in the sun. Beyond lay the first tents of the jaran army. Jiroannes was relieved to be free of the oppression of the walls and of Habakar habitations. In there, within the walls, in one offhand moment, he had been transformed from a common ambassador into the worst sort of criminal. He had raped the holiest woman in Habakar lands. He had offended their God mightily, and by their laws deserved to be executed.

"Look," said Mitya, pointing, "there is Bakhtiian out riding. Do you see his gold banner?"

Out here, beyond the walls, he reminded himself that he was a Vidiyan nobleman, answerable only to the laws of his own Great King. Still, to his horror, remorse and fear clawed at him.

"Qushid," he asked slowly, sure that if he did not choose his words carefully, the whole world would know at once of his crime, "what if such a woman did not die? What if she was taken captive by the army?"

When presented with questions that demanded thought rather than a rote answer, Qushid gained a rather slack-jawed look. Perhaps he really was a little stupid. Certainly he did not suspect a thing. "I don't know. The Almighty God wishes no bride who is not a virgin. I suppose she might kill herself, out of shame. That would be merciful."

"What if she didn't kill herself? Might she marry?"

"What man would wish to marry a stained woman?"

"If she is the king's cousin—? Might there not be some advantage to such an alliance?"

"What is a stained woman?" asked Mitya. "And anyway, I'm to marry the king's cousin, the princess, the one they sent out to my grandmother to foster until we're of age to marry. Bakhtiian says that if we mean to hold these lands for our children and our children's children, then we must weave ourselves into their hearts and into their laws and into their royal families as kin."

"Mitya," said Jiroannes suddenly, "I would be honored above all things to be asked by you to attend your court as ambassador."

Mitya smiled, looking heartened and pleased all at once. "I'd like that," he said, with the casual arrogance that characterized his people. Of course they expected the world to bow down to them; hadn't the gods granted them a heavenly sword with which to conquer foreign lands? Weren't the khaja falling before them like the wheat trampled beneath their horses' hooves?

They separated at the outskirts of camp, and Jiroannes rode with his two escorting guards to his own encampment. Once there, he called Lal to him.

"Bring me the woman," he said, and he went inside his tent to conduct the interview.

Lal brought her. She now wore Vidiyan silks, brighthued, brocaded with peacocks intertwined with flowering vines. She cowered in front of him, kneeling, head bent. Her hands lay folded, trembling, in her lap. Her complexion was pale and spotless. The skin of her hands was so soft that Jiroannes felt that just by rubbing it vigorously between his own hands he could chafe it and redden it. Under the silks, he knew that her body, shaved clean of all hair, was as silkily smooth as that of the finest concubine in Vidiya, where such women were raised from childhood and pampered and scented and oiled and bathed to a fine perfection fitting for a nobleman's use. But now he knew that this woman—the Javani—bore these marks not because she was a slave bred to concubinage but because she was of noble rank.

She did not look up at him. Stillness masked her expression. He could not read her at all, but he knew she cried a little, every night, and then wiped her tears away.

"Syrannus," he called, "bring ink and paper. I wish you to take a letter to my uncle." Syrannus entered and sat on a stool, parchment laid over a board balanced on his knees. "Syrannus, how much of the Habakar tongue can you speak?"

"A little, eminence. Perhaps Lal speaks more."

"Umm. Lal, ask this woman who she is."

"The Javani," she answered in a stifled voice when Lal put the question to her in halting words.

"Ask her if she escaped the burning of Hazjan."

At the name of the city, the Javani burst into tears, a sudden and copious weeping that surprised Jiroannes. She cast herself facedown on the carpets and blurted out a long string of sentences, groveling at Jiroannes's feet.

"What is she saying?" he asked Lal and Syrannus.

The boy and the old man regarded each other. In low voices, they debated, and at last Syrannus nodded and turned to his master. The Javani lapsed into silence. Her hands lay gripped in fists and her eyes were leaden with tears. Her black hair had slipped free of its veil and now spilled onto the carpet in disarray. Jiroannes loved her hair, and he found that the sight of it here, unbound, naked, aroused him.

"Eminence," said Syrannus, "we cannot be sure, but we are agreed that she is lamenting that she did not die, or could not die, or was afraid to die. Perhaps that she is ashamed that she preferred to live in shame rather than die honorably. But it is difficult to understand and unlikely in any case that a woman could entertain such masculine sentiments."

"Yet most men would have chosen to die, rather than live in disgrace," said Jiroannes thoughtfully, staring at the curve of her body under the soft silken fabric of her robes. "A woman might easily be weak enough to fear death more than shame. Still, I wish you to take a letter to my uncle, asking him for his permission to marry."

"His permission to marry?"

"Yes. I wish to marry this woman. Once I have ascertained that she is indeed who I believe her to be: a Habakar noblewoman of the royal line. With such an alliance, Syrannus, I can bind myself both to the Habakar royalty and to the advantages we can find there through trade with Vidiya, and to the young prince, who is going to marry into their family as well. If it is true that she was once a holy woman, then I can't in good conscience keep her as my concubine. And no one else will have her, whether as slave or concubine or wife. I think we can find both profit and blessing in this transaction. Lal, see if you can make her understand what I mean to do. Then take her away and see to her. And—" He hesitated.

"Certainly, eminence," said Lal, "if she is to be your wife, she cannot be expected to share a tent with a slave."

"Of course. Just what I was about to say. See that Samae is lodged somewhere else. Samae can act as her handmaiden for now, but I think—" He bit at his lower lip.

"Perhaps, eminence, I can find a woman in the guards' camp to act as her body servant. That way she may have a woman of her own people as her companion."

"Ah, a fine idea, Lal. But not a peasant woman. Indeed, perhaps one of the merchants left in the suburbs has a niece or daughter he would be willing to sell into our service."

Lal knelt beside the woman and, like a handler coaxing a spooked horse, spoke to her gently and soon enough led her out of the tent. Syrannus's pen scratched across the parchment. Jiroannes leaned back in his chair and sipped contentedly at the cool sweet tea Lal had brought him earlier.

"When you are done, Syrannus, we will go ask for an audience with Bakhtiian. No, with Mother Sakhalin, I think."

"With Mother Sakhalin, eminence?"

"You don't think I'm fool enough to marry her without getting permission from the jaran, do you? Or at least without advising them of the situation? Not while we live in their power. If they come to think well of me, then there will be fewer obstacles in my path four years from now."

"Four years from now, eminence?"

Jiroannes felt a surge of pleasure, seeing Syrannus at a loss for once. Always, before, he had felt that Syrannus knew better than he did what was going on; now, at last, Jiroannes felt that he was beginning to control his own life, to build his own destiny. There was more to life than a Companion's Sash. There was a greater world than that contained in Vidiya. Jiroannes intended to rise as high as he could, no matter how far it meant he had to travel. He had grown up in the Great King's court. And now he had seen the jaran. He was no fool. He could see to whom Heaven had granted her favor.

And what if the jaran collapsed and their conquests were scattered to the winds? What if the Habakar king or his nephew regained his lands? Well, then, Jiroannes still had possession of the Javani, "the king's ear and mouthpiece." Either way, he would benefit.

"Syrannus," he added, rising and pacing the length of the tent and back again, "we will go first to the Habakar priests. I know there are some in camp, hostages, guests, whatever they are called. They must identify her and give their blessing, and then, armed with that knowledge, we can present our petition to the old woman. Yes. Yes. This will do very well."

Syrannus's pen marked the parchment with his flowing script. Jiroannes sat back down and drank his tea.

CHAPTER TWELVE

"Now what?" asked David of the little council gathered in Charles's tent. "By Rajiv's calculations, the actor is 24.7 kilometers away from us, up in the hills."

"And," added Maggie, "we've got a shuttle available for rendezvous anytime in the next three days. It might have been possible to distract Grekov, but Nadine doesn't miss anything. I don't see how we're going to manage bringing down the shuttle *and* picking up Hyacinth, especially with her eagle eye upon us."

Inside the tent, there was room enough for them all to sit in the wood and canvas folding chairs that Charles favored, although Marco stood and Jo lounged on the floor. Rajiv sat hunched over the table, manipulating data on the modeler sunk within the table's surface.

"I've plotted their course," said Rajiv, "and it's not unreasonable to predict that they'll move another five to ten kilometers northeast tomorrow, which, depending on our course, could put them within ten to fifteen K range of us. But our paths will begin to diverge in another two days."

"Landing sites?" asked Charles.

Rajiv brought up a flat geological map that took over the entire smooth surface of the table. It was detailed to the ten-meter range, shaded to show elevation and vegetation and water patterns. "I've marked them here. But given that it's a Chapalii shuttle, we've got a fair amount of leeway. They can land with relative silence and minimal damage in most terrain."

"Why is the actor staying up in the hills?" asked Jo. "Wouldn't he be safer traveling north down through this valley?"

"Not if he'll get executed if he's caught," said Marco. "What about the people with him, Charles?"

Charles steepled his fingers together and rested his chin on his fingertips. "Difficult to know. Hyacinth and his stolen gear will have to come with us, of course. His companions can either travel on, on their own, or— No." He shook his head.

"We can't give them our protection?" asked David. "It's ridiculous that they were punished so severely for homosexuality. It isn't even a crime. But I suppose it's all of a piece, when you consider how primitive this planet is."

"Why, David," said Marco, "you're singing a different tune these days."

David shrugged.

"If we give them our protection," said Charles softly, "then what becomes of them once we leave? As we inevitably will. I've thought of that, David, but I don't see how we can manage it. Still, they're the least part of our problem. We need to bring in that shuttle and transfer the medical equipment for Cara onto the pack animals. Without alerting our escort." Charles grinned suddenly. David had long since realized that Charles enjoyed himself most when he confronted a seemingly insolvable problem. "Any suggestions?"

"Kill them all," said Marco facetiously. "That solves the problem."

"Except we have to explain it to Bakhtiian once we arrive at the army. Anyone else?"

"Well," said Jo, "that's not so far from the mark, though, Charles. We have to render them unconscious somehow. Drug them. I don't know. So we can send out an expedition to bring in the actor and pick up the supplies."

"But how do we explain how we found Hyacinth?" demanded Maggie.

"As you see," said Charles, "this kind of masquerade gets more and more difficult to bring off. Jo, can you drug them?"

"Probably. But how do we explain it to them when it wears off? They'd wonder, surely."

"Wait a minute," said David. "You know these people drink like fish. Get them drunk, add just enough of a dose of—whatever—to make them sleep late and wake up with terrible hangovers. If we can get within ten K range of Hyacinth, that should give us enough time to pick him up and rendezvous with the shuttle, and get back by midmorning. If we leave before dawn. Don't you think?"

They all regarded him openmouthed, all except Charles. Charles rose and paced over to the table, placing his hands palm open, flat, on the surface, examining the topographical model laid out before him. "That's perfect, David. Perfect."

"I admit it might work," began Maggie.

"Mags, your praise overwhelms me."

"Quiet, you. But what possible reason do they have to get drunk in the middle of a long trip south? And at the pace we're riding, too?"

Charles straightened up. He smiled. "A perfect reason. We haven't celebrated Nadine Orzhekov's marriage yet. Remiss of me, as her host. We've made good enough time that I can excuse an early stop tomorrow, and a late morning start the day after."

All of David's triumph in thinking up a brilliant idea burned away to ashes. Charles was right, of course: celebrating Nadine's marriage provided the perfect excuse. It didn't mean he had to like it. "Well, if that's settled," he said brusquely, "I've some things to attend to. Are we done?"

Charles glanced once, sharply, at him, but mercifully only nodded. David escaped out into the camp. He strode out to the fringe of camp, to the screen of straggling trees that hid the pack train. The animals grazed peacefully, some hobbled, some on lines. Packs stretched in neat rows along the ground. About one hundred meters away, a mob of horses milled beside a pond, jostling for drinking space. Three jaran riders supervised this chaos. David recognized two of them instantly. One was the quiet boy, Vasha. The other was Feodor Grekov.

He sighed. Was this what it meant to be in love? Purely, simply, David was jealous of Feodor Grekov. In the ten days since Nadine had rejoined their party, David had found it impossible to address the young man with any semblance of politeness, so he avoided him instead. Only Marco twitted him about it; perhaps only Marco noticed. No, Charles must know. Charles knew everything. But by and large, Charles respected privacy to an almost extravagant degree since he valued it so keenly for himself. Now David had leisure to reflect on Bakhtiian. No wonder Bakhtiian had looked daggers at him, all those months ago, thinking that David had slept with his wife. Then, David had feared that he had violated some taboo. Now he understood that Bakhtiian's anger stemmed from jealousy, from possessiveness, perhaps even from fear. And why shouldn't Bakhtiian be afraid? Tess belonged to David's kind, she belonged to Earth—to *Erthe*—not to the jaran.

Only, maybe she didn't. Maybe she did belong to the jaran now. Or at least, for now, for a time. Nadine didn't belong to the jaran; that was one thing that angered David. Nadine deserved better, deserved more than to be a brood mare for her uncle's convenience. She wanted more.

"David!" The voice made him wince. He spun, to see that he had not been paying attention well enough. If he had seen her coming, he would have fled. She grinned down at him from her seat on her horse. Dusk shadowed her, but she seemed cheerful enough. "Walking sentry duty tonight?" she asked. If she knew that her husband rode herd on the horses close by, she gave no sign of it. "I just spoke with the prince. I don't suppose, since he insisted, that I can refuse the honor of a celebration given by him."

"You don't want a celebration for your marriage?" David asked.

She shrugged and turned her face to one side. She had a fine profile, sharp and distinctive. He watched as her mouth twitched down into a frown, watched her rein herself in, watched her lips straighten and assume a smile again. "It's fitting," she said at last, in a toneless voice, "that a marriage should be celebrated with a feast and dancing and drink. I don't suppose we can have dancing; there aren't enough women. And there's scarcely enough interesting food for a feast. But the prince promises a rare wine, that he wishes to share in honor of the marriage. That's generous of him."

"Well," said David awkwardly, "we all like you, Dina."

Her gaze flashed to him, and away. She wasn't usually so coy. "You all like me," she said softly, "and pity me for what has happened." Abruptly, she reined her horse aside and rode away, out toward the sentry line.

David watched her go. He swore under his breath and walked back to camp.

The next day they camped in the late afternoon on the outskirts of a burned-out village that huddled up against the low hills. The vast gap of land—more than a valley, less than a plateau—through which they rode on their way south to the Habakar heartlands spread out around them, bounded by steep hills to the east and west and mountains to the south. Rajiv calculated that the actor had made his camp 9.4 kilometers away from them, up in the western foothills. He mapped out a path from the village to the signal emitted by the actor's transmitter.

Charles poured the wine himself, pressing the jaran riders to drink from the bottles Jo had spiked. David managed to swallow his ill-feeling long enough to participate in one toast to the happy couple. Then he left the party and went out to the horse lines.

"Go on," he said to the young man standing guard. "I'll watch tonight." The rider hesitated. They could both hear the distant sound of lusty singing. "I can't stomach the celebration," added David, appealing to the other man's sympathies, "since I—well, you know. Now she's married to another man."

The rider's expression softened. "Well, and you being khaja and all, I don't suppose you'd any hope to marry her, since she's Bakhtiian's niece. If you don't mind. . . . Just a sip, and then I'll come back."

David waved at him to go on. Then he waited. He set the perimeter alert on his knife and paced up and down the lines. The singing grew louder and less tuneful, then quieted, and finally ceased altogether. Eventually, about two hours after midnight, Marco and Charles appeared. They saddled up four horses and slung packs on two of the pack animals; at Morava, they had loaded two of the animals with packs filled with extra odds and ends, so that once they made the pickup there wouldn't seem to be any change in the amount of gear they carried. Then they set off.

Once out of sight of camp, leading the horses, they switched on lanterns to light their way. The steady glare lent a gray color to the landscape as they wound their way up into the hills. Rajiv had coded a pathfinder into Charles's slate, and it guided them up dried-out streambeds and along the curve of the hills, gradually working up into the wilderness. A few wild animals tripped their perimeter alerts. Otherwise, nothing stirred. The isolation mirrored David's mood.

Just before dawn, with a faint glow rising in the east, they led their train down a defile and halted in the shadow of a copse of trees. With a word, Marco shut off their lamps, shuttering them in the half light of dawn. Beyond the trees, set out on a rocky slope, stood a tent. An off-world tent, that much was obvious by its cut and weave and by the tracery of filaments woven into the canvas, shining like dew-laden spiderwebs against the khaki fabric.

Marco cast a glance down at his slate, hanging open from his belt. "There'a perimeter alert activated inside the tent. We've already triggered it."

"Let's wait a moment," said Charles. "We've no guarantee that some bandit hasn't murdered Hyacinth and stolen his gear."

David winced. No matter how stupid the actor had been, David could not believe that he deserved such an awful fate. He glanced at Charles, but in the dim light could not read Charles's expression—if indeed Charles let any emotion show at all on his face, anymore. "It's true we ignored the emergency signal that came— what?—weeks ago," he muttered. "We don't know what happened to him after that, or if he even survived."

"You know very well, David, that we couldn't send a shuttle down cold, without marking the ground first. He chose his exile. He knows what it means, that Rhui is interdicted. Marco. Alert the shuttle. I think this is an isolated enough spot for a safe landing." Charles surveyed the sky, lightening ever more in the east, and then looked directly at David. "You were going to say something?"

"You're a damned hypocrite, Charles."

Charles nodded, looking thoughtful. "It's true. So often people in my position are. I wonder if there's any remedy for it? I condemn that poor boy for a crime that I then turn around and commit myself."

"Doesn't it bother you?"

"I do what I must."

"Shhh," hissed Marco. "Someone's coming out of the tent."

They watched as a man dressed in jaran clothing emerged from the tent, wary, holding his saber in front of him. He glanced all round and then stared straight at the copse of trees, although surely he couldn't see them. Perhaps he could hear or smell the horses. A moment later another man ducked out of the tent, holding a knife in his left hand.

"I don't recognize either of them," said David in an undertone. The second man wore a dirty tunic over dirty trousers. What color the clothes had once been was impossible to tell. The man's hair was a coarse muddy blond.

"Look at those eyes," said Marco in an undertone. "I think that's Hyacinth. None of the natives in these parts have the epicanthic folds."

David stared, trying desperately to match his memory of Hyacinth with this filthy, coarse-looking man. He looked altered beyond imagining from the glamorous, golden-haired actor who had played Puck in *A Midsummer Night's Dream* with such athletic and sensual flair. Then the man flipped open his slate and keyed into it. Lights flashed, and a sudden image projected out from the screen, suspended in midair. It was a heat projection of the surrounding area, betraying their presence. The man's jaran companion did not even start at this sorcerous apparition.

"What the hell?" muttered Marco. "It looks like he's already broken the interdiction."

"Call down the shuttle," said Charles to Marco. He

took five steps forward, out into the open, and raised his voice. "I'm looking for the actor known as Hyacinth, legal name, Sven Rajput Nguyen."

The man with the slate jerked his head around at the sound of Charles's voice. He staggered forward three steps and then collapsed onto his knees, signing himself with the Goddess's circle of grace. "Oh, Goddess," he wept. "Oh, Goddess. I thought we would never find you."

Charles gestured to David and Marco, and they came out onto the slope, the horses and pack animals behind them. Light rose in the defile. The sun had come up, although it had not yet breached the high walls to glare down on them directly. Hyacinth struggled to his feet, ran forward, and threw himself prostrate on the gravel in front of Charles.

The first thing David noticed, even from two meters away, was the smell. Hyacinth stank like he hadn't had a bath in months, or even changed his clothes.

Charles knelt and raised the young man up gently. Behind, by the tent, the jaran rider stood and watched, his expression guarded. He did not sheathe his saber.

"I knew that if we kept riding north, we'd come to you. I knew you wouldn't abandon us. I told Yevgeni that you'd rescue us. Oh, Goddess, why couldn't you have heard the transmitter? Maybe you could have saved Valye." Hyacinth babbled on, one grimy hand gripping the sleeve of Charles's shirt as if he never meant to let it go.

Marco walked up beside them and pried Hyacinth loose. "You look the worse for the wear," he said mildly, letting go of the other man as soon as he had freed Charles.

"I hate this planet," said Hyacinth with a hatred so implacable that his tone sent a shiver down David's back. "I want to go home."

"I think," said Charles, "that we can grant your wish. What about your friend? What's his name? Yevgeni?"

"Yevgeni Usova." Hyacinth turned. "Yevgeni! Come here. You must meet the duke."

The other man obeyed, but he approached cautiously, though he sheathed his saber. "The *duke?*" Yevgeni halted six paces from Charles and regarded him measuringly. He was of the dark-haired strain of the jaran, David noted, with a blunt nose and brown eyes. He appeared marginally cleaner than Hyacinth, and he certainly didn't smell as rank.

"I mean the *Prince* of Jeds."

"How did you find us?" Yevgeni asked, evidently still suspicious of Charles and his little party. "Is this your entire party? Are you truly a sorcerer?"

"Yevgeni!" said Hyacinth impatiently. "I told you that we're not sorcerers."

"Then it is true that you come from a land that rests in the heavens? I know that Singers tell many strange stories, and have often visited the gods' lands, but I didn't know that you were also a Singer."

"A shaman?" Charles allowed himself a brief smile. "I'm not a shaman." He turned his bland gaze on Hyacinth. "So. What have you told him? What does he know?"

Hyacinth's eyes narrowed in suspicion. "How did you find us? You must have traced my signal. But that means—" He caught in his breath and David tensed, waiting for the explosion. When Hyacinth spoke again, he spoke in Anglais, hard and fast. "That means you must have picked up my emergency transmission. How could you not have responded? Yevgeni's sister *died* because no one responded."

Charles sighed. "May I remind you that you chose exile? You knew you were putting yourself at risk. You knew—"

"That Rhui is interdicted? Yes, I knew that. But you're here. The Company is here. That's breaking the interdiction. But I suppose that since you own this planet you can do what you damned well please!"

"Quite true. Now, how much does he know?" The timbre of Charles's voice had altered, and though he did not raise his voice at all, the words cracked over Hyacinth and reduced the young man to silence. "You're responsible for him, now, you know," added Charles. "If he knows too much, he can't go back."

"Goddess! Don't you know anything? He can't go back anyway. His exile is permanent. Without me, he'll die."

Charles glanced at Marco. "Time?"

"Twenty-three minutes."

"Well, then," said Charles. "Take him with you."

Yevgeni edged closer to Hyacinth. David could not tell whether the young rider's proximity was meant to protect Hyacinth or to seek shelter for himself. Startled, Hyacinth gaped at Charles and then turned his head in a smooth motion to stare at Yevgeni. Yevgeni arched an eyebrow, questioning. David admired his stoic silence, his patience, his ability to stand there and hear an argument in a language he couldn't understand and simply wait it out. Or perhaps he had long since grown resigned to death, to his fate, whatever it might prove to be. But David recognized the gleam in his eyes, underlying his composure. He was in love with Hyacinth, and he trusted him.

What a fate lay in store for him.

"I could take him with me?" Hyacinth asked haltingly.

"Indeed," said Charles, "I begin to think you're going to have to take him with you. That would be the easiest solution."

"Wait. You're not taking me back to the Company?"

"How do I explain to the jaran how I found you? No. The shuttle lands in twenty-two minutes. Take down your tent. You're going with them."

"Off planet." Hyacinth shut his eyes. A look of peace smoothed his expression. "Thank you. Thank you."

"I'll help you take down the tent," said Marco. "We don't have much time."

"Hyacinth," said Yevgeni in khush, "what is happening?"

Hyacinth turned, took hold of Yevgeni's hands, and kissed him on the mouth. "We're going home. We're leaving. You're coming with me."

Yevgeni disengaged his hands and glanced at once, sidelong, at Charles and David, as if to gauge their reaction to Hyacinth's show of affection. Marco had already walked over to the tent.

"I hope you understand," said Charles softly, to Hyacinth, "that the transition will be particularly difficult for him. He'll have no one but you. I'll arrange for a stipend for him, that much I can do, but you'll be the only person he knows. And life will seem—very strange—out there. Do you understand the burden I'm laying on you? Can you manage it?"

Hyacinth drew himself up. "I chose exile because of the burden I had already laid on him. They stripped him of his saber, of his horse, of his name, of his connection to the tribe. It's my fault he got exiled, and exile is tantamount to death in this world."

"In any world," said Charles softly. "When you come right down to it."

"Well, so I already accepted the burden. I'll promise to marry him, if that will make you trust me more."

"Do what you must. Remember, perhaps, once in a while, that the burden I carry with me always is something like the one you now bear. I'm sorry about his sister. I had no choice."

" 'I'll deliver all,' " murmured Hyacinth.

"Ah, that's a line from *The Tempest*. So says Prospero, when he promises to tell the story of how he came to the island and into his powers."

Hyacinth colored, easy to see even with the dirt caking his skin. "You know the play? We were working on it when I—left."

"It's been brought to my attention."

David stifled a grin, knowing that the poor actor couldn't possibly understand Charles's convoluted sense of humor, his always clear sense of the ugly ambivalence of his situation.

"Seventeen minutes," called Marco from the tent. "What do we do with the horses?"

"The problem with meddling," said Charles under his breath, "is that for every problem you solve, you create two more."

"Rather like the Hydra in Greek mythology," offered David, realizing that it was true, that the two refugees had a dozen horses with them. "Where did you get all of them?"

"We stole some from the army," said Hyacinth. "The rest we—we took in payment for Valye's life." He

seemed about to say more. Instead, he spun and hurried
away to help Marco with the tent. Yevgeni hesitated and
then turned to follow him.

"Yevgeni," said Charles. The young rider turned back.
"You're content to stay with him? You can return with us,
to the army. Or we can leave you here."

"I can't return to the army," said Yevgeni. "I've nowhere else to go. I'm content." But the look he cast toward Hyacinth betrayed the depth of his feeling, however
offhandedly he might have replied.

"Do you have any suggestions about what we might do
with the horses?"

Yevgeni looked puzzled. "But surely we'll need the
horses to ride?"

"No. You'll be leaving here by other means than
horses."

"Not with you?"

"Not with me. I can't take the horses with me. But if
I leave them here, free them—"

"I don't understand." Yevgeni shook his head. "Horses
are valuable. Why would you want to loose them? And
anyway, they need us to care for them. Even if we—why
can't you—?" He stumbled to a halt, looking confused.

"So it begins," said Charles in Anglais. "Do you have
any suggestions, David?"

David raised his hands, palms out. "Don't ask me. I'm
only an engineer. I know how to saddle one, and I can
ride, in a manner of speaking. Can they survive on their
own in the wild? I don't know."

"You're no damned help," muttered Charles, sounding
both amused and irritated. "Well, I see no choice but to
let them go and hope whatever refugees live in these hills
find them."

"We can't tell Nadine that we found them running
loose in the hills?"

Charles gave a curt nod, and Yevgeni, dismissed, hurried away to help Hyacinth and Marco. Charles regarded
David, his lips quirking up. "Do you really think she'd
accept that story? She's no fool."

"She's too damned smart," murmured David, "to get

stuck here on this planet. She's the one who should be leaving, not him."

"What makes you think she'd be happier out in space?"

"There's so much to know, to learn, to discover. . . ."

"There's so much to know, learn, and discover on Rhui, too. This is a rich planet, David." He shrugged. "Well, in any case, whether in her lifetime or later, they'll begin to leave, more and more of them."

David heard an odd note in Charles's voice. "What do you mean? I thought you were going to keep the interdiction in place, so that we can maintain a protected safe house for growing and shielding the next rebellion."

"It's only a matter of time. We're already breaking the interdiction. We're already affecting their development. 'Their understanding begins to swell, and the approaching tide/Will shortly fill the reasonable shores/That now lie foul and muddy.' "

"It sounds so awful, put like that. Is that another line from *The Tempest?*"

Charles nodded. The wind came up, and a low moaning rode in on it, the dawn wind.

Only it wasn't the wind. David caught the silver glint of the shuttle, circling in. Yevgeni leapt back, his hand on his saber. Marco ran to calm the horses. Charles lifted a hand, in sign, and instead, Marco cut them all free. They scattered in fright. David ran back and pulled down the heads of the animals they'd brought, holding them in place, trying to calm them with soft words. From this distance, he watched the shuttle brake in the air and begin its descent.

Marco and Hyacinth backed up, lugging Hyacinth's gear. Yevgeni froze, unable to move as he stared at the hulk above him. What did he think? That it was a dragon? A metal bird? A sorcerer's tame devil? A demon of the air? Hyacinth flung his rolled up tent on the ground and sprinted forward. By main force he dragged Yevgeni backward, out of the flash range. The poor man looked in shock, as well he might be.

The shuttle landed, spraying gravel and dirt. Its engines

whined high, canted sharply, and then cut off. The silence was deafening. With a pop, a hatch opened and a ramp extruded. A Chapalii male appeared. By his mauve robes, David guessed it was the merchant Hon Echido Keinaba. He descended and came forward to bow before Charles.

Hyacinth had a hold on Yevgeni's elbow. Only by that grip did the jaran rider stay upright. His face had gone dead pale. A deep, abiding pity filled David for the young man about to be thrown into a world he had not the slightest comprehension of.

Behind Hon Echido, two stewards emerged carrying perfect replicas of the packs already on the pack animals in Soerensen's train. David was too far away to follow the conversation that ensued, but the transaction was swift. The stewards deposited the packs at Charles's feet and, at his direction, hurried back on board with Hyacinth's gear. Hon Echido bowed to Charles and retreated back up the ramp.

Hyacinth spoke rapidly and earnestly to Yevgeni. Haltingly, one slow footstep followed by another, Yevgeni allowed himself to be led. He faltered at the foot of the ramp and stared, back stiff and ramrod straight, up into the maw of the ship. He put a hand on his saber hilt. Hyacinth gestured, spoke. What a vast reservoir of trust it must take for Yevgeni to go up there—that or simple fatalism. David shook his head. Perhaps he was overestimating Nadine; not her intelligence, not her courage, not her curiosity, but her ability to absorb something so utterly outside of her experience.

Yevgeni tested the ramp with one booted foot. He threw his head back and stared up at the blue dome of the sky, seeded with clouds, tinted by the rising sun, that arched above them. Then he turned right round and looked at Charles. He said something to Hyacinth. Hyacinth started, taken aback, and then abruptly grinned and replied. To David's astonishment, the young jaran rider dropped to his knees and bowed his head toward Charles in obeisance. After a moment, he rose and without further hesitation walked with Hyacinth up the ramp and into the ship.

The hatch closed. The engines sang to life. Flame singed the earth and the shuttle rose like light into the air. It yawed, steadied, turned, and circled up. David watched as it sped on its way, winking out at last just as the sun topped the far ridge and streamed bright light into the shadowed depths of the defile.

Charles and Marco arrived, each man lugging one of the saddle packs. They threw the old ones off the pack animals and cinched on the new.

"Shall we go?" asked Charles.

"But what did he ask Hyacinth?" David demanded. "That's what decided him in the end to get on the ship."

Charles grinned, looking like the old Charles, the Charles David had gone to university with. "He asked if I was one of the ten lords attendant on Father Wind, who rules Heaven." He gathered reins into his hand and mounted.

"Well, what did Hyacinth say?"

Charles shrugged.

Marco coughed into a hand, looking sly, enjoying himself. David felt a sudden camaraderie with these two men, the simple pleasure of their company, out on this secret adventure. Charles had a spark in his eyes, of mischief, of suppressed laughter. A horse neighed in the distance.

"He said, 'I and my fellows are ministers of fate.' "

Which was true enough. Marco and Charles were still chuckling, but David found the quote disturbing. They rode away. Behind them, gravel and dirt lay scorched and scattered, but the first rains would obliterate all traces of the ship. Had Yevgeni truly understood that he was leaving forever? It was no less a sundering than death would have been; but Hyacinth was right, exile was death for a tribeless man like Yevgeni. He had chosen a new tribe. He had chosen to go with the ministers of fate, with the lords of heaven; he had thrown in his lot with Hyacinth's people. He was no longer jaran.

The next day, Nadine's scouts picked up seven horses and brought them into camp that night when they swung in from their rounds. Three of the animals bore the clip in their right ear that marked them as jaran horses. If Nadine thought their sudden appearance strange, if she had any theories about them at all, she did not honor David with her confidence.

CHAPTER THIRTEEN

Vasil discovered that he could watch as many *rehearsals* as he wished, as long as he stood quietly to one side. Sometimes Ilyana came with him, but the hours wore on her, and she fled back to camp, to her mother, to her chores, to the other children. The Company usually attracted an audience, but it shifted as the day passed; no one stayed as long as he did.

He watched. There, the tall, coal-black woman paced out a recurring movement, the same action over and over again. The young man with mud-colored skin tapped at his drums, finding a pulse, working it in with the *scene* being rehearsed in front of him. On the platform, five of the *actors* sang, with their bodies, a part of the old jaran tale of the Daughter of the Sun and the first dyan. The man, Owen Zerentous—Vasil thought of him as the dyan of the Company—measured their singing from the side, where he stood with his arms folded over his chest, squinting at the actors on the platform. Now and again he spoke, or they spoke or asked a question; after that the actors would pause, shift their stances, and go back through the same part again. But always, how they spoke, how they gestured, altered subtly at these times.

Diana shone. She had the art of shining. Of the other four, Vasil could only recall the name of the man called Gwyn Jones, because Gwyn Jones was the best singer of them all. They were all fine singers. Vasil could see that; he had seen it. Diana was particularly good. But Gwyn Jones thought so completely with his body that impulse and action became one gesture. And all trained to a pulse that the musician heard and transmitted back to them.

Owen Zerentous cocked his head to one side and

abruptly turned to look at Vasil. Some thirty paces separated them, but Vasil felt that gaze beckon him. Zerentous lifted a hand. Clearly, he meant Vasil to come speak with him. Vasil walked over.

"I beg your pardon," said Zerentous politely but with a kind of detached presumption that Vasil would bow to his word, "you're Veselov, aren't you?" He didn't wait for an answer. "You've been interested in our work, I see. Perhaps you'd agree to help us for a moment."

"I'm not a Singer—" Vasil began, but Zerentous had already pulled his attention away from him.

"Diana, call him up to you as if to an audience."

Diana did not need to speak. She lifted a hand imperiously, as the Daughter of the Sun would do, should Vasil ever have the misfortune to meet her. The dyan who had fallen in love with the Sun's daughter had died an untimely death, of course; it was always dangerous to attract the attention of the gods. And yet, although the Daughter of the Sun beckoned him, she was also Diana. She was both. By such skill, by her ability to be both herself and the Sun's daughter, did she show her mastery of her art.

Vasil clambered up on to the platform and approached her, eyes lowered. Three paces from her he stopped. He gave her a glance sidelong, knowing he appeared to advantage with his eyes cast down, and then bent his head slightly, just slightly enough to show that he knew the respect due to a woman but without demeaning himself in any way, knowing his own power. They watched him, the actors and Zerentous, and whatever jaran audience lingered beyond. He enjoyed that they watched him.

"There," said Zerentous from the ground. "Did you get that, Gwyn? That's what you're missing. It's the modesty without losing the strength. Thank you, Veselov." Dismissed, Vasil retreated back down off the platform. "So, is it because she's a goddess that you approach her so humbly, or because she's a foreign woman?"

"She's a woman," replied Vasil, puzzled by the question. "Whether she's the Sun's daughter or a mortal woman makes no difference."

"Ah." Zerentous nodded, but the reaction mystified Vasil. "Run it again."

As Vasil watched, the actors sang again—no, they didn't actually sing, they played their parts. They acted. This time, Gwyn Jones imitated Vasil's own language of the body, his gestures, his stance, his lowered eyes, so expertly that Vasil was amazed.

"Better," said Zerentous. "But now make it your own, Gwyn."

They went on. After a bit, even standing so close, Vasil realized that they had forgotten him. Perhaps Zerentous was more like an etsana, truly, since an etsana often only noticed those of her people whom she had a special use for or those who shirked their duties. A dyan must know where each of his men rode, and where and how strongly they wielded their weapons that day. They called Zerentous a khaja word; *director,* that was it. Beyond, at the fringe of the Company camp, Ilyana appeared. She hopped impatiently, balancing first on one foot, then on the other, and when she saw that she had her father's attention, she beckoned to him. A summons.

He sighed and retreated. To one side of the platform, the tall woman paused and acknowledged his leaving with a nod of her head. Her notice heartened him. They had felt his presence. That was something.

"What is it, Yana?" He bent to kiss her.

"Mother Veselov wants to see you. Mama sent me to fetch you." She tilted her head back and examined him with that clear-eyed sight that characterized her. Vasil suspected that she knew very well the kind of man he was, but that she loved him anyway. "They're not pleased with you," she added by way of warning him.

"Oh?" That would have to be mended. It wouldn't take much time. He took her hand in his and they set off together, back toward the Veselov camp.

Yana shrugged. "You spend too much time here."

"Do you think so?"

She had a bright face, unscarred by sulkiness. Like her mother, she had learned to accept what life brought her; unlike her mother, she never seemed resigned to her fate, and she did not let the jars and jolting of life bother her. Where her little brother Valentin saw only the clouds, she saw the sun waiting to break through. Everyone liked her; she was, as she ought to be, a charming, brilliant child. "Well, it isn't so much what I think that matters, Papa, it's what Mother Veselov thinks."

"But *I* care what you think, little one."

They walked ten steps in silence. "Is it true that, a long time ago, that you and Bakhtiian—?" She faltered and gave him a sidewise glance, gauging his reaction.

Anger blazed up. How dare anyone disturb her with such rumors? But he did not let his anger show. "Who has said this?"

She shrugged again. "Sometimes I hear things. Once, someone teased Valentin with it, and Valentin just got angry and cried, so I had to protect him."

"What did you do?"

"I told him—the boy, not Valentin—that his mother was as ugly as an old cow, that his father was as stupid as a khaja soldier, and then I gave him a bloody lip."

Amused, Vasil allowed himself a brief smile. "Well, I suppose that served the purpose, but really, Yana, outright insult is never as effective as more subtle methods. Who was the boy?"

She rolled her eyes. "I'm not going to tell you that! I can take care of myself. I always have, you know."

The words stung him. "Of course you can take care of yourself, but I'm here now, little one."

"Yes. But you might leave again."

He flinched. It hurt, the matter-of-fact way she spoke. He stopped her. "I won't leave you or your mother or Valentin. Ever again. I promise." He gripped her by the shoulders to make sure she understood. He could not bear for her not to believe in him. She had to.

For an instant he thought she looked skeptical, but it wasn't so. Like her mother, she must love him more than anyone else. She smiled her loyal little smile and stretched up to kiss him. "Yes, Father," she said.

At Arina's tent, he had to wait outside for a time, cooling his heels, before Arina's young sister admitted him. Karolla sat beside Arina, as she had for ten days now; Karolla had practically lived in Arina's great tent ever since Arina had been carried back to camp on a litter, after being wounded in that skirmish. These days she paid more attention to Arina than she did to her own husband, and every now and then, when he thought about it, he resented it.

Vasil knelt beside the etsana. Arina gestured with her right hand. Ilyana and Karolla left the tent, leaving Vasil alone with his cousin. She was as pale as the moon and scarcely more substantial than the high clouds that streak the sky on a summer's day. But he recognized the set of her mouth and settled down for a good scolding.

"Vasil, I am minded as etsana of this tribe to ask the Elders to reconsider your election as dyan. I have never heard any complaint about your actions as dyan, but in truth, these days, Anton is dyan in everything but name, and I refuse to allow you to continue to hold the honor if you don't also accept the responsibility."

He bowed his head. Gods, how he hated these discussions.

"Have you nothing to say?"

He stared at his hands, which lay clasped on his thighs. Then he wondered if, by turning his right hand palm up, underneath the shield of his left hand, the arrangement might express a different emotion. Except the fingers of his right hand stuck out then, from under the left. Perhaps if he curled the right hand into a fist, hidden under the looser curl of his left hand—

"You seem distracted, Vasil." Though soft, her voice was sharp.

"I beg your pardon." He lifted his gaze. She lay propped on pillows with her braided hair snaking down along the curve of her tunic almost to her waist. His dear cousin. She had always supported him. He was glad she had not died.

"I'll permit you a few days to consider," Arina added. "Come speak to me once you've made up your mind."

This was the time to insinuate himself into her good graces again; he knew it with every fiber of his being. But he wanted to go back and watch the acting. He nodded, allowed himself to be dismissed, and left the tent.

Karolla waited for him outside. "Well?" she demanded. Then she took hold of his arm and led him aside. "Vasil!

You've been infected by some madness. She's going to make Anton dyan again."

"What of it? I never wanted to be dyan."

"You did once. When you came back to the army."

"Oh, that—" He broke off. When he came back to the army, he had been sure that Ilya would give in to him eventually, just as he always had before.

"Oh, that!" echoed Karolla scathingly. "She'll install her own brother as dyan instead of you. That's how far you've fallen. What will you do then? Become a common rider again?"

"A common rider? I think not."

"If not ride, then what? Why should Arina keep you in camp if you do nothing? Where will you go? Where will we go? You have no place here, Vasil, if you're not dyan. Or perhaps she'll take pity on you and allow you to ride in Kirill's new jahar, the one Bakhtiian is granting him. They say he's to ride south past the mountains and the great river, or east on the Golden Road, to discover which lands offer their submission freely to Bakhtiian and which must face his wrath."

He recoiled. "Ride under Kirill's command? Never."

"Then what? What, Vasil? Gods, you're of no use to anyone but yourself. You never think of anyone but yourself!"

"Karolla!" This was too much. *Karolla* could not doubt him. He grasped her hands and drew them up to his lips. "Never say so, my heart. *You* are—"

She wrenched herself away. "Don't embarrass me further by acting this way in public. What do you intend to do?" Quite suddenly, her eyes filled with tears, but she smothered them by wiping at her skin ruthlessly, so hard that it surely must hurt her. "Or do you still think Bakhtiian will take you in?"

Tess, pregnant, had a glow about her that made her look almost beautiful, and Vasil admired the way she moved with a rotund grace unimpaired by her swelling belly. Karolla, pregnant, simply developed blotchy skin, and she waddled already, often with one hand on her back.

Vasil folded his hands together and regarded his wife

with what he hoped was a measured expression. "I won't do anything rash, Karolla. I promise you that. If I must speak with Bakhtiian, then I'll do so."

Immediately he saw that he had said the wrong thing. Her mouth puckered up. She bit at her knuckles. Then she spun and walked away from him. She rolled more, a rocking, ungainly gait. Valentin darted out from behind the screen of a tent and, throwing a single hostile glance back at his father, grabbed a handful of her skirt into a hand and clung to his mother, walking along beside her. Vasil knew he should go after them. Karolla always gave in to his coaxing. But right now he felt—empty more than anything.

He turned and walked back out to the edge of camp. A jahar riding in blocked his path. He stopped to let them by, and there, riding at her ease at the front of the line, sat his newly-widowed sister. She caught sight of him and as quickly, dismissively, her gaze flicked away again. Her fine, handsome face was disfigured forever by the mark of a marriage that no longer fettered her. Petya had died twelve days ago, of wounds suffered in the battle to halt the Karkand governor's flight. Vasil himself had supervised the burning of Petya's body, two days ride out from the besieged city, in marshland, his spirit sent back to the gods along with those of twenty other riders from the Veselov jahar. His saber and his clothes—those not ruined by blood—Vasil returned to the one of Petya's three sisters who traveled with the Orzhekov camp; she had wept copiously. Vera had not mourned with one single tear, not even beside the pyre. Without the least sign of grief, she had watched her husband's body burn. The next day, it was her arrow shot that had brought Karkand's governor down at last, mired as he was by that time in boggy ground, his horse blown, his last loyal followers dead or straggling behind him. But even then, she had shown no emotion except perhaps disappointment that the chase was over.

The jahar passed him, and he hurried away back across camp. But by the time he came to the Company's camp, they had finished for the day. Already the sun sank below the far rim of hills. A sudden, restless discontent seized

Vasil. Its grip, like a strong hand, clutched hard at his chest. He did not want to go back to his tribe. Nothing held him here. He had, indeed, no place, no place to go, no place where he truly belonged.

In time, his wandering led him on a spiraling path in to the heart of the camp, to the Orzhekov encampment. Guards challenged him. He used Tess's name like a talisman, and none barred his way.

By now it was dark. He hesitated, past the innermost ring of guards, and instead traced a route that led by discreet shadows and hidden lines of sight around to the back of Tess's tent. Out beyond, at Sonia Orzhekov's tent, laughter and talking and singing swelled out on the night air. Back here, silence reigned. He took his chance, and snuck in, ducking down, crawling, by the little back entrance that Tess had not sewn shut, despite her threat, past the tent wall, sliding out beyond the inner wall of heavy tapestries into the inner chamber of Tess's tent.

A lantern burned. By its light, Vasil saw Ilya seated beside his bed. Ilya twisted around to stare. Vasil settled into a crouch, waiting, waiting for the reaction, for the burning anger, for the sharp sweetness of Ilya's glance, on him.

Instead, Ilya rose gracefully to his feet and touched two fingers to his lips: *silence*. There, at his feet, lay Tess, deep asleep on her side, her hair spilled out on the pillows, her shoulders bare above the blankets. Ilya walked quietly around her and paused by the entrance flap that led to the outer chamber, then vanished behind it. Vasil had no choice but to follow him.

"What do you want?" asked Ilya in a reasonable tone when Vasil emerged into the outer chamber. He stood at his ease with one hand brushing the khaja table that crowded the far end of the space.

Vasil prowled the chamber, and Ilya let him, watching him as he touched each item: the carved chest, the cabinet, the table and chair, the nested bronze cauldrons and the bronze stove, a knife, the lush tapestries lining the walls, the two ceramic cups and bronze beaker set on the table. All of it, an odd intermingling of jaran and khaja; not one piece of it out of place by a fingerbreadth.

"You've nothing rich here." Vasil lifted one of the ceramic cups. In the dim light, he traced the simple floral pattern that twined around the cup.

"I don't need riches. Heaven has granted me its favor. The gold I leave for the tribes under my command."

Vasil pressed the cup against his own cheek, as if its ribboned surface, held so often by Ilya or by Tess, could whisper secrets to him. "I don't understand you." He said it softly, provocatively.

Standing mostly in shadow, still Ilya burned. Unlike the actors, who channeled light through them and shone with its reflected glow, Ilya *was* the light.

He regarded Vasil gravely, by no sign betraying the least dismay at Vasil's presence. "No. Years ago I thought you did, but now I wonder."

Vasil set down the cup. It made a hollow tap as it met the surface of the table. "You never doubted me before."

"I loved you once, Vasil, and never doubted you then because I never saw you clearly. I love you still, in that memory. But it is ended."

"Ended! For you, perhaps, or so you say now, when it's convenient for you to do so."

"We've had this discussion a hundred times. I see no point in continuing it now. It is ended."

"Then what was it you gave me, that night in this tent? That wasn't love?"

Ilya moved, coming around the table. He stopped not even a full arm's length from Vasil, and his closeness was like balm. He lifted a hand and brushed his fingers down Vasil's cheek. His touch was painfully sweet. Then, on an exhalation of breath, he leaned forward and kissed Vasil once, briefly, on the mouth. And pulled away, and stepped back.

"That is all it was, the memory of love. Eleven years ago, I gave you up because I thought I had to. I—" He broke off. "You don't understand what I did. If you knew— No, never mind that now. The gods have their own way of punishing our arrogance. Only you must understand, that I deliberately sacrificed you, Vasil, in the Year of the Hawk. That year."

The ceremony of exile. Ilya had spared him one thing

alone, that day those many years ago, and that was the
audience of the entire tribe. He and his aunt had performed the ceremony of exile in front of the men of the
jahar. Vasil had always thought it the mark of Ilya's love,
that Ilya had shielded him from the greater humiliation.
Now he did not know what to think. He could not bear
that Ilya could stand here and speak to him so evenly, so
calmly. Gods, was it true? Did Ilya no longer love him?
He discovered that his hands shook, and he closed them
over the back of the chair to steady himself.

"I'm not sure you ever truly loved me, anyway," Ilya
added, grinding dirt into the fresh wound. "Not as love is
true, caring more for the other person, for who she is, in
and of herself, than for what she brings you."

"By what right do you stand there and judge me? How
can you know? Or is this by way of convincing yourself
that you never truly loved me either?"

"No, I loved you. That memory at least is true."

"And by such scraps I must feed myself now? That is
generous of you, Ilyakoria."

"Keep your voice down. I don't want to wake up
Tess."

"Because you don't want her to find us here together?"

"No, because she's tired. Gods, Vasil, Tess would be
the last person to condemn us for being here together. As
you must know." Outside, a bell rang three times, softly.
Ilya wrenched his gaze away from Vasil and listened for
a moment, head cocked to one side. "Send them in," he
said in a clear, cool voice.

Vasil knew an instant of such utter despair that he
thought his legs would give out beneath him. Only his
grip on the chair held him upright. It could be anyone,
coming in to speak to Bakhtiian. Had Vasil been just another visitor—a dyan, a rider, any man from the tribes—
Ilya would feel no embarrassment in being found with
him in the privacy of his wife's tent. Another man might
sit in conversation with Bakhtiian to all hours of the
night, without it being the least bit improper. And if Ilya
was now as willing to be found here alone with Vasil as
he would be if his companion was Yaroslav Sakhalin or

Kirill Zvertkov or Niko Sibirin or Anton Veselov—gods, what if it was true? What if Ilya no longer loved him?

The entrance flap swept aside and two figures came in.

"Dina!" Ilya started forward, amazed, and embraced his niece. "Have you just ridden in? Where is the prince?"

"About two days behind us, with the pack train. I rode ahead, Uncle." She hesitated. She broke away from him and turned to look directly at Vasil. Her eyebrows lifted.

Under her scathing, skeptical gaze, Vasil flushed.

"Who is this?" demanded Bakhtiian.

"I see I've come at just the right time. Where is Tess?"

"Sleeping. Come here. What's your name?"

Out from behind Nadine emerged a boy. He looked to be a few years older than Ilyana. With his black hair and dark eyes and narrow chin, he bore a striking resemblance to Nadine Orzhekov. Except that Nadine was not old enough to have a child that age. And her mother and younger brother had both been killed the same year Ilya had exiled Vasil.

"Vasha, this is Bakhtiian. Pay your respects."

The boy's chin trembled, but he drew himself up bravely enough. "I'm Vassily Kireyevsky. My mother was Inessa Kireyevsky."

"Inessa Kireyevsky! Gods." For a moment, Ilya simply stared at the boy.

As well he might. It was hardly an auspicious introduction. Vasil remembered Inessa as a nasty, selfish little beast who had foolishly believed she could make Ilya love her more than he loved Vasil. For an instant, Ilya's gaze met Vasil's. Oh, yes, they both recalled those days well enough.

Ilya turned a piercing gaze on his niece. "Perhaps you can explain, Dina. Why are you traveling with Inessa Kireyevsky's son?"

"His mother is dead. Mother Kireyevsky gave the boy into my hands, and I promised—I promised to bring him to you, and to see that he was safe."

"Why?"

Vasil watched the boy, who watched Bakhtiian. More than watched. The boy stared greedily at Ilya from under lowered lashes, just as a man weak with thirst stares at a cup of water being borne up to him.

Nadine smiled, looking wickedly pleased with herself. She reminded Vasil much more of her grandmother than of her mother; her mother Nataliia had taken after Petre Sokolov, who was a mild-tempered, even-going man, rather than Alyona Orzhekov. Vasil had never liked Ilya's mother, and he didn't much like the look in Nadine's eyes now.

"They didn't want him. His mother never married."

"But how could she have a child, then?" asked Vasil, surprised. A moment later, he felt the movement behind him.

"Isn't Inessa Kireyevsky the one you lay with out on the grass, under the stars?"

Without turning, Ilya replied. "You've a good memory, my wife."

"For some things." Tess came forward. Her calves and feet were bare, but a silken robe of gold covered the rest of her. The fine sheen of the fabric caught the light, shimmering as she moved forward through the chamber. With her unbound brown hair falling over her shoulders and the high curve of her belly under the glistening silk, she looked doubly exotic and nothing at all like a jaran woman.

"You're the khaja princess," said the boy abruptly, jerking his gaze from Bakhtiian to her.

"Yes. What's your name again? Vasha?"

"Vassily Kireyevsky."

"Well met, Nadine." Nadine hurried forward, and the two women kissed.

"You look as big as a tent," said Nadine.

"Thank you. You look sly. If Inessa Kireyevsky never married, then whose child is he? How old are you, Vasha?"

"I was born in the Year of the Hawk."

"And you've no father? Did your mother never marry?"

He hung his head in shame. "My mother never married. That's why my cousins wished to be rid of me."

No wonder, reflected Vasil, a little disgusted. What

place was there in a tribe for a child who had no father? The boy watched Ilya from under lowered eyelids, gauging his reaction.

"Inessa never married?" asked Ilya. "I find that hard to believe."

"Evidently it's true," said Nadine. She laid a hand on the boy's shoulder, a surprisingly protective gesture. "They didn't want him, Ilya, and they treated him poorly enough. I thought he'd be better off here. Especially since Inessa Kireyevsky claimed up until the day she died that you were the boy's father."

"How can I be his father? I never married her."

"Oh, my God," said Tess, sounding astonished and yet also enlightened. "Vasha, come here." Like a child used to obeying, the boy slid out from under Nadine's hand and walked over to Tess. Tess examined him in silence. And it was silent, all of a sudden. Not one of them spoke. They scarcely seemed to breathe. After a bit, she tilted his chin back with one finger and frowned down at his slender face. "It could be. There's a strong enough resemblance, once you look for it."

"But, Tess—"

"Don't be stupid, Ilya. How many times must I tell you? If you lie with a woman, there's a chance you'll get her pregnant whether you're her husband or not." She lifted her hand to touch the boy's dark hair. "Vasha, do you know why your mother never married?"

He looked back over his shoulder, at Ilya. "Because she thought that Bakhtiian was coming back to marry her. But he never did. And she never wanted anyone else." Then he flushed, as if he expected a scolding for his presumption. Ilya wore no expression at all. Nadine smirked.

Tess sighed. "Well, it's possible. I'm beginning to think it's true. And anyway, I've been waiting for this."

"Waiting for this?" demanded Nadine. "What do you mean?"

"Surely this was inevitable?" Tess regarded the others, puzzled. "You don't think so?" Her hand traced a path down the boy's neck and came to rest on his shoulder. He seemed to melt into the shelter she offered him.

Vasil struggled to make sense of what Tess had said.

Certainly, a man might get his lover pregnant—it was possible, but it went against every custom of the jaran to consider that man the child's father; a woman's husband was the father of her children. So it was; so had it always been; so had the gods decreed at the beginning of the world.

Ilya made a sudden, choked noise in his throat. "Gods, I didn't think she meant it when she told me she was pregnant. What woman would want to get pregnant without a husband?"

"A woman who wanted you very badly. Is it just a coincidence that he's named Vassily?"

Ilya flushed. The dim light covered the stain to his skin, but his body, the sudden stiffness in his shoulders, the way his right hand curled around the edge of the table and then let go, transmitted the emotion in the gesture. "I thought she was joking," he said roughly. "How was I to know she meant it?"

Vasil let go of the chair, only to find that his hands ached, he had gripped it so hard for so long. "Do you mean to say that you told her to name the child after me?" he asked in a hoarse voice.

The boy flashed an astonished glance toward Vasil and then sidled farther into the shelter of Tess's arm.

"Be that as it may," said Tess, "I think you did the right thing, Dina. Vasha. Is that what you wish? To be our son?"

The boy gaped at her. Vasil scarcely knew what to think.

"Tess!" Ilya looked astounded. "We can't take him in. That's absurd. I'll raise no objection if Nadine wishes to foster him, but—"

"This isn't your choice to make, Ilya. Or perhaps I should say, you already made the choice. You lay with her. She bore a child."

"But, Tess—"

"Why should she lie? For all those years, why should she lie? Look at him. Gods, Ilya, just look at him. He's your son."

"But—"

"Not by jaran law, it's true. But by the laws of Jeds,

whether bastard or not, this boy would be recognized as your son."

"This isn't Jeds, and neither are the laws of Jeds *my* laws."

"That may be, but by the laws of Jeds, and by the laws of Erthe, I acknowledge him as your son, and by that connection, as my son as well. And by the law of the jaran, by my stating it in front of witnesses, it becomes true."

As though felled by a bolt from heaven, the boy dropped to his knees in front of Tess and began to cry. Ilya took a halting step toward them, stopped, took another step, and froze.

"You think it's true, don't you?" Vasil murmured, absorbing this knowledge from Ilya's face, which, the gods knew, he could read well enough. Yet how could it be true? And how could they take in a shamed child and yet reject *him?* A hand touched his elbow. He jumped, startled.

"I think we should go, don't you?" asked Nadine with a falsely sweet smile on her face. She took him with a firm grip on the elbow and gave him no choice but to go with her.

Outside, the two guards looked amazed to see him emerge with her, as well they might, since they hadn't seen him go in. She led Vasil past them without a word, on into the night.

"How can it be true?" he demanded of her.

"Veselov, just because the jaran have one set of laws doesn't mean that the khaja hold to the same set of laws. Gods, though, I didn't know what Tess would do. For all I knew, she'd want Vasha strangled."

"Then you believe it, that the boy is Ilya's son? Ilya never had any intention of marrying Inessa Kireyevsky."

"I suppose you'd know. What were you doing in there tonight, anyway?"

"That's none of your concern!"

Nadine snorted. "I could make it my concern, if I wanted to, but I don't. Well, go on, Veselov. Get. Go home. I don't think you need my escort."

Yes, definitely, Nadine Orzhekov reminded him of Ilya's mother, except that Nadine didn't seem to have the

same ruthless ambition. Vasil hadn't been sorry when
Alyona Orzhekov had been murdered; neither had he
been surprised. Only, of course, the result of that awful
massacre had been his own exile. Sometimes, when you
wished too hard for something, you paid a bitter price.

Nadine left him standing there, just strode away, leaving him in the darkness. Stars blazed above, the lanterns
of heaven. The moon hung low, as sharp as a saber's
curve against the night sky. Far in the distance a scattering of lights marked the twin hills of the khaja city,
torches raised on the battlements. For a long time, Vasil
simply waited.

After a long while, the stars wheeling on their blind
path above him, he realized that he might wait out here
all night and through the day and on into night again, and
the one person he most wished for would make no rendezvous with him, here or anywhere. Like a weight, the
knowledge dragged at him. Like a sundering force, it severed forever the dream from the truth. Ilya would not ever
again meet him as anything or anyone, except as
Bakhtiian. Vasil thought that he might just as well die as
live without hope.

CHAPTER FOURTEEN

Out on the plains, the jaran army had not seemed so threatening to David. But now he had ridden along its wake; he had seen the Habakar countryside devastated by its passing. Here on a ridge looking far down at the broad fertile valley that harbored the city of Karkand, the tents of the jaran camp covered the lands surrounding the city like some ominous stain. Like an amoeba engulfing its prey. Like a gloved hand crushing a delicate flower within its fist.

"Pretty impressive," said Maggie, sitting astride her horse next to him. "You look philosophical."

"I'm waxing poetic. What in hell are we doing here anyway, Mags? This is insane."

"David." She hesitated. "Are you sure you're—coping well with Nadine's marriage? You've seemed rather moody since it happened, and you're usually pretty even-tempered. It's one of your wonderful qualities."

"Thank you." Luckily, Charles called the party forward at that moment, and the distraction served to get Maggie off his back. They rode down into the valley, under lowering clouds, only to find a welcoming committee. A group of about one hundred riders waited for them beyond the outskirts of the camp. A gold banner danced in the rising wind. Bakhtiian rode out to greet Charles, Tess on his left, Cara and Ursula on his right. Charles took it all coolly enough. He smiled at Tess. He nodded at Ursula. He met Cara's gaze, and whatever they read of each other satisfied them both.

Then Charles allowed Bakhtiian to escort him to a site suitable to a prince of his eminence. Bakhtiian had evidently set aside a prime bit of land for this purpose just

outside the main camp but close to both the hospital encampment and the Bharentous Repertory Company. An
awning awaited them, as well as children from the
Orzhekov tribe bearing food and drink. Bakhtiian dismounted and went at once to assist Tess from her horse.
Charles dismounted. David and the rest of his party followed his lead.

Out of the swirl of activity, Tess created order. Pillows
appeared. Riders took command of the pack train, un-
loading the animals. The change in Tess amazed David.
Her entire shape had altered, of course, though she didn't
look awkward with it but really rather beautiful. She approached Charles and hugged him, and then stepped back.
Charles actually broke; he actually grinned and rested his
right hand, tentatively, on her abdomen. He shook his
head, still smiling, and removed his hand.

"Oh, thank you," retorted Tess, although Charles had
not spoken a word. "Laugh at me." She slid a hand over
her pregnant belly, stroking it. The gesture looked habit-
ual.

"No, no," said Charles, "you look very—"

"Very rotund? Very fecund? Very abundant? I feel like
a ship. No, a ship is too agile. I feel like a barge. Cara assures me that with two months to go, I'm nowhere close
to being big yet." She kissed Charles on either cheek, in
the jaran style, her hands on his shoulders. "But I'm glad
to see you."

She looked glad to see him. Charles looked pleased.
Pleased! Charles, who rarely showed any emotion anymore. David had never seen the two of them look so at
ease with each other, not since Tess was a child and their
parents were still alive. Evidently, pregnancy agreed with
Tess.

Evidently, it agreed with Bakhtiian as well. He chatted
easily with Cara and Marco, letting Tess and Charles have
their little reunion in what privacy such a public place
could afford. Perhaps he believed that now that his wife
was pregnant with his child, there was no risk that she
would ever leave him.

In Anglais, Charles gave Tess a brief account of Hyacinth. Then he turned away from Tess to address

Bakhtiian. "I'm pleased to see you as well, Bakhtiian. There are matters I think you and I need to discuss."

What the hell? What game was Charles playing now?

Tess blinked. Cara arched her eyebrows. Marco frowned. Bakhtiian took it coolly enough. "I trust," he replied, "that you had a fruitful expedition to Morava. My niece tells me that a party of khepelli traders traveled all the way in from the coast to meet you there."

"Yes. I've managed to take one of their trading houses under my protection. With their help, I learned a few things that might be of interest to you as well, and might prove to be of benefit to both of us."

"Charles," began Tess. She looked white. She looked terrified.

"But," said Charles, "I'd like to have a few words with Owen and Ginny first, and perhaps the rest of the afternoon with Cara. We'll need some time to set up our camp as well. And tonight, a small celebration of our reunion."

"Of course," said Bakhtiian smoothly. "Children." He rounded them up ruthlessly. David noticed for the first time the boy, Vasha, among their numbers. The child stuck next to Sonia Orzhekov's daughter, Katerina, and he looked nervous. As well he might. What was he doing with the Orzhekov tribe? They trooped off, Bakhtiian herding them. A rider took his horse.

Tess lingered. "Charles!"

"I know what I'm doing."

"Well, you'd better fill me in."

"I will, Tess. I have quite a bit to say to you, in fact, and I'll need you in on the council as well. Now go on."

She hesitated. Then she looked at Cara, who had waited patiently through all this. Jo and Rajiv and Maggie had already retreated to the gear, sorting it out.

"It's true," said Cara quietly, not without humor, "that we might like a few moments to ourselves, little one."

Tess threw up her hands in exasperation. "You aren't going to do anything rash, are you?"

Charles blinked. "Do I ever?"

"You're impossible. Hello, David." Tess turned her back on her brother and came over to David, and kissed him.

"You're looking well."

"Thank you. I'm feeling well. You're not looking bad yourself. Is it true that you and Dina—oh, never mind. I'm sorry I mentioned it. I don't think Feodor Grekov is a good match for her, either. She doesn't respect him."

"Tess, I'd really prefer not to speak about it."

"I'm sorry. Truly, I'm sorry, if you feel so strongly." She rested a hand on his shoulder, companionably. "And I have a rather urgent request for you."

"For me?"

"Is it remotely possible that you can design—I don't know—within the limits of the interdiction, some kind of decent plumbing? Something you can teach the army engineers to build at every campsite? Something better than a ditch? Something not too difficult to build, not too time-consuming, but, God, I want something like the Company's necessary. I go over there every chance I get. And showers. Hot showers. Is there any chance you can devise—? It's not that they're dirty, the jaran. They're not. They're scrupulously clean in most ways. But still, the conditions. . . ."

"And you pregnant."

"Oh, tell me you understand."

"Not about being pregnant, but I can sympathize."

"Oh, David." She hugged him, as well as she could given her girth. "You're an angel."

"I haven't promised to do anything yet."

"But you will. You have to. You're an engineer, after all."

At that inopportune moment, Cara paused beside them. "And that reminds me, David, I need a better sanitation system for the hospital. Surely between that brain of yours and your modeler you can design—"

"Oy vey." David flung up his hands palm out as if they could ward him. "Let me breathe a moment. Let me set up the camp. Then I'll see. Cara, why don't you and Charles just go? I'll supervise the camp setup."

"Will you? Thank you, David. It *is* good to see you, you know. Charles and Marco are going over to the Company later, to give them the news about Hyacinth. I'll see you tonight, then." She and Charles left. Tess left. David got to work with the others, and with practiced ease, and the addition of Ursula, they set up the camp before night-fall.

After weeks journeying at an inhuman pace on horse-back across the endless, changing landscape of Rhui, David found himself relieved to come to a temporary halt, even in the primitive conditions of a siege. Karkand rose before them, made tiny by distance, but real, there to be touched. The palace of Morava loomed in the back of his mind like an illusion, seen on the horizon, coming no closer.

"Here, you old slug," said Maggie, jostling David where he sat, sore, tired, and grateful, in a chair, "help me hang lanterns all around here. Don't forget that we're having a party tonight."

"Goddess in Heaven." David dragged himself up. Maggie paused to rub his shoulders, and he sighed and drooped.

"Now don't you sit down again, or I'll stop."

"Don't stop. Why the actors? All that noise."

"Who knows what lurks in the heart of Charles? You, better than I. He has a position as prince to maintain, you know. Aren't princes meant to give parties? I don't know."

"It's true Charles is often at his best in a crowd. Better than me, certainly."

"You shy thing." She removed her hands from his back. "Here, now, give me a hand."

"Mags, you're an angel. Remind me never to ride that far that fast again. In fact, remind me never to travel any distance in anything other than a skimmer or a shuttle, would you?"

She snorted. "What, you didn't think it was romantic?"

"Not to my thighs and my rump it wasn't." They lit and hung lanterns at the four corners of the awning that thrust out in front of Charles's tent. Rajiv emerged from his tent and helped them. Jo and Ursula had gone to the hospital camp with the new equipment for Cara. As eve-ning fell, Charles returned from his peregrinations, alone.

"Well?" asked David. "Did you give Owen and Ginny the news? How did they take it?"

"They were relieved. Owen said, 'perhaps he'll be a better actor for the experience.' "

"No! He would. The man's a lunatic."

"Oh, I don't know. He's not unlike me."

"Or Cara, or any of you obsessive types. Where's Marco?"

Charles shrugged. "Marco seemed distracted. I'm not sure whether we'll see him again tonight or not."

"What, already off tomming it?"

"David, this time I'm beginning to wonder if there's more to it than that."

"What? You're not serious?"

But David could see that Charles was, indeed, serious. David followed him inside his tent, where he removed two bottles of whiskey from his precious horde. Only one bottle remained. "I don't know. Help me keep an eye on him, will you?"

David simply grunted in reply, too astonished by the thought of Marco seriously distracted by a woman to think of any words to express himself with. The tent flap swept aside behind them, and Tess and Cara walked in.

"So it's true?" Tess was saying to Cara in Anglais. "I'm not surprised, I suppose, but still, to have it confirmed by your tests. . . ."

"To have what confirmed?" asked Charles, turning around.

Cara glanced at Tess, as if for her permission to speak, but Tess went on. "The boy, Vasha. He's Ilya's illegitimate son by a woman he knew years ago. Cara has confirmed it by comparing VNTR regions."

"Vasha!" David gaped. "So that's why he looked like Dina. But, Tess, I saw him with the other Orzhekov children—"

"Well, of course, I took him in! Poor child. His mother is dead and his relatives didn't want him, which is no surprise, considering what a disgrace it is to have no father."

"But he has a—"

"Not by their laws. But because I adopted him as my son, then Ilya, who's his biological father, becomes his accepted father because Ilya is my husband." Then she hesitated. "Wasn't it the right thing to do?"

"I think so," said Cara firmly.

Charles thought about it for a while. "For the boy, certainly, I should think. Can he inherit?"

"Only through my line."

"Ah. Of course."

"But you know, Charles, the jaran have changed already, in little ways, since I've come to them. Who knows where it will stop? He's a very intense boy. Quiet, but that may just be the way he learned to survive. Time will tell how ambitious he is."

"But what about your child, Tess?" David asked.

She blinked at him. A moment later understanding flooded her features, and she chuckled. "What? I need to protect my children's inheritance rights by murdering him? How very Byzantine of you, David." She hesitated, appeared about to say something more, then did not.

But, of course, Tess's children had three inheritances to choose from: Rhui, Earth, and the Empire. Although their ability to inherit Charles's position was problematic, to say the least. Tess caught his eye and for that instant they spoke without words. David did not envy her her dilemma and yet he could not feel sorry for her either, not really, since she had not only chosen her own fate but seemed content with it.

She turned to Charles. "What happened at Morava?"

Charles unfolded a canvas chair. "Sit down. David, can you go outside and head off any inquiries for—what?—ten minutes? I want Tess and Cara to hear the basics now, so they can think about it before our council. Which I'd like to hold—oh, not tomorrow. The day after."

David nodded and retreated. He paused by the entrance to listen.

". . . and we do have the resources. We have Rhui entire."

"But the interdiction?"

"Will hold. It could take decades for us to process the information and to put a plan into place. The underlying structure, the foundation, has to be as strong as—as bedrock. It has to be invulnerable. So in a sense, Rhui is safer this way—"

"For now."

"How long do you really think the interdiction can stay in place? I can only hold off the inevitable for so long."

"No, you're right. I'm just being selfish. What about the dates on the Mushai, again? My God, Charles, I realize now that I must have learned simply one line of their language, that I was learning—what?—the male language, or something. It's like turning a corner in a hallway only to find that you've stepped into a whole 'nother world. Don't you realize that I'm perfectly placed to learn both the male and the female side, if that is in fact how their culture is structured?"

"Oh, yes," said Charles in his cool voice. "I realize it."

David slipped outside. Almost ran into Bakhtiian, who stood a meter from the entrance, listening. David choked back an exclamation.

"I beg your pardon," said Bakhtiian in a tone so colorless that a Chapalii lord would have been envious of it. "Is Tess—?" Then he hesitated, because if one listened, one could hear her voice as she spoke with Charles. But, of course, she spoke in a language Bakhtiian did not understand. "I hope," he added, looking David straight in the face, "that you will find time to attend me in the morning. I have some requests to make of you."

"Of course. If you'll excuse me." David retreated as quickly as he could. Goddess, what did Bakhtiian want of him? Was he still holding a grudge against him because he thought David had slept with his wife? And yet, faced with such an order—even though it was phrased as a request—David dared not disobey.

The actors arrived in a flurry of sound and movement. David retreated into the safety of their company, but he was sorry to note that Diana had not come over for the party. The evening passed in a blur of conversation, and he went to bed early.

In the morning, a young jaran rider waited at the edge of the encampment. Bakhtiian had, quite kindly, sent an escort.

"Mags, you *will* come with me."

"I will?"

"Yes, you will. I need a witness. I'm not going over alone."

"Oh, here," said Ursula, coming up. "I'll come with you, David. You're looking a little ashen about the gills. What's wrong?"

"Nothing!" David cast a last, hopeless glance at Maggie and allowed himself to be escorted away by Ursula and the jaran soldier. The soldier remained respectfully quiet on the long walk, but his presence allowed them to pass right through the rings of guards, straight to the awning under which Bakhtiian sat. David found himself ushered to the front immediately and was, for once, glad of Ursula's companionship.

"Ah." Bakhtiian beckoned David forward. Reluctantly, David went, keeping one eye on Ursula to see what she did and the other on Bakhtiian's sheathed saber. Tess was nowhere in sight. "Please. Sit down. You're an engineer, Tess tells me."

David cleared his throat. "Ah. Yes. I am." Ursula settled down beside David as if she were used to sitting in on Bakhtiian's councils.

"We have a need for engineers. Siege engineers. Perhaps you'll agree to ride out with me and survey the city. Any suggestions you have would be welcomed." Without more invitation than that, he rose and beckoned to his guard. Horses arrived, led by soldiers. David saw some khaja prisoners—or at least he assumed they were prisoners—mounted as well; presumably these were other engineers, culled from the ranks of the conquered. David felt compelled by events and by Bakhtiian's proximity to go along. Ursula did not hesitate.

"This is a wonderful opportunity," she said in a low voice to David as they mounted. "You have an entire city to experiment on. Von Clausewitz says that 'critical examination is not merely the appreciation of those means which have been actually employed, but also of all possible means, which therefore must be suggested in the first place.'"

"Ursula!" He was appalled. "There are people in that city. I don't think Charles meant his interdiction to hold only for them and not for the jaran as well."

"Oh, David, be reasonable. The city is besieged anyway. The war is already here."

"That doesn't make it right."

"Well, then, your contribution might save lives on both sides. If the jaran attack is effective enough, and swift enough, perhaps the khaja will surrender to save themselves."

"If that will indeed save them."

"You forget that I've been traveling with the army. Overall, the jaran are merciful to those who surrender."

"Are they now? I wonder what your conception of mercy is. I saw how devastated the lands were, behind us."

"That was Yaroslav Sakhalin's doing. Most of it, anyway."

"It's still against the interdiction."

"I beg your pardon," said Bakhtiian, riding up beside them. "I hope," he said, nodding toward David, "that you'll ride with me."

As they rode out, all David could think of was how stupid he had been to come here at all. He could have pled illness. He could even have asked Charles to make excuses for him, but then again, maybe Charles would not have done it. Maybe Charles wanted this—not the breaking of the interdiction, but the attempt, the act, the place where the line had to be drawn and his authority thrown up against Bakhtiian's, to prove once and for all who was really in charge. Was this how Tess felt, that she was a pawn tossed about from one side to the other in someone else's game?

They rode out of camp and alongside harvested fields striped with rows of fruit still ripening. Khaja peasants plowed a fallow field under, turning up the soil.

"I was remembering," said Bakhtiian suddenly, startling David, "when we first met."

Goddess, here it came. David recalled all too clearly that awful first meeting, when he and Tess had crawled out of his tent into the full sight of her husband.

"Do you recall that I asked you if you could do a portrait of my wife?"

A series of images flashed through David's mind: the

port and the thousand jaran horsemen arrayed along the shore to meet them; the horrible execution; he and Diana sitting in the quiet of camp, Diana watching while he sketched . . . Bakhtiian.

"Why, yes," he replied, remembering now how incongruous it had seemed at the time. "I did a sketch of you."

"Yes. You're a fine artist. I hope, now that you're with the army again, that you might find time to do the portrait."

David could not respond immediately. The quiet respect in Bakhtiian's voice for David's ability, the diffident request, the nature of the request itself, all combined with Bakhtiian's formidable presence and the all-too-evident wreckage that his army had left in its wake to confuse David as to the kind of man he was dealing with.

"My niece speaks highly of you," Bakhtiian added, as if this inducement might convince David to agree. "You've taught her a great deal about mapmaking."

Which he had. Thus breaking the interdiction. But that was different, wasn't it? Because she was different. David felt impelled to smile at his own hypocrisy. "I'd be pleased to do a portrait of your wife."

Bakhtiian nodded. He gestured to the khaja prisoners. "These four khaja soldiers are engineers. This woman is our interpreter. Ursula you know, of course. I hope you will be able to contribute to our discussion."

"I. . . . You understand, of course, that I'm subject to the prince. I must first have his permission to . . . to contribute anything." There, it was said.

Bakhtiian measured him, not without sympathy. "I understand." No doubt he did, on one level. After all, his army didn't share its secrets with its enemies either. "But today should give you ample time to observe."

They rode on, out to survey the walls of Karkand.

CHAPTER FIFTEEN

Sitting on the edge of the platform as day slid into evening, Diana unplaited her hair and combed her fingers through it. The Evening Star—which of the planets was it? she never could remember—pierced the darkening blue of the sky, and one by one other stars appeared. Rehearsal had tired her today, but she never minded that; it was a satisfying sort of fatigue.

"Di!" Quinn jogged up, breathless with excitement, and grabbed her hand. "Come with me!" Quinn yanked her forward, and Diana laughed and went with her to the Company tent.

"Look!" Quinn pointed. At first Diana only saw Owen, speaking quietly with Dejhuti and Seshat and Yomi. Joseph wandered up. Ginny arrived, notebook in one hand, pen in the other. Phillippe helped Anahita to a chair. Helen and Jean-Pierre gossiped with Gwyn over on the other side. Oriana stood in the entrance to the huge tent, half-hidden in its shadow.

"Am I missing something?" asked Hal, walking up beside Diana and Quinn. "Everyone's here."

"Except Hyacinth," murmured Diana. Then she spotted two figures crossing toward them from the main camp. At first the dusk disguised them, but then they emerged into the glow of the lanterns fixed at intervals around the camp.

Quinn squeezed Diana's hand. "Look, here comes the duke."

" 'With his eyes full of anger,' " replied Diana automatically.

Quinn rolled her eyes. "Are you quoting again?"

"That's *As You Like It,* you idiot."

"It may be, but unlike you, I don't retain entire plays in my memory for years at a time."

"Charles!" exclaimed Ginny. "How good to see you again. Hello, Marco. Did you just ride in? This afternoon? You made good time. Though I must say, you look none the worse for the wear."

With one thought, Diana and Quinn and Hal sidled closer toward the center of the scene.

"I don't suppose," said Yomi quietly, "that you have any news of Hyacinth, poor lad."

"In fact, I do."

He told them. The entire Company listened intently. Diana found her attention straying to Marco, who stood silently beside Soerensen. He glanced once at her and away as quickly, an exchange that reminded her incongruously of jaran men. Except that he looked nothing like jaran men. By League standards he was not a particularly tall man, but here his height and the breadth of his shoulders marked him as big.

"Thank goodness Hyacinth is safe," said Ginny at last. "I suppose that under the circumstances you couldn't have brought him back."

"No. I thought it best to simply remove him and his companion from Rhui altogether."

Owen sighed. "Which still leaves us one actor short. Well, we've managed so far, by the skin of our teeth."

"Remember, too," added Soerensen in his mild voice, "that we'll be leaving soon."

"Leaving soon!" Anahita roused herself, straightening up in her chair. "Thank goodness. I wish I'd gone with Hyacinth. I'd be quit of here now."

There was a short, embarrassed silence which Soerensen covered by going on. "Autumn's coming on. In order to maintain the charade, we must return to a port before ships stop sailing for the winter. Or else winter here, which I've no leisure to do."

"What about your sister?" asked Ginny.

"In any case," added Soerensen, "we might be leaving anytime within the next two or ten weeks, and possibly abruptly. Just so you can be prepared."

"Excuse me," said Diana in a low voice to Quinn and

Hal, and she escaped the assembly. She wandered back to her own tent and simply stood there, outside, staring at nothing. Two weeks, or ten weeks. What if they left before Anatoly returned? What if she never saw Anatoly again? She shivered. After the long hot nights of the summer, she had forgotten that it could get cold at night. But the season did turn, eventually; eventually, the year turned, and what had been young grew old, and what had sprouted fresh and green in the spring withered and died to make way for winter.

"Diana?"

Somehow, it didn't surprise her that Marco had followed her here. "Hello." She managed to say it without her voice shaking.

"I beg your pardon, if I'm disturbing you."

"No. No. I'm just— No, you're not."

He stood three paces from her. "I thought— You're well? You look well."

"Thank you. I'm well. I hope you are, too? I mean, we got a few reports, not much, but— Everything went as you hoped it would?"

"Better. It's nothing I can speak of, right now, but, yes, it went well."

"No, I understand. Of course, I understand. Was Hyacinth all right?"

"He was traumatized. I think he'll recover."

"Thank the Goddess for that. He took his jaran lover with him? Well, I don't envy him for that. Neither of them, really."

A sudden, awkward silence fell. "You don't—you don't mean to take Anatoly with you, when you go back?" He jerked a hand up, warding off any comment. "No, I beg your pardon. It's none of my concern."

"No, don't apologize. Please! Thank you for asking. You don't know what it's like. No one in the Company speaks of him anymore, not to me, at least. It's as if they think I'm embarrassed of him, or that I don't want him mentioned anymore, now that he's gone. And in the jaran camp, why, it's hardly worth mentioning, it's nothing unusual to them."

"He's gone?" Marco faltered on the question. "He didn't—"

"Oh, no, he's not dead. At least, I don't think he is. How can a person know, with the communications they have here? He went off months ago—*months* ago!—and he hasn't come back yet. I don't know when he'll come back. For all I know, we'll leave before he comes back."

He took a single step toward her, and halted.

"It just doesn't seem fair. And it makes me so damned angry. Why can't I know? How can the women stand to live this way? They could be separated for months, for years! There are tribes out on the plains that haven't seen their riders for years. Although in all fairness, I think there's some kind of a leave system, that after two or three years serving in the army, a man gets to go back to his tribe for a year. Or something, I'm not sure about the details." She broke off and felt a flush rise in her cheeks. "Goddess, I'm sorry. I'm babbling. It just seems like no one else cares. I don't want to bore you."

"You don't bore me, Diana."

Diana shut her eyes, wilting under the heat of that simple utterance. He could have said any words, those words, other words, nonsense words, and she would have known what he meant by them. What a stupid little infatuation she had had for him, before. Then he had seemed wild and strong and half a barbarian himself. Oh, the attraction remained. It had never eased. But she desired him as much now because he seemed familiar and safe to her, standing here on the outskirts of a truly barbarian encampment, as because of what he had once represented to her, an adventurer who had wandered in wild landscapes and faced death and fear with equal self-possession. And she was lonely, and she felt alone. She opened her eyes when she felt him take another step. He loomed before her.

"Diana? I'm sorry. I'm sorry for all the stupid things I said to you. I'm sorry you hurt now."

It took only a half step to move into his embrace, because his momentum still carried him forward into hers. They kissed.

Diana ceased feeling the cold, or the night breeze, or

anything except his hands on her back, and her thigh and hip pressed up against his, and the unsteady catch of his breathing against her chest. She was warm everywhere.

A dull ache prodded her ankle. After a moment, she identified it. One of the guide ropes of her tent cut across the skin. She shifted and, shifting, Marco sighing and gathering her back into him, she heard the distant echo of bells. Messenger bells. What if they brought news of Anatoly?

"Marco," she murmured into his lips. He drew his head back and lifted a hand to cup her chin.

"Golden fair," he whispered.

"I can't." It hurt, not the movement, because she moved gently, but the cold and the emptiness. "I can't, Marco. You must know that I want to, but I can't."

"Because you love him?" His voice cracked on the word "love."

She could not reply.

"Do you?" he demanded.

She could not say yes. She could not say no. She said nothing.

"If you don't know by now— Goddess, Diana, any fool could see that you only married him to get back at me or at best because you were infatuated with the idea of marrying a romantic native prince."

She flared, angry and embarrassed together. "Whatever it was," she said, stumbling over the words, "I just feel that I have to stay loyal to Anatoly until I know what's going to happen to him, and to me."

"Well, then," he pressed on stubbornly, "jaran women take lovers. It's accepted—it's even expected—in their culture."

"I know that *now*. And it's no wonder, if the men are always off riding for months at a time. I'm not surprised that they take lovers when they're always left behind. But I'm not jaran. I don't want to be jaran. I have to do what's true to me. It isn't you I'm rejecting, Marco. Please tell me you see that."

"Then if you don't want to be jaran, why in hell did you marry him?" He flinched away from her suddenly. "Oh, hell. I'm sorry," It hurt her worse to see him in pain than it had to feel herself alone again, not knowing if Anatoly would even return before she left. He dipped his chin down, like he was containing words he wished to say but refused to say. "I will respect your decision. I'll stay away from you."

"I didn't mean— Don't feel you have to stay away from me. At least come to see me. We can talk."

"Don't you understand, Diana? I love you. I can't pretend to be your friend. I can hardly stand to be this close to you as it is."

Diana had never imagined that Marco Burckhardt might be vulnerable. He had always seemed so self-contained, so confident. It shook her horribly to see him wounded.

"Good-bye," he said, and he walked away.

"Marco! Wait. I—do you remember, that handkerchief you loaned me? When you left for Morava? I never returned it to you. I still have it."

"Keep it," he said without turning around, and he vanished into the darkness that ringed the camp.

She hurt.

She just stood there and let it wash over her, as if that alone would do justice to his feelings, to what she'd done to him. Or had she done anything to him at all? They'd done nothing to each other that they hadn't done to themselves; made mistakes, behaved stupidly, acted without thinking through the consequences of the action. Maybe Marco had made an image of her, that first meeting, that proved just as false as the one she had made of him. She had let herself fall in love—or into an infatuation, at least—with Marco before she had the slightest knowledge of who he really was. And if that was true about Marco, how much more true it was about Anatoly. She couldn't even talk to Anatoly when she married him. She hadn't known him at all. The choice had seemed not rash but adventurous and brave at the time. Now, with clearer sight, it just seemed reckless. A true explorer treads cautiously and with a deep respect for the unknown land. She had charged blithely in, all unconscious of danger. Well, and had she suffered so much? Only in her heart. She tried to imagine Hyacinth, straying through the wilderness, seeing one of his companions die, and could not compare her suffering to his.

"Di? Di!" There came Quinn, of course. "You left so quickly. Soerensen invited us to his camp. They're having a little party, a reunion party, I suppose. Are you coming?"

"No, sorry, I'm not in the mood."

For once, Quinn gave up immediately and went away.

Diana ducked into her tent and stripped and lay down. She was tired, really tired now, in the heart as well as the body. But every time she shut her eyes she saw, not Anatoly, not Marco, but Vasil Veselov coming up to her on the stage, dropping his eyes, waiting there—acting— and it suddenly came to her the one element Gwyn hadn't caught yet, the one that would allow him to subsume completely the character of the dyan who loved the Sun's daughter. She threw on her clothes and scrambled out of the tent and ran.

The others had already left camp, but by the single lantern left lit for their return, she saw a shadow blurring the deeper shadows on the stage, and she knew it was him, practicing, still practicing.

"Gwyn! Gwyn, I've got it." She hopped up on the platform and he paused to listen to her. "It's not just what Owen said, about showing the modesty without losing the strength. It's about power contained. It's about the promise of power unleashed. It's as if, through her, you can reach your true power, just as somehow she can reach her true power through you, and the exchange is as much about that recognition of each other . . ." She lapsed into silence, puffing, out of breath, she was so excited. "Do you see what I'm trying to say?"

Gwyn considered. He never did rash things, not Gwyn. That remained one of his strengths, that he tread cautiously, that he considered, and when he did move, he placed his feet on the firmest ground. But he wasn't afraid to take chances.

"Let's try it," he said.

CHAPTER SIXTEEN

"Husband!"

Jiroannes flinched at the sound of his bride's voice. Samae jerked her hand away from his feet, which she had been massaging, and sank back to kneel at the foot of the couch. Jiroannes rose from his cushions and signaled to Lal to bring him a robe. As the boy tied the robe closed with a sash, she who had once been Javani entered through the enclosed walkway that now linked her tent with his. She wore the emerald silk peacock gown and a tiered gold headdress, like a conical cap, with an embroidered shawl draped from it down over her shoulders and a veil of silk covering her lower face. The silk was so sheer that he could see her expression through it; she wanted something. Again.

"Wife."

Her interpreter hovered anxiously three steps behind her.

"Husband, it is impossible that I continue to live in these vulgar conditions. I have sent my steward to find a suitable house within the suburbs, near the vegetable and fruit market. Meanwhile, my handmaiden has gone to purchase silks for my wardrobe. These peacocks are very pretty, I'm sure, but the quality of the weave is mediocre."

"Those silks were woven and embroidered in the women's quarters of my father's house!"

"Then I see that we will have to import Habakar weavers as well as the perfumer and the three cooks I have been forced to engage in order to afford a decent quality of living in this household."

"And how are we to travel with this city of retainers?

And pay for them? Lal, go tell Syrannus to send guards after the steward and the girl. None of these orders can go through."

Lal nodded and slipped out, leaving Jiroannes alone with his wife. He braced himself.

"The orders must go through! I demand it. It is insupportable that I live out here among these barbarians. There are decent houses lying empty within the outer walls, not what one of my birth expects, but they will do until better arrangements can be made."

"We're not leaving the camp. To do so would insult the jaran. I would think you, of all people, would see the idiocy in such a course. Or would you prefer I had not married you and merely cast you off to the tender mercies of your conquerors?"

What frightened Jiroannes about Laissa was how swiftly her personality had changed once the Habakar priests had sprinkled perfume and holy water over them and proclaimed them betrothed and married by the laws of their Almighty God. At his threat, she merely drew up her chin and stared scornfully at him.

"You would have been a fool to do so, and you're a fool to threaten me with it now. No merchant of my people would dare refuse to do business with me or with my husband's ministers. You will keep that in mind, I hope, if you wish to prosper in these lands. I think you're being unnecessarily sanguine about the possibility that these barbarians will hold on to their conquests. As Javani, it was one of my duties to study the records of my people, and let me assure you that barbarians have ridden through these lands before only to be chased out by our armies or by their own troubles back in the lands where they come from."

He had thought the Habakar a civilized people. Marriage to Laissa had disabused him of this notion. Their noblewomen learned to read and write and were encouraged to study arts such as mathematics and philosophy and poetry that only men were suited to engage in, and any woman might conduct business in her own name, although it was true that she must be under a husband's or father's or brother's protection.

"Furthermore," she continued relentlessly, "whatever may become of these barbarians, you certainly won't impress them with the paltry retinue that attends you now. If you wish for respect, then you must show that you deserve it. Your guards' camp was a disgrace when I toured it five days ago, children running everywhere, sluttish women unsupervised and unkempt, and no priest to watch over them. I hope it is in better condition now because of my efforts, but do I receive thanks for that? Certainly not. You complain that I brought in a priest of my people to hold the hand of the Almighty God over those of us in this camp. You refuse me sufficient quarters, and then complain when I act to improve them. If you wish me to entertain jaran noblewomen, I certainly cannot do so in that cramped, colorless little tent that I had to share with my handmaiden. I have managed to enlarge the tent—"

She had, at that. Her tent, attached to his by a covered walkway so that she needn't leave its seclusion, was twice the size of his own, now, and warrened with little rooms for sleeping and primping and administering and one with a cot for her handmaiden.

"—but I need more tapestries for the walls and more carpets. There is a certain kind of carpet from the south, near Salkh, which I should like four of, if they can be got. And some couches for visitors, and I refuse to serve anyone, even a barbarian woman, that swill you call tea. Furthermore—"

"Enough!"

"It is not enough! Furthermore—"

He cuffed her across the cheek. She gasped, and that quickly raised her right hand and slapped him. The blow didn't hurt—she wasn't strong enough for that—but it stung. "You dare strike me!"

Despite his anger, she didn't shrink back from him. "The Almighty God teaches us that a woman must bow to her husband as the angels bow to God, but if he strikes her without justification, then she may strike back."

"Without justification! A woman ought never to raise her voice to a man! Never! So has the Everlasting God proclaimed."

"Then you are barbarians, as I thought. I encourage

you to see how well you will prosper in Habakar lands without my assistance. I lived better than this before the jaran came, and had your guards not discovered my hiding place, I would have escaped and been treated among my own people as a woman of my station ought to be treated.

"Yet you were discovered, and if I judge rightly, you ought to have killed yourself rather than let yourself be dishonored."

Her chin quivered. Silk trembled over the bridge of her nose, and her eyes flashed. "So speaks the man who dishonored me. That is for the Almighty God to forgive, if He judges that I did not do my duty toward Him. Not for an unbeliever such as yourself."

"I hope you realize what forbearance I am showing in allowing you to bring a priest into my camp at all. It is only my respect for Bakhtiian's proclamation that all priests must be tolerated."

"It is only your respect for the power of Bakhtiian's army. It was, in any case, part of the marriage contract that you signed."

A contract witnessed by the Habakar priests and signed by him and by Laissa. As if a woman's word was worth anything, although evidently it was to these people. Still, by birth as reckoned by Habakar standards she ranked far above him; in Vidiya, he could never have hoped for so advantageous a match: She was cousin to the reigning king and to the king's nephew who, rumor said, was now raising an army in the southlands, and also to the princess whom Mitya expected to marry. The bitter truth was, she treated him like the commoner she considered him to be; although his family was an old and honorable house, they were not nobility. That he had been allowed to study in the palace school for boys was due to his uncle's high standing as a Companion to the Great King, and the fact that his uncle had once saved the Great King's father's life in a battle. And imagine, if Mitya became king here, then the king's wife and his own wife would be cousins!

"Well," he said, quashing an urge to touch his cheek, where she had slapped him, "I forbid any expedition to look for a villa within the walls, but if you need rugs and carpets, and silks for your wardrobe, you have my permission to send your steward out to the market." Her steward. She had a regular army of attendants, more than he had brought, certainly. Yet it was true that in some ways she made his life easier. She had taken over much of the day-to-day administering of the camp, which was by rights a servant's job. Evidently she thought it a woman's duty, and indeed, the Everlasting God proclaimed that women were the servants of men, so perhaps it was fitting.

The tent flap stirred and Lal appeared. "I beg your pardon, eminence. I thought to inquire if you had further orders for me before I left?"

Probably the boy had been listening outside. Jiroannes glanced at Laissa.

She bowed her head, but the show of humility did not fool him. "I abide by your command, husband."

"Lal, the mistress will direct you. Also, I mean to attend the performance this afternoon. Wife, you will accompany me. Although I'm sure you feel reluctant to leave your seclusion, I think it best that the jaran noblewomen see you with me again, out in the camp, so that they can be assured that we are fixed as man and wife."

"As you wish." She retreated to the door and glanced back—not at him, but at the still, silent form that was Samae, kneeling motionlessly, head bent submissively, at the foot of the couch. Then she was gone, Lal scurrying after her, into the women's quarters, a place that no man might follow Laissa into except her husband.

That sudden, lightning interest puzzled Jiroannes. Why should Laissa notice Samae? The girl now slept in the same tent as the two eunuchs, and now that he was married, Jiroannes had felt able to endure her touch again. He remained leery of bedding her so far, but he allowed her to massage him every day.

"Jat! Where is the boy, damn it? Samae, dress me."

She did so without word or sign of what she thought of her new favor in his eyes. Perhaps Samae's exotic beauty interested Laissa. Vidiyan women had their own diversions within the women's quarters, and what they did to keep themselves occupied did not merit a man's concern, as long as they did their duty by bearing him sons of his own seed.

In the afternoon he walked beside Laissa's covered litter, borne by two guardsmen and two servants of her own people, to the ground where the Company performed. Lal and Samae and Syrannus walked in attendance on him, and four handmaidens as well as the interpreter accompanied Laissa, so that when they came to settle themselves in front of the platform, they made quite an unwieldy little group.

After so long with the jaran, Jiroannes had learned to recognize the various ranks within the jaran; today many of their nobles gathered to attend the performance. Evidently, this dance was being danced for the first time, and Bakhtiian himself, accompanied by the Prince of Jeds, meant to attend as well. Mother Sakhalin hurried up, and Laissa, no fool, eased herself out of the litter to greet the old woman. Except, to his horror, she did not offer greetings at all. Instead, she and the old woman began haggling over right of place.

"Wife," he began, "naturally we will move to a different—"

Two heads turned. Both women stared at him, most brazenly, and he realized that they were enjoying themselves and that his opinion was not wanted. Fuming, he retreated to stand beside Syrannus.

"They're all barbarians," he muttered.

"Look, eminence, there is Bakhtiian. With his wife and the prince."

Mother Sakhalin and Laissa finished their argument, and Mother Sakhalin moved away to intercept Bakhtiian.

"Husband, we will sit here, as I said."

"But—"

"We are displacing one of the Ten Tribes, but the queen mother wishes them to learn a little humility on this occasion, so she has assented to our presence here. She also sees the expediency in honoring me as an ally in high favor. I hope you understand that this benefits your position as well."

Jiroannes only grunted in reply. They settled down, Laissa within the litter, one flap thrown askew so that she

could view the dancing platform as well as her husband.
Her handmaidens knelt around her. Lal laid pillows on
the ground for Jiroannes, and he settled there, Syrannus to
his right and the two slaves seated between him and the
litter. At the front of the audience, Bakhtiian sat down between his wife and the Prince of Jeds. Two girls helped
Mother Sakhalin sit on a pillow to the right of the prince.

A man entered onto the platform, three small drums
slung around his waist. He tapped on them, drawing out
a rhythm by whose beat a woman entered. But not just
any woman: this was Mother Sun, who sent her daughter
to the earth. Mitya had told Jiroannes this story. Now, the
actors danced it. It was as if they brought it to life: the
daughter's exile and the ten sisters she brought with her
to be her companions, who bore the first tribes of the
jaran; how she met the first dyan of the Sakhalin tribe;
how they loved, how they parted. The Daughter of the
Sun traveled away into dark lands, where she bore his
child, and he followed her, but in the end, as is the fate
of all mortal men, he died. And in the end, as must any
child of the heavens, she returned to her home in the
gods' lands.

They danced well. Their audience sat with deep respect, in rapt silence. Syrannus sat with hands folded in
his lap. Laissa, by her profile, was as busy surveying the
ranks of the jaran as watching the performance. A tear
trailed down Samae's face.

A tear! Jiroannes stared at the slave-girl. A girl still,
perhaps; she had been so young when his uncle had offered her to him at the marketplace that she had not yet
begun her woman's courses, although of course the merchant selling her had assured Jiroannes that she was a virgin. In five years, Jiroannes had never seen her cry. He
had never seen her show any feelings at all, except once
that flash of rebellion, as quickly stifled. Except once
when he had thought she had smiled at Mitya. Except
now, when a tear lined her cheek as she watched the performance.

What did he know about her? He knew more about Lal,
who was a common boy, son of a tavernkeeper and a
whore, sold into the palace service and lucky enough to

gain a place in Jiroannes's household, and who by dint of
hard work and ambition had risen fast. Already Laissa
considered him indispensable, and the boy was certainly
clever and industrious. But Samae—she had come from
Tadesh, the Gray Eminence's lands across the sea. She
had been taught the concubine's arts there, while still a
child—or she must have been, because she knew them,
and where else could she have learned them? She danced
finely. Perhaps she had once lived with such a company
of dancers—of *actors,* that was their proper name—when
she was a child; perhaps she remembered them; perhaps
she mourned what she had lost.

Stirred by a feeling he did not entirely understand,
Jiroannes reached out and patted her hand. She flinched
and jerked away from him, startled, her eyes wide. As
quickly, she pulled her hands in against her chest and
bowed her head and sat as still as stone. Jiroannes drew
away his hand and glanced up. Laissa watched him,
watched Samae, through her sheer veil, and a moment
later looked away.

Jiroannes grunted under his breath and returned his attention to the performance. Well, that would teach him to
try to understand women. The Everlasting God enjoined
men to rule women, not to understand them. Still, he
could not help but wonder what Samae saw in the
dance—in the *play*—to make her cry.

After the performance, Mitya trotted up, all flushed and
cheerful. "That was very fine, wasn't it!" he exclaimed.
Then he recalled his manners and bowed his head before
Laissa's presence. She acknowledged him coolly and sent
her interpreter to invite Mother Sakhalin to her tent for
refreshments. The handmaidens closed up the litter and
the guards bore her away.

Mitya watched her go, bemused. "It's a curious way to
travel. She can't see out, can she?"

"There are a few cunningly concealed slits in the fabric, but otherwise, no. In this fashion a woman can travel
from one place to another, when she must, without expos-
ing herself to the eyes of strangers."

"Oh." Mitya nodded, staring after the litter with a look
of incomprehension on his face. "Well. It *was* very fine,

what they did though, telling the tale like that." He glanced at Samae, glanced away, and fixed his attention on Jiroannes.

"Perhaps you would like to return with me to my tent for refreshments."

"Oh, certainly!"

In such charity they went, Syrannus behind them and the two slaves behind the old man. Under his own awning, Jiroannes seated Mitya on a pillow and excused himself to go inside for a moment so that Samae could rebind his turban, which had loosened at the back. He sat on the couch and she unwound the cloth from his head. His hair fell down around his shoulders and down to his waist, and Samae lifted the ribboned strands and wound them back up in fresh linen. The quiet lent a kind of intimacy to their endeavor, contrasted to the bustle outside as Laissa's servants prepared for the arrival of Mother Sakhalin.

"Samae," he said, surprising himself more than her, perhaps, "what did you do as a child? Who were your parents?"

Her hands stilled. She tensed, not so much in fear but in astonishment, or anticipation, or anger. How could he tell? He knew so little of her. He felt the tiny movements of her fingers, caught half in his hair and half in the complex folds of cloth wound around his hair.

"Husband!" Laissa swept in. "Move aside, girl!" She cuffed Samae hard on the right cheek, carelessly, but her eyes glinted as she surveyed the slave's retreat to the foot of the couch. "Come, come. I want you to greet Mother Sakhalin, and then you may retire to entertain the boy, the young prince. He is Bakhtiian's nephew? No, his cousin's son. How curious their customs are, but evidently he has no children by his own wives yet."

Jiroannes rose, the cloth tumbled in his hands. "It is a grave insult to interrupt a man with his hair unbound. Apologize instantly."

She took a step back, retreating from his anger. It reminded him of those first days, when she had been in his power entirely, when she had groveled before him. "I beg your pardon, husband. I was not aware—"

"Then you will learn. The Everlasting God commands us never to cut our hair and to conceal it from the eyes of strangers, just as we conceal the beauty and worth of our wives from those who might covet them. Do you understand?"

She bowed her head submissively. He clenched one hand into a fist and opened it. Her fear lent her a sudden attraction, and he felt the immediate, full force of desire. But he had a guest outside. "You may go." She turned to retreat, for once not answering back. "Wife." At his clipped tone, she froze and looked back over her shoulder. "I will punish my own slaves, when they deserve it. It is not your place to lay hands on them. Do you understand?"

Her gaze shifted past him, seeking Samae, and then darted back. "I understand," she replied in a low voice.

"I will entertain my own guest. How you choose to entertain women is no concern of mine. Be sure that they are gone by full dark, however, as I mean to come to your bed tonight, and I expect you to be waiting for me."

She dropped her gaze to stare at the carpet, and he saw that the prospect frightened her. This power he still held over her, who had been virgin and protected by her God from the appetites of men for so many years. Invested as Javani in the year she began her woman's courses, by the reckoning of her people she had reigned as priestess for over sixteen years before the jaran had burned the holy temple. Another woman would have borne many children in the intervening span and been aged and withered by the burdens of womanhood, but Laissa had remained young, her flesh unmarked by God's punishing Hand. So had the Everlasting God decreed, that women bear children as a punishment for their weak natures. Jiroannes intended to get many children on her.

She ducked her head and padded away into the safety of her own chambers.

"Samae." He said it softly. "Let me see your face." She did not move. He walked over to her and lifted her chin. Red stained her pale skin, where Laissa had hit her. Jiroannes smoothed his fingers over her cheek. "Never mind it. It will fade. Here, now, bind my turban back up, and then you may attend me and the prince. And you may go to him tonight, if you wish it."

Her gaze lifted to his face. She stared, eyes wide, and then recalled herself and averted her gaze. Her astonishment pleased him, and it fed his desire as well. Tomorrow night he would not go to Laissa's bed. Tomorrow night, perhaps, he would call for Samae to attend him once again. He sat down on the couch and let her minister to him. Was it his imagination, or did she perform her duties eagerly now, with a certain tenderness? He would find out more about her, who her parents were, why she had been sold into slavery, how she had come to learn the mysterious arts of the Tadeshi concubines, why she cried to see the actors perform their play. Quickly she performed her task and followed him outside, where she knelt in silence three paces behind him, eyes lowered, while Lal served tea and cakes to Jiroannes and Mitya. The two men chatted together, about the return of the Prince of Jeds, about the marriage of Bakhtiian's niece, about the siege of Karkand, about the relative merits of the weave of cloth from Habakar looms and how much the merchants trading this fine cloth to countries north and south ought to be taxed by the jaran on their profits.

CHAPTER SEVENTEEN

"I'm not welcome at this council, am I?"

Tess squatted down in front of the chest, lifted the lid, and rummaged inside. "Ilya, in all fairness, why should you be?" She found the length of gold cloth she was looking for and drew it out. "Charles wouldn't be welcome at your councils, either."

"There might be a time when it was appropriate for him to attend."

"There might be, it's true. I think I'll use this gold cloth to make a shirt for Vasha."

"A shirt for who?"

"You remember him. Your son."

"Tess, he is *not*—"

"Ilya."

In the silence, he paced while she heaved herself to her feet and went to the table, to unroll the bolt there, smoothing her hand over the fabric. "He's a good-looking boy," Ilya conceded at last, "and he seems well-mannered. Katya likes him."

"Katerina has befriended him, yes. But then, she's a generous girl, like her mother."

"Unlike me?"

Tess grinned suddenly and walked across to him. She took his hand. "I know it was abrupt of me to adopt him like that. But he looked so bedraggled and so pathetic. He's so young. Was his mother dark-featured as well?"

Ilya nodded absently, attention on the entrance flap, not on her. Outside, they heard Katerina calling out: "Vasha! Vasha! Come here!"

"But what are we going to do with him?" he asked at last.

"Raise him as our child."

"*Our* child? But it goes against all our traditions . . . by no custom of the jaran would he ever come to me. Even so, we can never know if he is truly my child."

"Do you doubt that he is? I don't. Oh, it's moving."

He spread both hands over her belly and they just stood there. A smile caught on his lips and he closed his eyes. "Yes, I feel it. Our child, Tess." He sighed, content, and drew his hands up to enclose both her hands between his. "Tess." He hesitated, glanced toward the entrance, and then back at her. When he spoke, she could barely hear him. "We traveled alongside their tribe for five months, and every night I slept in her tent. It was stupid of me, to show any woman such exclusive attention, but—"

"But?"

"Roskhel's tribe rode alongside ours for those same months, and I wanted away from my mother's tent. I hadn't a tent of my own, and anyway, Inessa was very pretty, so it was no hardship for me to lie with her every night. By the time we left them, she knew she was pregnant. Vasha is my child by the laws of Jeds, where such lines are followed through the man whose seed makes a woman pregnant. But we are not in Jeds. Nor do I rule there. By the laws of the jaran he is not my child, nor am I his father, except that I'm married to you, and that you adopted him as a foster-son."

He released her abruptly. A moment later Katerina burst into the tent. "Aunt Tess! Vasha, come here!"

The boy pushed through the opening hesitantly and halted right on the threshold as if he did not want to intrude, the heavy flap caught on his shoulders. Katerina grabbed his wrist and jerked him forward.

"Look. Vasha, show them!"

"Little one," said Ilya sternly, "he needn't show us anything he doesn't want to." He turned a steady gaze on Vasha, and the boy stared up at him.

Oh, yes, the resemblance was strong enough that anyone might guess just by looking at them together that they were father and son. And Vasha had the eyes, the same fire there, burning. He stared at his father as much with awe as with apprehension. Ilya looked vexed. Finally,

Vasha uncurled his right hand to display a finely-carved bone clasp, the kind one would use to close a saddlebag or a pouch.

"By the gods," Ilya murmured. He lifted it up and examined it. It was long and narrow, like a finger, curved, with a small hole at one end for a leather strip to lace through. He laughed out of sheer surprise. "My father gave me this. He carved it for me, as a present, when my first cycle of years had passed. Do you see the eagle, here? How his wings curl and drape around the clasp, as if he's embracing the winds?" Katya hung on her uncle's arm, staring. Vasha did not move, did not even close his hand or withdraw it. "Where did you get it?"

Vasha shrugged, dipping his chin down, staring at the carpet.

"Vasha! When I ask a question, I expect an answer."

The boy mumbled something.

"Gods, boy! I'm not going to punish you for it. I thought I'd lost this years ago, but I see that your mother merely stole it from me."

His gaze leapt up to Ilya. He glared. "She did not! She said you gave it to her!"

"I never gave it to her! And it happened more than once, that she'd take things from me and tell people I'd given them to her—" His voice dropped suddenly, in the face of Vasha's humiliated anger. "But perhaps I merely dropped it somewhere, and she found it and kept it to give to me again."

"Only you never came back," said the boy in a muted tone, looking down again.

"No, I never did. Well, here. I give it back to you, then."

"To me!" His gaze flashed up to Ilya and down again.

"As my father gifted me with it, so do I gift it to you."

"Oh," said Katerina.

Vasha did not move. Ilya placed the clasp on the boy's palm and closed his fingers over it. "Vasha, you are with us now. Let this be the seal between you and me, then, that . . . that we'll raise you as we would any son of ours." Still Vasha did not speak. Ilya glanced at Tess. "Well?" he demanded, as if she could help him.

"I have to go. Katya, I'm going to make a shirt for Vasha out of this cloth. Take it over to your mother and show it to her, please."

"Of course, Aunt Tess." Katya rolled up the cloth and hurried away.

Tess straightened her clothes over her belly. "Give me a kiss, little one," she said to Vasha. He started and came to kiss her, once on each cheek, in the formal way. She kissed him on the forehead as well, kissed Ilya on the cheek, and went to the entrance. There she paused on the threshold.

Ilya examined the boy as if he hadn't the least idea what to do with him. He coughed, glanced at Tess, and frowned. "Well. Do you know how to ride, Vasha?"

"Of course I know how to ride! How do you think I got here? Oh, I beg your pardon, I'm sorry. That was ill-mannered of me. Yes, I know how to ride."

Ilya sighed. He put out a hand as if to pat the boy on the shoulder, withdrew it, and then reached out again and awkwardly touched Vasha on the arm. "You'll ride out with me today, then. We'll go find you a mount."

Satisfied, Tess left them. She stopped to consult with Sonia about the shirt and then went on to Charles's encampment. She enjoyed the walk; she much preferred walking to riding these days, although she sometimes had to stop when her belly tightened up, all the muscles tensing, practicing for the event scheduled to occur in about seventy days. She was seven months pregnant now, with two months to go, more or less, Earth-time, although the year and month were longer here on Rhui.

Sometimes, especially late at night, she really thought the best thing would be to return to Jeds. But Cara could care for her as well here as at Jeds, really, especially with the new equipment Charles had brought with him, and it was too late by now to get her off-planet. What if she died?

But there was no point in worrying. She couldn't turn back now. What would come, would come. And she did have Cara, after all. Somehow, with Cara here, she couldn't imagine anything going wrong.

So what would happen after the baby came? These

days it seemed like a veil lay drawn between her here, now, and what lay after the baby's arrival. What did she want out of life anyway? Mostly she wanted to be finished with the pregnancy, which weighed on her like a kind of mental torpor, as if all the activity in her body, mental or otherwise, had been channeled into her womb. Yet for two days now the thought of the female Chapalii had nagged at her. All this time humanity had read old human patterns onto Chapalii culture: males who possessed all the status and did everything important and females who lived in seclusion, as second-class citizens. Now it appeared that they had been wrong; now it appeared that the Chapalii possessed two cultures. Yet surely the two cultures intertwined somehow. Surely the pattern was readable, if only the right person, with the right skills, could investigate. Tess knew quite well who the right person was.

Yet she did not want to leave Rhui. She did not want to leave the jaran. Charles lived in a world made cold by his obsession; by joining with him, her world, her surroundings, would be cold as well. She would have to leave the warmth of her family behind. Because the jaran were her family, now. Somehow, she had to find a way to work with Charles and yet remain on Rhui.

"Tess!"

"Oh, hello, Aleksi. Where did you come from?"

He ran up to her and settled into a walk. Pink flushed his cheeks. "Sonia told me where you'd gone. I thought—" He broke off.

"You thought what? What's wrong?"

"Nothing." But his expression belied the comment. He hesitated, and then words came out in a rush. "Tess, don't leave me behind when you go. When you leave. I've got no place here, except with you. Whatever there might be, out there, in the heavens, I'll gladly risk it, as long as I can stay with you."

"Aleksi!" She stopped. "I'm not leaving. Not yet, anyway."

"But someday—?"

"Yes." She said it reluctantly. "Yes, someday I'll leave the jaran."

"Then?"

She smiled sadly, thinking of Yuri, who had refused her offer to go with her to Jeds. Gods, it seemed long ago that he had died. "Aleksi, I promise that when I leave, I'll take you with me if that's what you truly want." His flush faded. His expression cleared. "You may as well come with me now. You already know too much as it is." He assented with a nod and walked beside her the rest of the way to Charles's tent.

Charles waited outside. He rose when he caught sight of her, and came to greet her. "You're looking well."

"Thank you."

He looked at Aleksi and then back at Tess.

"He knows already, Charles. I don't see the harm in letting Aleksi sit in on the council."

"You don't?"

"Believe me, Aleksi has no standing whatsoever in the tribes except what I've given him. He knows it. I know it. We can trust him." Beside her, Aleksi stood perfectly still, effacing himself in that way he'd learned over the years to avoid notice.

Charles studied the young man, and then Tess; he drew two fingers down the curve of his short beard, stroking it to a point at his chin. "What benefit?" he asked finally.

"Benefit! You would ask that. All right. This one. He has his own tent. When you leave, you can leave a modeler and communicator with him which he can keep in his tent, which I can then use without fear of it being discovered by Ilya or anyone else."

"This assumes that when I leave, you don't come with me."

"I'm not coming with you."

"Come inside. Everyone else is here." He turned to go in, turned back. "And you as well, Aleksi."

Aleksi glanced once, swiftly, at Tess. Tess knew well enough what the invitation meant: Aleksi had just stepped outside the boundaries of his old life and been accepted into a new one. He knew it, too. All of them knew that this was an invitation that would never be extended to Bakhtiian.

They ducked inside the tent. Tess sank gratefully into

the chair Cara offered her. She greeted everyone: Marco, David, Maggie, Jo, Rajiv, and Ursula. Aleksi crouched beside her, one hand on the back of her chair. Better that he be here, to mark that although she was part of this world, this council, she also had inseparable links to Rhui. She rested a hand on her abdomen. The fetus moved, rolling under her hand, under the cloth of her tunic, under the skin and the flesh. That link alone marked her forever, mother to a child half of one world, half of another.

"I think," said Charles into the silence, "that we need to consider the interdiction. We need to consider putting into place a matrix within which the plan of sabotage can develop and from which it can be launched at the appropriate time. Also, I'm running out of time. Now that I've proclaimed myself a player in court politics, I can't be absent for too long without losing—what? face?—without losing position, certainly, and without causing so much suspicion that the emperor might feel called upon to act, to investigate what I'm actually doing here on my interdicted world. Comments?"

"No doubt that you must go back soon," said Cara.

"I think we should pull everyone off Rhui," said Rajiv, "except those vital to the matrix."

"But if we pull everyone off," said Marco, "then won't the Chapalii be suspicious? We ought to let it go on as it always has, more or less."

"Marco, you only say that because you still have continents you want to explore."

"Selfishness is the root of human success in evolution, don't you think?"

Cara snorted.

"Quite the contrary," answered Rajiv, "cooperation has sustained human development."

"But groups can be selfish as well."

"Now, now," said Maggie, "let's keep to the subject at hand, if you please. For the sake of argument, let's say we keep the interdiction in place without any obvious changes. Where do we install our base of operations? Where do we channel all the information? Where do we build the matrix? Jeds? Morava? Both at once? Somewhere else?"

"A single fixed base of operations is always dangerous," said Ursula. "Easy to discover, easy to root out. I'd suggest two or three bases."

"But when we increase the number," objected Rajiv, "we increase the necessity for communicating between them, and that poses its own problems and its own dangers.

Maggie shook her head. "Rajiv, communication on Rhui is going to be a problem nevertheless. The interdiction works both for and against us in that way. But you'd know better than I how likely the Chapalii are to be monitoring all planetary communications and how thorough their coverage can be."

David coughed. "And while Morava might seem best because of its size and its banks, we don't know if there are other forms of monitoring going on there that we aren't—can't be—aware of. Yet we must stay in contact with Morava. It's vital to the plan, isn't it?"

Cara nodded. "Jeds provides a good landing point still, and an already established base of power on Rhui. Not to mention a good port, with trade routes spreading out all over the planet."

"Jo?" Charles asked.

She shrugged. "Nothing to offer yet. I've finished my report on the samples I took from Morava. I'm studying the samples Cara has taken from the jaran population now. We'll need Jeds in the link just for the laboratory facilities, for one thing. Even Morava doesn't have facilities we humans can use."

"Unless we bring Chapalii down onto Rhui."

"Marco!" David threw up his hands. "That's absurd. That would be breaking the interdiction all over again."

"David, they've already been at Morava. We've established now that Charles has a merchant house allied with him, established on Rhuian terms, I mean. Why shouldn't they visit Morava?"

"Which still hasn't answered the question of where to centralize operations," said Maggie.

"Tess," said Charles quietly, "you look like you have something to say."

The answer stared her in the face. It answered both her problems. Neatly. Perfectly. Almost too perfectly. She already knew how to build matrices, and what Charles wanted built here was not that different from any language. She already led a jahar of envoys. A steady stream of visitors, envoys, ambassadors, merchants, and philosophers came and went from the camp of the jaran army. Tess could authorize their movement within the camp; she had the authority to receive them, or to send them away, or to conduct her own missions, to send her own people to Jeds, to Morava, to anywhere she wanted. And the jaran moved, always. They never stayed in one place for long. She had allies within the jaran, and allies outside the jaran.

"Base it with me," she said softly, surprising everyone but Charles. Tess doubted she could ever surprise Charles. "Base it with the jaran."

CHAPTER EIGHTEEN

Sonia regarded the gold cloth with some misgiving. Certainly Tess had every right to adopt the boy into her tent; indeed, Tess herself had gained a place with the jaran by the same means. But the truth was that this was not a simple adoption. Vassily Kireyevsky *ought* to have stayed with his mother's relatives. She faulted the Kireyevsky tribe for casting him off, but it wasn't unheard of that a family would rid itself of an unwanted child by giving it to a family who had need of a servant or even a child to adopt. But a child who had no father could not then be sent to the man who had, perhaps, *sired* him—as if it could ever be proven.

Sonia made a face and rolled the cloth up again. She disliked that Rhuian word, "sired." Oh, she did not doubt that Vasha was Ilya's son—by Jedan law—but this was not Jeds. Mother Sakhalin's warnings seemed apt now. If the jaran took one step too many off the path the gods had given them to ride, then they would no longer be jaran. And why should Tess care what happened to this child, anyway? In Jeds, Sonia had read of noblewomen who murdered their husband's or father's bastards. What did Tess expect to come of taking in this child?

She signed and set the cloth aside. Looking up, she saw two riders and their escort halt at the edge of camp. A strange sense—not quite of foreboding but of dislocation—swept her, seeing her cousin and the boy together. There was something very alike about them. She got to her feet and went to greet them.

"Hello, Ilya. Vasha."

The boy stammered a greeting. He looked deeply embarrassed at having the luxury of handing over his reins to another man, who would tend to the horse for him; indeed, he looked embarrassed at having ridden such a handsome horse at all, since they had, of course, gone out on two of the khuhaylan Arabians.

"Go on, then," said Sonia, taking pity on him, "Katya is waiting for you. They're over there—" She waved toward her left, where Katya and Galina and a handful of other girls were practicing archery on the empty stretch of ground lying between the Orzhekov tents and the next tribe.

Vasha looked up at—Sonia could not quite bring herself to think, *his father*—Ilya, and Ilya gave the slightest lift of his chin, which the boy took for permission. He ran off.

"Well," said Sonia.

"It was not my choice!" Ilya exclaimed.

Sonia chuckled, resting a hand on his sleeve. "Ilyakoria, I would never tax you with something that so obviously has Tess's mark about it."

"I will never understand her," muttered Ilya, sounding vastly irritated.

"You do hate that," she agreed mildly. "And you would never have married her if you did understand her. Come. You look thirsty."

He also looked as if he wanted to talk. He walked with her and sat down under the awning of her tent. She brought komis for them both, and while they drank they watched the girls shoot.

"Vera Veselov wants every girl to ride for at least one season with the archers in the army," said Sonia. "I think she thinks of it as some kind of *birbas*, hunting the khaja as we hunt animals. Good training. But I and Mother Sakhalin and several other etsanas have argued against it. The experience will do some girls no good; others will prefer to ride for two years before it's time for them to marry. And there are women who have lost their husbands who have asked to join as well, but others who wish only to return to the plains. Right now we have enough volunteers, and we haven't even begun to draw young women from the tribes still out on the plains."

"Right now," said Ilya. "But eventually the novelty

will wear off, and then it will no longer be enough to have volunteers and a casual place alongside the rest of the army." His eyes narrowed. "Look."

Galina had given Vasha her bow. He obviously had handled a bow before, although he did not have the skill of the girls.

"Will you stop him?" Sonia asked quietly.

Ilya glanced at her. "How can I?"

The sun baked down on the children, but they appeared not to mind it. Their game interested them more.

"What will happen to him, Ilya?"

"I don't know. I scarcely know what to think of him." He hesitated. His lips quirked up into a half-smile. "I scarcely know what to think of myself. Am I a father or not? What do I do with such a child? What does Tess want me to do with him? Gods." He grimaced. "What does the child himself want? Or can he even know?"

The air lay still today, hot, oppressive, and crowding, as if it waited on some larger storm to break. But the sky remained blue, unsullied by clouds, and distant Karkand shimmered in the heat.

"Autumn will come soon enough," commented Sonia, "though I don't think it ever grows as cold here as it does on the plains."

Ilya watched the boy out beyond as he shot another round and then gave the bow back to Galina. "Sonia," he said. Faltered. Began again. "Sonia, don't you suppose that Aleksi should marry?"

The change of subject surprised her. "Ilya! It would break Tess's heart if he left camp." She regarded her cousin questioningly. Surely he understood his wife by now. "And in any case, Tess rules him with an iron hand, however light it may seem to others. He wouldn't go."

He shook his head. "I didn't mean that he should leave. Surely some woman can be found who might come to us."

"Ah," she said, understanding him now. "You think that if you bind Aleksi to camp as well, it will be yet another reason for Tess to stay."

He flashed her a look so filled with indignation that she laughed. How he hated it when people saw past his words and his authority to his feelings. He knew better, however, than to snap at her. "I don't—" he began, and stopped, because what she had said was true. He subsided into an offended silence that reminded her all at once of Nadine.

"Ilya," she added, taking pity on him, "be assured that for my own reasons I am keeping an eye out for a wife for Aleksi."

He did not deign to reply, but she saw that her answer mollified him.

Shadows lengthened around them, and the children ended their game. Katya and Galina and Vasha ran over to the tent and swamped the silence with their laughter. The two girls threw themselves down, unconscious of any need for dignity around their formidable cousin. But Vasha moved cautiously, like a foal testing its legs, and with a touching, stiff gravity that made Sonia actually feel a little sorry for whatever he had endured before. Clearly he was proud. As clearly, his Kireyevsky relatives had punished him for his pride, for him to be so leery of it now.

Katya gave a great sigh and rolled over onto her back. "You have to learn to *read* and *write,* Vasha. Doesn't he?" And she rolled her gaze over toward Ilya. Sonia sighed. Katya rode moods the way she rode horses; right now, she was on a racing tear.

"Oh," said Vasha, flashing a glance toward Ilya, and bit off a question.

"Katya! He doesn't *have* to!" retorted Galina. "You're being a bully."

"Does so," said Katya, and she sprang up and darted into Sonia's tent, emerging moments later with two books. "Shall we start with Aristoteles? Or Sister Casiara?" She set the books down in front of Vasha and opened them both.

Vasha stared down at the pages filled with tiny words, all of which were certainly incomprehensible to him. He was flushed. Sonia doubted if he even knew what *reading* and *writing* were, but he could never admit that here, now.

"Katerina, my dear," said Sonia, "Sister Casiara is a

little dry and dense as something to start off with, don't you think? I don't recall that even *you* have managed to read farther than the first chapter."

Katya scowled at her mother, but it was impossible to make her ashamed enough to blush. The little beast. How like her to generously befriend the boy and then embarrass him like this in front of the person he most wanted to impress.

"You all have far too much energy," said Ilya suddenly. "I think all three of you must be old enough now to attend the envoy's school along with Mitya. Afternoons." He looked at Sonia. "There aren't so many chores to do then." Sonia nodded, pleased that he understood how much she needed the children in the mornings, especially since Galina still spent many mornings with Dr. Hierakis. "Any fool can see that Vasha can't read Aristoteles or Sister Casiara," he added directly to Katya, "since he doesn't know Rhuian. Yet."

Vasha's shoulders had remained hunched all through this recital, but they lifted slightly now.

"Meanwhile, he must learn his letters. You two girls may teach him the letters Tess and Niko devised for khush, since I'm sure you know them all quite well now."

"Oh!" said Galina, looking disgusted. "You idiot!" she hissed at her cousin.

"As for you, my young scholar," Ilya added to Katerina, "you will write me a little book in the style of Aristoteles on the nature and kind of horses in this army."

Katya looked dumbfounded. Sonia was pretty sure that Katya had not a clue what Ilya was talking about. The girl set her hands on her hips. "What if I won't?"

"I don't suggest," said Ilya quietly, "that you disobey me, little one."

Beaten by superior horsemanship, Katya gave up the race. She made a horrible face and flopped down on her stomach. Galina giggled. Katya kicked her.

"Do you mean it?" Vasha asked in a small voice. "That I'm to learn to—" He hesitated, touching the paper with one finger. "So that I can learn to hear what these marks say?"

"Gods! Of course I mean it!"

Vasha flinched back. Ilya let out an exasperated sigh. Katya had one eye open and one shut, as if she was trying to decide whether to venture any more mischief.

"Oh, Vasha," Sonia interceded smoothly. "Since you're here, let me measure you against this cloth."

"What's it for?" he asked sulkily, and then his eyes widened as she unrolled the golden silk.

"May I help, Aunt Sonia?" asked Galina at once. "I recognize that piece. Isn't the weave fine?"

"Is Aunt Tess back yet?" asked Katya suddenly, evidently determined to make one last gallop or even, perhaps, to provoke a stampede. Sonia had a very good idea of how much Ilya disliked being kept out of any business Tess was involved in, especially when that business, that council, involved the Prince of Jeds. Sonia did not doubt that the council might last well into the night, and that Ilya might never learn the least scrap of information about what had gone on there. Sonia did not precisely distrust Tess's brother; on the whole, she guessed he was their ally more than their enemy, but he had yet to impress her as a person who cared much at all what the jaran thought of him. *As if he does not need us.*

Ilya stiffened. Here it came.

"But I don't understand," said Vasha tremulously, "how these little marks can speak?"

Sonia had to bite her tongue to stop from laughing out loud. Outmaneuvered and outraced.

"Oh, here," said Ilya, rising at once. "Come with me, Vasha. I've got a stylus and tablet. It's the only way to learn letters. I'll teach you."

Vasha leapt up, his face bright. Katya stuck her tongue out at him, looking sour.

"That will teach you," said Sonia to her daughter as soon as Ilya and the boy were out of earshot.

Katya ignored her mother. She had a stubborn set to her mouth now, and she pulled the Aristoteles over and opened it up and began the laborious process of sounding out the words. Sonia smiled.

"May I help you with the shirt?" Galina asked.

"Of course you may, my love."

Together they worked to make a shirt for Vasha. Beyond Karkand the sun set, staining red a trailing growth of clouds that had begun to gather on the horizon.

CHAPTER NINETEEN

Diana watched Marco surreptitiously. Outside, rain fell. Here in the Company tent, they all sat listening while Charles Soerensen and Owen and Ginny discussed the possibility of the Company breaking new ground.

"With my patronage, I think it's quite possible you could actually tour outside of League space."

"Think of it!" Diana recognized the gleam that lit Owen's eyes. She had seen it before. She had seen it that winter morning three and a half years ago when Ginny first broached the idea that they travel to Rhui. "Does theater even translate to nonhuman species? Are there links between all intelligent species, or are we simply myopic in thinking that all other forms of life must have some discernible relationship to our own?"

Soerensen sat between Owen and Ginny. Marco sat next to Owen. Marco glanced up at Diana and they looked away together.

"Would this be an exclusive contract?" Ginny asked.

Soerensen smiled. "No, not exactly. I want to encourage arts of all kinds to spread. I want to encourage humanity to move out into the Empire, now that—" He paused. They all waited for him, the entire Company—all but Hyacinth, who was gone, and Anahita, who had stayed in her tent. Anahita rarely met with the others now, except at rehearsal or a performance. Gwyn said that she had succumbed to her own spiritual hollowness.

"—now that we have the means to do so."

A "Hmm," said Owen, and Diana wondered what he was thinking.

"Hmm," said Ginny, echoing her husband. She cocked her head to one side, and she and Soerensen exchanged what Diana always called A Significant Glance. Diana had it in the back of her mind that Ginny had known Soerensen for quite a while, maybe even from before she had met Owen. Then Ginny surveyed her troupe, one by one: Oriana with her willowy, dark beauty; quiet Phillippe; Dejhuti, who looked half asleep but never was; Seshat, born into the profession, who had lived it and breathed it all her life; Helen and Jean-Pierre, who were snappish but good-hearted; sweet, silly Quinn. Yomi and Joseph sat patiently; everyone knew that they provided the foundation on which Owen and Ginny built. Ginny hesitated, looking at her son, but Hal for once met her gaze with curiosity not antagonism. Next to Diana, Gwyn sat, leaning forward over his knees, chin perched on his intertwined fingers; he looked alert, brimming with controlled energy, and he examined Ginny and Soerensen in turn, as if he read something from them, something that met with his approval. Last, Ginny met Diana's gaze. She nodded, once, with finality.

"They'll do," she said. "We'll see about Hyacinth, and we'll have to do new auditions as well. Given that we'll have fewer physical constraints, I'd like to add a few actors, and definitely we'll need more crew."

"Definitely," echoed Yomi with a sigh of relief.

"Good," said Soerensen briskly. He rose. "Once we're off planet, we'll deal with the particulars."

The meeting broke up.

Diana leaned toward Gwyn. "Am I missing something?" she whispered. "This is all very exciting, but somehow I feel we're not being told everything."

"Think about it." The others got to their feet around them. A few braved the elements, following Soerensen out into the sodden outdoors. Others lingered inside, chatting, while Joseph brewed tea. Gwyn kept his voice low. "Soerensen doesn't do anything without a reason—that is, without a deeper reason. Humans have never been allowed to travel much outside of League space. Those of us who are allowed to might be able to find out things."

"Oooh. Spies!"

"Sssh. This isn't a game, Di."

"Sorry. But we're actors, not soldiers or diplomats."

"Exactly." Then he grinned. "What better cover? And what better people to play roles?"

"No! You don't really think—?"

He shrugged. "Maybe I'm wrong. One's thinking becomes a little warped after an extended stay in prison. Excuse me." He rose and caught Ginny's arm before she walked outside, and they went out together, Gwyn shrugging his cloak on. A finger of cool, damp breeze brushed Diana's face and dissolved in the heat of the tent. An eddy of movement had trapped Marco between Oriana and Hal. He sidled past them toward the entrance. Diana jumped to her feet and pulled the flap aside for him, and followed him out.

"Thank you," he said without looking at her. They stood under the awning. She slung on her cloak and hitched the hood up over her head. Rain drenched the ground. A wind threw mist under the awning, and out beyond the muddy canvas groundcloth on which they stood, the earth was soaked and weeping rivulets of water. "The soil doesn't absorb the rain very well, does it?" asked Marco. Whether the rain beyond or her presence made him reluctant to leave the shelter of the awning, she did not know. He still didn't look at her. The clouds lowered dull and gray over them. The sheeting rain blurred the distant shapes of tents. Gwyn and Ginny stood talking under the awning of her and Owen's tent, stamping the mud off their boots and shaking water from their cloaks. Farther away, they saw Soerensen trudging through the rain into camp, his shoulders hunched, his pale hair slicked down against his head.

"It must be the rainy season," said Diana, and then she laughed, because it was such a stupid comment.

"I must go." He did not move.

"Marco. Are we going to become spies?"

He flung his head back, startled, and then he chuckled. He reached out and with one finger tilted her chin back and smoothed his finger over her lips. His skin was surprisingly warm. "Only if you wish it, golden fair." He traced her cheek and jaw with his hand and as abruptly closed the hand into a fist and drew it away from her face. "Forgive me."

"No." She captured the hand in one of hers. "There's nothing to forgive. It's true, you know, that I have a right here to take a lover if I wish to." His eyes flared slightly as he watched her. "How soon are we leaving?"

"I can't say. We could leave anytime. Two days. Ten. Twenty. But it will be soon."

"And the Company will go with Soerensen?"

"Yes. What will you do, Diana?"

"What do you mean?"

"Well—" He did not try to free his hand, but she felt his fingers move within her grasp. "Anatoly—"

"The Company is my life, Marco. If they go, I go with them. Or did you think I was like Tess Soerensen? That I meant to stay with the jaran?"

"I didn't think—I mean, I didn't know—it's not my business to ask, is it?"

She heard Hal and Ori at the entrance, and she dropped Marco's hand, but neither of them came out. "Di!" called Hal from inside. "Did you want some tea? Goddess, this weather is disgusting."

"Come to my tent tonight," said Diana quickly, in an undertone.

"Di! Where are you?" The tent flap rustled aside. Hal stuck his head out. "Oh," he said, and ducked inside again.

They stood in silence, serenaded by the incessant pounding of rain. One corner of the awning sagged down under an accumulating pool, and with a rush the balance tipped and a waterfall began a slow trickle out of the pool, flooded with a tearing splash, and emptied.

Diana sneezed. "I beg your pardon! As if I would want to live like this for the rest of my life anyway!"

"Diana." His voice was taut. "Do you mean it?"

"I wouldn't say it if I didn't mean it!"

"I beg your pardon. I only—"

"I know what I said before. I know it was only six days ago. But it's over, Marco. I mean, what are we talking about now? We're talking about touring into Chapalii space! We're leaving Rhui. I can't hang on to here forever. I'll have to let go, I'll have to let him go."

"You might be able to get a dispensation from Charles to let him come with you." He said it reluctantly.

"Come with me? Do you think he'd want to?"

"I don't know. Diana, I'm not the best person to ask that of. I'm not exactly a disinterested party."

"No, I'm sorry. That was cruel of me."

"Not cruel." He took in a breath and let it out. "I would—" He broke off, shook his head, and started again. "I would like to— Of course, I— Oh, Goddess, I'm making a hash of this. The answer is yes. Excuse me." He jerked the thong of his hat up tight and strode out abruptly into the rain.

Diana stared after him. But it was just as well. Her chest had gone tight with a sudden pounding. She had asked him; he had said yes. And he was just as flustered as she was. She watched him slog away through the mud. A smaller figure, a child, ran toward them through the pelting rain, fair head bent under the onslaught. Marco paused as the child raced by him and then he trudged on in the direction Soerensen had disappeared. The child began a detour toward Diana's tent, but when Diana raised her hand, the figure halted, slipping in the mud, and jogged toward her.

It was one of the girls from the Veselov tribe. She halted outside the awning.

"Oh, here," said Diana. "Come underneath."

The girl did so gratefully. "Mother Veselov sent me," she said after she'd caught her breath. Her hair was soaked through, but the rain slid off her long felt coat and dripped onto the ground. "A messenger came in. From Anatoly Sakhalin's jahar. They'll be here today."

Today.

Wind whipped a sheet of rain in under the cover of the awning, spraying Diana's face. She tugged her cloak around her. "Haven't you anything to wear on your head?" she demanded.

"Oh, of course I do, but it was all so fast, Mother Veselov calling me in, and so I just ran. It'll dry. I don't mind."

I don't mind. They none of them complained about the hardships. It was one thing to live under these conditions for a short time; that was endurable. But to live under them always. Diana could not imagine how Tess Soerensen could choose to live here, year after year. Or how she could even want to have a child under these conditions. But then, she wasn't Tess Soerensen, and Anatoly, for all his undoubted charms, was nothing like Ilyakoria Bakhtiian.

"I don't know what to do," said Diana in Anglais.

The girl smiled up at her, blinking drops of water off her pale eyelashes.

But it was worse just to stand here undecided. "I'll go with you," Diana said abruptly. They forged out into the rain. It hammered on her head, and soon enough she regretted that she hadn't thought to get the girl a hat. Mud slathered her boots. Few people moved about; wisely, they had chosen to stay in their tents.

"Mother Veselov said to take you to the Sakhalin encampment," said the girl as they slogged along. "Anyway, the jahar will have to report in to Bakhtiian before anything else."

"And Anatoly will have to report in to his grandmother."

"Well, of course!"

Halfway through camp, they found themselves caught in a swirl of movement along the avenue that led from the outskirts of the camp straight in to the central encampments. A troop of horsemen rode by. They were spattered with mud and drenched by the rain, windblown and yet impressive, unbowed by the weather. In better weather, Diana thought they would have formed a triumphal procession, but as it was, only a handful of jaran ventured out to watch them go by. Where had they come from?

She saw the prisoners all at once, three cloaked women and a small child riding on caparisoned horses. Riders surrounded them, but the prisoners paid no heed to their presence or even, seemingly, to the camp through which they rode. They looked thoroughly dispirited. The eldest woman's nose ran with mucus, streaking her face, and she coughed deep from her lungs as they passed where Diana stood. Mud sucked and squelched under the hooves of the horses.

Then Diana saw the king. He could be nothing else. Even brown with mud, his surcoat glinted with gold where the rain washed the mud away in patches. He wore a crown, too, fixed somehow to his head so that when he fell, stumbling, sliding in the mud, struggling up again, it did not fall off. It was more like a mockery of a crown, because of that. A belt of ropes at his waist tied him to the harness of two horses, which were ridden at a taut rope's length on either side of him. Just in front of Diana he slipped and fell to his hands and knees, and the riders kept moving, so that the ropes dragged him on through the mud. He wept, scrabbling to gain purchase, but he could not get up.

She could not stand to watch him. Whatever else he might be, he did not deserve this kind of treatment; it was inhuman. She dashed forward and yelled at the riders to stop. They obeyed immediately, unthinkingly. They stared, astonished, as she bent down beside the man and laid a hand on his arm. He flinched away from her.

"Here, let me help you up," she said in khush, though she doubted he could understand her. Perhaps her tone reassured him; perhaps her woman's voice amazed him. Perhaps he had long since given up hope. In any case, he did not resist as she helped him to his feet.

Lines etched his face. White streaks ran through his hair and his beard, where it wasn't splashed with mud. Tears and rain melded together on his face, so that it was impossible to tell one from the other. His nose was red. His mouth quivered. He stared at her. A strangled noise came from his throat, and more sound, like choked words, and when his lips parted to reveal red-stained teeth, she realized that his tongue had been cut out.

Like a wave, revulsion washed over her, revulsion for the act and pity for the man. The rain poured down. Water seeped into her boots. She felt chilled to the bone.

"What is going on? Who gave you permission to stop?"

The king cowered, ducking his head and lifting an arm to ward off a blow. Diana turned.

Standing, Anatoly was no taller than she was. On a horse, he loomed above her. The horse itself invested him with power. His saber, his spear, the weight of his armor, invested him with authority. Flanked by his captains, he glared down at her, and she knew, in that instant, what it felt like to be a woman—any person, indeed—trapped and cornered by the conquering nomads. Like savages, like devils, ruthless and driven, they stood ready to strike down anything or anyone that blocked their path.

"Diana!" Without looking away from her, he spoke to one of his captains. "Mirtsov, get a horse for my wife."

It was done. Given no choice, she let go of the king and mounted up on a gray mare, next to Anatoly. "The girl—" she said, and faltered.

"Mirtsov, take the girl up behind you and escort her to her family. The rest of you— Go on!" His men started forward again. The king stumbled along between them. Anatoly waited, reining in his horse, until the others had splashed past them, and then he started forward as well. Diana rode beside him. He said nothing. He looked angry. She studied him, noting how he had grown a straggling beard, how his fair hair was caught back in a short braid to keep it out of his face. Of the leather segments hanging from his cuirass to protect his thighs, three looked new, as if his armor had been repaired recently; as if he had been in a battle not too long ago. His red silk surcoat was frayed at the hem and mended all down the left side. She saw no trace of the cheerful young man who had left her more than three months ago; this man looked like Anatoly Sakhalin, proud and handsome, but he looked aloof and heartless and hard as well, as if out there in the hostile territory he and his men had ridden through, hunting down the king, he had become a predator in truth.

They rode together in silence until they came to the ring of guards that surrounded Bakhtiian's encampment. With an escort of ten riders, plus the prisoners and the king still bound by ropes, Anatoly passed through with Diana and they came to a halt on the muddy stretch of ground that fronted the awning of Tess Soerensen's tent. Bakhtiian emerged from the tent.

"Bakhtiian, I have brought to you the coat, the crown, and the head of the Habakar king," said Anatoly.

"Still attached, I see," said Bakhtiian mildly. The king

simply stood there, looking stupefied. "Who are these others?"

"They attended the king. Wife and sister and daughter, perhaps. The child belongs to the young woman. There were two other children, but they died along the way. They were already sick when we found them. He ran like a coward, Bakhtiian, and in the end, he tried to barter the life of every woman and man in his jahar in order to save his own. He wasn't worth the trouble."

Diana saw how Bakhtiian looked up from the king with a sharp glance to examine Anatoly. "That may be so, but he killed my envoys and blinded Josef. Thus must he and his city serve as an example to the rest. It was well done, Anatoly. You may hand him over to my riders. Send your captains to my niece immediately. She'll want intelligence, all your observations, on the lands you passed through. You yourself may attend me tomorrow." With that, Bakhtiian retreated back inside his tent.

Thus dismissed, Anatoly handed the prisoners over to Bakhtiian's guards and dismissed his own men in their turn, to return to their camps and families.

"I must go pay my respects to my grandmother," he said, only now turning to regard Diana. His steely expression made her nervous. The rain had slackened finally, and drops glistened in the exposed fur lining of his hat. His helmet hung on a strap from his belt. The armor made him look burly and thuggish. What on Earth had possessed her to marry him in the first place? Well, nothing on Earth, of course. The picture had seemed much more romantic at first. Now it merely seemed primitive and brutal.

He guided his horse around and they rode back through the ring of guards and crossed a narrow strip of field and came into the Sakhalin encampment. Clearly, someone had alerted Mother Sakhalin to their coming. She waited under the awning of her great tent. Anatoly dismounted, handed the reins over to an adolescent boy, and went to greet her with the formal kiss to each cheek. Diana swung down and followed, hesitating at the edge of the awning.

"Grandson. You are welcome back into camp. I'm not sure what your wife has arranged. . . ."

Diana felt like an idiot, as she was sure Mother Sakhalin intended her to. "I didn't know—I just found out that Anatoly had returned."

"Ah. Well, then, Anatoly, I have water and a tub for you to bathe in. You look filthy. Your cousins will help you remove your armor, and they'll see that it's cleaned." Several boys hovered anxiously off to one side; at her words, they hurried forward, evidently eager to help their famous cousin, the youngest man in the army to have a command of his own. Diana wrung her hands. Anatoly glanced at her once, twice, and all the while kept up an easy flow of small talk with his grandmother.

". . . and the water is still hot, so you must beware. Mother Hierakis has shown our healers how if we boil all the water we'll have fewer fevers in camp."

"Have there been fewer fevers in camp?" he asked.

"The khaja die in greater numbers than we do, it is true, but they are weak in any case. Still, Mother Hierakis is a great healer, and one must not discount her words."

Stripped down to his red silk shirt and black trousers and boots, Anatoly looked suddenly much more—human. He handed his saber and sheath away to one of the boys, and he looked suddenly much more—gentle. His clothes smelled of sweat and of grime, but the sodden scent of rain dampened even that, although Diana imagined that he hadn't bathed in weeks. Not on such a journey as he had ridden.

"Boris and Piotr will help you with the bath, if you wish," said Mother Sakhalin. Two boys waited, each bearing a saddle pack.

Anatoly's gaze flashed to Diana and away. "If that is your command, Grandmother, of course, but I had hoped that you might allow Diana to attend me."

"Your wife has her own tent, and if it was not ready for you—" She sighed.

"Grandmother." The dread conqueror softened, settling a dirty hand on the old woman's sleeve. "Please."

She gave way at once, before his blue eyes and pleading expression. "For you, Anatoly, but for no one else would I allow it!"

"Of course, Grandmother. You're too good to me." He kissed her again on either cheek.

"Hmmph." She stood aside and gestured for them to go past, into the tent. Anatoly grabbed the saddlebags from the boys and went inside. Diana had no choice but to go with him.

Mother Sakhalin's tent was huge, twice the size of any other tent in camp. To the right of the entrance a rust-red curtain embroidered with three leaping stags screened off a spacious alcove. A metal tub sat on a pile of carpets within, and a weary-looking old man poured a last pitcher of streaming water into the tub. Seeing Anatoly, he ducked his head and limped hurriedly out of the alcove.

"He's not jaran," said Diana, staring after him. The curtain fell into place behind him, shielding them from the rest of the tent. On this side, a herd of horses raced over a golden field toward the rising sun.

"He was a Habakar general," said Anatoly, glancing that way as well. "Now he is Grandmother's servant. She is kind to him, considering that he deserted his army on the field."

"Oh," murmured Diana, not knowing what else to say. She clasped her hands at her waist and stood there.

Anatoly tossed down the saddlebags and stripped. Diana just watched him. He paused, between pulling off his shirt and unbuckling his belt, and glanced at her, and grinned.

"Send one of the boys in to take these things away, if you can't stand to touch them. Did you bring anything for me to wear?"

"No, I—I'm sorry. I didn't think."

"Oh, never mind it. Grandmother will have thought of it."

"Yes," said Diana bitterly, "she always does think of everything."

"There's much you could learn from her, Diana. No etsana runs her camp as well as my grandmother runs hers." He stripped out of his trousers and tested the water with a foot. "Ah," he said, in a way that made her suddenly, achingly aware that he was naked, and close by her. He slid into the tub, which was barely large enough for him to stretch out his legs. Diana took a step toward him without realizing it, halted, and then walked over and knelt beside the tub.

"Where's the—" he began. Diana found the stuff they used for soap and started to hand it to him, then set it down, threw off her cloak, and rolled up the sleeves of her tunic. "Here, could you unbraid my hair? Gods, it's gotten long. I used to wear it that way when I was younger, but not since I joined the army."

"You all wear it like Bakhtiian, now."

Even with his hair as filthy as it was, she could not help but tangle her fingers in it as she unwound the braid. He sighed and lay back against her hands. She dipped a hand in the hot water and started to wash him, his neck, his back, his arms.

"How far did you ride?" she asked in a low voice, aware of his skin under her hands, of the gritty scrape of soap against dirt and sweat, of water sloughing off him. "Where did you find the king?"

"A long way. It would take the army—oh—one hundred and twenty days perhaps to travel as far as we rode southwest. In the end, the khaja bastard tried to row out across a lake. I think there was an island out there, and maybe his gods." He chuckled. "But I was damned if I would let him get away after all that. I threw off my armor and rode after the boat."

"Do you know how to swim?"

"Swim? Oh, in the water, you mean? No. My horse did."

"But you might have drowned!" One hand, slick with soap, lay open on his chest. He caught the other in a now-clean hand and rubbed it against his beard. He smiled and shut his eyes.

"But I can't die. When I saw you, after that battle, I thought you were an angel sent down by the gods from the heavens to take me up to their lands. The gods know my wounds were bad enough that they might have killed me, but they didn't, because you were there. As long as you're with me, I can't die. So why should I fear?"

Diana buried her face in his neck. Tears burned at the back of her eyes. Absently, he stroked her arm with his other hand. "When the king's men saw we were coming after them, even into the water, they threw him overboard, hoping to gain mercy for themselves. I'm surprised they rode with him that far. He'd abandoned his children and family already. So we caught him and brought him back. There were plenty of riches, too, with his family, but those will go to Bakhtiian."

"You sent me some things, the necklace, the earrings, by a messenger."

"Well, those were fairly won. Do you see the scar on my left thigh?"

She saw it, white and jagged but cleanly healed. She sank her hand into the water and ran it down his leg. He shivered all over and said something meaningless, and she drew her hand back up to his chest and kept washing him. "Did it gain them mercy?"

"Who?"

"The men who were with the king, giving him up like that."

"Of course not. If they'd break allegiance to their own king, their dyan, then how are we to be expected to trust them? Diana, why did you lift him up off the ground?"

She pulled her hands away from him. As he shifted in the tub, arching back to look at her, the water slipped about him, lapping against his legs and the side of the tub. "I felt pity for him."

"But he brought the gods' wrath down on himself three times! First by killing our envoys, second by running away from battle, and third by abandoning his children. These khaja eat birds, you know." He shuddered. "Savages. I only left him alive because I knew Bakhtiian wanted him. Here, can you find my razor? I'd like to shave."

She rummaged in the bags and found the razor. He reclined and watched her through half-closed lids, the barest smile on his face. He looked content enough, having done his duty to Bakhtiian, gained glory in the doing of it, and come home to his beautiful wife. But he didn't look smug, just at ease. Goddess help her, the truth was there for her to see, as bitter as it was. Even knowing how casually he had killed, how simple and pitiless his judgments were, how appalling, compared to what compassion and mercy she believed was due any human soul, still she cared for him.

"You look sad," he said, puzzled.

Still, she would leave here, Rhui, the jaran, him. She had to. Her work lay elsewhere. "What would you do, if you weren't a rider?"

"What would I do? But I am a rider, Diana. What would you do if you weren't an *actor?*"

But I am an actor. She brought the razor back to him and watched him as he shaved. Then, because it gave her pleasure, because it gave him pleasure, she washed his hair. After that, she found the ceramic pitchers of warm water that the servant had left by the tub. "Stand up so I can rinse you. Look how filthy that water is." But she did not look at the water, only at him.

Clean, he stepped out of the tub. "Now," he said.

"Anatoly! Your grandmother—"

"—will not send us out into the rain this night, you can be sure. It's a long walk from here to your tent, my heart. Shhh." Rain drummed softly on the roof of the tent. "You see, she left pillows and a blanket along the wall, there. It's raining again."

Only much later, when he lay sleeping beside her, did she remember Marco. Had he come by her tent that night, only to find her gone? Anatoly stirred and shifted, opened his eyes, and smiled to find her there.

"Elinu," he said. My angel.

CHAPTER TWENTY

Their tour of the engineering works led them under the ground, down to where the sappers worked. The khaja laborers pressed back against the damp earth walls of the gallery as Aleksi and his escort ducked by them.

"Once we're under the wall," said David, "we'll burn the props and the fall of the mine will cause the wall to collapse."

Aleksi did not like being underground, nor in such a closed space. The other jaran men liked it less. Only Ursula seemed more excited than nervous, peering around in the wavering lantern light, breathing in the dank, stuffy air, lifting one hand to touch the earth a hand's-span above her head, but then, everyone knew that she was a little mad.

David wore a loose cotton shirt pulled up to expose his arms. Dirt stained the cloth, and sweat darkened it all down his back. He glanced at the others and bent to whisper to Aleksi. "We've twenty feet to go to the wall. But ten feet out and four to the side there's another tunnel coming. They're countermining. We're going to need to post some kind of guard down here. Those sabers aren't going to work down here, or your lances, or bows."

"Short swords and short spears," said Ursula. "Thrusting weapons, mostly. You won't be doing much cutting in these close quarters. 'The best use of the companion sword is in a confined space.'"

"David," murmured Aleksi, "how do you know there's another tunnel? Is it from your box, your machine?"

"Yes. We can measure it—oh, I can't explain it now. We've seen everything we can down here. Let's go back up."

They edged back past the laborers. Aleksi noted how David said a few words, here and there, to the khaja men stuck down here. All of the people in Charles's party were like that: they spoke to everyone, even to the khaja, however briefly. Only Ursula behaved like a normal person, interested only in the task at hand. After all, when the attack began, most of these laborers would die in the front lines, taking the brunt of the assault.

They wound back through the mines and climbed up until they came out into a trench covered by thick hides, and thence out along a rampart built to screen the mine entrance from arrows. From here, Aleksi looked out over the grassy sward that separated the outlying district from the massive walls of the inner city of Karkand. Once, he supposed, animals had grazed here. Now nothing stirred. Pennants fluttered on the walls above. A few figures moved, patrolling the heights.

With a sharp thud, a siege engine fired, casting a missile into the city. Up until yesterday, they had thrown rocks and dead animals and corpses in. Now, with the Habakar king in Bakhtiian's hands, they had stepped up the assault. Aleksi himself had watched at dawn when the first pot of burning naphtha had been launched. The sun sank in the west, lighting the walls with red fire. In the district where the palace towers gleamed, a thread of smoke flared up. By the southern curve of the walls another column of smoke rose.

"Down," said David abruptly, shoving on Aleksi's shoulder. As Aleksi ducked, he heard the distant echo of a *thunk,* and he rose to see a cloud of dirt and splintered wood rise in the air behind them, in the suburbs, and dissipate, falling back to earth. The defenders of Karkand had their own siege engines, but unfortunately for them, the jaran camp lay far out of their reach. The defenders could only attack the well-defended siege engines brought up to fire on them, or those portions of their own suburbs that lay within range of their catapults. Still, as the preparations for the assault grew up, ringing the inner city, the defenders stepped up their fire as well.

"Shall we go?" Aleksi asked. "This khaja warfare

leaves a bad taste in the mouth. I'd rather fight out in the open."

"It's true that, as Sun Tzu says, 'Attacking a Fortified Area is an Art of last resort,' " said Ursula, "but you have to adapt yourself to the conditions that present themselves. Are you coming, David?"

The engineer drew a hand across his brow, wiping off sweat. "No. I've a few more things to supervise here. We need more guards here, too. Some equipped for the tunnels, and another jahar. There was a sortie out from the eastern portal last night, according to the laborers. The auxiliaries posted here had a hard time of it. I don't want any more of my workmen killed."

"*Your* workmen?" Ursula asked, with a grin that Aleksi could not interpret.

"Charles gave me a free hand. Indeed, he urged me to do what I could." David glanced at Aleksi and then away. "Let's not discuss this here, Ursula."

She saluted him mockingly and followed Aleksi out to where riders waited with their horses. That was another thing that puzzled Aleksi about these people from the heavens: He could not tell where each one stood according to the others. One might defer to another and then be deferred to by that same person. The prince was clearly in charge, yet he deferred in his turn, at times, and the members of his party usually treated him as casually as they treated each other. Was this how the gods behaved in the heavens, among their own kind? But they weren't gods— Tess assured him of that, and he could see it for himself.

They rode out through the suburbs. Here, beyond reach of the Karkand catapults, siege towers rose, built by conscripted laborers marched in from the countryside and from as far away as Gangana and guarded by the Farisa auxiliaries who hated their former Habakar masters and who had been overjoyed to throw in their lot with the jaran. The wheels of the towers rose almost twice Aleksi's height and were as thick as the length of his arm. Farther back, they built the scaffolding for the Habakar king.

At the gate of the outer wall, the grain marketplace did a brisk business, heavily guarded by jaran riders. Passing through the gate, they came to the huge churned-up field where once a portion of the jaran camp had lain. Much of the camp had moved a morning's ride out from the city, having used up the forage and muddied the water beyond repair. Also, there were rumors that the King's nephew had gathered an army and was even now marching north, to lift the siege. Aleksi knew that Bakhtiian fretted over Tess's safety. Still, Sakhalin ought to stop the king's nephew. And the governor of Karkand had not escaped to join the royal prince. Now and again riders slipped out from Karkand and eluded the jaran net, but such small parties could at best bring intelligence to the Habakar prince and none of them rode as fast as the jaran couriers.

At camp, Ursula left Aleksi to go to Soerensen's encampment. Aleksi rode on past ambassador's row and up to Tess's tent. A council had gathered before the awning. Yesterday the clouds had cleared away, but the air still smelled of rain and the ground had only just begun to dry out. It was a bad time to mount a siege. Aleksi left his horse with his escort and walked around to listen in on the council.

"—despite Mother Hierakis's directions, we're seeing more fevers."

"This rain makes fighting difficult."

"Nevertheless," said Bakhtiian, "it is time to take the city. We have the king, and I don't want to winter here." He glanced at Tess, and Aleksi felt sure that Bakhtiian also did not want his wife to bear their child here. Tess looked a little pale. Sonia sat next to her, and Mitya beyond Sonia. Josef sat next to Ilya, and next to Josef sat Kirill Zvertkov, who had been elevated rather quickly to such a place of honor.

Aleksi sank onto his haunches at the far edge of the awning and settled in to watch. A little later Ursula arrived, with David in tow, and the council shifted to accommodate them. They began to discuss how best to launch and sustain the assault on Karkand's walls, and what to do with the Habakar king. Tess got to her feet and retreated back into her tent. Aleksi rose and circled around and slipped in the back entrance.

"Are you all right?" he asked, seeing that she was already resting on the pillows. Her paleness frightened him.

"Yes. Just tired. I'm just so tired today."

"Shall I get the doctor?"

Tess shook her head. "You could get me something to drink. Cara's at the hospital. She had a horrible argument with Ilya this morning over how many resources she ought to put into tending to the khaja laborers. Ilya wanted nothing done with them, but Cara told him that if he wanted to rule all people then he had to treat them all as his people. Gods, he was furious—spitting furious." She smiled fleetingly at her memory of the scene. "But what could he do? She's right."

"She is?"

"Aleksi!" She sighed. "I hate it here. I just want to get away from here. I want to go back to the plains." He brought her water and sat beside her. They listened as the council droned on outside. He felt comfortable with her, and he could tell that his presence, quiet and steady, comforted her. She shut her eyes and after a while she slept.

Aleksi ducked outside. Bakhtiian glanced back at him, and Aleksi nodded, to show that Tess was safe. Bakhtiian turned back to the discussion of scaling ladders and the assault on the towers, of shields and infantry, of mining and the vulnerability of mudbrick walls.

"As at Hazjan, we must bring the archers into firing range behind cover, and much of the early assault will be done on foot with some of our troops mixed in with the Farisa auxiliary behind the cover provided by the laborers. If we can get the gates open, then we can send squads in, but otherwise, as we've done before, we'll use khaja warcraft to take the city. I see no point in further discussion. How soon will the mines be ready?"

"Oh, ah . . ." David glanced around and then, reluctantly, spoke. "Certainly in two days I can—"

"One day. Tomorrow we will roll the king out on the scaffolding onto the ground before the main gates of the city. He'll be left there until we kill him or he dies by other means. They'll have one day to consider him. We'll start the assault at dawn, day after next." Bakhtiian rose. "Excuse me, Josef. Kirill, Mitya, attend me." He strode off, Kirill at his side, Mitya two steps behind, leaving the council sitting in silence for a moment before they all burst into talk and rose themselves, hurrying off, some after Bakhtiian, some to their own commands.

Sonia paused beside Aleksi. "He's moody," she observed.

"Bakhtiian?"

"Yes. He's worried about the reports from the south. He doesn't like sitting here in one place. He knows the army is better off in the field. Anyway, they're going to wheel the khaja king out on a cart in front of the walls and offer to kill him quickly if Karkand will surrender."

"And if the city won't surrender?"

She shrugged. "He doesn't deserve a merciful death for what he did to our envoys and to Josef." She looked past Aleksi toward Josef Raevsky, who sat patiently, waiting for Ivan to come help him away. "Do you think I should marry him?"

"Marry who? The Habakar king? That wouldn't be very merciful for him, would it?"

"Aleksi!" She laughed. "No, Josef."

"Josef!"

"It would mean less work for us, if he slept in my tent, since he's with us most of the time anyway. And a fair reward, for all he's given, to marry into Ilya's family."

"Do you love him, Sonia?"

"No, but I like him very well, and the children do, too. When are you going to mark Raysia Grekov, Aleksi?"

His heart skipped a beat. "Never. I'm not going to marry." He paused to catch his breath and had a sudden intuition that he ought to be honest with her. "You must know I don't want to leave the Orzhekov tribe."

Sonia considered him. "True enough. And we already have one of the Grekovs in our camp now. Two would be too many."

He grabbed hold of this distraction. "Don't you like the Grekovs?"

"They've gotten a little above themselves since Feodor married Nadine. Haven't you noticed it?" Aleksi shrugged. "Well, I'll look and see if I can find a young woman who might come to our tribe. Maybe one who's lost her husband."

It took him a moment to understand what she meant. "Sonia!" Why should she do this for him? Not just to make him happy, surely. "Is there some other reason you want me to marry?" he asked suspiciously.

"Yes. I need more help. Another woman in camp would be welcome."

Stung by her honesty, he snapped at her. "Get servants!"

"Tess won't have them," she said reasonably.

"But you have authority over camp, through your mother."

"That is true, but all the same, if Tess doesn't want a thing to happen, it does not happen. She told me once she finds them too much like slaves to be comfortable with having any about. Aleksi, you might trust me that I do this for you as well as for the tribe."

It was hard to stay angry at Sonia. And it was true that she had always treated him well. "You could use more help," he agreed, placated by her even tone. He hesitated. "And it's true I wouldn't mind being married." She accepted his confession equably. "If you can find someone, and I like her, then I'll mark her."

"Thank you." Sonia kissed him on the cheek and, seeing Ivan crouch beside Josef, went over to them.

An unfamiliar emotion settled on him as he watched Sonia kneel beside Josef and solicitously help the blind man to his feet. Josef did not need her help to stand, of course, but what man would refuse it? It took Aleksi a moment to name the feeling: Envy. He envied Josef the simple kindness Sonia showed him now. Gods, it hurt, like his heart had cracked. He fought to seal it up. He forced himself to watch them dispassionately.

Sonia guided Josef around to the square tent, set back behind the two great tents, where Josef and Tess conducted their jahar of envoys and accepted petitions from khaja supplicants. Josef was a good man, still dignified, and only a few years older than Bakhtiian, and he had been a brilliant general, every bit Yaroslav Sakhalin's equal, until the expedition to Habakar. Sonia was right.

The Habakar king didn't deserve a merciful death. Ursula had suggested that they pour molten silver down his throat until he died. In fact, Tess had left the council right after Ursula had made that suggestion. Would Tess try to talk Bakhtiian out of killing the king? And yet, Bakhtiian had to show the khaja that they could not kill his envoys, and he had to show the jaran that such an insult would not go unpunished. Even if Tess urged him to show mercy, even if he wanted to, he could not.

If Tess was appalled enough by the sight, would she leave with her brother and go back to Jeds? No, not to Jeds; to Erthe. Jeds was a khaja place. Erthe—*Earth*—was in the heavens. Soerensen meant to leave soon; how soon, Aleksi did not know. Perhaps no one knew but Soerensen himself. Certainly, Bakhtiian did not know. Aleksi supposed that Soerensen could not really leave until Karkand had fallen, since Bakhtiian had no troops to spare him for an escort. Except, if Earth lay in the heavens, then maybe the prince did not travel there by horse or by ship. Maybe he did not want an escort.

Aleksi ducked back inside the tent and checked on Tess, but she still slept. He lingered there, reaching out to touch her hair the way Anastasia had touched his hair all those years ago, soothing him to sleep. Tears stung his eyes. He blinked them back and wrenched himself away. And went to see the doctor.

The tall woman with skin the color of riverbank mud greeted him. "Oh. Aleksi. I'll see if Dr. Hierakis can come out." She returned a moment later and showed him all the way in to the inner chamber.

Dr. Hierakis glanced up from the counter. She smiled, and her smile warmed him. "Hello, Aleksi." The machine that made pictures was on. It showed a strange spiraling pattern, doubled, like the spirals embroidered onto pillows and woven into tent walls. "Jo, can you finish these measurements? We'll do the correlation later, but I think we've reached an endpoint here. I'm not getting any results I haven't gotten before. We need something altogether new, and I don't think we're going to get it from this pool. Aleksi, how is Tess?"

He started, jerking his gaze away from the spirals. "Tired."

"Hmm. In a bad way, or do you judge her just tired?"

"I think she didn't like to hear the talk about how the king will be killed."

"Ah. No doubt." She stepped away from the counter, leaving room for Joanna Singh to take her place. "Why did you come by?"

He hesitated. She felt his hesitation and, kindly, she placed a hand on his sleeve. Embarrassed, he eased his arm away and yet he stood as close to her as he dared. And in any case, she held the answers to his questions. "Doctor. I know you're leaving soon—"

"I'm leaving when Tess is safely delivered of a healthy child."

"But the prince—"

"May leave sooner if he has to, it's true."

"But how will he go? How do you travel, in the heavens?"

Dr. Hierakis chuckled, and Jo Singh cast a glance back over her shoulder, looking surprised at his question. Then she turned back to her work. "Here, come with me, Aleksi." They went into the outer chamber, and she gestured to the table. He sat, though he still did not like sitting in chairs. "If you traveled from Karkand to Jeds, you could travel by horse, or you could travel by horse to a port and then travel by sea. If you traveled to, say, the Gray Eminence's lands, that they call Tadesh, you would have to sail in a ship because there's a great ocean between his lands and these lands."

Aleksi nodded. "Yes. I've seen a map that Tess drew. It showed a great sea as broad as the land itself. But Earth is in the heavens."

"Well, think of the stars as lands. Well, no. Think of the stars as lanterns, and around some of these bright lanterns worlds like this one orbit. Earth is such a world, like Rhui, with lands and seas on it. We sail in ships from world to world."

"Is there water out there? Vast seas? Is that what the ships sail on?"

"Think of it as an ocean of night. If I had time, I'd

show you some programs, a stellar map. But I don't. I'm due at the hospital. Do you know how soon Bakhtiian intends to start the main assault?"

"Oh, yes. It was just decided this afternoon. Day after next, at dawn."

"Ah. Then we've much to prepare for. Well, Aleksi, keep an eye on Tess for me. Keep well." She hesitated and then, to his astonishment, she kissed him on either cheek, in the formal way, and left. He sat for a moment, just staring. She had left some of her warmth with him. Surely Dr. Hierakis had no reason to be nice to him except simple kindness. Unless by winning him to her side she hoped to win Tess back to the prince. He sighed, gazing at the lantern that wasn't a lantern—was that how the sun looked?—and wished mightily that he knew how to see these maps for himself, to understand what kind of ship might sail the ocean between the worlds.

Outside, twilight had lowered down over camp. At last, he strolled back to the Orzhekov encampment, wondering what kind of a woman Sonia would find for him to marry.

The assault began as the first hint of light paled the eastern horizon. Aleksi stood beside Tess on the ramparts of the outer wall and watched as, far away along the inner walls, flaming arrows arched into Karkand. He watched as the artillery flung trails of fire and sparks over the walls. As the sun breached the horizon, the siege towers rumbled forward and battering rams rolled into place, their crews sheltered by stiff screens of hide.

"Oh, God." Tess sank into the chair that Mitya, who now stood up to the left in the height of a watchtower, had carried up onto the wall for her. Since the parapets on the outer walls faced outward, to protect the suburbs from an outside attack, these walls served as a good vantage point from which to observe the jaran attack on the inner city.

"Tess, you don't need to watch," said Aleksi. "You can go back to camp."

"No." She looked grim. "I need to watch. I won't turn my eyes away from this." She folded her hands over her abdomen, laced her fingers together, and an instant later unlaced them and stood up again. "Why couldn't you people just have stayed out on the plains where you belong? Why did I have to fall in love with *him*, damn it? Why couldn't I have married a nice sweet jaran man like Kirill?"

"Couldn't you have married Kirill?"

"I'm not talking to you!" She shook her head. "I'm sorry, Aleksi. I just don't understand why we must always be blessed and cursed together."

"But if the gods only cursed us, then we would hate them. And if they only blessed us, then—well, then we'd care nothing for their laws because we'd respect nothing but our own pleasure."

She sank back into the chair. "Oof. Oh, I hate this." She took in a deep breath and let it out slowly, rubbing her belly. "It was meant to be a rhetorical question, but I suppose that answers it as well as anything does."

"And that is why you are blessed and cursed? Are there no wars on Earth?"

"There are no longer wars like this. That's something we learned at long last to stop. But Charles—well, in the end, what he's planning may well lead to the same kind of thing. Who am I to judge what I see here? 'More nor less to others paying/Than by self offenses weighing.' So I watch, though it hurts. But I refuse just to look the other way, knowing what I married into."

"Hurts?"

"All I can think of is all the people who are going to die, and the pain they'll suffer."

"Oh." Aleksi crouched down beside her chair. She rested a hand on his hair, and he leaned against her, melting into this sign of her affection.

In the distance, the first line of siege towers jolted into the walls. They sat too far away to see anything but a tiny blur of movement; dust rose—or was that the blur of arrows?—and smoke streamed up into the clear morning sky. To Aleksi's ears, the attack sounded like the distant roar of a cataract. Above, on the battlements, Mitya stared toward the conflagration. A small gold banner whipped in the wind above his head, snapping rhythmically. Next to him, his dark shadow, stood Vasha, the boy's gold shirt like an echo of the banner. Katerina and Galina had also come to watch, but the rest of the children had stayed with the camp.

"Well," added Aleksi after a while, "the gods send us to our fate. They sent you to Bakhtiian, after all."

She blanched and removed her hand.

"Tess? Are you well?" he demanded, alarmed.

"It's not that. It's true, what you say. We might as well have been sent by the gods to aid Bakhtiian in his victories. Look at the modifications David made to the catapults, changing them from the lever to the counterpoise system. Look at Cara's hospital. Gods, look at Ursula, advising him with all of her textbook knowledge."

"What is *textbook?* Has she fought in such wars before? Certainly she knows a great deal, and Bakhtiian listens to her advice."

"She's only studied war before now, but still, the breadth of her knowledge ... it's inevitable that her knowledge, given to him, alters the balance of power."

"But then if it's true that the gods favor Bakhtiian, why should we be surprised that the jaran are always victorious?"

She only shook her head, but as much as if she agreed with his comment as disagreed. She stood up again and paced down the length of the wall toward the tower, turned, and returned to Aleksi. Their escort ranged out around the base of the tower: Anatoly Sakhalin's jahar, resplendent in their armor and red silk surcoats, lances gleaming in the first light of the sun. Behind the jahar lay fields and the jaran camp; between them and the inner walls stretched the now deserted suburbs, emptied out by the army.

"Aleksi, go ride to see him."

"To see who?"

"Ilya. I'm just restless. I just—feel strange; I'm afraid that something bad might happen to him today. Just go and make sure that he's well and then come back to me."

She needed him. Heartened, and yet disturbed by her mood, Aleksi examined her. Finally he rested a hand on her shoulder. "Very well. I'll go. Shall I send someone up to sit with you?"

"Mitya and the girls are close by. Go on." She smiled at him, grateful, and he felt content.

He left. Below, he mounted, reported to Sakhalin, and rode out. He circled the outermost walls, crossing a stretch of fields and bypassing a straggle of refugees thrown out of the suburbs, passed back into the outer city, and came at last to a rise overlooking the great main gates of the inner city. Here, Bakhtiian had stationed himself and his jahar. His gold banner lifted in the wind, stirring gently, and every rider's spear bore a pennon of gold silk. No one spoke here; they only watched, and the pennants fluttered and snapped in the breeze. These ranks of riders wore gold and red surcoats, richly embroidered; their burnished helmets bore a tuft of horsetail, and the harness of their gray horses was ornamented with tassels and gold braid.

At the height of the rise, two riders sat side by side looking out of place in the midst of such panoply because they were so plainly outfitted. Bakhtiian wore lamellar armor covered with a plain red surcoat, and his stallion was distinguished only by the fact that it was the only black in the troop. He sat with his helmet tucked under one arm and turned his head to address a comment to Charles Soerensen, who wore a heavy quilted coat, belted at the waist, and no other armor. They might have been any two kings, allied in conquest, watching over their latest victory.

As Aleksi rode up to them, he considered what Tess had said. Perhaps they were. Although Charles Soerensen had no army here, and apparently no great army in his city of Jeds, perhaps he commanded stronger forces than soldiers.

"Aleksi!" Bakhtiian beckoned him over as soon as he saw him. "What are you doing here?" Soerensen turned his head to regard Aleksi as well.

"Tess was restless."

"She can't come in this close. I forbid it." Bakhtiian looked out toward the great gate. From this vantage point, the figures fighting up against the wall appeared to be the height of Aleksi's hand. Two troops of horsemen armored only in heavy coats and brocaded robes waited between

Bakhtiian's jahar and the troops besieging the wall. The arrow fire itself obscured the walls. The siege tower burned. Men swarmed up ladders, only to fall, stricken, or be drenched with steaming liquid. The constant pounding of the siege engines sent stones falling like rain into the city. Columns of smoke rose from inside the walls, and Aleksi saw, for the first time, the lick of flames on the roof of a minaret that stood within the walls. To the far right, missiles hurled from the siege engines crumbled the ramparts of a long stretch of wall. Like a still eddy in the midst, the scaffolding on which they had trussed up the Habakar king sat about two hundred paces away from the main gate. Aleksi could not see the king from this angle, to know whether the monarch was dead or alive. Certainly the heat of arrow fire around the gates was withering.

All at once, far to the right, to the north and west, a roar went up from the jaran army. In seeming concert, a rumble shook through the ground and to the left a portion of the wall sagged and gave way. Clouds of dust streamed into the sky. Bakhtiian drew his saber. Flags rose, passing the order down the line. A distant mass of Farisa auxiliaries, their wicker shields held angled in front of their bodies, charged forward toward the collapsed wall.

A small gate within the main gate opened. Khaja soldiers poured out, racing toward their king. Foot soldiers fanned out in a line and then men on horseback raced out, charging for the scaffolding. At once, the jaran troop below started forward, and a line of archers fired into the khaja ranks.

Bakhtiian turned. "Konstans. Go." About a third of the jahar detached itself from the group and drove forward, heading for the sortie.

"You send your own men?" Soerensen asked.

"The other jahar is lightly armored. They can't sustain under the fire from the walls. In any case, the insult remains against me."

"Ah."

Jaran fire peppered the ranks of the khaja riders and foot soldiers alike, from the women shielded by the front line of the troop. "That's the Veselov jahar," said Aleksi.

"So it is," said Bakhtiian. "No doubt their dyan will choose caution and pull them back."

Already Konstans's unit pressed forward past the back ranks of the Veselov jahar, which split to either side to give them room to pass. But the foremost of the khaja horsemen had already reached the scaffolding, and four men flung themselves down off their horses and climbed to free their king.

A single rider broke away from the front rank of the Veselov jahar, spearing straight for the khaja ranks. They spun to face him, but he made it somehow through a barrage of arrows and leapt off of his horse onto the scaffolding, saber drawn, fighting. As two khaja warriors dragged the limp body of their king toward the horses, two more khaja arrived to confront the lone jaran man.

The pounding of hooves threw up dust, obscuring the scene below as Konstans and his riders charged into the enemy ranks beyond the scaffolding. Out of the cloud, figures appeared, running for the gate. A riderless horse caparisoned in the Habakar manner bolted free of the melee, followed by another. A man weighted down in armor stumbled wildly toward the small gate, but it closed before him.

The jaran unit emerged from the dust, wheeled, and drove back through. Arrows rained down from the walls, like a second cloud, like a storm of rain.

Out of the chaos the gold pennons appeared again, riding away from the walls. In their midst, they dragged along on the ground a figure dressed all in gold, gold surcoat, gold crown, tumbling in their wake—dead already or killed in the sortie, who could tell? Out of arrow's range one of the riders turned back in his saddle and cut the rope free, leaving the corpse all forlorn out on the churned-up field. By the time the unit rejoined Bakhtiian, enough dust had settled that Aleksi could see the scatter of bodies strewn haphazardly between the gates and the scaffolding. Veselov's jahar had pulled back out of catapult range. One of the archers set an arrow alight and fired; the arrow lodged at the top of the scaffolding, and flames licked at the pitch-covered wood. Three bodies lay at the base, two in khaja armor, one jaran.

"Konstans!"

Layered with dust and spattered with blood, Konstans rode up beside Bakhtiian. His face bore a cheerful grin. "That got the bastards."

"Casualties?"

"A few, but we got everyone back except for him." He nodded toward the lone jaran corpse.

"Who is it? It was foolhardy, but bravely done."

"Veselov."

"Anton Veselov!"

"No." Konstans glanced at Soerensen, at Aleksi, at the scaffolding that was smoking and really taking fire now, and then back at Bakhtiian. "Vasil Veselov."

Perhaps Tess could have read the expression that crossed Bakhtiian's face at that moment. Aleksi could not. Rage? Agony? Relief?

"Aleksi." Bakhtiian's voice was as cold as the winter wind. "Ride forward and tell Anton Veselov that he is dyan now."

Then, below, the jaran man moved, raising himself up on his elbows, and struggled away from the scaffolding back toward the jaran lines. His legs dragged behind him in the dust.

At once, four riders broke free from the Veselov jahar and rode for him. Arrows rained down from the walls. Bakhtiian swore, and his stallion shifted, reading his mood. He clapped on his helmet. And stopped.

"Konstans! Aleksi!"

Aleksi and Konstans exchanged a lightning-swift glance. As one, they rode forward, breaking into a gallop.

"Here," shouted Aleksi, detouring for the back of the troop. "Give me a shield. Konstans!"

They grabbed the great rectangular wicker shields used to protect the archers and rode on. Of the four riders racing for Veselov, one had fallen and another was hit. Konstans cursed, almost overbalanced by the awkward shield. Aleksi raced forward, gaining speed, gaining on the others. There, in the lead, that was Anton Veselov; he reached his cousin and bent down, hanging from his saddle to grab Vasil's outstretched arm. An arrow pierced his mount's shoulder, and the animal screamed and spun, almost trampling Vasil.

Then Aleksi and Konstans arrived. "Go ahead!" Aleksi shouted. "We'll cover your backs." He swung his horse around and balanced the wicker shield on his back. Konstans did likewise. The fourth rider swung down and hoisted Vasil up over his mount, got back on, and in this wise they sprinted out of arrow range. A rock thudded to the ground, spewing dirt, and another, and then they were out of catapult range.

Up on the rise, neither Bakhtiian nor his jahar moved but only watched as the riders straggled in with the two injured men thrown over the horses like sacks, and half of the horses limping and squealing. Vasil's eyes had rolled back. He looked dead.

"I need a new mount," said Anton Veselov. "Take them back to the hospital." He glanced up toward the rise, toward Bakhtiian, and then down at his cousin. Vasil's legs were a mass of wounds, scored with blood. Two arrows stuck out at an awful angle from his left thigh. His right shoulder weeped blood. His face was pale and his left cheek torn by a ragged, ugly cut.

"You're in command now, Veselov," said Aleksi, tossing the wicker shield to the ground. He counted seven arrows stuck in its fiber, and two shallow wounds in his mount's rump. Konstans's shield had ten arrows lodged in it. "I'll escort them partway, if you wish."

Anton stared at him a moment. A roar rose up from the left. The Farisa auxiliaries wavered, driven back from the breach in the wall by a scathing round of archery and catapult fire. Flags signaled. Anton started. "Archers, reinforce left," he shouted. He urged his new mount up to the horse across which Vasil lay and jerked the staff of command from Vasil's belt. "Damned fool," he said to his cousin's lifeless form. "But maybe you're better off dead. Go on, then," he said to Aleksi.

Konstans nodded at Aleksi and rode off, returning to Bakhtiian. Aleksi guided the others forward, and the lines parted to let them through. Up on the rise, Bakhtiian watched them go and then turned away as a rider bearing the green pennant of Raevsky's jahar galloped up to him. They fell into conference.

Aleksi rode beside Vasil, but the wounded man did not stir except as the movements of the horse jostled him. But he still breathed. Blood dripped from him onto the ground, leaving a trail. Aleksi parted from the wounded soldiers at the river and, alone, he made his way back to Tess's position.

He gave the reins of his horse to one of Sakhalin's men and took the stairs two at a time up to the walkway. There Tess sat in the chair, staring fixedly toward the battle. Mitya knelt at her feet, holding her hand. Smoke and dust obscured the city. Fires flared up in four different places within the walls.

"Tess?" All at once, fear seized his heart. "Tess!"

Slowly, slowly, she turned to look at him. He heard voices behind him, Katerina calling, "This way! This way! Hurry!"

Tess was deadly pale, as pale as Vasil had been. Mitya jumped to his feet. "Thank the gods," he said.

"Tess!" Aleksi sprinted up to her and flung himself at her feet. He went hot and cold together in sheer, stark terror. "What's wrong?"

"Aleksi." Her voice was hoarse and unsteady. "I'm bleeding."

Up on the tower battlements, Vasha stood alone, gazing raptly at the battle. Katerina appeared on the ramparts, leading four soldiers carrying a litter.

Tess shut her eyes and opened them again. "Damn it," she muttered. She rubbed a hand over her lower belly. "Damn it." She started to get to her feet.

"No!" said Mitya. "No, Aunt Tess. We'll carry you. Don't move."

"He's right," said Aleksi, standing up as Tess rose. His hands, on her arm, shook. "We'll carry you to the hospital."

"No. To Cara's tent." A strange expression crossed her face. Her shoulders curled in and her left hand clenched up by her chin. "Breathe slow," she said to herself, but her breath came ragged. "Let it pass."

Then, without warning, she swore, a single word. Wa-

ter gushed down her legs, staining her boots and the loose
belled ends of her women's trousers.

Aleksi stared in horror. His fear for her paralyzed him.
He could only stand and shake, clutching Tess by the
arm. Mitya gasped. Katerina ran up beside them.

"Quick!" she exclaimed, surveying the situation with a
comprehensive glance. "Quick, you idiots! Get her on the
litter. The baby's coming!"

ACT FIVE

"These our actors,
As I foretold you, were all spirits and
Are melted into air, into thin air:
And, like the baseless fabric of this vision,
The cloud-capp'd towers, the gorgeous palaces,
The solemn temples, the great globe itself,
Yea, all which it inherit, shall dissolve . . ."

—SHAKESPEARE,
The Tempest

CHAPTER TWENTY-ONE

Beyond, the battle raged. Charles Soerensen watched it without any pleasure, but he watched it nevertheless. "If I were to die," he said to his companion, "and Tess inherit Jeds, then you would gain Jeds by more peaceful means than this."

Ilyakoria Bakhtiian glanced at him, then back at the battle. The fighting was fierce over the ruins of the wall, but neither side gained ground. "You would not have put yourself in my power if you thought I coveted Jeds, by whatever means I meant to use to get it. And I can't marry every princess. Nor would I want to."

"There are other means than marriage."

"There are, but with what power should I enforce them? The Great King of Vidiya will not grant me his throne simply because I ask him for it."

"Do you want his throne?"

Bakhtiian still wore his helmet. He had not taken it off since the death of the Habakar king and the removal of the injured jaran soldiers. Out on the field before the gates, bodies littered the ground surrounding the smoldering remains of the scaffolding. "I want an alliance with him."

"For now. Who is to say what you will want later?"

Now Bakhtiian turned his head to look directly at Charles. "Jeds is a rich city, with ships that sail to ports across the seas, and it boasts a fine university, but my army could ride across the extent of the lands Jeds calls her own in two days. How can you understand what I might want?"

"Because trade is as powerful as land. What makes these cities rich, here in Habakar? Not just farming. Not just the metals and the crafts. Merchants caravan through here, and the governor of each city demands a toll, a tax, from each merchant. Jedan ships sail to more ports than you know of, and the more of that trade, the more of the seas, they control, the richer we become."

"So it *was* to negotiate trading rights that you sent Tess over the seas. She *was* spying on the khepellis."

"Is that what she told you?"

"I'm asking you."

A messenger rode up, blue pennant snapping from his upraised lance. He reported to Kirill Zvertkov, who was stationed at the far left of the jahar. The two men spoke together, and then Zvertkov sent him away. Over the distance, the blond rider and Bakhtiian looked toward each other; Zvertkov lifted his spear once, twice, and a third time. A hundred riders split off from Bakhtiian's jahar and rode away after the messenger. Bakhtiian watched them go and then turned back to Soerensen.

"The Chapalii control the seas," said Charles.

"They built Morava."

"They built it, yes."

"Do they want it back?"

"I don't know what lies in the mind of their emperor."

"They are zayinu. It's true that they might not think like we do. I often didn't understand them, when I escorted their priests to the shrine. And if they want these lands—*my* lands?"

"If they want these lands back, they will take them."

"They are so strong?"

Charles glanced up into the sky, but the clear blue was roiled by smoke and dust from the battle. He looked back down to regard Bakhtiian with an even gaze. "They are stronger than you with your army and I with my ships."

"Stronger than I with my army and you with your ships, if we had an alliance?"

"Ah," said Charles. His lips quirked up, not quite into a smile. "If we had an alliance. Don't we already?"

"Because of Tess? Quite the reverse, I thought."

"But don't you see, Bakhtiian, that Tess links us. In the jaran, she is your wife and also the adopted daughter of your aunt who is, as I understand it, a powerful ruler in her own right. In Jeds, she is my heir."

"But in Jeds, if you had a child, that child would be your heir."

"I won't have a child."

"How can you know? You're still young—no older than me, I'd wager."

"I cannot have a child."

"I beg your pardon."

"No pardon necessary. It's a simple fact. I can't have a child, because any child that I have would be killed."

"Killed!" Bakhtiian looked astounded. Inside the city, a wooden tower built up against the walls collapsed in flames, and like an echo, a siege tower far to the right buckled and splintered and sagged into ruin. Men fell from its heights, or scrambled, screaming, from the wreckage. Smoke billowed up into the sky, obscuring the entire stretch of wall. The catapults kept up their fire, a constant, numbing harmony to the roar of battle.

"The children Tess has will be my heirs."

Bakhtiian took off his helmet and shook out his hair in the breeze. The acrid scent of burning, the pall of dust, tinged the air. "*My* children."

"Exactly. So you see, Bakhtiian, that we are already allied by many forces, by our own ambitions, by the threat of the Chapalii, by the children Tess will bear, by your education at the university my father founded and I built."

Bakhtiian considered in silence, and at last he spoke. "There is one thing I've never understood. Tess said that when you're not in Jeds, you sail to *Erthe*. Your mother came from that country, and so do many of the people in your party. Tess went there to study. Do you rule there? Was your mother the queen? Is that why she married your father, the Prince of Jeds?"

Charles shook his head. "They do not govern on Earth as they do in Jeds or in Habakar lands. They rule, well, more like the jaran in the tribes: there is a council, and one woman or man who administers."

"And you are that man."

"Yes."

"But also Prince of Jeds."

"Yes."

"How can you be both? Why visit Erthe at all when you rule entire in Jeds?"

"Why live with your aunt's tribe?"

Bakhtiian grinned. "Any man must respect his mother's and his aunt's wishes."

"So it is with us as well. I am a child of two countries, just as the child Tess is carrying will be a child of two countries. But there is one other thing that Tess did not, perhaps, explain to you."

Bakhtiian lifted one expressive eyebrow. "No doubt."

Charles chuckled. "I beg your pardon. It was in deference to my orders that she kept her secrets. If I may?"

"Soerensen, I have learned more from you today than I have in three years from Tess. Why now?"

"Because of what I learned at the palace—the shrine—of Morava. Bakhtiian, Earth does not rule itself. It is part of the Chapalii Empire, where it lies, far across the seas. We rule within our lands, by their favor, but they rule us completely."

"But Jeds—"

"They are not yet concerned with Jeds."

"Tess said that the khepellis had only recently learned about the shrine itself." Bakhtiian stared, musing, at the city, at the figures struggling on the walls, at the archers below and above firing sheets of arrows, at the flames inside the city, at the trampled corpse of the Habakar king. The thud of artillery serenaded them. Yet Bakhtiian did not really seem to be watching the battle but rather something beyond it. "Gods. Then why—?" He broke off. "You mean to free yourselves, to free Erthe, from their rule."

"Of course."

"Of course," Bakhtiian echoed. "Of course. And you want my help."

"We of Earth can't war with the Chapalii outright. They're too strong."

"Though they rule you, you aren't part of their empire, not in truth. Not in your hearts."

"Not at all."

Bakhtiian considered Karkand. For a while his gaze rested on the Farisa auxiliaries, taking the brunt of the attack over the mined wall. "It's true that a land may be won by war, but to hold on to it takes subtler skills. To hold on to what you've won, and to unite it. Since the khepelli are zayinu, there is even less reason to love them or to accept their rule. What profit for me in this alliance?"

"What do you want?"

"I want Jeds."

Charles laughed. "I thought you didn't covet Jeds."

"I only said that you must not think I did, to put yourself in my power. If I said the word, my men would kill you."

"True," said Charles coolly. "But you'd still be no closer to having Jeds."

Bakhtiian's lips twitched up into a smile. "It's true that Tess would repudiate me in an instant if I killed you. Well, then, if I can't have Jeds, then I want all the lands that lie between."

"I can't promise you them. And I didn't say that I wasn't willing to bargain with Jeds."

Stones lobbed out from the city fell harmlessly onto the ground a hundred paces in front of them, spewing clots of dirt into the air. A clay pot filled with water struck earth and broke into shards; the water spattered and steamed over the churned-up soil.

Bakhtiian stared at Charles, eyes wide and questioning. "But then—" He broke off and twisted around in his saddle.

"Bakhtiian!" A rider hailed him. The next instant, two other riders appeared, galloping, driving their mounts hard. They resolved into two of the Orzhekov children, the brother and sister, Mitya and Galina.

Bakhtiian muttered a word under his breath. His stallion shifted restlessly beneath him, sidestepping.

As they rode closer, the children could be seen to have pale faces and a drawn look about their mouths. Still, Bakhtiian held his place, waiting for them to attend him.

Mitya held back so that his sister could take right of place before Bakhtiian. She reined her mare in beside him.

"Cousin! It's Tess!" She broke off and cast a glance back at her brother. He nodded.

"Go on," said Bakhtiian sharply.

Galina gulped and went on. "The baby's coming early."

Charles swore. "I must go back. Are you coming?"

Bakhtiian did not reply. A huge stone flung from Karkand struck the ground about eighty paces in front of them. The impact shuddered through the soil. Dirt sprayed out.

Konstans rode up beside Bakhtiian. "They're getting better range. Perhaps we'd better move back."

Bakhtiian flashed a furious glance toward Konstans. "I do not move back! We hold our position." He was taut with suppressed emotion. "Mitya, you will stay with me. Galina, go with the prince."

"You're not coming with me?" Charles demanded.

Bakhtiian turned his dark stare toward Soerensen. "Don't you think I want to go? But I have a duty to my army. I must remain here, to be seen, until nightfall."

"Ah," said Charles. "I understand."

"Yes," said Bakhtiian softly, "I think you do. Go. I will come when I can." He was pale, and his horse minced under him. "Konstans, get Mitya some armor and take him back behind the lines until he's suitably outfitted to sit up here with me."

"Of course." Konstans rode away with the boy.

"Well, then," said Charles.

"Keep her well," said Bakhtiian. His voice slipped and broke on hoarseness.

"Cara will be with her. Nightfall, then." He reined his horse aside and followed Galina toward camp. Behind, Bakhtiian fastened on his helmet, clenched his hands on the reins, and stared out at the assault. Inside the walls a minaret burned, flames leaping up its delicate neck to scorch and engulf the ornamented tower. A din rose from the city like the distant clamor of the ocean: the blare of trumpets, the roar of flames, the constant arrhythmic thunk of catapult fire, the bellowing of animals, a multitude of sobs and cries all blended with the clash of the armies and the screams of the wounded and the pounding of stone against stone as artillery battered down the walls of Karkand. The sun sank toward the west, and as sunset came, the light ran like blood along the western hills.

CHAPTER TWENTY-TWO

David could not bear to go anywhere near the siege, now that he'd done his work so well. He could not bring himself to observe the fruits of his labors, since it had cost him nothing, and others—jaran soldiers, khaja civilians—so much. He condemned himself as a coward and a hypocrite. As penance, he worked triage in the hospital with Marco and Gwyn Jones. The wounded came in in a steady stream. Three times David almost fainted from the sight of blood and gaping flesh. After the third time, a numbness settled over him and he could follow Marco about, helping him hold down the screaming wounded, refilling the three leather flasks he carried—one with water, one with alcohol, and one with a jaran concoction, a blend of herbs in tea that dulled pain. At the water jars, he met Diana Brooke-Holt. Blood spattered her tunic, and she gave him a pained smile, filled her flasks, and went back out to the ranks of wounded.

Now and again David lugged some poor soul into the surgery where Cara and the best of the jaran healers worked. Jo Singh had set up several huge copper pots of water to boil, to sterilize instruments. After depositing his unconscious patient on a table, David took a break from the wounded for a while and cleaned the crude instruments and boiled them and lifted them out to dry with a set of metal tongs.

He was standing there, sweating from the steam and the heat of the coals, when Gwyn Jones and a jaran woman brought in a stretcher. A blond man lay on it, looking more dead than alive.

Cara glanced up. Her eyes widened. "Vasil! Here, Gwyn, I'm done here. Bring him to me."

The transfer was made. "He's badly wounded," said Gwyn. "Do you think he'll make it?"

"You know him?" Cara's tone was sharp.

A ghostly smile passed over Gwyn's lips. "Not in that way, if that's what you mean. He comes to watch the acting. He has—what should I call it?—charisma, I suppose. And he's a handsome man." He paused, wiping his hands down his stained trousers. David could see the jaran man's face where he lay, unconscious, on his back on the table: a huge gash had ripped one cheek open, and his forehead was bloody and torn. His other wounds looked worse. "Or he was, at any rate. Will he live?"

"I don't know." She turned to examine him, and her two young jaran assistants huddled around her, aiding her, observing her.

David steeled himself and went back outside. In truth, the noise bothered him more than the blood. Some of them moaned, a reedy, grating sound. Some of them screamed as if they meant to rub their throats raw. Others lay there in stoic silence, suffering their agonies without a word. A few whispered, begging for water. Under a huge canopy lay those Marco deemed would not survive or were too badly wounded to benefit from the crude surgery available. Jaran attendants moved among them, relatives, perhaps, providing succor. David saw Diana there as well, carrying two flasks, soothing the dying with her gentle hands and voice. Oh, Goddess, he was tired. He found a corner of ground and shut his eyes. Mercifully, he slept at once.

The thunder of hooves woke him. A rider dismounted, saw David, and ran over to him. It was Tess's adopted brother, Aleksi.

"Where is the doctor?" he demanded. He looked wild-eyed, not at all composed as he usually was.

"She's—what's wrong?"

"Tess. The child is coming early."

"Oh, hell! I'll go tell Cara. Where is Tess?"

"I took her to the doctor's tent."

David sprinted for the surgery tent and burst inside. "Cara!"

She did not look up, "What is it, David?"

"Aleksi just rode in," he said in Anglais. "He says that Tess has gone into premature labor."

Cara's head jerked up. Blood trickled over her fingers where they rested on her patient's hips. "Let me finish here. Jo, you'll be in charge of equipment, Sibirin of the healers, until I can return. David, go with Aleksi."

David ran back outside. Aleksi had already commandeered another horse. "Where is the doctor?" Aleksi snapped.

"Coming in five minutes."

"She has to come *now!*"

"I'll come now. She's finishing with a patient. Come on."

They rode off together, across the hospital grounds and on through into the center of camp, where Cara's tent lay close by Tess's. They gave their horses to Vasha and went inside. In the inner chamber, Tess lay on her left side on the examination table, breathing evenly. She looked pale but otherwise composed. Maggie stood beside her, holding her hand.

"Tess!"

She twisted her head to look behind her. "David. Where did you come from?"

"Goddess! Let we wash myself first. What happened?"

"My water broke." The color leached from her face suddenly, and when she spoke, her voice was tiny. "Is Cara coming?"

"Yes. Let me wash. Aleksi, come with me."

"David, I'm scared."

"I know." He felt a great sinking gap in his chest at her words. Her fear terrified him. "Cara will be here soon."

"We sent Mitya and Galina to tell Bakhtiian and Charles," said Maggie. She rubbed Tess's hands between hers. "Katerina went to get her mother."

David went over to the counter, where the sterilizing unit lay. "Here, Aleksi, help me move this to the outer chamber." They lugged it out. Tess watched them go. David set it down and triggered it. "Now, do what I do. Listen, Aleksi, you're going to have to run interference."

"Interference?" Aleksi kept glancing back toward the inner chamber.

"I don't know what Cara intends. I suppose it depends on how the delivery goes, but Tess is so early. . . . You're going to have to keep your people out of there."

"Ah." Having a job to do seemed to steady Aleksi's nerves. "Dr. Hierakis will use her machines to help Tess and the baby."

"If she has to. Charles is going to be furious."

"Why?"

David looked up in surprise. "Well, Charles wanted Tess in Jeds. It's dangerous. . . ."

"I know childbirth is difficult for women, and that they die at times, and early babies usually die at once, of course, but Tess—" Aleksi's expression pinched in, and David saw how frightened the young rider was. "The doctor doesn't think Tess is going to die, does she?" His voice broke.

"Aleksi." He hesitated. He didn't know what to say.

"Is it because she isn't in the heavens? Was she never meant to have a child down here? Oh, gods." He lapsed into silence. David finished the sterilization procedure, and Aleksi mimicked him stiffly, jerkily. His whole body betrayed his agony.

David took in a deep breath. "Now. You go in and sit with Tess, and send Maggie out to sterilize. I'll have to do some arranging here—"

Aleksi went in at once. Maggie emerged. "Oh, Mags, this is awful. Let me see. We'll move some things aside, here, and get out this cloth. Oh, can you go outside and set several pots to boiling? We'll need lots of hot water, more as a cover than anything." Maggie nodded and hurried outside. In the inner chamber, Tess and Aleksi spoke to each other quietly. David could not make out their words.

At last, *at last,* Cara strode in. She stopped, surveyed the chamber, nodded once briskly, and then ran her hands and outer clothes through the sterilizer. She ran a damp cloth over her face and pulled a cap over her hair. "David, I'll want you to attend and Aleksi will have to keep everyone out." David followed her inside, and Aleksi retreated. "Well, Tess, what happened? I see. No, stay on your side. Let me attach this monitor here. Don't move, I'm running a scan."

David watched as Cara ran the scan down over Tess's body. Tess faced away from them, lying quietly, working hard on breathing slowly. Cara's hand stopped dead over Tess's abdomen. An expression of horror passed over Cara's face. She made a tiny sound in her throat and fiddled with her fingers on the scanner, and ran it again.

"Cara, what is it?" Tess began to crane her neck back to look.

"Don't move!" Cara snapped. She sidestepped over to the counter, slotted the scanner into the flat modeler, and read the screen.

"Is the baby all right?"

"Fine. Listen, Tess, there's no telling how long this will take, but I'm afraid it'll be fast. Ah, here comes a contraction. Does it hurt?"

Tess took in seven tense breaths and let them out before she spoke. "Not much. And they're short."

"But damned effective. That's often the case with premature labor. Goddess, you're only twenty-nine weeks. Tess, if we were on Earth, I'd have few worries about saving the baby. But you realize—"

Tess shut her eyes. "Are you telling me it's going to die?"

"The conditions—"

"It's my fault for refusing to leave!"

"No, Tess! We're not throwing around blame here. You seem to forget there is another person involved in this transaction: yourself. Tess." She came over and took a tight hold on Tess's hands. "Tess." She bent and kissed her. David admired Cara's calmness, her ability to bury her emotions in order to act professionally. It was what made her so effective. "There's no guarantee that you'll react, or when it will hit if you do, or how badly, but I want you to promise me that you'll believe that I'll pull you through, that you'll trust me to do that."

Another contraction came. David could recognize them now by the look of concentration Tess got on her face, a kind of dropping away from everyone and everything else. It faded.

Tess lay her face on Cara's hand. Her own hands gripped tight onto Cara's fingers. "I trust you, Cara," she said in a whisper.

"Oh, my little girl," murmured Cara. A single tear slid down her cheek. "Why are you so damned stubborn?"

Tess did not reply.

Voices outside. A moment later, thrusting the flap aside, Charles strode in.

"Have you washed?" Cara demanded.

He halted, turned, and went back out.

"Did Ilya come with him?" Tess asked in a small voice.

The flap stirred again, and Maggie pushed through. She raised her hands up. "Sealed and approved. What can I do, Cara?"

"Sit here with Tess while I go argue with Charles." Cara bent and kissed Tess again, and eased her hands away. "David, come with me."

"What are you going to argue about?" Tess asked, managing a tenuous smile.

"The Soerensen family stubbornness. I don't want him to do anything rash."

"Oh, gods, Cara. Don't let him intervene now."

"We'll do what we have to, Tess. Don't argue with me. David?"

In the outer chamber, Charles had thrown off his quilted coat and stood leaning over the table, keying in to a slate laid out on the flat surface.

"What are you doing?" asked Cara.

"Calling in a shuttle."

"Charles!"

He looked up at them, and David saw how drawn, how tense, his expression was. "This is Tess, Cara."

"This planet is interdicted, Charles. Do you intend to call a shuttle down in the middle of camp?"

"If I have to."

"Against Tess's express wishes?"

"If I judge that she's incompetent to decide, yes."

"Charles!" exclaimed David.

"I meant at this moment, under these conditions, dammit. Don't argue with me." He continued keying in.

"All right," said Cara. "Let's compromise. Call one in

but keep it circling at a high enough altitude that it won't be spotted, unless they think it's some kind of a bird. There's no guarantee you can even get it here before she delivers in any case. She's already over halfway to full dilation."

"There's still the baby to consider. Surely this early it'll need special care that you can't provide. Most of your provisions were made for Tess's care, not for this premature a child."

"The point is moot, Charles." Her voice cracked.

He straightened. "What do you mean?" His eyes narrowed.

Even this far from the siege, David could smell smoke on the air, the perfume of distant burning, a hint of dust tickling his nose. He sneezed.

Impatiently, Cara wiped another tear from her cheek. When she spoke, she spoke in a whisper. "No heartbeat. She went into labor because the fetus died."

David felt sick with anger and shock. His throat tensed, choked, and he couldn't swallow.

"Sometime in the last twenty-four hours," Cara went on, her voice still soft, slipping into a cool, clinical mode although a third tear, and a fourth, trailed down her face. "There's preliminary evidence that the placenta ripped away from the uterine lining, but I don't know yet. Charles."

He sat down. He said—nothing.

"Is Bakhtiian here?"

Still he said nothing. He covered his face with his hands and rested there, not moving.

David felt impelled to do something, anything. He walked to the entrance and peeked outside. Aleksi attended the great pots of water warming over two fires. He glanced back, saw David, and lifted a hand in acknowledgment. Already a crowd of children had gathered, and beyond them, a line of guards ringed the camp, Anatoly Sakhalin's jahar, guarding Bakhtiian's wife. A woman broke through the line and jogged toward them. David let the curtain fall and turned back. "Incoming," he said. "It's Sonia. I know she's going to want to see Tess."

"Here, Charles," said Cara briskly. "Go in and pull the

curtains over the countertop, and disguise the table. Let me see. David, what can I do with her? I need to start an IV, so I'll need some excuse to get Sonia outside after she's seen Tess."

Charles lowered his hands. "Does Tess know? About the baby?"

"No."

"Why not?"

"Because she's got enough ahead of her as it is. I didn't think—"

"I'll tell her." He rose.

"Charles! You will not!"

He was angry now. "She has a right to know *now*. Or do you think it's better for her to go through it and then find out? That we make that decision for her?"

Cara rounded on him. "Why, Charles, this is new. That's your usual mode of operation, isn't it? Hoard all the vital information to yourself. Make the decisions for others."

"You're very protective and self-righteous all of a sudden."

"I'll thank you," said David curtly, "not to argue. Don't be stupid. Now, what do we do about Sonia? Where is Bakhtiian?"

Charles moved abruptly. He crossed the chamber and embraced Cara, and they stood together for a long moment, silent.

"I'm sorry," murmured Cara.

He just shook his head. David thought his heart would break, to see their sorrow. Then Charles kissed her and they separated. Charles sighed, crossed back to the table, and slid the slate into its slot underneath the wood grain surface. "Bakhtiian has to stay with the army until nightfall. Listen. Give me a few moments alone with Tess. Then send Sonia in to me, and I'll let her talk to her. I'll find some way that the two of us, Sonia and I, can go outside. There's no point in me attending Tess, Cara. I can't contribute anything except grief and anxiety and that won't do you any good."

Cara nodded. Charles went inside, and a moment later

Maggie emerged from the inner chamber. The bells tinkled on the entrance flap, and Sonia swept in.

"I beg your pardon," she said to Cara, "for charging in. But Tess—" She was pale, her lips set with worry.

From the inner chamber, they heard Tess start to cry, soft, despairing sobs. Sonia went white.

"Go on," said Cara gently.

Sonia rushed in.

David and Maggie and Cara looked at each other. Tess sobbed. Sonia spoke soothing words to her, and once Charles spoke, softly.

"Well," said Cara suddenly. "We've work to do. Maggie, I'm going to need Jo. There's one thing I have to do, and it's going to take all of our skill to pull it off."

"What do you mean?" Maggie asked.

"You'll switch with Jo at the surgery," Cara continued, so preoccupied now that David wondered if she'd even heard Maggie's question. "You know the routine in the surgery well enough. If you can't stomach it, then—well, Sibirin can order things perfectly well."

"I can handle it," said Maggie. She looked at David, asking a question with her eyes, but he could only stare back. He had no answer either, for anything. He heaved his shoulders in a sigh and drew a hand back over his hair. His fingers tangled in his name braids, and as they smacked together and stilled, he mouthed a prayer.

"I'll go, then," said Maggie, and she left.

"What about me?" David asked quietly.

"We build what we can out of tragedy," said Cara in a soft voice. "I can't let this opportunity go by."

"What opportunity? Cara, you sound like you're trying to talk yourself into something."

Charles pushed the curtain aside and poked his head through. "Cara, are you coming back? The contractions are picking up. Sonia and are I going out to get some things for the baby." Behind him, David saw Sonia bend down and kiss Tess, and embrace her, holding her. Then she straightened and came over to Charles.

"Yes, we'll need one of our stoves, and a cradle, and a scarf and blankets to wrap it in. If it can live at all, if it's as early as it seems, then we'll need to keep it warm.

Some goat's milk, perhaps." She met Cara's gaze. "I'll arrange all this."

"That would be wonderful," said Cara. "I'll attend to Tess."

There was a pause. Then Sonia took hold of Cara's hand, briefly, and let it go. "There is no healer in this camp I would trust as I trust you," she said. Charles waved her forward and she preceded him out.

Cara crossed through into the inner chamber. The room lay swathed in cloth, which draped the counters and shielded the table readouts. Two holographic lanterns lit the space, suspended from the corners. "Increase illumination," said Cara, and the light brightened.

Tess lay on the table with her eyes closed. Tears streaked her face. "Oh, God," she said. "All for nothing."

"Hush, child," said Cara. She smoothed Tess's hair down tenderly and let her hand linger on Tess's cheek. "Let's get these clothes off you."

"One's coming," said Tess. "Shouldn't it hurt more than this? It doesn't really hurt at all."

"Except in the heart, my child. David, can you help me with her trousers? We'll need to prop you up, Tess, here at the end of the table, for the delivery. Maybe David can just sit behind you."

"What about Jo?" David asked.

Cara shook her head. "At the rate Tess is dilating, Jo may not get here in time. Gloves. Stool."

"Another one," said Tess.

"David, go get Aleksi." David dashed into the other chamber, called outside, and ran back in. "I'll need a second covering, here at the end of the bed," Cara continued as if he hadn't moved.

"It's changing. It's going lower. Cara, is this what's supposed to happen?"

"Yes. Breathe evenly. Lay back, I've got to examine you. This will be uncomfortable. David, uncover the counter and start the procedure that's listed on the monitor." Bells tinkled. Aleksi and Jo came in together. "Sterilize," said Cara, and they went out and came back in. "Jo, thank goodness." Jo nodded and went over to the counter. "Aleksi, sit with Tess."

David moved aside to make room for Jo and looked back to see Aleksi staring at them in amazement.

"Where's Ilya?" Tess asked. "Another one."

"He'll be here," said Cara. "He'll be here."

"But the men are supposed to leave camp," said Aleksi. "It's bad luck for a man to watch a child's birthing."

"Aleksi, you may leave if you wish. I need your help, and jaran customs aren't our customs. Which will it be?"

"Oh, stay, Aleksi," said Tess, and Aleksi went to her at once. She let out her breath all at once, and her voice took on a sudden intensity. "Cara, I have to push."

David watched, feeling useless. Jo worked on with efficient fury, linking equipment, setting up the IV. Aleksi helped Tess sit up, leaning into her, linking his arms under her arms and over her chest, so that she could prop herself up on him. Cara waited.

It didn't take very long for the baby to come, and it was no wonder. In two pushes the head crowned, and on the third the body eased out into Cara's waiting hands. Its skin had a strange bluish-gray color, smeared with some whitish substance, and the body was perfectly formed: miniature fingers and toes, testicles, button nose, and perfect rosebud lips, crowned by a shockingly black crop of hair. It was a tiny little thing, so tiny.

So still.

Aleksi buried his face against Tess's hair.

Cara cut the cord.

Tess stared. "Cara," she said. "It's so hot in here. Could you get me a blanket, I'm freezing." She shuddered, all through her frame. Her eyes rolled up, and she sagged back against Aleksi.

"David! Take the baby. I've got to deliver the placenta."

"I can't!" Still and dead, the baby barely stretched longer than Cara's cupped hands. It was bloody, too, streaks of it that echoed the streaks of blood along Tess's thighs.

"You must, David." Cara's voice cracked over him, and he obeyed blindly, through tears, taking the tiny thing from her and wrapping it in a white square of cloth that

Jo handed him without looking at him. The body was warm and soft, cooling as he held it. One little hand peeped out of the cloth, each minute finger tipped with a white nail. He covered it hastily, binding it in under the cloth.

He felt dazed. A numbing roar descended on him, and he watched as through a haze while Cara and Jo fussed over Tess, hooked her up to this and that, flicked on the modeler, cut off her tunic, set into a glass dish the strange veined blood-red creature that was the placenta. Tess's image appeared, floating in the air at the foot of the bed, turning, pulsing critical red all along its length.

Voices sounded outside. Cara did not even look up. David shook with exhaustion and realized that he was squeezing the bundle in his arms. He was filled suddenly with such revulsion that he thought he might well be sick.

"Think, you idiot," he said under his breath. Bells chimed.

"I don't think—" someone said, protesting.

"I will see Tess!" said Bakhtiian.

Without thinking, David stepped to the curtain and eased himself through so that the curtain sealed shut behind him. "Don't go in!" he said. And came up short, facing Bakhtiian.

Rajiv stood wringing his hands a pace behind the other man. "Oh, thank goodness, David!" he exclaimed. Then, like a coward, he turned and hurried back outside.

David made himself look at Bakhtiian, but Bakhtiian only stared at the bundle in David's arms. He smelled of smoke and dust, and his clothes still bore the impression of his armor. His face was ashen. Slowly, he held out his hands. David gave him the child.

He cradled it against his chest. Easy enough, that was, since the bundle did not reach from his elbow to his hand. With the other hand, carefully, he unwrapped the cloth. The hair showed first, all course and black, and then the impossibly perfect face, still and shuttered. The tiny arms, the fingers, the chest, the legs, and the tiny tiny little toes. He said nothing; he did nothing but breathe. Then, more carefully than David had, he wrapped the little body back up and hugged it closer against him. He raised haunted eyes to David's face.

"Tess?"

"I don't know," said David. "I don't know. Dr. Hierakis is with her. We can't disturb her." He braced himself for a torrent of protest, but Bakhtiian said nothing. David glanced back toward the curtain. He heard Cara and Jo, speaking terse, quiet phrases that David himself barely understood and Bakhtiian certainly could not understand: IV, anesthesia, transfusion, systolic pressure, basal temperature, placenta abruptio, antibody sensitization.

In the middle of the room, Ilya Bakhtiian stood silent, crying, holding his dead son.

CHAPTER TWENTY-THREE

Jiroannes sat under the shelter of his awning, a blanket over his legs, his torso and arms encased in a fine brocade coat, and watched the glow in the west where the sun sank down over the hills and blended its light with smoke and fire from distant Karkand. He sipped at hot tea. Steam rose from the porcelain cup; this cup alone, of all that Syrannus had so carefully packed back at his uncle's villa, still remained fit for him to drink from. All the others had been chipped or broken or stained. Vines and peacocks circled the rim, a delicate round of painting. The aroma of the tea soothed him. Around him, the camp was quiet. At last.

He shuddered. He had not known that a woman could shriek that loudly, or that a woman who so clearly feared his attentions in the bed would show such anger when he informed her that he intended to visit elsewhere that night. As if it was any right of hers to dictate where he found his pleasure. But perhaps Syrannus had been right all along. The old man had, in his mild way, cautioned against the marriage. And yet, Laissa's audience with Mother Sakhalin had proved successful, or at least, so Laissa had reported. With the Habakar king in the hands of Bakhtiian, Habakar merchants streamed to Jiroannes's camp to beg for an audience with the princess Jiroannes had married. No, Syrannus had been wrong: The alliance would serve him well.

"Eminence?" Lal scurried toward him, bearing a thin-necked porcelain pitcher glazed white and etched with flowers. "May I pour you more tea?"

Jiroannes nodded. As Lal bent, Jiroannes saw a mottling on the boy's dark skin. "What is this?" he asked, reaching up to touch the bruise with one finger.

"It is nothing, eminence."

"It is a bruise. Where did you get it?"

Lal kept his eyes cast down. "It is nothing, eminence."

"I command you to tell me."

Lal finished pouring and backed away two steps. "The mistress struck me, eminence, when I entered her chambers after . . ." He faltered.

"After we argued." Wind stirred the awning. Beyond, smoke obscured much of the western curve of the sky, but above, stars began to show in the high bank of the heavens. It was frustrating enough never to know what was going on in camp, except that the jaran had at last assaulted Karkand. Jiroannes felt strongly that Mitya noticed and cared for him, but he doubted if Bakhtiian even remembered that a Vidiyan ambassador abided in his train. In order to complete his mission, he needed Bakhtiian's notice. And now—now Laissa had the audacity to strike *his* servants. It was all too much.

"Lal, you will cease waiting on my wife. It is insufferable that she treat you in such a fashion. Henceforth, you will serve me alone and cease going into the women's quarters. I'm sure that will be a relief to you, in any case."

Lal sank to his knees, balancing the pitcher in trembling hands. "I beg of you, eminence, it was nothing."

"You *want* to continue to serve her?" Jiroannes was astounded. "After she, a mere woman, treated you in such a way?"

"Eminence." Lal bent his head and shoulders, curving over the pitcher. From the guards' camp, Jiroannes heard a hacking cough and a baby's whimper. Darkness shielded the hills. The smoldering haze of the besieged city illuminated the western horizon. "I am not a man. My mother sold me into the palace service when I was still a boy, and after they cut me, I knew that only in the women's quarters could I rise to a position of importance. Eunuchs are not allowed to hold any office higher than that of attendant of the sash in a lord's household, and never any administrative office." In the lantern light,

Jiroannes studied the boy's beardless cheeks. "You have treated me well, eminence. You have been generous and kind, but you know it's true that while I can't become an offical in the Great King's court, I am welcome within the women's quarters."

Jiroannes tilted his head back. The underside of the awning lay dark above him, but he knew the scene well enough, having seen it created in the slave workshop abutting the women's quarters in his uncle's house: fine Vidiyan lords in their Companion's sashes riding to battle flanked by flags and standards and the Great King seated under a parasol, observing the march. A moment's reflection assured him that Lal was right: a eunuch was not considered a fit servant in a man's household, except as a body servant, and certainly not in the household of a Companion of the Great King. A eunuch might tie a lord's sash, but neither eunuch nor woman was allowed to hold the parasol over the Great King's head. Eunuchs belonged in the women's quarters, as go-betweens, as guards, as master of the gate and master of the treasury, as ministers seeing to the administration within the cloistered walls.

"Very well," he said at last. "But you remain under my protection."

"You are all that is magnanimous, eminence."

Jiroannes drained his tea, and Lal poured more into the cup. The warm liquid soothed him, and he felt the truth of Lal's words. He had been kind and generous to his slaves, and yet, one still eluded him. "Lal, send Samae to me."

Lal bowed his head and retreated. Soon enough, Samae appeared, dressed in striped trousers and a quilted damask robe, and knelt before Jiroannes, head bent in submission. Her hair had grown long enough to twine into a braid at the ends, fastened off with a silk ribbon. She folded her fine-boned hands in her lap and sat so still that the only movement he could see, on her, was the stirring of the ends of her hair on her collar. The carpet sank under her knees, forming a dark hollow.

"Samae, why did you refuse your freedom, when Bakhtiian himself granted it to you?"

At first she said nothing. Wind rustled through the tasseled fringe of the awning and shuddered the walls of his tent. He smelled smoke from the guards' camp; or was that a taint on the wind, blown in from Karkand?

"I am a slave, master," she said at last. Her voice was scarcely louder than the wind's rustle. *Her voice.* It was deeper than he had imagined it would be.

"But I command you to accept your freedom."

"Only the gods command me, master." She doubled over and touched her forehead to the carpet and lay there for the space of twelve heartbeats before lifting her head up again. "I am a slave by their law."

"By their law? What gods? What law is this?"

Under her lashes, she lifted her gaze to look at him. She had liquid brown eyes, dark and slanted against the pale ivory of her skin. "It is death to speak their name. Their laws are cruel, and they hate us for our ugliness."

"Samae, surely I do not understand you correctly," he said, exasperated. "The Everlasting God has given man laws in order that we may live as befits His Word. He shepherds us, in our ignorance, for we are His creation."

"We are clay," murmured Samae, as if she had not heard him, "clay and unclean water, and nothing else."

Jiroannes was too appalled to speak. Here he had thought that the great Tadesh Empire was a civilized country; certainly their concubines and dancers and metalwork and pottery were of the finest quality.

"When my grandfather's grandmother begged for their pity, because she was barren, they granted her wish but with this price: that one child from each generation be sold into slavery. I am the child the gods chose."

"But—" He took a sip of tea and choked on it. "Even a slave has certain rights, as we read in the words of the Everlasting God and his three prophets. Among those rights, the right to be freed."

"I am a slave," said Samae in her stubborn, soft, deep voice, "so that my family will remain free of the curse of barrenness. I will not bring this curse back on them. I cannot. Freedom is forbidden us, who are slaves by the gods' will."

"So if I command you to be free, you will not accept?"

She bent double again, brushing her forehead on the stiff carpet. "You are my master on this earth of clay, but the gods rule me."

Jiroannes realized that she was not bowing to him, but to her gods. A sudden compulsion seized him: to know her, to know of her, to make her speak her thoughts aloud, to fathom what lay behind her blank expression. "Then you serve the gods as your master?"

She remained bent over. Her voice emerged, muffled, out of the collar of her damask coat. "We cannot serve the gods, since they despise us."

"But if you're so much beneath their notice, then why bother to obey their laws at all?"

"They punish those who rebel against them."

Jiroannes let out a great sigh. He lifted his cup up, and Jat padded out of the shadows and took it away. Without knowing why, he extended a hand and brushed his fingers back along her hair and toyed with the ribbon holding her braid fast. "Why did you cry, when we saw the *play*—the dancers who speak with both words and hands?"

"Because the jaran believe their gods are kind."

"I don't understand."

The radiance along the western horizon swelled and brightened and then faded back down to a luminescent glow. "The woman came from the heavens, did she not? And the man loved her, and he got her with child. So she gave him a sword that she had stolen from her mother, the sun. But a sword brought from heaven bears two edges. For each blessing, it brings you also a curse."

Her voice had a hollow unearthliness that made him nervous. He jerked his hand away from her hair. The wind picked up. Golden tassels danced and fluttered, spinning, along the awning. His sleeve quivered, like an animal shifting in sleep and then settling. "Why should you care, in any case," he asked, "that the jaran believe their gods are kind?"

She did not speak for a long while. At last, she lifted her head enough that he could see her pale cheeks and the dark slash of her mouth. The lantern light caught the glistening of tears on her cheeks, and tears welling in her

eyes gave those eyes the brilliance of jewels. "Because
they will learn otherwise," she whispered.

"But why——?" But he knew, to see her face, why she
cared. She had lived long enough in Tadesh, perhaps even
with her family, to learn their dances, the secret of which
passed down only within their own race. Then, sold into
slavery, she had sailed alone over the wide seas and come
into a foreign country and been sold again, into the hands
of a foreign master. Alone, at the mercy of her gods, it
was no wonder he had never seen her smile. The only
wonder was that he had never seen her cry before now.
But she had never cared about him. He was only her master on this earth of clay. Probably she had never cared
about anyone or anything in Vidiya; had not cared until
she came to the jaran. Until she saw their women walking
free. Until she was sent to the tent of a boy newly come
to manhood.

"I will undertake to treat you more kindly," he said,
wanting suddenly for her to think well of him. "It's too
bad the jaran don't allow slaves in their camps, or I'd
give you to Prince Mitya as a gift."

She gasped, harsh, as if he had hit her. Her hands
moved frantically in a sign, warding him off. Or not him,
perhaps, but the notice of her gods. She struck her forehead to the carpet once, twice, a third time, keening in a
thin, muted voice, and then fell silent, and stilled.

Jiroannes stared at her, taken aback. "Go in to my
tent," he said brusquely. "You'll attend me when I'm
ready for bed."

With no expression on her face, she rose, bowed, and
retreated into his tent. Jiroannes swore under his breath,
flung the blanket off his legs, and stood up. Jat padded
forward and eased it off the carpet, and briskly folded it
up, and vanished back into the shadows. Jiroannes strode
to the edge of the carpet. The tassels spun over his head,
gold thread glinting and sparking in the lantern light. Beyond, the camp of the jaran army stretched on endlessly
into the night. A few campfires burned, in his guards' encampment, along ambassador's row, and farther on, into
the main camp. Stars glistened above, as unobtainable as
Samae. He saw now that he would never be anything to

her but her temporary master, to be suffered while she served out her penance, which could only end, for her, when she died. Perhaps he would give her to Mitya, or into Mitya's household. Perhaps he could explain the situation to Mother Sakhalin and ask her to advise him. Mitya would marry the Habakar princess, of course, but surely a man was allowed a secondary wife or a concubine. Surely some provision could be made for her. Yes, that was the right choice.

Determined, he spun and walked back across the carpet. The plush gave beneath his boots, and he had to step up, a little, inside his tent, where the carpets were piled five deep. A gauzy silk curtain screened off his bedchamber from the front portion of his tent, and as he crossed past his writing table, he saw a lantern shining through the fine silk, and movements silhouetted like the dancing of actors against the translucent fabric.

Like a play, he watched it unfold before him, at first in surprise and then in horror.

Samae knelt at the foot of his bed. Laissa, standing, extended her arm and offered the slave girl a cup. She said: "Drink this." Samae took the cup and drank it down without hesitation.

Jiroannes lunged forward and pushed past the beaded entrance into his bedchamber in time to see Samae drop the cup and clutch her throat, clawing at her neck. She gagged and gasped and choked, and her pale complexion faded to an obscene gray color. One hand groped out. She grasped at the drapery ringing the bed, but the fine silk fabric slipped through her fingers and she fell, retching, but all that emerged from her mouth was a hoarse, rattling sound.

She gasped and choked out three words. "He is safe." As she doubled over, the embroidered quilt caught on her bronze slave's bracelet and slid down off the bed, half over, half under her. She lay still. Her head lay cushioned on crumpled quilt. Against the fine white silk embroidered with red leopards and blue peacocks outlined in gold, her black hair made a stark line, like coarse, unraveled thread.

"She was stupid as well as ugly," said Laissa impassively. "You're better off without her."

Jiroannes could not make himself move. "What have you done?"

"Just so we understand each other, husband, I have poisoned her. I will supply you with concubines from now on, girls who are more suitable to our household. You will have to marry again, of course, but I expect that you will include me in the negotiation for your secondary wives."

Samae's damask coat was the same peacock blue as the draperies that shrouded the bed. A lantern hung from each carved bed post, each one a cunningly wrought bronze bowl girdled with an elaborate screen through which the light shone.

"I could have you killed for this!"

"This is commoner's behavior, these histrionics." Her voice was dispassionate. "I sought to provide you with a lesson. You will treat me with the respect I deserve. I run this household now, and with my influence, you and I can attain eminence at court. I warned the jaran queen that you might prove difficult. Be assured that without my goodwill you won't leave this camp with the alliance your Great King so sorely desires. Why else would he send you so far?"

The truth was, Jiroannes was beginning to have doubts about Vidiya's army and its ability to hold off the jaran army, if things came to war. He suspected that his future lay with the jaran, not with the Great King's court. But he wasn't going to let Laissa know that. "You're a fool, Laissa. I meant to give her—" He jerked his chin toward Samae's body. "—to the young prince."

"Find him another slave-girl, then. There's little enough to choose between them."

The shadows stirred, down in the tunnel that linked his tent to hers. Jiroannes caught a glimpse, sliding away, of an observer: It was Lal. Maybe Lal had been trying to warn him all along. Maybe Lal had already thrown his lot in with *her* camp. She had stuffed the household full of retainers loyal to her; she controlled the kitchens; the guards' camp was by now probably riddled with her informants. She was a princess.

"I'll await you in my chambers," she said. "If you cared for the girl, and she for you, then I'm sorry for it. Had you gotten her with child, I'd have had to kill her anyway."

She eased her robes away from the corpse and turned and marched away down her tunnel, into her domain. She had sewn tiny bells around the hem of her veil and hood, perhaps in imitation of the jaran women, and they tinkled merrily as she vanished into the dark billowing hall. Lal hesitated, there in the shadows, and then followed her.

Jiroannes stared at the body. Samae had fallen on the cup—his last porcelain cup, shattered into bits under her shoulder. A hand lay limp on silk, stretched out as if tracing the golden line of a peacock's feathered glory.

Laissa was wrong, of course. Samae hadn't cared for him at all.

"He is safe." Samae had known it was poison. She had taken it willingly. The blessing for her, to go to Mitya, whom she cared for, would then become a curse to the prince; she had taken the poison to spare him.

It had been a long time since Jiroannes felt called upon to pray. He sank to his knees now and bent his chin to his chest and spread his hands on his thighs, palms open to God, and prayed a long reverent prayer of thanks to the Everlasting God, who judged His servants with more mercy than Samae's gods had judged her.

CHAPTER TWENTY-FOUR

From nothing, she could suddenly hear.

"Signs are stable. We pulled her through, Jo, at least through the worst of it."

"Should I go tell—"

"No. Remember, to Bakhtiian, we'd have no way of telling until she woke up."

"Ah. Not that I want to go out there anyway. Cara, he won't let go of the child. He's been holding on to it for over four hours. Don't you find that a little macabre?"

"Let him sit, Jo. Charles is sitting with him. He needs to mourn it before he can let it go."

"David went out to—"

Their voices faded.

* * *

"I went through this once before," said Ilya into the shuttered silence.

"You lost a child?"

Ilya glanced at Charles, startled. "Yes, that, too—a child. Not my own. My sister's." He did not look down at the still bundle cradled in his left arm. "I meant with Tess. Forty-five days I went not knowing whether she had lived or died. She was wounded in a skirmish—"

"The scar on her abdomen."

"Yes, that's right. I had to take the khepellis to the coast, to the port, so I had to leave her before I knew if she would live. Forty-five days." He lapsed into silence again.

The lantern on the tabletop burned. Cara had in her tent one luxury: three pillows with soft satin coverings that could be tied together to form a hedonistic reading cushion. The light caught the fabric at such an angle that the satin gleamed. A single leather-bound book, *Shakespeare: The Complete Works* lettered in gold on its spine, lay on one of the pillows, tossed casually down. Otherwise, the chamber was spartan: a chest for clothes, a table, two wooden folding chairs, and a small cabinet for cooking utensils and odds and ends. Silence hung over them, dense. An occasional word or phrase drifted through from the inner chamber and once the sound of a short laugh being swallowed into a cough. What transpired in there might otherwise have been a thousand kilometers away, it remained so distant from the two waiting men.

"I lost my parents," said Charles suddenly. "Do you ever wonder—" He broke off.

"I wonder a great deal," said Ilya softly. "Most of it is fruitless, though."

"Your wondering?" Charles asked. Bakhtiian did not answer, but the silence seemed as much of a reply as any words he could have spoken.

A slow, erratic drip sounded from outside, along one corner of the tent.

"Why did you allow her to marry me?" Bakhtiian asked suddenly.

"I didn't. I'd have stopped it if I'd been able to. If I'd known. Not because of you, you understand. But because of who she is, and why I need her."

"And if she dies?"

"She won't die. Cara is taking care of her." Charles turned his head to stare at the curtain, the veil that closed them off from Tess. "She won't die. She can't."

"You don't want her to." Ilya bent his head and touched his face to the cloth that shrouded his child.

Charles did not move, but he shifted in his chair, restless, uneasy. "No, I don't want her to," he admitted.

"Well," said Ilya, raising his head, "neither do I. Why is it that you and I suppose that if we want something, it must come to pass?"

Charles's lips quirked up into a smile so colored by grief that it felt almost as if other people had been brought by that tiny expression into the hushed solitude of the chamber. "There's an old saying: 'be careful what you wish for; you might get it.' "

"Oh, gods." A quaver shook Ilya's voice. "The bargains we make with the gods never fall out as we think they will."

Charles stood up abruptly and went over to the chest. Rummaging within, he drew out a bottle and two glass tumblers. "Here." He returned to the table and poured out a round. "Have a drink."

* * *

This time, when she woke, she saw the blurred edges of the lantern in the corner, illuminating an oval of plain canvas fabric. She saw a figure move, recognized it as Cara, and fell back under.

* * *

". . . and then after the rebellion failed, I thought I would be executed. But they made me a duke—it's a nobleman's title within their imperial hierarchy—instead."

"Is that so strange? If you want to unite an empire, and you only enslave the people you conquer, doesn't it make sense that in time they'll rebel against you? But if you make them part of your court, then in time they'll become loyal to you. That's why Mitya must marry the Habakar princess. Then her father will support us, to protect her, and her children will rule and yet be both jaran and khaja."

"As your children will be— Oh, God, I beg your pardon. I'm so incredibly sorry."

Ilya stared at the haze of lantern light. He felt lightheaded, with exhaustion, with alcohol, with grief, and the sensation gave the lantern a blurred, magical substanceless look to his eyes, as if it didn't really exist at all. He tried to speak, once, but nothing came out. He tried again. "The gods will judge whether I may ever have a child, or whether I already bargained my children away."

Charles shut his eyes. "I gave up the chance to have children before I knew I had done it. Only I didn't know it until the day my parents were killed. They weren't killed, I mean. They were murdered. It was made to look like an accident—a crash—they were traveling in a ... carriage—but their agents left just enough evidence that I would know who was responsible. That I would know the emperor himself had ordered it, as a lesson. The only reason I didn't lose Tess that day is that she happened to get the flu and stayed home with our aunt. How could I dare have a child under those conditions? I couldn't protect a child, not against them. Maybe Tess *is* better off here. She's safe here."

"Safe," said Ilya under his breath. He cupped his free hand over the round arc of the baby's shrouded head.

"She will live," said Charles. "You must believe me."

"I want to believe you. The gods alone know how much I want to believe you. I'm sorry, about your parents."

"Here. Have another drink. Do you ever wonder—? God, I don't know what possessed me to tell you that. I must be getting drunk."

"Because the khepellis killed your parents, because of you?"

"I killed them. Cause and effect. The blame lies nowhere else. I made the choice, knowing it would put them in danger. I risked them, and I lost them. They were wonderful people. They always supported me. They loved me." He hesitated and went on haltingly. "I loved them. But I had to make the choice. I had to choose the rebellion, I had to choose the dukedom, I had to choose Jeds, and I have to choose to continue, now."

"You told me because I understand," said Ilya so softly that his words evaporated on the still air as a whisper of warmth vanishes in the cold of deep winter, out on the plains. "Eleven years ago, I bargained with the gods. I knew that my vision for the tribes was the right one, but I was young, and I wasn't sure I could convince the Elders to follow me. Why should they listen to a dyan as young and inexperienced as I was? I was afraid—afraid they would reject me, and afraid of losing my vision. But I knew I was right. So I committed sacrilege."

A scrape of shoe sounded from the inner chamber.

Both men tensed, expectant, but nothing happened, no one emerged.

"I killed a bird." His hands shielded his dead son's body, although by now it was, of course, too late to shield the child from the fate he had brought on it. "I offered a hawk on the altar of Grandmother Night, She Who Will Bargain if you are desperate enough to call on her. I killed it, and I poured its blood on the soil. I offered her my dearest one, if she would make my vision succeed. But you see, I meant to offer Vasil, because I was willing to give him up. Not to kill him; I didn't mean that, or maybe I did, but I told myself I meant only to send him away. To exile him."

The lantern burned, constant, with only the barest flickering on the wick within its globe. "She agreed to the bargain. Grandmother Night never refuses a bargain. And then she took them all, one by one, everyone I loved best. My parents, my sister, my nephew. She only spared Nadine that day to mock me. She took my cousin, Yuri. And now my son. And She'll take Tess, if She can get her. She'll take her back to the gods' lands, and we'll have to burn her, and I'll never—I'll lose her forever. Do you ever wonder if the price was worth paying?"

Charles shook his head, just a little, eyes half closed. A sound caught in his throat. "I kept trying to ask you that. We're so certain of our vision. But it is right. It is right. And yet, how many people will die? Some because they follow us, because they believe in us, and some on the other side of the conflagration we've started."

"But what else can we do? The gods have called us to our path."

They considered the path in silence. Nothing stirred. It was so quiet outside that they might as well have been camped in the middle of a wilderness, they two alone, fixed at some point no other woman or man had yet explored out to. Or in a clearing that some other, like them, had sat in, equally alone, and then turned back or forged on.

* * *

The urge to speak, to establish herself in the time-line, was so powerful that once she saw the lantern light again she opened her mouth and spoke. She spoke, she heard the words in her head, but her ears registered nothing. Her body existed, but nothing moved. She was aware but paralyzed.

"How long has it been?" she said. "How long was I out?"

Cara moved past her line of sight. Jo bent over a burnished counter, tapping her fingers on the modeler. Neither of them heard her. She couldn't hear herself.

Everything faded out again.

* * *

"I don't understand, though," said Charles, pouring them out another tumbler of whiskey. "I thought your parents and family were killed by another dyan, a rival. Isn't that—common? When there's a war going on? How did the gods come into it?"

"We don't harm women and children in the sanctity of camp! Gods, you khaja are savages! I beg your pardon."

"No. No offense taken. I apologize if I offended you. It was poorly said, on my part."

"No, I'm sorry. How could you understand? No one knows what happened that night. My aunt suspects, she alone, but we've never spoken of it. My mother discovered me, out there in the darkness, and she had Khara Roskhel with her. She often had him with her. They were lovers for as long as I could remember. And they found me, with the bird still struggling in its death throes, with its blood pooling on the ground.

"Well, Roskhel was outraged. Up until that moment, he had supported me. Then he saw what I was, what I was willing to give, that I had committed sacrilege, and all for my vision. Some already called me gods-touched, then. That night he called me cursed. He said to my mother, 'Now you must repudiate him, because you see what he is.' I knew at that moment that everything was in vain. I thought that Grandmother Night was laughing at me, by making me sacrifice myself and lose my vision, all at once, all together. Gods, we so foolishly think we understand the gods. Her price was much subtler and more cruel.

"You see, my mother smiled. She thought it was exciting that I was willing to break our holiest law in order to achieve my ambition. All the years of my childhood I had been a disappointment to her. Now, she was happy. She saw herself, her ambition, in me. And Roskhel said that he saw now that the taint spread through the entire family. He left. A few months later he rode into camp with his jahar and killed them, killed the corruption: my mother, who was the only woman he had ever loved; my father, whom the gods themselves had called to make a marriage that was never peaceful; my sister, who was the sweetest, most generous soul, and her little boy, who was far too young to be blamed for the rest of us. But he was my heir.

"So I tricked Roskhel down and I killed him myself, with my own hands.

"But my family was still dead. And yet, Grandmother Night kept her side of the bargain. The Elders listened to me. I united the jaran." His voice dropped so low that Charles had to lean forward, straining, in order to hear him. "I have never lost a battle. My riders have taken terrible casualties; I've been wounded myself, and once we were forced to retreat, but even then, in losing, we won." He stopped speaking abruptly and stared at nothing; at the past, perhaps, whose hand still worked in the present.

"It's strange, how it works," murmured Charles. "In leading a rebellion that failed, I gained a stronger position within the Empire. One that now might allow me to win Earth's freedom. What we think is failure sometimes leads to success."

"Perhaps. The gods aren't yet done with us." Ilya's hand sought out the tumbler and he raised it to his lips and downed it. He shuddered. "Gods, this is strong." He blinked. "But I don't understand how both your parents could have been killed by the khepellis. You said they don't yet know about Jeds—and wasn't your father—? Your father was the Prince of Jeds, the nephew of the old Prince Casimund. How could he have been in Erthe?

Wait." He set down the glass and brushed his free hand impatiently through his hair. "Your father, the first Charles, was killed in Jeds. I know the story. They were laying the foundation for the university, and some quarried stones fell and killed him. But you said your parents were killed in a carriage accident in Erthe."

"My mother was killed—" Charles broke off. He covered his eyes with a hand and swore under his breath. "I've forgotten what I told you. My mother was killed in that accident."

"Tess said the same thing once, that her parents were killed—her mother and her father. And she didn't mean the Prince of Jeds, only I just realized that now." Ilya stood up suddenly, swaying a little, and took considered steps to the entrance. He pushed the flap aside with his free hand. Bells chimed softly. He stared out at the night. Two fires burned out beyond the tent, low now, almost coals, and the single figure tending them turned expectantly at the sound of the bells. It was Aleksi. The young rider waited patiently and then heaved his shoulders with resignation and turned away again, back to the kettles and the water simmering over the flames.

Ilya stepped out under the awning. The night wind hit him, a cold swell. The cloth in his arms stirred. Charles appeared.

"Well," said Charles. "You've discovered our secret." He staggered, just a step, and halted beside Bakhtiian.

"The Prince of Jeds wasn't your father. But he was married to your mother. He acknowledged you as his children, you and Tess. Because he loved her, because he needed heirs—well, after all, a woman's husband is the rightful father of her children."

Charles was silent.

"But by Jedan law," Ilya finished, "that means you're not the rightful heir to the princedom. And neither is Tess."

"No," said Charles. "By right of birth, no, we're not. But we needed Jeds, so we took it, when the opportunity came. That's the plain truth. Old Prince Casimund had no heirs but his nephews. It had to go to someone. I've no excuses for what we did, except to say that we've been good stewards."

For the first time, Ilya smiled, but it was a wry expression, filled with pain. "What, you don't think I'm going to judge you, do you?"

"How did you guess?"

"It always pays to listen. Do you hear that? It's very distant—a horse neighing. They don't like being separated from the herd."

The vista granted them from under Cara's awning was of the sky, half clouded over now, and a dull red illumination along the western horizon. Darkness blotted out the camp, except for what few fires burned through the night, among the tents. "There's an old story, an old legend," said Ilya, "that the Singers tell, about why there are so many fair-haired jaran and so few dark ones. The Orzhekovs are a fair-haired family. All my cousins are fair-haired, and their children, their husbands, my aunt. My mother was fair-haired, and she married a fair-haired man—my father, Petre Sokolov, the Singer. My sister Natalia was fair-haired. She married a dark-haired man, her first husband, and their first child was dark—that is, Nadine. And I am dark. And this child has dark hair. Do you know who was a dark-featured man?"

"Oh," said Charles in a low voice. "The boy, Vasha. He's dark-haired. Tess told me that you acknowledged him as your son, even though by jaran law he isn't—he can't be."

"Inessa—his mother—was also dark. But, yes, by the laws of Jeds, Vasha is my son." He stroked the cloth bundle, stroked it, and said nothing for a long long while. They watched the clouds drift along the heavens. Aleksi sat as still as stone out by the fires. The awning sagged down and sighed up, and sagged down again, as the wind breathed on it.

"From the days before she married, and for all the years she was married, my mother and Khara Roskhel were lovers. He was dark-haired, like me."

Through the flap, thrown askew, the lantern gave dim illumination to the chamber and dimmer light yet to the two men standing just outside. Like a beacon, it marked them, throwing vague shadows out from them into the night.

"By the laws of Jeds," said Ilya slowly, "Khara Roskhel might have been my father."

* * *

"How long have I been under?" Tess asked, and was relieved to hear her own voice both inside and outside of her head.

At once, Cara appeared beside her. "Aha! We've got you back. Jo, drape all the counters, cover everything, and then go get Charles and Bakhtiian."

"But how long?" Tess insisted.

"About seven hours. I'm so pleased to see you, my dear. Just lie quiet. You're stable. Everything is fine, Tess. Everything is fine."

CHAPTER TWENTY-FIVE

Night enveloped the city of Karkand. The hellish noise of the day's fighting had evaporated into the darkness, though echoes of it remained. Within the walls, a minaret still burned. Outside the walls, four siege towers smoldered, three of them collapsed into ruins. Beyond the range of catapults and arrows, Nadine heard knocking and pounding: the laborers built anew for the next day's assault.

Smoke obscured the stars, here close to the city, and on the eastern horizon clouds streaked the sky, blotting out the moon. Otherwise, silence lay like a blanket over them. Nadine gave command of her jahar over to Yermolov, took three auxiliaries to bear torches to light her way, and went in search of her uncle.

Her jahar had been stationed halfway round the inner city walls, almost opposite the main gates, and she rode back through the abandoned outlying districts. In these suburbs, quiet reigned. Many of the trees and houses nearest the inner city walls had been demolished, either by catapult fire or by laborers or soldiers scrounging for materials to build, for food, for shelter, or for firewood. A line of men stood patiently in a dark plaza, waiting for their turn at a public well. The two jaran guards lifted their hands, acknowledging Nadine as she passed by.

Farther along, she skirted a flat field on which a new set of siege towers and artillery rose or were repaired. She paused to watch, and there, escorted by four men bearing torches, she saw David ben Unbutu on his rounds. She rode over to him.

"David! Well met." She smiled and lifted a hand in greeting as she pulled up beside him. His torchbearers edged away from her. David spun around, startled. "Your engines did good work today."

"Dina! I didn't see you."

The wavering torchlight gave him an ashen appearance, but then she realized that a fine white powder covered his hands and that streaks of it lightened his black skin. "You're out late," she said. She felt inordinately pleased to see him; his pleasant open face was such a relief to look at after watching the siege all day, after arguing with Feodor yet again at dawn over her decision to ride out with her jahar.

"Most of my work is done at night." said David. He glanced to either side. The torchbearers—khaja laborers all—had averted their faces from the exchange. "Preparing for—" He shuddered, cutting off his words. "You didn't see any fighting, Dina? You look no worse for the wear. I'm glad of that."

"*Saw* plenty of it. We're too heavily armored, my jahar, to be of any use in these conditions, except what archers we now have with us. But we can protect against sorties that come out beyond the gates, and if those khaja bastards look over the walls, they see how many of us there are. That ought to encourage them to surrender."

A smile came and went on David's face, and he looked uncomfortable.

"If you'll excuse me. I'm off to report to my uncle."

"Dina."

"What is it? What's wrong?" she demanded. He waved his torchbearers away impatiently and looked meaningfully at hers. "Go on," she said, and they moved a few steps away. Her horse shifted restlessly, disliking the dark, and Nadine dismounted and stood at its head.

"Tess had the baby. It's—there's no way to say this gently, except to say I'm sorry. It's dead."

"Oh, gods." She was shocked and saddened, mostly, but a second voice nagged at her: If the baby had lived, there might have been less pressure on her to contribute heirs. No matter what Ilya said, Nadine suspected that his children could inherit over any she bore, especially if they showed promise for command. "Where is she?"

"In Dr. Hierakis's tent. You ought to go. . . ."

"I'll go. Thank you, David."

"For what?" he asked bleakly. She took a step toward him, reached up, and kissed him lightly on the lips. "Nadine!" he whispered fiercely, and pulled back from her.

She sighed and mounted again. Her torchbearers hurried back to her, and she rode on. She did not ride directly to camp. Instead, she detoured along her original route and came to the main gates near midnight. Torches ringed the fallen stretch of wall, and now and again arrows sped out and thudded dully against the shields, but there was otherwise no movement along the collapsed wall except for an occasional slide of loose bricks.

"Zvertkov! Well met!" She hailed the rider, and he turned his horse aside and came to meet her.

"Orzhekov. Your position?"

"Quiet, for now."

"You heard about Tess?"

"I heard."

They said nothing for a while, ruminating in silence over the ways of the gods.

"We've a courier in from Vershinin," said Zvertkov at last. "He's turned south. Grekov's jahar will ride to Karkand to replace him."

"Garrisons?"

"They left Izursky's jahar to patrol the area, but we can't afford the men. There isn't much resistance left there in any case."

"Zvertkov!" This from a rider at the far end of the line. "Messenger riding in!"

Torchlight bobbed along the uneven ground, heading for their position. Nadine heard the bells before she could make out the figures. Soon enough the sound resolved into three men running with torches in their hands and a single mounted rider. He pulled up before them. His horse was lathered, and he himself look exhausted.

"Gennady Besselov. Sakhalin's command."

"Sakhalin!"

"There's a khaja force marching north to relieve Karkand, under the command of the king's nephew."

"The Habakar king is dead," said Zvertkov. "The nephew may well be the king, now."

The courier shrugged. "Whatever he is, he's good enough on the field, for a khaja, and he's got twenty thousand well-trained men with him. Sakhalin could only spare two thousand of his army to harry him as he marched north; it was that, or lose the ground we've gained so far in the southern lands, which was hard enough won to begin with."

"I'll take you to my uncle," said Nadine, and she looked at Kirill for confirmation. Zvertkov nodded. She led the messenger away.

The man regaled her with stories of Sakhalin's advance southward and how stubborn the southern Habakar inhabitants were—except they called themselves Xiriki-khai, and some of them spoke a different language. The Habakar prince's mother was a Xiriki-khai princess, and the merchants they had captured said that she had herself as a girl led an army and thus gained the title "Lion Queen," and that it was her heart and courage the boy had inherited. The torchbearers trudged on beside them.

Once in camp Nadine found riders to send the message out that a council would meet immediately. They found Anatoly Sakhalin's jahar ringing the tent of the doctor at a discreet distance. Nadine left the horses and the torchbearers with them. Closer in, Aleksi sat alone beside twin fires. Nadine led the courier between the fires, for their purifying heat to sear away any untoward contamination she or the man might bring with them, and Aleksi motioned at her to go on. It was late, past midnight and turning toward morning. A woman emerged from the tent, holding a swaddled bundle in one arm.

"Aleksi! Oh, I beg your pardon." It was Joanna Singh, one of Soerensen's assistants. She nodded at Nadine and eyed the courier, who stared at her in astonishment—at her height and her brown skin—before remembering his manners and looking away. "Would you like to go in? Your uncle is inside. Aleksi, can you get some of the riders out there to help? We need a bonfire. Cara wants to cremate the child as soon as possible. You'll need to get Sonia Orzhekov back here, too."

Nadine regarded the tiny bundle with curiosity. Was that the baby? Besselov waited patiently. Since they spoke in Rhuian, he couldn't understand them. "Besselov," said Nadine, "you'll have to wait out here. I'll go get Bakhtiian." She left the courier by the fires and ducked inside. The bells sewn onto the entrance flap sang, warning those inside that she was coming in. "Jo?" That was Dr. Hierakis. "Can you send for—? Oh, Nadine."

Nadine examined the chamber with interest, but it did not look that different from the outer chamber of Tess's tent: some khaja furniture and little else. A glass bottle sat, almost empty, on the table, with a crystal tumbler on either side. A book lay on a cushion, and a second book peeped out from the carved cabinet that stood against the far wall; the polished wood grain looked elegant compared to the plain fabric that made up the walls of this tent. Not a rich tent, by any means, but it was practical, and Nadine supposed that Dr. Hierakis prized practicality above luxury.

Light shone from farther in, from the private inner chamber into which no person but blood family or lover was ever admitted. The curtain between the two rooms had been thrown back. By the glow of two lanterns hanging from the corners of the chamber, Nadine saw a striking tableau.

For some reason, the doctor had shrouded her sleeping chamber with cloth, heaps of it, piled up and spread out everywhere, muting the edges in the room. Within all this fabric, almost seeming to float on it, Tess lay. Her entire left side was covered by gleaming silver silk. Nadine could not see Tess's left hand, but her right hand grasped Ilya's hands where he knelt beside her. He gazed up at her. Dried tears streaked his face. The prince stood down toward Tess's feet with one hand resting on her legs, which were also concealed by a silklike fabric that gleamed white under lantern light. At Tess's head hovered the doctor. Nadine could not see her left hand, but the doctor's right hand lay open on the silvery silk, the contrast making her hand seem almost as dark as David's.

Somehow, with Tess and Bakhtiian framed between the

doctor and the prince, the picture held an ominous quality for Nadine, as if they—Tess and Ilya—acted out their parts within boundaries they were themselves not aware of. The prince and the doctor seemed like sinister figures to her, like demons in one of the old tales, working their plots in human guise. She shook herself, driving the thought away. In these dark hours, the interregnum between midnight and dawn, between one day and the next, ghosts touched the mind and whispered secrets that were usually lies. No wonder they wanted to burn the dead child now: better that its spirit fly away to heaven before dawn, better not to let it see the light of day when it had only known night than to risk its lingering here. These hours belonged to Grandmother Night, and it was never wise to draw Grandmother Night's attention to oneself. She was just, but rarely merciful.

The tableau broke. Bakhtiian looked back over his shoulder at Nadine and rose at once. He bent to kiss Tess on either cheek and disengaged his hands from hers.

"I want to see the child, just once, before he goes," she said. Nadine thought her voice surprisingly strong. Ilya nodded. The doctor nodded. Tess shut her eyes and seemed at once to fall back asleep.

Ilya backed three steps away from her, and turned and left the chamber. The prince moved to close the curtain behind him. The inner chamber vanished from their sight.

"What news?" demanded Ilya.

Nadine could see that his temper was uncertain. "I brought a courier. He's waiting outside."

Without replying, Ilya left the tent. He stopped dead at the sight of Joanna Singh holding the shrouded child, and then walked past her over to Gennady Besselov. Singh went back into the tent. Bakhtiian grilled the courier for a long while. After a bit, Zvertkov appeared and listened in on the discussion, asking a few questions himself. When Sonia arrived, she brought Josef Raevsky with her, and the Orzhekov children, who immediately ran off to help build the pyre. The stack of wood rose rapidly. More commanders filtered in, holding their council there, out beyond the awning of Dr. Hierakis's tent while riders and children built the pyre. And there—damn it all anyway—there came Feodor.

"Dina! What's going on? Is it true that Tess Soerensen lost the child? Gods!" He stared at the pyre. "And there's a force riding north? A khaja army?"

"Yes, Feodor. Now will you hush? I'm trying to listen." The discussion ran fast and furious, but for once Nadine could hear her uncle steering it forcefully in one direction. He wanted to ride out now, destroy the Habakar prince's army in the field, and then return to deal with Karkand. For once, others objected and he thrust aside their arguments.

"But the distance—"

"We'll take remounts, of course. We can surprise him. He'll never expect us to meet him so quickly."

"What if there's stiffer resistance from Karkand? What if they've a strong force holed up inside that attacks while the bulk of the army is gone?"

"Zvertkov will remain here to deal with them. He can decoy them into thinking the army is as large as ever. And—" He cast a look around, and it lit on Feodor. "Grekov! You'll remain here as well. Your uncle will be riding in soon, and his force and the auxiliaries can keep them quiet until we return. The siege engineers can keep up their firing. If we destroy much of the inner city without fighting, that will only demoralize them more."

"But—"

"There, Dina," said Feodor in an undertone. "We'll stay in camp. He's half crazed with grief, can't you see that?"

Nadine surveyed her husband with disgust. "I'm not staying in camp. I'm riding with him."

"You can't know that! And anyway, you're married now. You can't put yourself at risk."

"He didn't take away my command. Gods, Feodor, my jahar is still my jahar."

"He left me in charge of the army here. I can order you to stay."

"He didn't leave you in charge of the army! I'm beginning to think you only married me as a ploy to advance your family. Now leave me alone!" She shouldered him aside and pushed through the crowd to stand beside her uncle. Bakhtiian glanced down at her, marking her attendance.

"I'll want your jahar, too, Orzhekov. With Vershinin's troops, my own, and Sakhalin's two thousand, that will give us almost equal numbers, and enough armored to carry the center. Very well, we'll leave as soon as—" But here he stopped suddenly, just broke off, and could not go on. The commanders attending him glanced each at the others, and as one, without further words, they retreated, leaving him alone.

"It's ready," said Aleksi, coming back from the flat field about fifty paces in front of the tent.

The prince came out of the tent, bearing the child. They had changed the shroud to one of fine damask linen, folded in an elaborately elegant pattern, so neatly tucked in to itself that it seemed more the work of an artist than anything. He handed the bundle to Bakhtiian. At once, Ilya walked away from the others, out to the pyre. Everyone shrank away from him, his expression was so grim. Farther, like a muted, gleaming shoreline, Anatoly Sakhalin's guard stood watch.

Soerensen followed him out, bearing two torches. They flared in the darkness. Their fitful light illuminated the scene.

Ilya halted at the base of the pyre. He did not move for the longest time, as if he simply could not bear to let go of the child. At last he put one foot on the pyre. Then he took hold of a corner of the shroud, to unwrap it for one last look.

The prince stepped forward so quickly that the torch flames shuddered and danced. Ilya flung his head up, but whatever Soerensen said convinced him to leave the child undisturbed.

He climbed up onto the stack and laid the child down in the very center. Kneeling, he remained there for a long while. Whether he spoke, to the gods, to the baby, or stayed silent, Nadine could not tell from this distance. But his back seemed bowed under the weight of his grief.

At last he stood up and climbed back down. Soerensen handed him a torch. They stood, each at one end of the

pyre, and Nadine felt, watching them, that between themselves this gesture had a meaning that the rest of those
watching could not fathom. Josef Raevsky held one arm
around Sonia, who wept. Kirill stood silent to one side,
next to Aleksi. Niko Sibirin had come up from the hospital, and he wiped a tear from his eye and hugged his wife.
The children—Mitya, Galina, Ivan, Katerina, and Kolia—
all stared, but only Galina cried. Vasha Kireyevsky
waited farther out, half hidden in the darkness, and
Nadine could not see the expression on his face. Feodor
loitered to one side, attention caught between the men at
the pyre and Nadine.

They put the torches to the wood. Flame leapt up. The
pyre burned.

They walked back together, the two men. For an instant, Nadine thought their expressions a perfect match.
Then Bakhtiian caught sight of Mitya.

"Cousin, my armor," he snapped. His armor was
brought, and in the roaring light of the bonfire, he tied on
his cuirass and slung his helmet over his shoulder.
Konstans appeared, leading his horse, and Vladimir and
one hundred of his jahar waited, lit by torches, in the
half-light thrown off by his son's funeral pyre. A thin
thread of light limned the eastern horizon.

"Nadine?" he demanded. "You'll attend me."

She cast a glance back to see Feodor fuming, hands
clenched, before she mounted on a horse brought by
Anatoly Sakhalin himself.

"You will watch over my wife," said Bakhtiian to
Sakhalin.

"At your command," said Sakhalin. His eyes glinted,
reflecting off the firelight. Nadine wondered if he was
disappointed to be left behind.

They rode. Dawn came, and they picked up the pace,
switching mounts frequently. They rode steadily throughout that day. The clouds burned off and the sun glared
down, unseasonably hot. When night came, Bakhtiian
drove them on. Nadine dozed in her saddle. She woke on
and off, once when scouts came in and rode alongside
Bakhtiian, delivering a succinct appraisal of the ground
between here and the Habakar army. At daybreak, they

reached the vanguard of Yaroslav Sakhalin's scouting net, and these scouts gave Bakhtiian a breakdown of the khaja forces and their disposition on the march. It had cooled overnight and they passed easily over several fields before the sun, rising in the sky, broke through the haze to bake down again.

They rode three abreast through a steep defile and over a range of rolling hills washed green by the rains. Two villages they passed, but nothing stirred there, either because the inhabitants had fled or because they had barred themselves within their houses. They traveled through the hills all day, passing twice through broad, flat valleys, changing mounts, driving on.

At dusk, more scouts joined up with them, and they rode south while Bakhtiian conferred with them. Twilight came, and then night, and finally, near midnight, one of Sakhalin's young commanders rode in and greeted Bakhtiian. Vershinin and his men were sent left, to complete the encirclement. Out there in the darkness, not so far ahead of them, the Habakar army lay bivouacked. A line of scouts went out to watch the khaja army, and the rest hunkered down for what remained of the night. Most simply lay down on the cold ground and slept. The horses huddled in groups.

Nadine could not sleep. She rode out with her uncle and the young Sakhalin commander to the crest of a hill overlooking the broad field on which the Habakar army had camped. Fires burned in two rings around the encampment, one on the outside, one within the tent encampments.

"Every night," said the young commander, "they stop before nightfall and dig a ditch around their encampment and a wall of dirt inside that, and they build fires on the earth wall."

"So that horsemen can't surprise them." Bakhtiian surveyed the field beyond. The night sky was brilliant with stars.

"Their prince must be a wise commander," said the Prince of Jeds' soldier, Ursula.

"Wise, indeed," said Bakhtiian. "We'll pull back be-

fore his march in the morning until we reach the first o
the valleys we passed, where we'll form for battle."

"Ah," said the young commander, "my scouts know
that ground. If we surround him there and leave him only
one way to retreat, southward where the path is widest
we can pick off his men as they run."

"If they run," murmured Ursula. "Your men have ridden far, Bakhtiian. They and the horses must be exhausted. Two hundred kilometers in two days!"

"What's a *kilometer?*" asked Nadine.

"My men and my horses will do what I ask of them,"
said Ilya.

They retreated back to the lines. Before dawn, the army
roused and began to pull back the way they'd come
Nadine, in the rearguard, could hear the rattle and pound
of the Habakar army as it followed their tracks. Now and
again she heard shouts and screams and the sing of arrows as the young commander's men harried them, but as
the jaran army struck up into the hills, most of her unit
joined up with Bakhtiian, leaving only a line of scouts in
the rear.

By midday they fell back into position in a wide field.
the armored riders massed in the center, the light troops
out on the wings and in the rear. Bakhtiian had brought
four units of archers with him, many of them inexperienced girls not much older than Mitya mixed in with riders and those archers who had fought before.

Out of the hills, down into the valley, marched the
Habakar army. The prince's banner shone, white with a
blue lion, under the noonday sun. At first, to Nadine's
sight, the khaja army flashed with a confusing profusion
of colors. Men in imperial blue marched in neat ranks.
Rank upon rank of chestnut horses caparisoned in gold
followed them, and around the prince clustered men in
silver and purple surcoats wearing plumed helmets and
riding white horses. Their striped pennons drooped from
their lances. Rows of shields glinted in the unit behind
the prince, stretching out to each side, burnished armor
shining in the sun. Spears bristled above the heads of
these men, tipped with blades and hooks.

Ilya let the khaja army march down onto the field. Already Sakhalin's young commander had drawn his troops back and to either side, far out of range and mostly out of sight, to cast around to eventually encircle the unit.

The Habakar army spread out to take positions, but before they could settle, Ilya lifted his lance up once, twice, a third time, and the center moved forward to meet the enemy. Archers rode up within their ranks and began firing. Arrows sang into the khaja, and then, just before impact, the archers turned tail back within the ranks. From behind, Vershinin's lighter troops and two units of archers swung around to either flank. It was here that the attack concentrated.

Nadine sat next to her uncle. The noise and cries of soldiers and animals mixed with the sound of weapons clashing.

"Orzhekov. There, a gap to the right. I want you to drive through and reach the prince. Konstans—now, the charge."

Nadine lifted her spear and her riders moved forward with her. To her left, she saw the bulk of her uncle's personal guard riding forward parallel to her, gold banner flying, gold and red surcoats a bright glare in the sunlight. The sight of them gave her heart. She stood a little in the saddle, thrusting her legs forward, and tucked her spear under her right arm. An imperial blue infantry unit held its ground in front of her jahar, and behind it rode the blue lion, fluttering in the breeze.

They held to a steady pace, gaining ground, and then some fifty paces from the line she kicked her horse to a pounding gallop and her men howled, a deafening ululation, and they hit the khaja line.

She plowed over the first man, who vanished into the maelstrom, and lost her spear to a flailing hook and pull from a knot of infantry men who had held together under the weight of the charge. Yermolov and Yartseva rode on either side of her, and then a sword cut into Yartseva and a hook dragged him down from his horse. A face, a man thrusting at her horse's head with his spear, appeared to her right. She cut at his arm as she passed but could not look back. As she recovered her saber, blood sprayed her armor—not her own blood but the blood of the soldier she must have hit.

A square of some nine men blocked the path in front of her, but at once four more riders, three still with their spears, joined her and Yermolov. Four of the nine khaja soldiers wavered and scattered, faced with the charge of horses. A spear thrust for her leg; she deflected it. Yermolov shuddered in the saddle, rocked back by a blow, and for an instant Nadine thought he would be toppled from his saddle. She parried; a man with his face screened by mail threw his spear at her. She knocked it away and then he was bowled over from the side by the hooves and spear of another rider. His dark eyes met hers for an instant, pain and anger and fear melded, and then he disappeared beneath the horses.

A moment later she came out into an empty zone. Ahead of her, the blue lion of the prince whirled away in a clot of fighting. Behind, the charge had disintegrated into confusion; unhorsed riders dueled: There was Yartseva, fending off a soldier in imperial blue, but then a line of horses obscured her sight of him, and when they passed, she could not see him.

Shrieks and moans; horses screamed and, to her left, a mare struggled up to its feet and collapsed again in a pool of blood.

"Orzhekov!" That was Yermolov, reining in beside her. "Form up the men. We've got to reach the prince."

A shower of arrows shaded the sun, arching over her head and falling with a sharp resounding clatter into the ranks of the Habakar prince. She saw, for one instant, Vershinin, far away topping a swell and then he rode down into—what?—she could not tell.

Behind her, bodies littered the field, most of them still moving or writhing, groaning in pain. Riderless horses reared and circled and stumbled over the dead and wounded.

The ranks of her jahar formed around her. Yermolov thrust a spear into her hand, and she sheathed her bloody saber.

They rode into the chaos surrounding the Habakar prince. A line of Habakar horsemen wheeled to meet their charge, but somehow the two units simply passed between each other. Nadine cast a glance back over her shoulder; she caught a glimpse of another wave of her jahar some fifty paces behind, narrowing the gap. The Habakar riders milled, turning this way and then that.

A rider shouted a warning. Nadine parried a blow with the haft of her spear and then thrust hard. The spear stuck in the man's segmented armor and she flung herself back to let it ride past her, and drew her saber. Cut to her right as an unhorsed man attacked her. The Habakar soldiers were mobbed in groups, infantry and cavalry side by side, disorganized, and they began to give way before her troops.

Except there, some hundred paces in front, bobbed the green pennant of Vershinin's jahar, and to her left she saw the gold banner that marked Bakhtiian's own guards. The white horsehair plume of Konstans' helmet trembled as he pressed forward through the ranks. Then he was hidden by a sheet of fighting. The arrow fire had stopped, at least into these ranks. She heard its sound from farther away, accompanying the louder crash of metal weapons.

They battled forward. Here, though disorganized, the Habakar resistance proved fierce. The clot around the prince's blue lion shrank, and shrank, but each gain was hard won. Yermolov fell, and then a rider to her left. All at once, she came up beside Konstans. He grinned at her. Blood spattered his face and surcoat, and blood leaked from an arrow wound in his horse's withers.

"The stubborn bastard won't surrender!" he shouted. She could barely hear him. "Here!" he cried. "Pull your jahar back. We're getting pressed too close together."

Obediently, she shouted aloud and found a flag to signal the withdrawal. Bit by bit, she pulled her jahar back and at last, coming out into the open, they formed back into ranks. What was left of them. She judged she had lost a third of her men.

The field lay open under the sky, churned into mud. Wounded and dead lay everywhere, in some places heaped in piles where they'd fallen over each other; in others, a single form lay tumbled alone on a sodden stretch of ground. From here, Nadine could see off to the

north the line of riders and the gold banner that marked
Bakhtiian's position. To the south she could not see, but
she heard cries and the clamor of battle retreating away
up into the hills. The clot around the Habakar prince
shrank, and shrank, under the deadly press of two jahars.
Abruptly, by a signal Nadine did not see, the jaran riders
pulled away and a unit of archers rode up and began firing at will into the last knot of defenders.

"We'll ride south," said Nadine, surveying her men.
They rode, and for a while they hunted, cutting down the
fleeing Habakar soldiers, those who had gotten that far.

But as afternoon lowered toward evening, Nadine
turned them back and returned to the field to hunt for
their own wounded and to round up those horses that
could be saved. Already many of the light troops wandered the field, killing the Habakar wounded and stripping and marking the dead. A steady line of casualties
walked or rode toward Bakhtiian's position, but Nadine
noted that his gold banner had moved.

She found him by the corpse of the Habakar prince.

He glanced up, seeing her. He looked tired. "He fought
bravely enough," he said, although Nadine was not sure
he was really speaking to her, to his niece, at all. She had
a strange feeling that he was speaking to Tess, almost as
if he was defending himself to her. "But he refused to
surrender. Had he led the army on the field outside Qurat,
the victory might not have gone our way so easily."

Vershinin's nephew was stripping the body, and Nadine
examined the dead Habakar prince with some interest—
with his chest-length black beard, dark hair looped in
double braids, and his throat red with his own blood. Not
particularly handsome, but so few of the khaja were; still,
he looked strong, and the wounds his body had
suffered—some fresh, some old scars—proved his courage in battle. Evidently he had cut his own throat rather
than surrender to the jaran. Or the arrow in his eye might
have killed him. Of his guard, none lived.

"Vershinin," Bakhtiian continued, "I'll leave you to
follow after, but I'm returning to Karkand with my guard
now. I'll leave you three healers who've been trained by
Dr. Hierakis. They'll judge those who can survive the

journey back to the hospital, and those it would be more merciful to kill now."

Nadine got leave for a few minutes to find her men among the wounded. She marked them, and was relieved to find over half those who had been missing, although at least one she judged would not make it back to camp. She found Yermolov; a chance cut by a khaja axman had severed the straps of his thigh armor, and a better aimed one had cut his exposed leg down to the bone, but already a healer cleaned mud and cloth out of it, muttering about something called *sepsis*.

"What is *sepsis*, Mother?" Nadine asked the elderly woman.

"There, you're done to fight again, young man," said the woman to Yermolov, who wasn't all that young except perhaps in comparison to her. She grunted and got to her feet and crossed a patch of baked-dry mud to crouch down beside a wounded archer. Two young men trailed after her, burdened with strips of cloth, with pouches filled with water, and a paste of herbal ointment. "Commander," she said, looking briefly up at Nadine, "it's what kills most of these men, or used to, at least. Dokhtor Hierakis has shown us how the wounds become infected with dirt and khaja blood, and so if we stop the infection, then the wound is likely to heal cleanly."

"Ah." Nadine left her to her work. "Yermolov, I'll leave you to come with Vershinin. You'll take command of those of my jahar who are wounded."

He nodded, and she changed to a remount and found her uncle again. It was dark by now. He had formed up his unit—most of whom had come through the battle with minor wounds or none at all—and was saying good-bye to the young Sakhalin commander and to Vershinin. Nadine waited patiently through the conference. She had no urgent desire to return to camp, but she could see that Ilya was obsessed with getting back to Karkand.

They started off. Nadine felt numb with exhaustion, and the torches bobbing up and down alongside her and all along the line disoriented her, making her dizzy. She rode without speaking, her jahar strung out in front of her where she rode beside her uncle.

"Dina," said Ilya suddenly. He rode one of his re-mounts, a shaggy tarpan, and one of his guardsmen walked along to his left, bearing a torch to light the horse's way. "I shouldn't have let you come with me. You're more valuable to me alive than dead."

"Thank you," she said dryly. "Feodor reminds me of that all the time."

"As well he might, since you're more valuable to the Grekov tribe alive than dead, too. But you fought well, in any case." They rode for a while in silence. A new torch-bearer came to take the place of the other one, and they switched mounts and went on.

"Dina." The torchlight illuminated part of his face, shifting on him, highlighting first his eyes, then his mouth, then the straight line of his nose, then his beard, then his eyes again. Otherwise, he rode in darkness. "Why should Soerensen offer me Jeds? If Erthe defeats the khepellis, then won't Erthe itself be a threat to us?"

"Erthe lies far over the seas, Uncle. Surely they'd need many ships in order to bring an army here."

"But what if it's the khepellis who have these ships? We know they can travel to any port along the coasts we know. And if the khepellis are as great a threat as Soerensen says they are, then we must unite against them. What if they want all the lands where humans now live?"

Nadine found herself a little confused by the conversation, since part of what he said made no sense to her. It sounded as if he had been negotiating with the Prince of Jeds. Over what, she wondered. "Then you really do believe that they're zayinu? I never saw any khepellis. Those that came to Morava at the prince's behest arrived after I left."

"They're zayinu. They're not like us. But how can Soerensen possess the loyalty of one of their merchant houses?" He said nothing for a long while. Nadine dozed.

His voice startled her awake, though he spoke softly. "What if they want all the lands, from the plains north and east along the Golden Road, from Vidiya to Habakar all the way south to Jeds and even the lands that lie south from there? All the armies must unite against them. We must prepare for that. Someone who understands the threat must prepare for that."

The night wore on. At last he called a halt and let them rest, men and horses alike, but in the morning they set off again, driven by Bakhtiian at a steady pace back toward Karkand.

CHAPTER TWENTY-SIX

He dreamed of a snow-swept landscape, of a single tree in a hollow, a scrap of cloth lying on the ground and a pathetic little fire burning but giving off no heat. His sister lay unmoving, pale gray, on the ground. For days she had tossed and turned in the grip of some demon, speaking words he could not understand. He had tried desperately to feed her with what little food he could gather from the winter-starved land, had tried to give her water, had tried to keep her warm. But at last the demon had drained her of life and now her last breath leaked out, too weak even to puff steam into the cold air. Her chest stopped moving, and her limbs went flaccid and, later, went stiff. He was alone in the wilderness.

"Don't leave me!" Aleksi gasped, and jerked up to find himself tangled in his own blankets, in his own tent. Sweat dampened him. The night air cooled his chest and back. He shivered. He forced himself to lie back down, but he could not sleep. At last, he rose and dressed and shrugged on a felt coat and walked outside. In the distance, he heard the arrhythmic thump of the artillery firing and the delayed crash of the missiles landing. In the four days since Bakhtiian had left, the noise had continued at such a constant rate that it was only now, in the predawn quiet of the camp, that Aleksi noticed it.

At Dr. Hierakis's tent, he hunkered down on his haunches just outside the awning and waited, knowing now that she had machines inside her tent that alerted her to his presence. Soon enough, the bells sounded as the doctor thrust aside the entrance flap and peered out.

"Aleksi! Why do you insist on sitting out there! You may come in without permission from me. I've told you time and again—and it would grant me some much-needed sleep." He rose and smiled sheepishly but did not reply, merely followed her into her tent. "You can hang your coat up over that hook." He did so gratefully. In her tent he was never too hot or too cold; it was as airy and comfortable as the great felt tents belonging to the etsanas. "Go on in," she added, impatiently. She lay down on a cot folded out beside the table. "Tess is asleep."

He went into the inner chamber. The counters gleamed softly in the light from the false lanterns. Tess slept, and beyond, on a black surface set within one countertop, colors pulsed in time to her breathing and her heartbeat. Feeling safe, Aleksi settled down on the floor beside her and rested his head against the couch on which she lay, and dozed.

"Aleksi? Where did you come from?"

He snapped his eyes open and looked up. Tess lay on her right side, gazing down at him. "I couldn't sleep," he said.

She sighed and reached down to touch him, but whether to reassure herself or him, Aleksi could not be sure. "What time is it?" she asked.

Since she had fallen under the sleep that the doctor called *anesthesia,* Tess had been obsessed with knowing the time of day. "I don't know. I came before dawn. Not too long after dawn by now, I'd judge."

"Then Jo should be coming in—" She stopped and they both listened, hearing the bells and then a conversation. A moment later the doctor came in to them.

"Color's good," she said cheerfully. "Readings good. We're going to take you off the system today. I hereby pronounce you Out of Danger."

"Insofar as any of us are out of danger," Tess murmured, and Cara shot her a sharp glance and then smiled wryly.

"A wise observation, my child. Jo will do the dirty work. I'm going to do my rounds at the hospital. Tess, I want you to stay with me today and tonight, and then tomorrow you can return to your tent. You can sit, you can walk a little bit—in fact I recommend it—but nothing more strenuous than that."

"I obey." Tess smiled. Aleksi was amazed at how strong she looked. Her face was still rounder than usual, and her skin was pulled taut and shiny on her arms, a little swollen, but the doctor dismissed that as *water retention* and said it would go away in a hand more of days.

Jo came in, and the doctor left. Soon enough, Jo had disengaged Tess from the couch. "Aleksi," Jo said, leading him over to the black screen, "I'm going back to the hospital. You see this pad here. I've coded it specially for you. If you press your right hand over this, it will send a signal to me and to Dr. Hierakis that one of us must return immediately. Only put your hand there if Tess somehow falls ill."

"I understand." He examined the pad with interest. It looked more like a kind of false skin, lacquered, except it looked slick as well. Jo left.

"I want to go outside," said Tess. Aleksi shadowed her, but her legs seemed steady enough. At once he saw where she was headed: to the remains of the funeral pyre that now lay as cold ashes and a few pieces of charred wood fifty paces out from the awning. Nervous, he walked with her, but when she stopped she simply surveyed the circle of ground dispassionately. There were, thank the gods, no bones; either someone had raked the coals or an early baby burned more completely then an adult. All at once Tess bent down and rummaged in the ashes. She held up a scrap of damask linen, smaller than her palm. The singed edges framed a single red rose. She stared at it for a long while and then closed her hand over it and turned away.

"Bakhtiian wept," said Aleksi in a low voice.

Her mouth pinched tight, but she showed no other emotion as they walked back to the doctor's tent. He brought a folding chair out for her and she sat. As soon as she sat down, Anatoly Sakhalin approached to pay his respects. Others filtered by, and eventually Sonia appeared and chased everyone else away.

"You're looking well," Sonia said carefully.

"I'm feeling well. Is there any news from the army?"

"None yet, that I know of. Aleksi, sit down. Tess, I've been giving some thought to Aleksi marrying. Indeed,

I've had my eye on a particular young woman for some time now. Her name is Svetlana Tagansky. She's from one of the Veselov granddaughter tribes, and her husband died in the fighting at Hazjan. She was brought in to wet-nurse Lavrenti while Arina was so weak—Svetlana lost her own infant to a fever—" Sonia broke off. "Oh, Tess." She laid a hand on Tess's arm, but Tess's expression remained blank. Her distraction worried Aleksi. Sonia exchanged a glance with him, but Aleksi could only shrug. Sonia withdrew her hand, looking troubled. "But I need your permission to approach her, Tess."

"Oh." Tess blinked. Aleksi wondered if she had heard a word that Sonia had said. He held his breath, hoping she would agree. "But Aleksi can't marry. He has to have his own tent." The disappointment felt sharp, but he said nothing.

"But men don't own their own tents. I would have thought you'd want him to get married and have a respectable wife."

Tess twisted around and regarded Aleksi. "What do you want, Aleksi?"

"Every man ought to be married," he said slowly, "if he can be."

"Yes, that's what the jaran say, but what do you *want?*"

Aleksi had a sudden feeling that Tess did not want him to get married. He didn't know what to do: tell her the truth and possibly offend her, or placate her with a lie? Like a wave, the memory of his nightmare washed over him. Tess was all he had; of course he must do what she wished. "Of . . . of course I don't care about being married," he stammered. "I'd much rather have my own tent—"

"You're lying," Tess snapped. "I asked you what you wanted, not what you think I want to hear. Do me the favor, Aleksi, of telling me the truth. I don't like this."

The cold edge of her anger shocked him into silence.

"Well?" she demanded.

He wrung his hands together. "I would like to get married," he said under his breath.

"What?"

"I would like to get married to a kind, respectable woman, one I liked."

"That's settled then, Sonia," she said in a curt voice. "Where is Josef? I have work to do."

"Don't you want to meet her first?" Sonia asked, looking affronted. "Know something about her and her family? See if you'll get along?"

"Aleksi will make up his own mind. I don't need to be involved."

"Well!" Sonia rose and shook out her skirts. "I see that this is not the right time to discuss it. If you'll excuse me."

"What's wrong with her?" Tess demanded as Sonia stalked away. Aleksi sighed and resigned himself to an unpleasant day. But at least she had agreed he might marry. That cheered him.

They sat outside for a while longer. Then, abruptly, Tess stood and went back into the doctor's tent. Aleksi followed and found her seated at the table. She spoke three words in Anglais, and a latticework appeared above the tabletop. Tiny symbols spread out along the lattice, interwoven in a maze. With one hand tapping onto a screen and the other tapping impatiently on the smooth tabletop, Tess began to manipulate the symbols. She moved them around at a dizzying rate, muttering under her breath, speaking aloud sometimes in a strange, alien language.

"What are you doing?" Aleksi asked.

She did not even glance up at him. "Trying to figure out how the Chapalii language works. I thought I understood it pretty well, but now I see that I overlooked half of it. More than half, maybe. I hate it when a language doesn't fall into place for me." She pressed her lips together and laid a rainbow of colors over the lattice, shrank segments down and dragged them away to the edges, and began to build a new lattice in the middle. It reminded Aleksi of watching David ben Unbutu direct the building of a siege tower or a siege engine, only her architecture was more insubstantial.

The bells chimed, and Charles Soerensen walked in. He acknowledged Aleksi with a nod and then stood there and watched his sister for the longest time.

She grunted finally, annoyed with something, and looked up at him. "Oh. Hello."

"Cara said you're out of danger."

"I suppose. I feel bloated. And my—" She broke off and crossed her arms over her chest. "Anyway, I've got some ideas here, but I don't have enough information. I'd like to interview—well, just speak with—some female Chapalii. Do you think I never came across any before because they don't move freely outside of Chapalii enclaves, or because my status as your heir made me an honorary male? If you'd treated me as your sister, not as your heir, would I have found access into their side of the culture? Is it even that separate, or is it somehow woven in with the male culture in ways we don't understand? We still often think of the universe as dualistic and forget how simplistic that philosophy is. Especially when we're dealing with what is alien to us."

"Good questions," said Charles. "I can't answer them."

"I should leave Rhui." Tess stared into the floating pattern she had created. "I can't do this here."

A thrill of fear ran through Aleksi. But Tess had promised to take him with her. She meant that, didn't she? He bit down on his tongue to stop himself asking her right here, right now. It wasn't an auspicious time.

"I thought you were going to stay on Rhui and act as the information conduit here, for my saboteur network," said Charles evenly.

"I'm sure you can make other arrangements. And it won't work anyway. Aleksi is going to get married, so he won't have a tent. I don't have anywhere to hide the equipment I'll need."

Charles crossed the chamber and halted behind her, resting his hands on the back of her chair. She stood up at once and moved away from him. "But, Tess, I've been thinking about this. Ursula wants to stay, too. We'll give her one of these large tents, and then there'll be no problem with keeping any such equipment concealed."

Aleksi didn't like the way Tess was standing. Her back had a stubborn, angry line to it. She did not turn to look at her brother. "Ursula! By what right can she stay here? Isn't that meddling a bit far with the interdiction?"

Charles sighed. "Tess. The interdiction is all shot to hell as it is."

Now she spun. Her face was white. "What did you tell Ilya?"

"I told him the truth—"

She flushed red. "You told him the truth! You might as well have stuck the knife in his heart and killed him!"

"I told him the truth," Charles repeated patiently, "in terms by which he could understand it. Tess, don't you understand?" He twisted his head to regard the lattice-work glowing above the table, and he spoke two words. The latticework faded to black and out of black a sphere grew and formed, a blue ball laced with white wisps, like smoke or clouds, and muddy patches. "That is the planet you live on, Aleksi," he said. "We call it Rhui, for no good reason except that it was the name of the first indigenous language any of us learned, who came here."

The ball rotated slowly, floating in nothing. Aleksi reached out toward it. He felt a tingle as his hand neared its bright surface, but where his hand met the field, the field blurred and vanished until he withdrew his hand again.

"Tess," said Charles softly. "I must sacrifice the interdiction in the end for the sake of the rebellion. It may take ten years. It may take one hundred. I don't know whether the choice is right or wrong. I only know that I must do it."

She did not reply. Aleksi watched her profile. Her face was taut, strained, and she looked angry, just so angry, not at Charles really, or at anyone. But maybe it was easier to be angry than to mourn her dead child.

"Tess," Charles added in that same quiet, implacable voice, "I want you to stay here."

She snorted. "You've changed your tune. That wasn't what you came here for in the first place."

Aleksi watched as the prince's lips pulled up into a wry smile. "I didn't get where I am today by refusing to alter my plans when it was necessary to. Even a river changes course from time to time."

"That's all very well, but I don't want to stay anymore. I want to go—" She choked on a word, could not say it.

"Go home?" Charles asked.

"Go back. I want to go back to Earth. Oh, just leave me alone!" Her arms were pressed tight against her chest, and Aleksi saw that her tunic over her right breast was damp. She shifted her arms to hide the spreading stain.

"Let me go get Cara," said the prince, and Aleksi was amazed to see him retreat from the engagement.

"I don't want to see Cara!" Tess shouted after him.

The sphere floating above the table vanished, snapped into oblivion, as soon as the prince lifted the tent flap. Aleksi heard horses, and Soerensen paused half in and half out of the tent, squinting into the sun. "Thank the Goddess," the prince murmured. "The cavalry arrives just in time." He swept out. The entrance flap rang down behind him.

Tess stared into the shadowed corner.

Bells chimed. Looking travel-worn, Bakhtiian came in. "Tess?" He looked so tired that Aleksi was amazed he could stand up. He circled the table and stopped behind Tess. He rested his hands on her shoulders and leaned his head against hers.

"You smell," she muttered.

He turned her around. "You're all wet," he said, sounding mystified, touching a finger to the front of her tunic. Then he said, "Oh," in an altered voice as he realized what it was from.

Tess burst into tears, sobs that wracked her body.

Aleksi judged it prudent to leave.

Outside, the prince waited, listening. "Well," Soerensen said, "she's crying. That ought to help."

"She must mourn the child," said Aleksi, "before she can give it up."

"Very wise," agreed Soerensen.

Very wise, thought Aleksi, a little perplexed by this praise. A sudden image of Anastasia's face rose unbidden in his mind, her sharp brown eyes and narrow face, the stubborn quiver of her chin and the simple generosity of her smile, the sheer brutal strength with which she had driven them on. She was as clear to him across the gulf of years as the day he last saw her, as the day he left her

empty on the grass and went on alone. Gods, he hated the
pain of seeing her. Better not to think of her at all—

Soerensen cocked his head to one side, watching
Aleksi.

But he had to think of her. He had chained her to himself for all these years. It was time to give her up.

Tears rose and he let them run silently down his
cheeks, sure that Tess's brother—who was by some
strange link his own brother—would not judge him for
his grief. And Charles Soerensen ducked his head and
looked up again, and tears ran down his face as well.

"Oh, hell," said Soerensen. "I hate this."

And thus they stood together a while longer, not needing to say anything else.

At last Soerensen broke the silence. "Aleksi, do you
think Tess meant it, about leaving Rhui?"

Aleksi considered the question for a while. The prince
allowed him the silence in which to do so. "No. I don't
think so. That was just her grief talking. They can always
have another child, can't they?"

Soerensen blinked. Aleksi read, briefly, in the prince's
face that an idea had emerged. "Well," said Soerensen,
musing. "I wonder. I think I will go talk to Cara."

Aleksi watched him walk away. He felt—gods!—he
felt at peace with himself in a quiet way. Riders milled
out beyond, but they dissipated quickly, returning to their
own tents, to wash, to eat, to sleep; to prepare for the next
battle. Aleksi strolled aimlessly out through camp, and
soon enough he discovered that his path had taken him to
the Veselov tribe. He hailed a passing child and sent the
girl in to convey his greetings to Mother Veselov. The girl
ran off, returning quickly with Mother Veselov's request
that Aleksi come in to see her.

He found Arina Veselov reclining on pillows in the
outer chamber of her great tent. She was pale still, but
she greeted him with a smile.

"Aleksi Soerensen," she said, nodding as he sat down
before her. "I am pleased to see you. What news of Tess?
Is she well? How is she recovering?" She glanced at her
own little son, who lay on a pillow at her feet, pushing
himself up on his arms and grunting as he tried to crawl.

Aleksi gave her a report, drawing it out. Arina considered it all gravely, as well she might, since she had come close enough to losing her own son, another early child.

"Ah," she said, lifting a hand to interrupt him. "Here is Svetlana. Yes, Lana, Lavrenti is ready for you."

A young woman with pale blonde hair drawn back in four braids ducked inside the tent and knelt to pick up Lavrenti. The child gurgled and flopped down on his face and then pushed up again, scooting toward Svetlana. Aleksi watched her from under lowered lids. She had a bright face and an easy manner, and she paused long enough to examine Aleksi carefully before she scooped up the baby and carried him off outside. He knew he was blushing, but he tried to convince himself that Mother Veselov would not notice.

She coughed into her hand. He glanced up at her in time to see her hide a smile. "Svetlana is an industrious young woman," said Mother Veselov casually, "good with children, and handsome, too, I think. She lost her baby this summer to a fever, but she has another child, a healthy girl of about four winters. She also has a younger brother and sister who came with her when their mother died last year. They're both very strong, and the younger sister is a fine archer already. The brother is good with horses and fights well, although he isn't old enough to ride with the army yet. They don't come from an important family, it's true, but their aunt is a good weaver and they have a cousin who's risen to become a second in the Veselov jahar."

"Oh," said Aleksi, stricken to dumbness. He felt a pang, knowing he could never marry Raysia Grekov; but then he thought of the smile that had played on the lips of Svetlana Tagansky, as she had measured her prospective husband, and he felt that he might endure her company easily enough.

"Go on." Mother Veselov waved him away. "Tell Tess that she must come to me, when she can, since I'm not allowed to walk yet." She sighed, and Aleksi could see the ready sympathy on her face for Tess's loss. "Go on," she repeated. "You've seen what you came to see. May the gods watch over you in the battle tomorrow."

He bowed his head and thanked her for her blessing. Outside, Svetlana Tagansky loitered under the awning. She smiled at him as he passed, and modestly, risking a glance straight at her, he smiled back. She had brilliant blue eyes, as fiercely bright as if fire lit them. A girl of about Kolia's age hung at her skirts, and farther off, two adolescents, a girl and a boy, stood staring at him. Aleksi had a feeling that the sudden addition of a family, so many and so varied, might well help Tess get over her grief. Or at least, it would keep her too busy to dwell on it. Even the prospect of a difficult and perilous battle tomorrow could not ruin his good spirits.

CHAPTER TWENTY-SEVEN

Vasil lay in an agony of pain, some of it physical. He had to stop himself from touching his face again, reading with his fingers the evidence of the wound that had destroyed his beauty. He raised himself on his left arm and tried yet again to get his legs to work, but they did not. He could see them, lumps underneath the blanket, and he could feel them, feel their presence, but he could not get them to move at all. He had only the vaguest memories of the event that had brought him here, to this blanket on the ground under an awning, here at the hospital. He remembered only succumbing to an overwhelming impulse to stop the Habakar king from being rescued: If he, Vasil, could spare Ilya that insult, then surely Ilya would be beholden to him; surely Ilya would turn to him in gratitude.

Dr. Hierakis came down the aisle of wounded toward him, kneeling beside each patient, speaking a few words, examining them. A man two blankets down from Vasil moaned, helpless against the pain assaulting him, and his young sister, who attended him day and night, dabbed a damp cloth on his brow and spoke softly to him. It was all she could do. Others cried only at night, when they thought the rest were sleeping. But really, the men here had it best: They had received some kind of surgery and were expected to recover, and most of them had a relative who helped nurse them until such time as they could be released to their tribe. Vasil suspected that under another awning lay men who simply waited to die. He suspected that he ought to have lain under that other awning, but that other forces, other people, had decreed that he lie here. A young healer had told him that Dr. Hierakis herself had performed the surgery that had saved his life.

Reflexively, Vasil reached up and brushed his fingers along the ragged gash that had laid open his left cheek from his chin almost to his eye. It hurt, and it still oozed.

"Don't touch that, please," said Dr. Hierakis, crouching beside him. "You won't do it any good if you worry it like that."

"Gods," he said harshly, "what does it matter? I'd be better off dead, anyway."

"Possibly," said the doctor curtly, and he flushed at her tone. "You're going to have to find a different way to kill yourself next time, though, since I don't think you're going to be riding any time soon."

He lay back down and stared at the awning. The fabric was, thank the gods, colorful enough, with the light shining through the pattern of squares set within circles set within a frame of squares. She pushed the blanket aside and examined his various wounds; a fine collection—she said so herself, in that dry, sarcastic tone she used. He winced when she touched his shoulder; winced at her hand on his abdomen, but below the hips he felt nothing but the weight of his legs and a steady, numbing ache. At last she shook her head and sat back on her heels.

"What's wrong?" he asked.

She sighed. As was fitting, the men on either side of him had turned their heads away to afford the healer and her patient privacy in these close quarters. "Vasil." She sighed again. The awning rose, filled with air, and bottomed out again. A few squares of sunlight dappled the ground, piercing through the palest colors in the design. "I don't know if you'll ever ride again, or even if you'll walk."

He gazed at her, at her serious expression, and then he realized what she had just said. "What about my face?" he demanded. "Will it ever heal?"

Her eyes widened. "It will heal, in time."

"But I'll always be scarred."

"Yes. It's going to be a bad scar, too. I won't lie to you."

"Gods," he murmured. What had she said? 'You're going to have to find a different way to kill yourself.' He had never done anything as rash in his life as riding out alone into that skirmish. He had always been cautious. But it was true enough that he hadn't cared any more whether he lived or died. But then why had he struggled back toward the jahar? Why had he cared enough to want to live? He should have just given in and let Grandmother Night take him, but every time in his life that Grandmother Night's hands reached out to gather him in, he had fled from her. Maybe Ilya was right. Maybe he didn't love Ilya more than he loved his own life.

"I'd be better off dead," he murmured, but even as he said it, he knew he did not believe his own words.

"You have visitors," said the doctor. "I'll leave you now." She rose and stepped away, and he saw Ilya approaching him down the aisle, flanked by his usual retinue.

Vasil grabbed the edge of the blanket, covering the laceration, and he turned his face to the side so that his right side, the unmarked side, showed.

Bakhtiian's retinue halted some ways down the aisle and dispersed to walk among the wounded. Ilya came on alone. He was pale with exhaustion and with some other overwhelming emotion. His eyes were dark with it, and the mark of marriage on his left cheek glared vividly against his dark skin. And yet, on Ilya, the scar did not mar his beauty; it had simply become part of him. His steps slowed as he caught sight of Vasil, and he halted beside him and knelt.

"Veselov," he said roughly. Stopped. He reached out and took hold of the blanket, to draw it down. Vasil gripped it tighter and pulled away from him. Ilya let go and sat back. "You saved my honor, in the battle," he said in a low voice, in the formal style, "at great cost to yourself. Is there some favor I may show you, to repay you?"

"What I want, you will never give me," said Vasil. Tears burned at his eyes but did not fall. "There is nothing else I want."

"It was bravely done," said Ilya in a whisper, eyes cast down. "You ought to have died."

"I ought to have died many times in the last eleven years. But I never did."

A smile touched Ilya's lips and passed away into noth-

ing. "No, you never did. By such means does Grandmother Night work Her justice."

Vasil shuddered, to hear Her name spoken in daylight,
and he shifted farther away from Ilya. And then realized
that he had done so. "There's nothing more I want from
you," he said finally, hoarsely, "except to see that my
wife and children always have a tribe and a tent of their
own."

Bakhtiian lost even more color. Vasil listened to the
ragged sound of Ilya's breathing while he controlled himself; at last he spoke. "Tess lost the child. We burned it,
five days past."

Vasil felt the comment like a wound to his heart. All
that pain in Ilya, and it was for the dead child, not for
him. At that moment, he hated Ilya, hated him fiercely
and without forgiveness. He had a sudden memory of the
day when he had stood beside the couch where Ilya lay,
his body empty and his soul taken up to the gods' lands,
and Dr. Hierakis had read him words and he had spoken
them back to her. " 'How would you be,' " he murmured,
recalling the lines, " 'if She, which is the top of judgment, should but judge you as you are?' "

Ilya's gaze jumped to Vasil's face. The fire that lit
Bakhtiian's eyes now was fueled by grief and helpless
fury, and Vasil felt a sudden, surprising pity for the khaja
who were sure to bear the brunt of Bakhtiian's anger at
the gods for taking from him the child he so desired.

But when Ilya spoke, his words only bewildered Vasil.
"If you only knew," he said softly, voice rough with pain,
"you would be glad to be rid of me."

"You will never understand me," whispered Vasil. He
closed his free hand into a fist and held the blanket taut,
concealing his face, with the other. "I want no favor from
you. Be assured that I will not bother you again. Good-
bye."

He gained some satisfaction from the hurt that passed
over Ilya's face and was as quickly controlled. Bakhtiian
rose and left him. Vasil forced himself not to watch him
go, not to follow his exit, and so he was startled when another man cleared his throat beside him and knelt, and addressed him.

"Veselov. I just heard you were badly injured. I'm so sorry." Owen Zerentous sat there, looking concerned and intent, regarding Vasil with that keen eye of his. "Dr. Hierakis tallied up your injuries for me. They're an impressive lot, and some of them are quite serious."

"Your concern honors me," muttered Vasil, mystified by Zerentous's presence.

"You can't ride again, can you?"

"The doctor says not."

Then they sat for a while. Squares of light shifted on the wounded soldiers as the wind moved the awning up and down. A boy walked down the aisles, seeking his brother; a wife knelt beside her husband and farther away, a husband wept beside his injured wife. Vasil smelled like a faint perfume the bitter scent of *ulyan,* the herb the jaran burned with the dead. Zerentous regarded the air. The director sat perfectly still, except for his right hand, which twisted at intervals in the cup made by his left hand.

"I have this idea," said Zerentous finally, and lapsed back into silence. From watching rehearsals, Vasil had learned that Zerentous often worked this way; that he thought aloud, not in words but in the way he projected the fact that he was ruminating over some idea of great moment. The actors simply waited him out, having long since learned patience. Vasil, of course, had nothing better to do. "I approached the prince, and he seemed to think we could work something out. But it makes a perfect coda to the experiment we've conducted this past year, don't you think?"

"I don't know," said Vasil, curious now in spite of his pain.

"Well, wouldn't you like to be an actor?" Zerentous demanded. "At least to try?"

The emotion that hit and swelled over Vasil was worse than the physical pain he endured, worse than the agony he had brought on himself by repudiating Ilya once and for all: It was hope. "An actor!"

"Oh, it won't be easy. You've some instinctive talents, but there'd be much much work to be done, training, practice, endless rehearsals, and even with the Company to support you, you're far behind them in skills right now. Still, to have brought our theater here and then to bring one of you back, to see how you might reflect our tradition back at us, how you might interpret it, that would be fascinating!"

"But—I'd have to leave the jaran."

"We'd be your tribe. We theater people always have been a tribe unto ourselves."

"But my family—?"

"Can't they come? Are they fixed here?"

Vasil winced as a pain stabbed up from his hips and splintered into a thousand pieces all the way up his backbone. "No," he said, gasping a little. "No, not at all. They live only on the sufferance granted them by my cousin. My wife long ago left her tribe, and my children only have her. But could they—?"

"Oh, they could come too," said Zerentous blithely. "We'll fix some kind of pension on them. You needn't worry about leaving them behind. What do you say?" Zerentous was clearly in the grip of his obsession now. His dark face shone.

"But the doctor says I can't walk."

Zerentous coughed into his hand and glanced around, the gesture so acting-like that Vasil almost smiled. He bent down closer to Vasil. "We're going back to our country," he said in a low, conspiratorial voice. "To Erthe. There, you'll find that . . . we can do things there . . . it won't matter. Truly. It won't."

Vasil felt sick with hope and despair intermingled. He felt as if the gods themselves had conspired to offer him his heart's desire and yet make it impossible for him to grasp it. Like Ilya, who had never really been his, because the gods had already marked him as theirs.

"I can't be an actor," he said finally.

"Why not?" Zerentous demanded, looking affronted.

Vasil took in a deep breath, for courage, and pulled the blanket down and turned his lacerated face to the air.

"Well?" demanded Zerentous again. The director's gaze had flicked onto the gash and then returned to stare into Vasil's eyes. The force of his gaze was immense, like a weight bearing down on Vasil. "Why not?"

"But . . ." Vasil faltered. "My face."

"Oh." Zerentous dismissed the terrible disfigurement with a wave of one hand. "I said it won't matter. We have arts of healing—we can erase it. You must believe me. More than that I can't say now. Veselov, what I'm offering you will be safe for you and your family. What's left you here—if you're crippled—I can't guess. Stay here if you will. Or come with me and the Company. The choice is yours."

There was, in Owen Zerentous, a certainty that Vasil found attractive. He was so sure of himself and of his vision.

"Yes," Vasil said before he realized himself that he meant to say it. "I'll go with you."

CHAPTER TWENTY-EIGHT

Before dawn, many partings.

Diana had stayed up half the night, helping Anatoly and two boys from the Sakhalin camp polish his armor. She had persuaded him to come to bed at last, but she slept far more restlessly than he did, and she woke before him, before dawn. A kind of bitter fatalism had descended on her, and she lay curled around him and watched him breathe. Today they launched the final assault on Karkand. Everyone expected the fighting to be prolonged and bloody, and Diana knew that Anatoly meant to throw himself and his men into the thick of it. She had a horrible premonition that he was going to die.

He was a heavy sleeper. When she ran a hand down his arm he did not stir. From outside, she heard horses and conversation and the creak of leather armor. He opened his eyes and sat up.

"Diana!" He started to scramble to his feet, then flung an arm around her and kissed her warmly. He murmured something, sweet phrases, and then jumped up and dressed. She hurried and dressed and followed him outside. Already, the same two boys had arrived, waiting for the honor of helping him into his armor. Diana wanted to help, but it was a privilege reserved for the adolescent boys and she knew better than to interfere. She held on to his helmet instead, running her fingers through the black plume that ornamented its peak while she watched the boys tie Anatoly into his armor and check for the fourth time all the iron and lacquered-leather strips that made up the body of his armor. For her was reserved the honor of belting on his saber. She did so gravely, and handed him his helmet. He put it on. A boy brought his horse, and Anatoly mounted. The other boy gave him his spear and, last, one of Bakhtiian's officers rode up and handed to Anatoly his staff of command.

Anatoly smiled down at Diana. He looked utterly confident. He looked magnificent, with his fair hair and his gleaming, plumed helmet, his polished armor and bright silk surcoat. He reined his horse aside and rode away, leaving her there. She watched him go. A horrible weight pressed against her chest, like a stone caught in her heart. She was convinced that she would never see him alive again. A bleak agony settled onto her, and she felt that every emotion except dread had been washed away with the first light of morning.

The boys had already excused themselves and run away to other duties. In such a camp, on such a day as this, no one had patience for idle hands. Diana went back into her tent. Shrugging on her old khaki tunic, she set out for the hospital. In the distance, she heard the steady thudding of the siege engines, hurling stones and flaming arrows into Karkand.

* * *

Ursula greeted David with a cheerful wave as he passed her on his way to Cara's tent. She had risen so far in Bakhtiian's estimation that she now had her own little entourage, including an adolescent boy and girl who helped her arm herself in her lamellar cuirass. David himself had deigned to borrow a heavy felt coat and a khaja helmet for the day's work. He tossed the helmet on the carpet under the awning of Cara's tent and went inside. In the inner chamber, he stopped short. Bright lights shone over the counter, and a transparent wall had been rolled down behind Cara and Jo where they bent over the counter, separating them from the rest of the room. He caught a glimpse of something tiny and pale, under their hands, and all at once he felt bile in his throat and he knew he was going to throw up.

"Out," said Cara without turning around. He retreated into the outer chamber and sat down heavily in a chair, panting. "What do you want?" she demanded from the other room, her voice penetrating the distance easily.

"I thought they burned it." He barely managed to choke out the words. "Cara, how *could* you?"

But even as he said it, he knew how and why she could, why she had to. As an engineer, he understood the necessity for finding out why a structure had failed.

"But that doesn't mean I have to like it," he added and felt nauseated again, seeing the tiny perfect fingernails on a minuscule hand.

Cara emerged from the back. She examined him but did not, mercifully, attempt to touch him. "I know," she said softly, "but it was too valuable simply to cast away."

"How did you manage the switch—? Never mind. I don't want to know. Does Tess know?"

"Of course not! And if you tell her, David, I'll flay you alive." Neither spoke for a moment. Cara suddenly wiped roughly at her cheeks with the back of a hand. "Dammit," she said, her voice thick. "You know how much it hurts, David. I just can't afford to cry. Not for the baby, not for any of them—all of them, every one I lose and all the ones I can't save."

"Oh, Cara," he said, and got up and hugged her. "I'll never tell."

Cara wept efficiently. She allowed herself three minutes and then she marshaled her forces, wiped her eyes, and washed her hands. "Where are you off to, in that coat?"

"I'm going down to the line. Tess wants Rajiv. Do you know where he is?"

"He went over to the actors last night," called Jo from the inner chamber, sounding repulsively jovial considering what it was she was doing. "I think he's having an affair with one of them. Here, Cara, that will do it. I think we've got everything that we can do now. I'll take it from here."

"Good," said Cara. "Go ahead and freeze it and pack it for Jeds." David shuddered. "What does Tess want Rajiv for?"

"Rajiv promised to help her; they're going to work on setting up the information network, the initial matrix. I guess Tess needs something to keep her busy today. Not that I blame her."

Cara dried her hands on a towel. She rummaged in her chest and pulled out a tunic, stripped off the one she was wearing, and changed into the other one. "So she is staying on Rhui? Charles was worried that she might change her mind."

"After all the trouble he went to, intending to convince her to return to Earth?"

"She's more use to him here."

David grunted. "No doubt. What's he waiting for, Cara?"

"Who, Charles? I don't know what you mean."

"What's he up to? I think he's plotting something."

"Charles is always plotting something."

"Yes, but something else is going on, something beyond the saboteur network. Something to do with Rhui."

"Ask him, David. If you'll excuse me, I'm off to the hospital. Where we'll doubtless be quite busy very very soon." But, as if to take the sting from her words, she rested a hand on his shoulder before she left.

David followed her out. Ursula had already gone, but out beyond the tent waited David's own little entourage, assigned to him for the duration of the battle: ten archers, ten riders, two of the khaja engineers, and two boys to act as messengers. He sighed. He didn't want to go down to the city, but he felt obliged to. He had helped create the mines; he had helped design and build the engines and towers; he felt the responsibility not so much to Bakhtiian, but to the conscripted laborers whose sweat had built these siegeworks and who might well pay with their lives today. Maybe, if they performed well, he could argue to Bakhtiian that they deserved some kind of legal position within the army or at least to retain some of their old status as Habakar citizens. If he could couch it in the right terms, perhaps he could persuade Bakhtiian that it was to his advantage to make them feel as if they were part of the jaran army rather than just subject to it.

He mounted his horse and rode with his escort in the faint light heralding dawn out through camp, through the distant outer walls that ringed the suburbs of Karkand, down along colonnaded avenues toward the besieged inner city.

* * *

"Ummm," said Nadine low in her throat, rolling her husband over in the blankets.

"Dina!" Feodor murmured. "Stop that!" All the while doing nothing whatsoever to halt her actions, and a few things that encouraged them.

There was silence for some time, broken only by the sound of their breathing and the occasional muttered comment, and the increasing noise of activity outside as the camp woke and prepared for battle.

Nadine sighed and sat back finally, running a hand through his tangled hair and combing it through her fingers. "I like you much better like this," she said.

He cast a sudden, angry glance at her and sat up to let her braid his hair back. She bound the braids with blue ribbons embroidered with gold thread and brought him three gold necklaces and a polished and embossed belt of god plates to wear over his red shirt. She even tied the gold tassels onto his boots.

"That's better." She regarded him with a sardonic lift to her mouth. "Now you look fit to be my husband."

He flushed. "Like a prize you won looting some city?" he demanded. "You don't need to throw it in my face every day, Dina. I know you didn't want to marry me."

She shrugged on her own shirt, belted it with a plain leather belt, and tugged on her boots. "I have to go. I'm to meet my uncle at the main gates. Aren't you riding out with your uncle today?"

When he did not reply, she looked up at him in surprise. He was staring at the carpet, cheeks stained red.

"What's wrong, Feodor?"

He flung his head back, glaring at her defiantly. "You'll find out anyway. Someone will tell you. My uncle is leaving me behind with the contingent that's left to guard camp."

"Ah," said Nadine. "He doesn't want to risk losing his new status in the army."

"I had nothing to do with it! I didn't ask to be left behind!"

"Gods, Feodor, I know you're not afraid of battle. You have scars enough to prove you're not. But your uncle is still being cautious. You're not a prize for me; you're a prize for the Grekov tribe, and they'll do everything in their power to keep you intact."

"You have no right to insult me or my family, Dina." He was so angry that his voice shook.

She smiled. "I can do what I like. Now, if you'll excuse me."

But when she brushed past him to go outside, he grabbed her arm. "No. You'll apologize. My uncle has proved his worth to Bakhtiian."

"What? Are you going to tell me that your uncle and aunt didn't encourage you to mark me? That they didn't goad you into it? How else could they have achieved such advantage in the tribes?" His hand clenched so hard on her arm that it hurt, but she refused to submit herself to the indignity of trying to break free from his grasp.

"Maybe no other man wanted you."

"I've had as many lovers as any other woman," she retorted, stung by his words.

"Wanting a woman as a lover is not the same as wanting her as a wife. Even with everything a man would gain from marrying you, I don't think any man but me wanted to marry you."

Now she did twist out of his grasp, wrenching herself away. "Have you finished insulting me? May I go now, Husband?"

"Go and get yourself killed! It makes no difference to me!"

"Why should it? In a few more years Galina will be ready to marry, and if you're quick enough, you can replace me with her!"

She stormed out of the tent and found herself faced with a little audience: Vasha Kireyevsky and Katya and Galina Orzhekov, busy helping Bakhtiian into his armor. All four of them glanced her way and then away, pretending that they hadn't heard a thing. She set her mouth and ignored them, calling over two of the Danov grand-

children to help her into her armor. Soon enough, Feodor
emerged from the tent. He was pale now, and he flushed
immediately, knowing as well as Nadine had that their argument must have carried well outside her tent.

With his eyes lowered, he came up to her. "I brought
your saber," he murmured. He dropped his voice even
further, and motioned with one hand, and the two boys
helping her sidled away. "I'm sorry. I didn't mean it. Let
me tie on your saber for you."

Seeing him thus, looking so mild, Nadine felt a sudden
rush of affection for him. "I'm sorry, Feodor. I'm sorry
that your uncle is being so stupid. I can talk to Ilya—"

His gaze lifted at once to her face. "No! Don't you humiliate me, too."

"I didn't mean to humiliate you! I just—"

"Oh, Grekov," said Bakhtiian casually from ten strides
away. He shrugged his shoulders up and down twice to
settle his armor into place, then leaned down and whispered something into Katerina's ear. She nodded and ran
off. Vasha circled Bakhtiian, eyeing the overlaid strips of
the armor for any that might have caught or stuck together. Galina brought him his helmet. "Mitya will be riding out with me today, and I need a trusted captain to
carry the Habakar prince's banner behind him, to remind
our army and the khaja army in Karkand that Mitya is
now the heir to this country. I have sent Katya to tell your
uncle that I need you for this honor."

Nadine flushed. She felt humiliated by her uncle's gesture, but when she looked at Feodor, she was appalled to
find him smiling, appeased by Bakhtiian's attention.

"Of course," he said brightly and turned away from her
to get his armor.

"Dina," said her uncle gently, "your jahar is waiting
for you."

She glared at him but had no choice but to go. What
right had he to interfere with her and her husband? Every
right, of course, since he needed an heir. She mounted
and received her staff of command and surveyed her
troops, all of them ready to ride. Smoke curled up in the
western sky as the sun breached the horizon. All around,
horses shifted and harness creaked and bells jingled, and

riders spoke to each other in low tones, waiting for the call to battle.

* * *

Tess felt wrung into nothing, that morning when she woke. Yesterday she had sobbed for what seemed like hours, and all that while Ilya had held her against him; soon enough she had realized that she was holding him up as much as he was holding her. In him, she had felt that same helpless, furious grief; he was the only other person who understood, who could ever understand, the terrible sick emptiness left in her by the death of their son. After a while she had felt, not better, but resigned to the long bitter agony of mourning.

He had left her for a time, to go visit the wounded. She had returned to her own tent, to find her healing there, because she knew she was better quit of Cara's tent now. And when he returned from his tour of the hospital that night, he had come to her and sat before her, and he had said, "Tess, there is something I must tell you. I must tell you of my bargain with Grandmother Night."

Now, lying awake at dawn, listening as he moved about in the outer chamber, she thought of the lantern light on him as he spoke softly but clearly, telling her the tale. It had the ring of an ancient tale told by a Singer, and the cadences of his voice lent it a rarified quality so that at the end she felt freed of an old weight rather than burdened by a new one. Like any confession, it had cleansed him, and, thank God, he had slept soundly afterward.

She heard him go outside. She stretched, feeling stiff, and then got to her feet and dressed slowly, aching all over but otherwise feeling strong. Her wrists looked suddenly small to her. She ran her hands down her ankles and found them back to their normal size as well. Her abdomen still hung in folds, and her breasts hurt, heavy with milk that no child needed, but that would pass, in time.

She sighed, heartfelt, wiped a tear from her cheek, and went outside. Ilya stood there, glorious in his armor. Tess paused outside the entrance flap just to gaze on him. He was looking toward Nadine's tent, where Feodor Grekov was being helped into his armor by two of the Danov grandchildren. Behind Ilya, in the distance, his jahar waited, pennants flapping in the dawn breeze, armor gleaming; his golden banner shifted and curled in the wind.

"Hello," said Vasha shyly and came to kiss her on either cheek, still formal with her as he was with everyone except perhaps Katya.

Ilya turned and smiled, seeing her, and Tess felt tears come to her eyes, because she loved him so much.

"Tess," he said, and came to her and took her hands and bent to kiss her. "My heart." He never needed to say more than that. That he loved her was written everywhere on him, in his expression, in the line of his body as he leaned toward her, in his voice.

"I brought you your saber," she said. She belted it on him. It seemed to her a moment's insanity, that scene with Charles when she had told him she wanted to leave Rhui; but then, perhaps it had been. Grief seen clearly can be overcome, though never forgotten; it was only when denying it that it distorted your vision.

"Tess," he said in a low voice, "do you forgive me?"

"Forgive you for what?" she asked, bewildered.

He cast his eyes down, looking incongruously humble. "For the sacrifice. For my arrogance in believing that I could cheat Grandmother Night. For what I did to my family, and our son."

What had he done, truly, but try to bring his dreams to life and, against all his expectations, succeed? What had he done that was different than what Charles had done, risking his own family and losing it? Losing the child had been a simple cast of fate, falling on the wrong side, but she could not possibly explain that to him. What could she explain? "Of course, I forgive you, Ilya. But it's not my forgiveness you need; it's the etsanas and the Elders who must judge you for that."

He frowned and looked directly at her. "That is true enough," he said softly, "but without your forgiveness, Tess, the rest is worth nothing to me."

She swallowed past the lump in her throat and laid one

hand on his chest, feeling the hard ridges of armor under the silky smoothness of his red surcoat. "Can you forgive me the lie, about Jeds?" she asked in a low voice. Yet even as she said it, she knew she had not done lying to him, and never would be done.

He looked startled. "Of course, I forgive you. You remained loyal to your brother, where your duty lay. Who am I to judge who ought to rule in khaja lands?"

Tess had to laugh. "Who are you to judge, Ilya, except perhaps to judge yourself the only fit ruler?"

"You're laughing at me. Tess." He just looked at her for a long while. Then he spun and walked out to his horse. Mitya waited, resplendent in a gold and blue surcoat that reflected half Ilya's banner and half the blue lion of the dead prince. Feodor rode behind Mitya, the banner pole fixed against his saddle. Vladimir held Ilya's gold banner, and Konstans Barshai—with his white-plumed helmet—and Kirill Zvertkov—with his bad arm awkward at his side—flanked Bakhtiian.

Ilya mounted and twisted in the saddle to salute Tess with his horse-tail staff. As one, the jahar started forward. Under a forest of spears they rode out, silk and iron, and leather lacquered until it gleamed, fluttering pennants and rank upon rank of sabers. Nadine rode past with her jahar, proud and confident of victory. A column of archers followed behind them, and then Anatoly Sakhalin's jahar, riders and archers together, brilliant in the dawn.

Quiet descended on the camp.

"Where is Aleksi?" asked Sonia, coming up beside Tess and taking hold of her hand.

Tess leaned into Sonia, letting Sonia's warmth and strength be her comfort. "I sent him out to escort Charles along the lines. It's beautiful to watch them go, isn't it? Yet what they'll bring will be terrible."

They stood for a time in silence. Their years together had brought them that as much as anything: the ability to find peace in each other, and the contentment of a friend who judged you solely on yourself, and nothing more, and nothing less.

"Well," said Sonia at last, "there's much to do. I

brought Svetlana Tagansky to visit, but now Aleksi is gone."

"Sonia. I'm sorry I snapped at you yesterday."

"Oh, Tess. I understand."

Tess smiled and brushed away a tear. "I know you do. Ilya and I started to make our peace with him, the little one—" She thought of him as Yuri, but she never dared say it aloud; a child born dead was never given a name, among the jaran, but it comforted Tess to know he had one, if only in her own heart. It consoled her to give the baby that link to the other Yuri, whom she had also lost. "Well. Let me meet Svetlana. Oh, look, here is Rajiv." Rajiv came up then, with Maggie and Gwyn Jones in tow. "Sonia, I'll come to your tent soon."

Sonia greeted the others, excused herself, and left.

Tess turned to the newcomers. "Hello, Rajiv. Maggie." She paused and regarded Gwyn Jones dubiously.

"He's clear," said Rajiv. "He knows what we're doing. He had a few clever ideas, too. I thought we'd bring him in at the first iteration."

"You have some ideas?" Tess asked. "I don't mean to be—"

"Skeptical?" Jones grinned. "But I *am* just an actor? No, it's all right. I was in prison before I studied acting, and—well, let's just say I've learned a few things that might be of use. Consider me a recruit for the cause."

"Rajiv, do you have the modeler with you?" Tess asked. Rajiv nodded. "Then go on in, but you'll have to use the inner chamber. If you can rig a perimeter alert and track it for—well, you'll know what to do. I've one more duty to perform, and then I'll come in." Thus dismissed, they disappeared inside the tent.

The camp was empty of soldiers now except for a single circle of guards around the Orzhekov encampment and a series of guards and scouts around the main camp itself, stretching out into the countryside so that no force might come upon camp or army unaware.

Under the awning of Sonia's tent stood a young woman, a child, and two adolescents, one girl, one boy. The young woman chatted easily with Josef Raevsky, seeming unembarrassed by his disfigurement, and Tess liked her for that at once. The dawn wind stilled. A thin streak of clouds paled the western horizon, but Tess could not be sure yet if they were true clouds, or smoke. Faintly, far off, she heard the steady thunk of the artillery, firing on Karkand.

Tess rubbed her arms across her breasts, they ached so badly, and then regretted it immediately, because it made the milk let down. She swore under her breath and just stood there for a while, pressing hard against the nipples with her forearms. Tears brimmed in her eyes and spilled down. The leakage stopped quickly; already it had diminished, and soon it would dry up altogether.

"Oh, God," she said on a long sigh, wiping her face yet again. She gathered together her self-possession and went to meet the woman whom Sonia had chosen for Aleksi to marry.

* * *

Aleksi passed by the Veselov jahar riding out, Anton Veselov in the lead, his cousin Vera leading the archers at the back. Ambassador's row was quiet as its tenants waited for the outcome of the battle. In the Company encampment, no one stirred, although he saw the woman, the *playwright,* sitting under the awning of her tent, writing furiously. She did not even look up as he rode past and crossed a trampled margin and came into the encampment belonging to the Prince of Jeds.

Charles Soerensen waited for him, outfitted this day in a light cuirass of leather, with a smooth round khaja helmet strapped onto his head. Marco Burckhardt stood beside him, wearing a felt coat instead of a cuirass. Seeing Aleksi, they mounted the fine Arabian mares that Bakhtiian had given them.

"You'll escort us to Bakhtiian?" Charles asked.

Aleksi nodded. "But we'll have to hurry if we want to catch up with him"

"Hold on," said Marco curtly. He blinked three times and tilted his head. "Incoming," he said at the same time as Soerensen abruptly dismounted and threw the reins to Marco before darting inside his tent.

Ten heartbeats later he stuck his head out. "Aleksi. I need you."

Like Bakhtiian, Soerensen did not give orders unless he meant them to be obeyed instantly. Aleksi gave his horse over to Marco and, with only the briefest hesitation at the threshold, went into the prince's tent.

A woman he had never seen before sat at the table. She had black hair and pale brown skin set off by the shimmering blue shirt she wore: Aleksi stopped and gaped. She had no body below the waist. She only *seemed* to be sitting at the table. The prince stood bent over the table, marking words on a piece of paper.

"Repeat that charge for me," he said.

The woman spoke, and Aleksi realized all at once that she was not *there* any more than the lantern illuminating Dr. Hierakis's tent was there. She was an illusion. She did not exist. Yet the prince acted as though she did. "The Protocol Office has detained Hon Echido and other representatives from the Keinaba house for breaking the interdiction of Rhui on four charges: the lesser charges of trespass and of impersonating Rhuian natives and the greater charges of taking with them a female and the actual act of violating the Interdiction order of their own overlord."

"Where the hell—?" muttered the prince. "And who instigated this, do you have any idea?"

The woman moved her eyes and to Aleksi's horror he realized that she was *looking at him.* "Who is this?" she asked.

It was like being under the scrutiny of the gods. Maybe she *was* one of the gods, manifesting from the heavens to oversee her children on the earth.

"That," said the prince, not looking up, "is Tess's brother Aleksi."

"Oh," said the woman. "Hello, Aleksi. I'm Suzanne. Pleased to meet you." Then she grinned, betraying her humanity. Aleksi did not think that gods introduced themselves.

"Well met," he said reflexively, and was rewarded by a second smile before her attention moved back to the prince.

"The Protocol Office can, of course, act on the emperor's behest or even its own behest, but in this case it seems to have been the officers stationed on Earth who moved against Keinaba, in which case—"

"In which case," interrupted Soerensen, "it was Naroshi who put them up to it."

The woman shrugged. "He did say he would keep an eye on you."

The prince smiled suddenly, an ironic quirk of the lips. "So I can't say that he didn't warn me? This is all very well, but I'm going to have to come back now."

"Yes," Suzanne agreed, looking quite serious. "You must. You're the only one who can extricate them."

"And the information Echido alone holds, not to mention that ke, is far, far too valuable to fall into Naroshi's hands, since we don't know how much he knows, or how much he learned when his agents were at Morava, or whether they even got hold of a cylinder like Tess did. Suzanne, think of the consequences!"

"I'm thinking," she said gravely.

"This could destroy everything we've started to build, Aleksi." He straightened up. He looked, to Aleksi, somehow brighter and more vital than he had before this strange communication, as if the challenge animated him. As if this sort of challenge was what he lived for. "I have two notes here, one for Cara and one for Tess. Find a courier, someone trustworthy, to take the messages to them— there should still be actors in the Company camp, if need be. I'll need you back *at once,* because we have to leave now. Suzanne, how will you pick me up?"

"Already arranged from this end," said Suzanne briskly. "The question is how *you* can make the rendezvous."

The prince looked again at Aleksi, and Aleksi hurriedly retreated outside.

"Well?" demanded Marco.

Aleksi hesitated. "Suzanne. Is she one of your kind? From the heavens?"

Marco raised an eyebrow. "Suzanne called? Goddess, it must be urgent."

Aleksi ran over to the Company camp. There he found

the playwright. She was so engrossed in her work that she did not even look up when he stopped beside her.

"I beg your pardon," he said.

She glanced up. "Oh. Hello. Aleksi, isn't it?"

"I beg your pardon," he repeated, "but the prince has asked that I give these messages to you to send on to his sister and to the doctor. He's leaving."

"He's *leaving?*" asked the playwright. "Oh, my." Aleksi was afraid she would ask him to explain, but she merely took the notes and marched off in the direction of her tent. He jogged back to Soerensen's tent to find that the prince had already mounted and was waiting for him.

"Now," said Soerensen before Aleksi had settled into the saddle, "we must ride at first toward the battle, as if we're headed in, so people will think that's where we've gone. But then we have to somehow leave without being seen and make our way out to these coordinates—we'll be headed north-northeast, into the near hills, to meet the shuttle."

"What is a *shuttle?*" asked Aleksi.

"It's a kind of a ship. Can you manage it?"

"Yes," said Aleksi. "I can manage it. But why must we go so secretly?"

Soerensen looked out at the camp. "Damn it," he said to no one in particular. "But it has to be done."

"What has to be done?" asked Marco mildly.

Soerensen urged his horse forward, and Aleksi and Marco came up on either side of him. "Today, the Prince of Jeds has to die."

CHAPTER TWENTY-NINE

Dawn came. David watched as the siege engines fired, and fired again. Clay pots filled with naphtha were launched into the city, and smoke began to rise up from within the walls into the heavens. He wiped sweat from his brow and helped a limping man back away from the engine, and sent another to take his place.

The rumble of the towers rolling into place reached his ears, and the higher sound of metal on metal, the clash of arms. He had no good view of the walls. He did not want one. Already wounded men—khaja laborers all—struggled back from the front lines, those that could. David knew well enough that others lay alive but wounded under the killing rain of arrows, helpless to get themselves free. If they were lucky, once the battle moved beyond the walls, they could be rescued. Cara had laid down the law firmly enough for Bakhtiian: All persons in the jaran army received care or none did. David wondered what would happen when Cara got hold of the first wounded enemy soldiers, assuming that any lived long enough to get so far.

Suddenly, a man shouted a warning and two riders escorting David shoved him down. There was a crash. Splinters flew through the air. A man screamed out in pain. Debris peppered David's helmet, and dust coated his vision.

He scrambled up and ran forward. A lucky hit for the Karkand engineers: They had hit a siege engine far enough back from the lines that no one had thought it within range. Four men lay tangled in the wreckage, bleeding, moaning; one was silent and twisted at a horrific angle.

David coughed through the dust. "I need men to carry these wounded out!" Laborers had scattered back from the hit, terrified. Now, heartened by his presence, they hurried forward to aid him. David tested the mechanism, but it had been thoroughly smashed.

"We'll give this one up," he shouted. "Here, move that one back ten paces, and I want screens over the men there."

Riders and khaja laborers ran to do his bidding. He had a sudden flash, watching them work together, that this was why he had come out here today to help kill poor innocents on the other side of the wall: so that in time, all of them could learn to work together. It was a poor excuse for a rationalization, but it helped him live with himself.

The other engines fired on with renewed vigor. David took himself back and sat down to try and figure out the trajectory of the rock, to see if they could target the enemy's artillery.

* * *

Ursula el Kawakami braced herself as the tower shuddered forward toward the wall. Inside, it was dark and stuffy; she felt the others pressed around her, about half of them Farisa auxiliaries and half jaran riders—unmounted now, of course—who had volunteered for the first assault, mostly young men from granddaughter tribes and servant families, hoping to win a name for themselves and a greater share of the loot. From outside, she heard the steady hammering of arrows against the wooden tower and she smelled burning pitch: They were trying to set the tower on fire, but it was covered with leather soaked in water and a lotion called *firebane*, and she doubted it would catch.

What did it matter, anyway? For all of her life, Ursula had wanted nothing more than to fight in battle. Not for her the martial arts craze that had swept through League space, offering aggressive young men and women an outlet. War was an ugly, primitive business, and an unacceptable means for resolving conflict. Everyone knew that.

Ursula supposed it might even be true, but she hadn't cared. From childhood on she had closeted herself in the net and immersed herself in accounts of Salamanca and Crecy, Cannae and Tyre, the bloody trenches of Verdun and the battle of the Pelennor Fields.

A thud shook the tower, slamming her into the side. She tucked and took the impact on her shoulder, and her armor absorbed much of it. The men were really packed too close here to fall down. Above her, she heard the sing of arrows from the covered platform at the top of the tower: the archers, spraying fire down onto the wall. From below, she heard shrieks and cries from the men rolling the great tower forward as stones rained down on them from the walls. Still, the tower advanced.

With a jolt, the wheels met the base of the wall. At once, Ursula sprang into action. She shouted and two auxiliaries cranked out the door, and as if by magic the plank reached and reached—not quite there—and then slapped down onto the parapet of the great wall of Karkand, making a bridge. Early morning light streamed in on them.

With two men on either side of her, Ursula led the charge. She howled. They took up her call and ran, to hit the Habakar defenders before they could foray out onto the bridge. The wood jounced under her feet, and she felt men behind, pounding after them. Arrows showered over them, toward the wall, and a spray of arrows peppered them from the defenders, but their armor was strong. And Ursula had drilled these units, in any case, in the use of shields and swords and spears in close formation.

Three Habakar soldiers scrambled up onto the bridge, but Ursula and the jaran man next to her hit them hard and simply shoved them back. They fell over the side, falling hard on the ramp. Men scattered away from them. Ursula jumped down, landing hard, and set about herself with her sword. She hacked through the first rank, pushing them back. Shields rose in front of her and she shoved and pounded at them, cut at faces and arms and exposed chests. An arrow stuck in her shield; another stuck in the armor covering her right thigh, and then the arrow fire ceased to bother her.

A spear thrust. She flinched away and felt the spear impact her companion. He fell, screaming, and she shouted: "Close up ranks! Close up!" And stepped over the fallen man and kept pressing forward. Another shieldman came forward next to her, and a man on the other side, and they took step by slow step forward, pushing, catching blows and turning them aside, striking—there!—and a man crumpled before them. She took a great stride, to get over his body, and moved forward.

Behind, she heard shouts. "Move up! There! Fire a volley!" Swords battered on shields. Men yelled. Feet thudded on the stone ramparts, and smoke and dust rose from the city, clinging to the walls and throwing the acrid scent of burning into her face. A roar of sound swelled up from the city itself, the blare of trumpets, the ringing of bells, the bellowing of pack animals, the neighing of horses, shouts and sobs and the clatter of wagons and troops of horsemen all soaring on the wind and blending with the din of battle.

Distantly, she heard: "They're coming up the other side. Krukov is falling back!" But the enemy line before her wavered and she pressed forward.

"Fall back! Fall back!" The words came closer here, just behind her.

She risked a glance behind. By the bridge, fighting swirled and, on the bridge itself, men stood still, staring, stuck out there while arrow fire blurred over them, shattered into them. The archers atop the platform fired in sheets, but it wasn't enough.

"Open up that bridge!" she shouted, but they could not hear her. "Close ranks!" she cried, and stepped back, letting another man come forward in her place as she pushed back through her own line.

Beyond, on the other side of the bridge, Habakar soldiers in blue and white shoved steadily into the jaran incursion, pushing them back. Ursula felt a cold rage descend on her. How dare they ruin her perfect tactics? A rush onto the parapet, down the ramps, and open the great gates; like Godfrey at Jerusalem, letting the Crusader hordes in to sack the city.

"Move forward! Let those men down! Advance, you

fools!" What was it von Clausewitz said? 'There is nothing in War which is of greater importance than obedience.' "Advance!"

A spear thrust. She ducked instinctively away from it, and it took her two entire heartbeats to register the point that penetrated her back. The Habakar had broken through behind. She staggered. Another blow hit her hard, and she spun full into their charge across the scattered bodies of her own men.

Pain blossomed, hazing the world to white. In one instant, she realized an arrow had pierced her cheek. In the next—

* * *

When the men battling their way over the collapsed section of Karkand's wall saw the golden banner heralding Bakhtiian's arrival, they roared and shoved forward into the breach. Nadine watched them. Ahead, the golden banner of the jaran and the blue lion of Habakar rode high together over the ranks of Bakhtiian's jahar. A commander rode up and delivered his report and rode away. Bakhtiian went on.

Nadine was getting bored. Evidently Bakhtiian had decided to circle the city with his jahar, so that at every point his own men, and the Habakar defenders, would be aware of his presence, and of the death of the Habakar prince. But as part of his entourage, Nadine did not find the circuit amusing. The morning was half gone already. She was bored and she was angry and she was beginning to get a headache from the noise and the dust and the agony of waiting for action. She looked back over her shoulder and could just see Anatoly Sakhalin in the ranks behind, eating the dust kicked up by her jahar's horses. Surely he was enduring this honor no better than she was.

In front of the great gates, the Veselov jahar waited on the flats just out of catapult range. Two siege towers flanked the gates. One had caught fire, though men still battled over the bridge, and the other was too obscured by arrow fire and smoke for Nadine to see. Leaving Mitya on the height, Bakhtiian rode down with one hundred men to where Anton Veselov and his riders and archers waited.

As if they had only been waiting for him to appear, the small gate within the great gates swung open and Habakar soldiers streamed out; first a few on foot, and then armored cavalry, charging straight for the gold banner.

"Forward!" shouted Nadine. She urged her horse down the slope. A swarm of Habakar soldiers smashed into Veselov's jahar, beating their way toward the gold banner. But instead of heading for the conflagration itself, she whipped her mount for the gates. Her riders followed her. They broke through the line of Habakar infantry fanned out from the gate and pressed forward.

Nadine slashed down to her right and cut a man off his feet. More soldiers raced out through the small gate, forming into ranks. Ahead, the siege tower loomed, and she squinted up to see men retreating back along the bridge, back toward the tower, being forced back by the defenders.

A man speared at her, and she batted the thrust aside and cut him down. Her horse squealed, throwing its head away from a boil of dust, and she had to fight it until it steadied under her hands. A rider pounded up beside her and reined his horse in. The front lines of her jahar had gone on, leaving her in an eddy behind them. Habakar soldiers lay strewn in their wake.

"Sakhalin!" she shouted.

"I'll take my men through the gate!" he yelled.

"You're crazy!" Then she grinned. "I'll reinforce the tower. We'll meet at the gates!"

Anatoly Sakhalin saluted her with his saber and they parted in the chaos of battle. She pushed through to the front and pulled as many of her men as she could away from the melee. There, she saw Anatoly Sakhalin charging with twenty riders at his back for the small gate, hacking his way through the defenders. And then he was through, disappeared into Karkand.

"Forward!" They galloped for the tower, and she threw herself off her horse and ducked inside. "Grab shields where you find them!" she shouted to the men pounding after her. She scrambled up the ladders, and her heart thudded fiercely and she gasped for air by the time they got to the top.

To find their own army shrinking back from the defenders.

She jumped out onto the bridge. An arrow hit her, sticking in her armor. Far below, men labored at a battering ram, and others ran scaling ladders forward. The height made her dizzy. She laughed and bent to tug a shield from a fallen man. Her men pressed forward with her, and they shoved back the Habakar defenders and reached the wall. One jaran man still stood upright, staggering under wounds. They surrounded him and swept past, shrieking and yelling so that their own voices deafened her to anything else.

At once she saw the danger, that there were two approaches to the bridge. "Split into two. You, just hold that section of wall. Don't give way. To the stairs!"

Under their onslaught, the Habakar soldiers gave ground step by bloody step and then, like a dam breaking, abruptly gave way entirely.

"Forward!" They took the stairs with a fury. One poor fool tried to take the steps two at a time and overbalanced under his own weight and tumbled head over heels, crashing down and taking four of the enemy with him.

At the base of the wall, a maze of streets spread out before them, but Nadine navigated by the sound of weapons clashing.

"This way!" She led them at a jog, leaving contingents to guard the side streets, and emerged at last into a market square fronting the main gates. Anatoly Sakhalin and one rider were all that was left, mounted, of his assault; they laid about themselves. Then Sakhalin's horse staggered under a blow and collapsed, throwing Sakhalin.

"Stay together!" she shouted, seeing two men break forward from the line to try to rescue Sakhalin. "Open the gates!" A whirlpool of fighting flowed past her, and she cut at a soldier dueling calmly with an unhorsed rider. He went down, and the rider turned, raised his saber— and recognized her and spun to join up with her troops.

A great creaking shuddered through the ground. The

gates began to open. Nadine pressed forward with her
line into the center of the square, sweeping resistance
aside, pressing everyone back so that there would be
room for the rest of Sakhalin's jahar to flood in. She
stepped over a body and then detoured around a downed
jaran horse. A man struggled up from the ground.

"Orzhekov!" Anatoly Sakhalin grinned at her.

"Gods, I thought you were dead!"

"Not a scratch. The gods sent an angel to watch over
me. Move aside!" The gates opened, and his jahar clattered in. What was left of the Habakar defenders fled,
leaving the jaran in possession of the gates and the market square. On the walls above, jaran men and Farisa auxiliaries swarmed, and archers took up position to shoot
down onto the roofs of nearby houses. "A horse!"
shouted Sakhalin. He swung up on a mount. "To the citadel!"

Nadine sprang up the stairs siding the gate until she
came to the parapet on top. Out on the flats, the golden
banner rode high, and the sun it reflected rode higher
still, at its apex. She watched as her uncle moved safely
away, toward the south, to rally his army at the next gate.
Below, the Veselov jahar rode forward, following
Sakhalin into Karkand. Nadine hurried down to meet
them.

Vera Veselov rode at their head. "Where is your dyan?"
Nadine called from the stairs.

Vera glanced up at her and lifted the staff of command
in her right hand. "Anton is dead. Killed in the sortie.
Men! I want half of you dismounted and to the left. We'll
take each street on foot, clean out every house. Drive the
women and children out onto the street and kill any man
you find."

Behind Veselov's jahar, Farisa auxiliaries waited to enter.

"Orzhekov!" One of her men appeared, leading a horse
for her.

She mounted and gathered her troops together with a
lift of her staff. "We'll follow Sakhalin to the citadel!"
She cried. "Risanovsky, ride to the engineers. No firing

into the city, and we'll need the siege engines drawn up to the citadel."

Soon enough she saw that Vera Veselov had the right of it. She dismounted half of her men and sent them in mixed groups to clear the streets. Fires burned and smoke choked them, mingled with dust, but the defense proved haphazard. She rode around a corner into a blizzard of arrow fire and jerked her horse back into cover and sent twenty men to root it out. She listened as they clashed. Beside her, a rider dragged a screaming, kicking woman out of her mudbrick hovel and left her on the ground, where she lay, black hair streaked with dust, stunned and terrified on the threshold. A clot of women cowered at a well, sheltering their children. Three Habakar men lay dead at their feet.

A messenger rode up. "Orzhekov!" He wore the gold surcoat and gold plume of Bakhtiian's jahar. "Orders to all dyans. Burn the city."

She nodded. "It's not safe to go forward yet," she said.

Already, the next street over, roofs caught fire, thatch flaming. Smoke roiled over them. The women at the well wailed and two riders drove them away from the well and kept after them until they fled away toward the gates, out of the city. A wagon trundled past, driven by an old woman, emptied of everything except blankets and a crowd of weeping children. Two riders commandeered the wagon, sending the old woman and the children on, on foot, and piled it high with valuables stripped from the houses. A baby cried.

The messenger cocked his head to one side. "Do you hear that?" he asked. The baby cried on, an awkward, reedy scream. Abruptly, he dismounted and paced down the street. Nadine watched him, bemused. One of her riders trotted out from around the corner to give her the all clear; they had found and killed the Habakar archers.

Fire leapt and crackled on a nearby roof. In the warren of streets beyond, mudbrick collapsed into a tower of dust. In the distance, she saw a minaret licked by flames. The messenger ducked into a house and, just as he entered, its roof went up in flames.

"Go!" said Nadine, pointing, and her trooper dashed

down, but before he reached the house the messenger ran back out, body bent over a scrap of cloth as sparks showered down on him. The roof collapsed in behind him. He jogged up to Nadine and swung back on his horse and then displayed his prize: a little red-faced infant shrieking its lungs out.

"Barbarians!" he said with a grunt of disgust. "Leaving their own children to die."

"Take it back to the hospital," said Nadine. "I'll pass the orders on down the line."

A troop of horsemen clattered past. Refugees streamed in the other direction, ducking away from the jaran riders, running, stumbling, and sobbing, dropping wooden chests and cloth bundles in their haste. A jeweled necklace lay spilled in the dirt. A rider picked the necklace up with the point of his spear and let it slide down the haft into his hands. He glanced over to see Nadine and the messenger watching him, then shook the necklace free and tossed it to the men loading the wagon.

"Take that horse!" shouted Nadine, seeing a Habakar woman leading a fine mare, and her riders summarily took the horse away. The woman was wise enough not to protest. The messenger left, riding with the infant in the crook of his arm. Nadine headed on into the city.

By now it was midafternoon and the resistance had worn away almost to nothing. Fires rose on all sides, and auxiliaries and archers stripped houses and loaded purloined wagons high with the riches of Karkand. It was time to press on quickly. She called in her jahar, pleased to see that she had almost four hundreds still with her, the others wounded or scattered behind. They formed up and rode on up the hill to the great square that fronted the citadel. This close, the walls looked thick and forbidding, impregnable.

To her surprise, all was quiet here, except for the constant growling noise of the conflagration in the city.

She found Anatoly Sakhalin with about fifty riders. "What's going on?"

"Bakhtiian is by the outer gates of the citadel, negotiating with the commander. On the other side of us."

"Negotiating with him?"

"He's agreed to spare the women and children if the garrison will surrender."

"Ah," said Nadine. "But surely from those walls they can see the refugees leaving the city. They must know that some are being spared in any case."

Anatoly shrugged. "How can we know what khaja think like? They make no sense to me." Then he looked abruptly guilty for saying it. As if to draw attention away from the comment, he glanced back. From this height, halfway up the hill on which the citadel lay massed, the city spread out in a maze of spirals and circling streets beneath them, all the way down to the great walls and over to the height where the royal palace lay sprawled across the sister hill. The city burned. A third of it was already obscured by smoke.

Nadine stared, realizing all at once how huge Karkand really was, how elaborate. Minarets thrust up into the sky, ornamented with delicate lacework that slowly disappeared into smoke and flame. The royal palace bore tiles all along its western front, gleaming in the late afternoon sun, but even as she watched, smoke began to curl up from its environs. Gardens lay green under the light of day. A colonnaded avenue led in pale splendor to a vast temple inscribed with tilework that formed huge letters, the words of their god. People milled in clumps, as small as insects, scattered everywhere she could make out from her vantage point. At a distant gate, she saw a steady stream of refugees leaving the city. Farther, the suburbs ringed the inner city, hazed now by the dust and the smoke, obscuring their white villas and verdant parks. Metal flashed against the sun as riders moved in the far distance, and here and there on the walls, where some skirmish fought itself to an end. No city she had ever seen, not even Jeds, was as beautiful as Karkand as it died.

Anatoly shrugged, turning his gaze back to the citadel, where the blue lion flag of the Habakar royal family still fluttered in the wind. "It's going to take a long time to burn," he said.

At the height of the citadel, the blue lion flag shuddered and began to descend. Nadine caught in her breath.

A man appeared on the parapet, high above, and in his right hand he bore Bakhtiian's gold standard.

Anatoly swore under his breath and urged his horse forward. Just as he reached the thick gates, they swung open. Nadine was shocked to see her uncle ride through them, Konstans Barshai and Kirill Zvertkov on his left and Mitya on his right. On foot, in front of him, walked three Habakar priests and a soldier in a fine nobleman's surcoat and rich armor, heads bared to the sun.

Bakhtiian saw Nadine, and he beckoned to her. She rode up to him and fell in beside Mitya. They rode out of the square, paced by their prisoners, and down the great colonnaded avenue until they came at last to the huge temple that lay between the citadel and the palace.

It was a glorious thing, the temple of the Habakar god, so profusely tiled along its walls and up its minareted sides that Nadine wondered how long it had taken to build and decorate. Arches filigreed with elaborate screens gave access onto the inner grounds, and through the arches she saw a green courtyard bordered by slender columns, their capitals wreathed in leaves. She wished suddenly, fiercely, that David could be here to survey it, to draw it, to keep its memory alive.

In the square in front of the temple lay a fountain built so cunningly that the play of the water splashing down level to level raised rainbows in the air. An unveiled, white-robed woman sat, head bowed, on the edge of the pool at the base of the fountain, a ceramic pitcher and two shallow wooden bowls resting beside her.

Their party came to a halt before the fountain. Bakhtiian looked on the huge temple with an expression that Nadine could not read. He did not look triumphant to her, though his victory that day had been momentous.

Stiff with fright, the priestess dipped a bowl into the pool, rose from her seat, and brought the water to Bakhtiian. Her hands trembled as she lifted the bowl up, cupped in her pale delicate fingers, offering it to him. He accepted it, took three sips, and handed the bowl to Mitya, who drank off the rest. Then Bakhtiian urged his horse forward to the pool and let it drink. The white-robed woman went as pale as death, watching the stallion drink from her fountain, and a moment later she collapsed to the ground in a faint. The Habakar priests wrung their hands, terrified and distraught, but they did not object to this impiety.

Bakhtiian pulled his horse away and motioned to the rest to water their own mounts. He moved up beside his prisoners. Shadows drew out across the courtyard, thrown by the minarets and the ring of tall columns. The horses drank noisily from the pool, serenaded by the pleasant murmur of the fountain and the muted dissonance of the bedlam in the city beyond. Plumes of smoke clouded the sky. The sun sank toward the western hills in a haze of red fire.

"You may leave," Bakhtiian said. "That much mercy I will grant you and your people." His expression remained fixed and distant.

"But, Lord," protested one of the priests, the eldest of them, "the holy books of the Everlasting God, which reside in the temple . . ." He bent his head over his hands. Nadine saw tears in his eyes and a look of bitter despair on his face. The others whispered fiercely to him. The nobleman knelt and bowed his head, not to Bakhtiian, but to the temple itself, as if saying farewell to it.

"Books!" Bakhtiian's gaze jumped back to the priests for an instant. "Konstans. Give these priests wagons, so that they may save their books. Take five hundred men and strip everything else that is valuable from the building."

"But, Lord, our temple took years beyond counting to build. And the palace—" The others hissed at him, but the old man set his mouth and continued. "Let him kill me if he wills. I am old enough to die without fear. Lord, surely once you have taken what you wish, we can return to our homes. Surely you or the young prince—" He glanced up at Mitya and away, as if he feared his impudence in looking directly upon the young prince might be punished, "—will wish to rule from here."

"Karkand is no more," said Bakhtiian in a quiet voice, deceptively quiet, Nadine understood now, seeing in his face the depths of his rage and of his anguish. "Nothing will be left of her once I am through. No one will live here, no thing will grow here, where I lost my son."

CHAPTER THIRTY

Aleksi knew how to get places without being seen. Charles Soerensen knew how to be seen. Once they had ridden far enough in toward the battle, once the prince had been recognized and waved forward by enough people, Aleksi got them lost and brought them out on a different side of Karkand, three jaran riders of no particular importance headed out on patrol. He did not find it difficult to avoid jaran patrols. But the khaja who had been driven from the outlying districts of Karkand flooded every path and road and least byway, and in the end they cut up into the hills early and wound a laborious way through the scrub until they came at last to a small defile hidden between two ridges.

"Here," said Charles, and they dismounted and led the horses down the steep hillside to the flat grassy floor. It was midafternoon by now, and already shadows covered the western flank of the little valley. They stood there, resting while they watched the horses graze.

"We're only about eight kilometers from camp," said Marco, "had we ridden straight here, but we rode over twice that. Goddess, what a lot of refugees."

"Let's hope," said Soerensen quietly, regarding the sky pensively, "that none of them decide to hide in the hills until we're gone. Or at least, in these hills."

Marco sighed. "Just think of all the people still left inside the city. I wonder what will happen to them."

The prince folded his arms on his chest and regarded the other man. A breeze slid through the grass. Here, in this peaceful valley, it was hard to remember that a battle raged a short ride away.

Marco clenched his hands. "Or what will happen to the people in camp if Bakhtiian loses." He looked white.

"I'm sorry, Marco," said Soerensen, more quietly still.

"You're sorry!" demanded Marco. "You're the one who abandoned Tess!"

"And Cara and David and all the rest of them, true. But I have faith that Bakhtiian will win. Hell, I have to believe it. And in any case, that's not really who we're talking about."

Marco swore and stalked off to talk to the horses who were, no doubt, more soothing company.

"Romance," said the prince, looking after him," is vastly overrated." He sat down and reclined on one elbow.

Aleksi crouched down beside him. "Is Erthe really such a place as this?" he asked, waving toward the ridges and the silent stretch of grass and brush lying within the valley walls. "Or is it like the plains? And if it lies up in the heavens, why can't we see it?"

Soerensen smiled. "You remind me of Tess," he said. "Hell, you remind me of me."

The simple words provoked a sudden flush of happiness in Aleksi. By this, he was acknowledged. He could not help himself. He smiled back.

The prince chuckled. "Well, we have about two hours until the shuttle is due in. Let me see." He settled into a more comfortable position. "I'm not a very good storyteller, and I don't have any visual aids ..."

"Oh, I don't mind," said Aleksi hastily. "Tell me a simple story first. Tell me about—" He hesitated, stunned for a moment by his own audacity. But Tess was his sister and, by some measure, Charles Soerensen his brother. "Tell me about your mother and your father and your tribe."

"My mother and my father and my tribe," mused the prince. "Well, then, let me start with the story of how they met—or at least, how they told it to me. I heard a different story from my mother's sister, which I'm afraid I believe more." But by his grin as he spoke, Aleksi saw that both these stories rose from love. Content, Aleksi settled in to listen.

* * *

The sun had fallen below the western ridge and twilight cloaked the valley when Marco left the horses suddenly and ran over to them, interrupting Soerensen right as he was getting to the part where Tess was born.

"Perimeter alert," said Marco. "We've got two riders approaching." He had a huge black stone attached to his wrist, and he stared into it now as a Singer might stare into feathers and bones to read omens.

"Refugees?" the prince asked, climbing to his feet. "Damn."

"I don't— No. They've got homing equipment. Must be ours."

Aleksi heard the horses before he saw them, picking their way down the western ridge. Soon enough he could make out their riders as well: One person walked, leading both horses, and a second clung to the saddle of her fine mare.

"Tess!" Aleksi said her name on the same breath the prince did. Then Marco said, "Maggie! What the hell—?" They all stared.

Zhashi looked no worse for wear, although not surprisingly she wasn't happy about going down an unfamiliar slope at twilight, but Tess looked awful. They reached the valley floor and Aleksi ran to help Tess down off the mare.

She collapsed into his arms and just hung against him while Maggie took the horses out to the others and hobbled them.

"And what the hell," Tess demanded of her brother as he hurried up to her, "do you think you're doing?" Her voice was strong, but still she clung to Aleksi. He wondered if she could even stand by herself.

"I might ask the same of you," Soerensen said, looking shocked, but he did not move to take her out of Aleksi's grasp. "Are you trying to kill yourself?"

"What? You don't want me to? You still have too many uses for me?"

"I'm *asking* because I care, damn it!" he exclaimed, and Aleksi was astonished to hear how hurt he sounded.

She did not reply immediately. Instead, she tested her

feet on the ground and Aleksi helped her to sit down. Her face shone gray in the dusk. She still had to lean against him, even then. "Oh, God," she said. "It just happened so fast. God, I'm exhausted."

"As well you should be," interjected Marco. "Goddess, Tess, it's hard enough to leave without worrying that *you* might—" He broke off and knelt down beside her, hugging her, and Aleksi let her go. "Why did you come after us?"

"That's a stupid question," said Tess. "I receive a note that states that urgent news from Odys forces Charles to leave Rhui at once, and you don't think I'd—" She paused for breath. Marco let go of her and stood up. "I need something to drink." Aleksi offered her water from his flask. She drank and gave the flask back to him. "If you're leaving this way, you must be leaving for good. Forever. It doesn't take any great brilliance to read your mind, Charles."

Aleksi was amazed by her tone of voice, and by the prince's expression, like that of a master of saber who has just realized that his apprentice can match him now. "It doesn't?" he demanded. "Then how am I to negotiate the maze of Chapalii politics?"

"By not underestimating your opponent, first of all. What am I to tell Ilya? That you disappeared? Right out from under his army?"

With dusk, the wind had dropped. Now it picked up again, a faint moan through the air.

"We've got incoming," said Marco.

Tess set her fists on the ground and took in three deep breaths. She heaved herself to her feet. Soerensen caught her by the arm and helped her up. "No, I'm all right. Just tired. So what am I to tell Ilya?"

"That I'm dead."

"How do I prove it? It isn't easy to fake a death, Charles. I won't have a body. At least a dozen people know I left camp, against their wild protests, and I refused any escort except Maggie's. I had to take messenger's bells and a seal to get past patrols without any questions. Ilya will hear all about that, I can assure you."

"You could come with me," said the prince.

She cocked her head to one side. Fear washed through Aleksi, and he took a step toward her. If she went, by the gods, he would go with her. But Tess only grinned. "No, I couldn't. You know that as well as I do."

Soerensen sighed and rested a hand on her shoulder— the gesture looked both awkward and intimate. "Tess," he said slowly, "I do regret how little time I've ever had just for you. I'm sorry."

Her eyes widened. "So you really *are* leaving Rhui for good."

"Yes! I don't have any choice. Listen!" He bent toward her and repeated to her the words that the woman Suzanne had told him. Aleksi realized that they had raised their voices to talk over the rising roar of the wind. How had the wind come up so suddenly? A few clouds lay torn across the sky, building in the west and concealing patches of stars, but there was no sign of imminent storm. The horses flung up their heads and pulled at their reins, nervous, and Maggie stayed with them, calming them.

Tess listened to her brother's recital in silence, and when he was done, she simply nodded her head. "Yes," she agreed. "You have to go."

As with one thought, the four khaja looked up into the heavens. It wasn't wind at all. Aleksi tilted his head back and stared.

It was a creature, a bird—not a bird—some monster— not a monster. The prince had said a ship was coming. And Dr. Hierakis had told him about ships that sailed the ocean of night, as it was night now, fallen all around them. A huge shadow blotted out the stars, and the air sang in a bellowing howl around Aleksi as the ship sank like a bird sailing in on the wings of Father Wind and settled onto the ground.

Dust sprayed out. Maggie's mare bolted and crashed down, constrained by the hobble, and struggled back up to its feet. Marco and Aleksi ran over to help Maggie, and the three of them led the animals back to Tess and the prince, fighting them, soothing them until they calmed, ears back, and resigned themselves to the presence of the beast. It roared; that was its voice, then. The swirling air was its breath, hot like summer, hammering at him, tearing at his clothes.

They showed no fear at all.

"What happened to Karkand?" Charles shouted, straining against the screaming voice of the ship.

"I don't know. Last I heard the jaran broke into the city. That's all I know. You really can't come back now, can you?" She sagged, just slightly, and Aleksi left the horses to Marco and Maggie and went to her. She cast him a glance, relieved and grateful, and let him hold her up. She shook, she was so exhausted.

"No." The wind pounded at Soerensen's back where he stood facing Tess, his back to the ship. It hulked there; small lights caught and winked on it, like eyes opening and closing. "There must be no link between me and Rhui until we're ready to launch the next rebellion, not anything else for dukes like Naroshi to grab hold of. I have to work as far into the Chapalii court as I can. In a way, I'll be providing the distraction. Because once the rebellion is launched, we'll need Rhui."

"You have Rhui," she yelled back. She squinted into the tearing gale, blinking back grit, and lifted an arm to protect her face.

"More than that." His pale hair whipped and danced in the breath of the ship. "You have to unite Rhui, as far as you can, you and Bakhtiian, his descendants, if it takes that long. So when the interdiction lifts, as it must, when we need its resources for the rebellion, we'll have some kind of central authority. But one that's grown slowly, without alerting the Chapalii. Without that central authority to coordinate our efforts on planet, it will be far too inefficient to exploit her resources with the speed and initial secrecy we'll need to make the rebellion work."

"We're such damned hypocrites!" The ship screamed behind her, and the wind battered them in waves. "By what right do we meddle on Rhui like this? By what right do *you?* You leave, but in turn you make Rhui the heart of your plans. And yet you made the interdiction in the first place. Now you're breaking it worse than anyone else. By what right?"

A single bright white light speared out from the ship.

It illuminated the prince and Tess as if the sun had risen on them alone, leaving the rest of the world in darkness.

"By the promise I made to free humanity," the prince said. His face was shadowed though light spilled around him, but hers was all lit, white and angry, and then she rolled her eyes and laughed.

"I'll never be free of you, Charles."

"Never," he agreed. "We never are free from ourselves and our heritage." Abruptly, he wrung his hands together, a gesture that showed how deeply this parting hurt him. Only he wasn't wringing his hands; he was pulling the signet ring off of his right middle finger. "This is yours, the sigil of the Prince of Jeds. I left the gold chain of office in my tent, and Baron Santer in Jeds holds the scepter in trust, until you return."

She pushed herself away from Aleksi and took the ring from Charles and stared at it as if she had never seen it before. "How am I supposed to prove all this? When am I supposed to ride to Jeds? Is there any guarantee that Baron Santer will remember me, or be willing to give up his regency? And how in hell are Ilya and I supposed to unite Rhui, anyway?"

He lifted his hands, palms up, and smiled. "Tess, I never said it would be easy."

She laughed. "Damn you!"

"The prince is dead," said Marco, his voice almost obliterated by the ship's voice. "God save the prince."

"Marco," said Maggie. "Go to hell."

"No doubt I will."

The ship coughed. Only it didn't cough. Its mouth opened and a golden glow penetrated the night, washing into the hard white glare that illuminated Tess and her brother. A ramp pushed out from the maw of the beast, a bridge linking the heavens and the earth. A figure appeared in the glow and hurried down the ramp. An angel? One of Father Wind's attendants?

It resolved into a man like any man, except for the strange cut of his clothes and the blithe way he strode out of the ship and ignored its screaming howl and the battering wind. Marco hailed him, and the two men shook hands—that strange Erthe greeting—and he came over to Soerensen.

"Ah, Javier, how are you?" said Soerensen. "This is Tess. I don't believe you've ever met. Javier Lu Shen." Formal greetings were exchanged.

"Hold on," said Tess, turning first to look at the horses and then back to the new man. "Javier, can you ride?"

"Ride?" Soerensen turned to his sister. "What are you thinking about, Tess?"

"Charles, I have to tell Ilya something. He'll never believe you're dead unless he has more witnesses and a credible story of how you—God, it's impossible. But what if I tell him the truth, in terms he'd understand? You already laid down half the smokescreen, you know, by pretending to ride into the battle. So if I tell Ilya that you're dying here, as Prince of Jeds, in order to go back to Earth—to Erthe—to fight the khepelli, and if Ilya tells the army that you're dead, who will question him?"

"Yes. I had thought that far. But what has this to do with whether Javier can ride?"

"A horse?" Javier demanded. "Do you mean a horse? One of those things? I've never ridden one."

"You'll learn," said Tess with a brief smile. "I did." She turned back to her brother. "Charles, you have to go on the shuttle. But if Marco and Javier ride north and swing back to Abala Port, where you came in last spring, and sail to Jeds, then they can go out on the shuttle through Jeds."

"Which means that Marco can deliver the news of my death to Baron Santer."

"Yes! And meanwhile, Ilya will get the report that two khaja men, you and Marco, rode through jaran territory and left by ship. For Erthe."

"This is all very convoluted, Tess," protested Charles. Poor Javier looked appalled.

"How else can I explain it to Ilya? I've got the messenger bells and messenger seal—they'll provide Marco and Javier with safe passage, new mounts, and supplies. They can ride as quickly as—well, as Javier learns. Speed and secrecy. Isn't that what we need? To prepare Rhui for the rebellion? You leave, Ilya knows enough to satisfy him, knows that he's part of the conspiracy, and he can say you died in the battle today. Cara can confirm it. We can burn some poor nameless soul as your body, and it's done."

"But what about Marco?" asked Charles. "Does Marco want to ride all that way?"

"What about me?" wailed Javier.

"I don't mind," said Marco in a low voice, barely audible above the roar of the ship. "I'm leaving camp anyway. What do I care? It has to be done. I think it's a good idea."

"Javier doesn't look anything like me," said Charles.

"That's true, but you're both khaja." Tess dismissed this objection with a wave of her hand. "If he wears a hood and none of the patrols ever gets a close look at him, and they pass along quickly, then how much of the physical description will ever get back to us? None of the patrols or tribes you'll pass will have seen you before anyway. It will do. It's the best we can do. Trade clothes. You'll be fine. I'm right in this, Charles. You know I am."

He considered her. The trees tossed in the wind, and leaves tore free from branches and swirled away into the night. "Convoluted," said Soerensen, "and worthy of a Chapalii duke's heir. We'll see if you can pull it off."

"But, Charles," said Tess sweetly, with a wicked gleam in her eyes, "you don't really have a choice, do you? By this ring, you've given me authority on this planet. So I order you to do as I say. Damn you, anyway. We're just pawns to you, Ilya and I, aren't we?"

His lips quirked up, and he laughed. "Don't forget how chess is played. With patience and cunning and wit, as well as the right strategy, a pawn can become the most powerful piece in the game."

He bent and kissed her, once on each cheek, in the formal jaran style. He said farewell to the others, to Aleksi, and then he and Javier turned and walked back to the ship. Aleksi watched as he vanished into the golden light of the interior.

Tess's legs gave out, and she collapsed to the ground. Aleksi dropped down beside her immediately, scared for her, but she nodded her head against him and just sat there, breathing shallowly.

"Tess!" Maggie exclaimed.

Tess shook her head and lifted—with great effort—one hand as a signal that she was all right.

Soerensen emerged from the ship, except it wasn't Soerensen but the other man, dressed in his clothes and in his jaran armor, helmet strapped awkwardly onto his head. The maw closed behind him. The white light snapped off, bathing them in darkness.

"Why me?" he asked as he came up to them. Then he saw Tess. "Oh, my. M. Soerensen, are you—?"

A high-pitched whine pierced the roar of the beast, and the ground trembled under Aleksi's feet. The horses pulled away, and Maggie and Marco tugged them down and tried to reassure them with their voices, only the ship howled and all at once bucked up and as slow as if Father Wind's invisible hand lifted it, it rose up into the night, jewel eyes winking open and closed, open and closed.

Tess tucked her head down. The wind washed over her, where she sat huddled on the ground. Maggie fought her two horses, dragging on them as they whinnied and tried to jerk free, to bolt, even though they couldn't bolt because they were hobbled. The hot breath of the ship slapped Aleksi's face, and the creature spun and showed a new face to him, gleaming pale in the starlight, and rose up into the night, blinking, blotting out stars, and rumbled and roared, and the wind howled down, and the trees bent under its force, and dust clotted the air, and he choked on the grit and shut his eyes and held onto Tess.

And the roar lightened and faded and the wind dropped and a low moan rang through the night air. Stars winked in and out, and then only the wind blew and the night lay silent under the stars. The canopy of clouds grew in the west. The horses calmed.

"Now what?" asked Marco, his voice a ringing shout in the quiet.

"You'd better go now," said Tess, her voice as soft as Marco's had been inadvertently loud. Aleksi showed Marco how to bind on the vest of bells. Tess roused herself for long enough to discuss with Marco routes and strategies, and at last the two men left, leading their horses up the confining slope, heading northeast. The muted ring of bells faded into the night.

Weakly, Tess brushed dry grass off her trousers. She lifted her hand and squinted at the ring on her middle finger. "My God," she said, to no one.

"Is that how the gods travel in the heavens?" Aleksi asked, looking from her up into the sky. Were any of those stars the ship? Were all of them ships? But, no, the doctor had said they were worlds—or not worlds, but suns. He shook his head. He was too tired to sort it all out now.

Tess sighed. "They're just machines, Aleksi."

"I've got a perimeter alert," said Maggie. "Horses and men."

Aleksi leapt to his feet and drew his saber. Maggie pulled a knife from her belt. Slowly, Tess drew her saber and rested it on her knees, but anyone could see she hadn't the strength to wield it.

But it was only a group of jaran riders, twelve of them, picking their way down the western slope. It didn't surprise Aleksi to see how astounded they looked when they discovered that they had stumbled upon a daughter of Mother Orzhekov, the woman who was also, of course, Bakhtiian's wife.

"We saw a strange light in the sky," said their captain.

"I saw it, too," said Tess, without moving from the ground. "It was an omen."

"We'll escort you back to camp, then."

"Tomorrow," she said. "I just can't go any farther tonight."

So they spent the night in the little valley, Tess sleeping on coats and under blankets provided by the riders, guarded by a ring of fires, and in the morning they remarked on the strange burn on the ground in the center of the valley and saddled their horses and formed up around Tess. If they thought it strange to have found her out here, practically alone, they did not discuss their thoughts with Aleksi. Tess was pale and still horribly tired. They rode back toward Karkand slowly, stopping frequently. The

day was overcast, and the light had an eerie yellow quality to it.

Soon enough they began to pass refugees from the city.
At first clumps of them, cowering away from the patrol.
A woman carried a baby on her back and held another
child by the hand. An old woman stumbled along, weak
and crying, and a little boy dragged a bundle behind him
and followed in her wake. Larger groups, families,
trudged along the road. Children wailed. A broken-down
old horse bore an injured woman slumped over its neck,
her thigh a bloody mass of tissue, open to the air. They
had nothing but the clothes on their backs, and a few of
the lucky ones, a handful of possessions wrapped in cloth,
whatever they had grabbed before being driven from the
city. A gray-haired woman walked under the weight of a
silk bundle. A tall woman with a strong, dark face
stopped to shift a pack of roughspun cloth to a better position on her back. A baby shrieked. A woman clad in
rich damask linen sobbed with each step, holding a hand
to her throat. Two girls held a limping crone between
them, helping her along. Most kept their heads bowed.
An adolescent girl, her face veiled, balanced a large ceramic vase on her head, walking steadily, only her eyes
showing dark and angry as she watched the riders pass.

Tess wept, to see them struggling along.

As they rode on, as morning passed to midday and
midday into afternoon, the trickle became a stream, the
stream a flood. Hordes of them; Aleksi had not known so
many people, even khaja, could live together in one
place. No wonder they were weak, crammed like insects
into a rotted stump or an old hollow log. They walked,
heads bowed. A layer of ash covered their clothes, and at
their backs smoke rose into the heavens, a dark blot
against the gray clouds far above. As the riders neared the
jaran camp, they could see Karkand burning.

"My God," said Tess. "Isn't there a rise, where we can
look?"

It was a relief to veer away from the road and along a
trampled field until they reached a low ridge which gave
them a vantage of the city.

Karkand burned. A huge black funnel of smoke marked

it, and spits of flame. Aleksi watched the lines of refugees, like tiny insects, leaving the city along the roads
and out through the fields. He saw the riders, moving
among them, and wagons trundling away toward the jaran
camp. In the middle of the blazing city, the huge dome of
the temple glowed red with fire. Clouds of heat shimmered out from it, and the intense glow of the flames cast
a hot, violent light up into the sky. As they watched, the
dome collapsed into a monstrous cloud of ash and smoke
that billowed into the air and shrouded the western horizon so that they could not even see the setting sun.

"Goddess save us," murmured Maggie. "Why did he
order this? The whole city is going, all of it, even the
suburbs are in flames. And it was so beautiful. Now it
looks like a funeral pyre."

Tears streaked Tess's face. "Don't you see?" she asked,
shaking her head. "It *is* a funeral pyre. For our son. For
everyone who died today, for everyone who will die. For
Charles." She wiped her face with the back of one hand,
but it only streaked grime over her cheeks, blending with
her tears. "For Rhui."

"Look." Aleksi pointed at the same time that the patrol
captain did. "There is Bakhtiian's banner. He must be riding out to look for you."

"We'll wait for him here," said Tess.

So they met on the ridge, Tess and Bakhtiian, he with
the pall of the dying city at his back, she with her face to
it.

He said nothing, only drew his horse in beside her and
raised one eyebrow, questioning. He looked remarkably
neat for a man who had just destroyed a city and defeated
an entire kingdom, with his armor newly polished and his
surcoat untorn and marked only by a fine layer of ash. He
wore his victory with pride but without gloating.

Tess lifted her right hand, to show him the ring. "I am
now the Prince of Jeds."

He regarded her measuringly, as he might measure any
threat to his power. "Where is your brother?"

"He's dead."

He took the news with no change of expression. "We

still have no treaty between your lands and mine," he said quietly.

"That's true." She looked beyond him, toward Karkand. "I have seen what you and I must do: We must unite all the lands against the coming of the khepelli, whether while we live or when our grandchildren rule. What can you offer me, Bakhtiian, in return for my alliance?"

His mouth lifted, not quite into a smile. He twisted for the first time and cast a glance back toward the conflagration. Then he turned back to gaze on her again.

He drew his saber and held it up between them. "My army, which is my sword. And my vision, which was granted to me by the gods. That is all I have, and everything I have."

Tess stared at the inferno that was Karkand. Over the night and on that day's journey, she had seemed to Aleksi to change somehow, as if the ring her brother had given her had altered her forever. She was still Tess, but she was also a prince now, invested with a greater power than anyone here but Aleksi and Maggie, and she herself, knew. It was almost as if Karkand was her own pyre, burning away what she once was and creating her anew.

"Your army and your vision," she said, meeting her husband's gaze. "That will do."

CHAPTER THIRTY-ONE

Fine ash rained down on David's head. He brushed at his hair, but it was useless. It coated everything, fine white ash and grittier black chunks. His boots crunched on it, and the beautiful woven patterns of the jaran tents lay hidden beneath it. He coughed, and coughed again, and finally gave up and held a scrap of cloth over his mouth and nose.

Although it was late afternoon, some of the encampments were breaking up, loading their goods into wagons and heading south to escape the constant shower. He arrived at their own camp just as Maggie rode in, looking soot-stained and tired.

"David!" She swung down from her horse and beckoned him over. A jaran boy ran up and took the horse from her, and Maggie wiped her nose with the back of her hand and sneezed. "Goddess, this is terrible. David. Have you heard about Charles?"

David blinked through his exhaustion. "What about Charles? I've been gone from camp since yesterday dawn, since they launched the assault."

"Charles left."

He thought he had heard her wrong. "Left?"

Heavy clouds covered the sky, but the quality of sunlight was peculiar, a warm yellow light instead of the silvery gray of the usual overcast day. The air was dry and smelled of burning. "He left Rhui."

"Is there a chair?" David asked, sure that he was simply so tired that he was hallucinating. "I think I need to sit down. Why?"

"Duke Naroshi had Hon Echido and a few other members of Keinaba House detained for breaking the interdic-

tion. Only Charles can sort it out. But if Naroshi is
watching him, then he can't risk returning to Rhui. He
doesn't want there to be any chance that the Chapalii
catch on to what we're doing, at least not by trailing him.
So he handed his signet ring over to Tess, and he left on
a shuttle last evening."

"On a shuttle?" David retreated under the awning of
Charles's tent, and there, groping, he found a chair and
sank down into it. "Oy vey," he muttered. "So much for
the interdiction."

"Oh, the Rhuians don't know about the shuttle. He's
officially dead, as far as the Rhuian natives are concerned. And Tess remains officially deceased off-planet.
But on Rhui, Tess is now Prince of Jeds. *We* have to make
our own way back to Jeds—damn him, I wish I could
have gone with him. And the actors. They'll have to
know as well. I'm not sure what Tess intends, but I think
Charles wants her and Bakhtiian to centralize as much of
the planet—or at least this continent, I suppose—as they
can, so that when he begins the new rebellion he'll be
able to bring Rhui wholesale into the League with little
resistance."

"All the same," said David. "So much for the interdiction. Maybe it was a vain hope." Even under the awning,
the breeze wafted flakes and fine chunks of charcoal
along to land on the carpet. A singed scrap of parchment
rolled in on a gust of wind and sank and came to rest
against David's boot. Reflexively, he picked it up. "Look
at this, Maggie," he said, raising it up for her to see.

It was a page from a book or a manuscript: a gor-
geously painted miniature of a hunting scene, lions and
gazelles in flight and horsemen in pursuit, their mounts
lovingly portrayed; a piebald, two chestnuts, three blacks,
and a dappled gray harnessed with gold bridles and saddles. Through the rocks and bushes behind the mounted
men trudged servants bearing two fringed litters in which
sat veiled women in rich damask robes. Stylized rows of
the angular Habakar script bordered the edge of the painting, where they hadn't been burned away.

"We *are* going to destroy her in the end." As he said it,

he felt the truth of the words, and he felt a deep and abiding sadness for what was bound to be lost.

Maggie took the parchment page from him and smoothed it out. "I'll preserve this," she said. "I'd say that the jaran army is already well on its way to destroying Karkand, and the kingdom, too, I suppose, although they did leave Hamrat and some other cities unmolested."

"No," said David softly. "I meant Rhui."

She grunted. "Well, it's too late to have regrets now. Oh, David. It was bound to happen. At least they'll have a running start. And it will take decades to build up the saboteur network. Where is Ursula, anyway?"

"I haven't seen her since yesterday dawn."

"Let her know, if you see her. I'm going to see Cara and give her the details." She strode away.

With the heavy cloud cover and the screen of smoke along the western horizon, afternoon hazed early into twilight. David cleaned himself up as best he could and crawled into his tent. The camp was deserted. He supposed that Cara and Jo were still at the hospital; certainly they had enough to do. Rajiv—well, wasn't Rajiv having an affair with one of the actors? He leaned back on his bedroll and shut his eyes, but instead of peace he saw the beautiful painting, curled black at the edges, smudged by grit. What had Charles said? "And the approaching tide/ Will shortly fill the reasonable shores/That now lie foul and muddy." But who was to say which was more contaminated, the swelling tide or the waiting shoreline?

"David?" *Her* voice, a whisper.

"Dina!" The next instant, she had ducked inside the tent. Then, checking her movement, she paused and crouched at the entrance. There was no light in here. He saw her only as a dark shadow against the paler wall of canvas. "Dina. What are you doing here?"

"I don't know." But she shifted and sat, blocking the entrance. "I wanted to see you. My uncle says that the Prince of Jeds is dead."

David swallowed. When he spoke, he found that his voice shook. "Yes. Yes, he's dead. Tess is prince now."

"Tess reigns there, Ilya here," Nadine murmured. "How long until they want to unite their princedoms and all the lands that lie between? David, are you leaving, then? You and the others?"

"I—it's all very abrupt. Yes, we'll have to, as soon as we can get to a port, get ship to Jeds."

"Tess, too? Will she leave for Jeds?"

"I don't think so. I don't know—it's all so sudden."

Even within the tent, the smell of soot and fire and smoke permeated everything. Yet he felt her presence just as strongly, not a meter from him, as still and silent as she sat. It was so unlike her to be so subdued.

When she spoke at last, her voice was so quiet he barely heard it. "May I stay, tonight? And on other nights, now and again, until you've gone?"

He wanted to ask about her husband, but he dared not. He wanted to ask, but he didn't want to know, and in any case, weren't jaran women free to take lovers if they wished to? He wanted her to stay. Tonight especially, after the horrible two days he had spent; for the comfort, yes, but for her more than anything, because he cared for her.

No, it was worse than that. He loved her, but he could not admit it, not to her, not to anyone; barely to himself. So wouldn't a clean break be easiest? Wouldn't it be harder, dragging it out like this, however many days or weeks they spent with the army, with her, until he left for good?

Even as he sat there, torn, she scooted forward. As soon as she touched him, her fingers brushing up his arm to his shoulder and curving around to the base of his neck, to touch, each one separately, his four name braids, he spoke without meaning to.

"Yes."

*   *   *

By the evening of the second day, Diana was relieved and more than relieved when Dr. Hierakis dismissed her from her duties and told her to go back to the Company camp and sleep. Two days and a night of an unremitting stream of casualties had worn her down to a thread.

Gwyn walked with her through camp, his right hand

light on her elbow. "This ash is disgusting," he said, just to talk, she suspected, to have a normal conversation after hour upon hour of tending to bloodied and mutilated soldiers. Karkand lit the western horizon, a dull, ugly glow.

"Yes," Diana agreed, playing into the part, "it's terrible."

"Hey! Wait for me!" Hal jogged up behind them, falling in beside Diana.

"Is there anyone else?" Diana asked.

"No," said Hal. "We're the only ones who can stomach it for that long. Why should they anyway, if they don't want to?"

"How can they not?" demanded Diana. "How can they stand and watch when there's something they could be doing?"

"Di." Hal hesitated.

At once, she knew he'd had news of Anatoly. "What is it?"

"No, I just heard, from a rider—"

"Go on."

"Just a rumor. It's probably not true."

"Go on!"

"That Sakhalin led a charge in through the main gates of the city, and his jahar got caught behind the lines and massacred. But you know it's all confused. Half the army is still out in the city."

Gwyn glanced toward the western horizon. "Surely not *in* the city still."

"I don't know. Goddess, I didn't want to tell you, but I thought you ought to know what people were saying. What the reports were."

"Thank you," said Diana grimly. But it was what she had expected all along. All day she had waited for this news. She accepted it bleakly, without surprise. Gwyn's hand tightened on her elbow, and a moment later Hal closed in beside her and rested a hand on her back, so that it was as if they two supported her, the grieving widow. It was some comfort.

At camp, Owen and Ginny had called a meeting inside the big tent, although it was mild outside. Only inside the tents were they free from the constant fall of ash. Gwyn and Hal made a little shield around Diana that only Quinn was allowed to penetrate. Quinn sank down beside Diana and draped an arm over Diana's shoulders, and Diana sighed and leaned her head on Quinn's tunic.

Owen was all on fire. He was focused, and pacing.

"We have two important pieces of news," said Ginny, after Yomi had called everyone to order. "Charles Soerensen left Rhui abruptly, by shuttle, last night."

Anahita, sitting in her usual sullen silence, flared to life. "And he didn't offer to take us with him? The selfish bastard."

"Anahita, shut up," said Ginny mildly. "So, the Company line is that he's dead, and that his sister is now prince. Owen and I just spoke with her in her camp. Poor thing. She'd ridden quite a ways, and her just having lost the baby." She frowned, glanced at her son, and paused.

"We're starting a new experiment," said Owen into her silence, in his fiercest voice, which Diana knew betokened some great roiling plan. "I want your cooperation. I'm bringing a new actor into the troupe. A jaran man. I got a dispensation from Tess Soerensen to take him and his family off planet with us. I want to see how he adapts to theater, coming from the background that he does."

"What?" Hal murmured, "like a rat negotiating a maze? Dad, don't you think that's a little cruel?"

Owen blinked. "Cruel? What curious words you use, Henry. Well, there's nothing for him here. He'll be crippled for life if he stays here. Why shouldn't he come with us? He'll be wonderful. It will take work, and you'll all have to be very generous for a while—"

"But who is it?" asked Quinn.

"It's Vasil Veselov, isn't it?" asked Diana. She looked at Gwyn, and he at her, and they both nodded, together.

"Hold on," said Ginny. "We haven't done with the first bit, yet. Tess Soerensen will be escorting us to a port, so that we and those of Soerensen's party who didn't leave with him can return to Jeds and thence to Earth. Oh, and Veselov's family will be joining us once we leave this area. He has a wife and two small children."

"Ginny," said Diana, "did anyone ask Karolla if she wanted to leave the tribes?"

"Karolla? Who is Karolla?"

"She's Veselov's wife."

Ginny shrugged. "I don't know, but Tess said that she had cleared it all with the headwoman of the Veselov tribe. Let me see. Burckhardt left with Soerensen, or not with him precisely—never mind. Yomi, what other details do they need?"

Yomi discussed logistics for a while, but Diana could not concentrate. She felt a kind of numb relief that Marco Burckhardt was gone, insofar as she could feel anything. Mostly she felt hollow. Someone would come, tomorrow, the day after, a week from now, bringing Anatoly's body. Then she felt faint, sick with horror. What if they had already burned him? What if the jaran dead had just been left in Karkand, if Bakhtiian had used the city itself for the funeral pyre for his soldiers? She tried desperately to picture Anatoly exactly as she had last seen him, proud and confident as he rode away into battle, but she could not bring the image into focus.

"Di? Are you all right?" Quinn whispered.

"I just need some air," she said, rising abruptly. "No, I'll be fine. No one needs to come with me."

"Let her go," Gwyn said. She pushed past the others and out underneath the awning. At long last the wind was dying, though ash still pattered quietly onto the cloth above her, a light, shushing sound. What did it matter, anyway, if the ash fell on her? What if some fragment of it was his remains, come to touch her one final time? She headed out into it, walking back to her tent through the darkness.

And there he was, the rider, standing beside his horse outside her tent, waiting to give her the news of her husband's death. She hadn't expected the message so soon.

"There's no point in even washing," he said, seeing her approach, "under all this dirt. Of course, the khaja would pour filth down on us." He took off his helmet, shook out his hair, and drew his fingers through the plume. "Everything, just everything is covered with it. Grandmother is going to move her camp south. The winds are blowing north and east, so it ought to be clear a day's ride in that

direction. And anyway, Bakhtiian will have to send part
of his army south to Salkh soon enough, to my uncle."

Diana stopped dead.

"Where did those boys go off to?" Anatoly continued.
"They were just here. Can you light the lantern?"

She could not speak.

"Oho, there they are. Viktor! You imp. Come get this
damned stuff off me. Bring that lantern!" He laughed.
"Look at them. They grabbed some khaja shields. No, no,
you idiots. You can't cut as if you're on horseback when
you're on foot."

The two boys panted up with a younger boy in tow.
They threw down their shields and helped Anatoly out of
his armor and stowed it under the shields to protect it
from further ashfall. Then Anatoly took the lantern from
them and ordered them away. He went into the tent.

Diana could not move.

A moment later, he ducked out again. "Diana?" He
walked over to her. "Come on." He grabbed her hand and
tugged her in, and she went. His grip was firm enough.
He wasn't a ghost.

"Is there something for me to drink?" he asked as he
tugged off his boots. "I'm famished. I came straight from
the field here, as soon as I could. I would have sent a
message, but—oh, Diana, I'm sorry if you were worried.
But you know I can't be hurt in battle. The gods sent you
to me."

This once, thank the Goddess, there was food and drink
for him in the tent, although not, of course, anything as
elaborate as his grandmother would have served him. But
he was content.

He was content. She watched him eat. Obviously he
was starving, but he ate neatly and efficiently. When he
sighed, replete, and reclined on the carpet, smiling at her,
she felt wretched.

"Diana?" His face changed at once. "You've heard,
then, haven't you? About the Prince of Jeds?"

"Yes," she whispered.

"Who else? One of the Vershinin sons died. Anton
Veselov is dead, too, and the amazing thing is that Mother
Veselov asked that their cousin Vera be named dyan. But

the Veselov riders demanded it! Evidently she took the staff of command out of her cousin's hand as he died and led them wisely enough through the rest of the battle. It was my men who brought the madwoman's body in. They found her up on the walls."

"The madwoman?" She was too stupified by his presence to understand what he was talking about.

"The prince's soldier—"

"Ursula el Kawakami is dead?" The conversation seemed unreal to her. Anatoly was dead; it was impossible that he was here, now, not one meter from her, regarding her with his beautiful, expressive eyes.

"You hadn't heard? Diana." He reached out and caught her wrist and drew her down beside him. He was warm and solid. She pressed her face against his chest. He smelled of smoke. "It's all right, Diana. I know what you're thinking. The prince's entourage must return to Jeds, and your Company with them. I know that you have to go with them. Grandmother still thinks I married beneath me, but she doesn't understand that you're a Singer, that the gods have called you. How else could you be both yourself and the Daughter of the Sun? Or Mekhala, or Mekhala's sister, or the youngest daughter of the headwoman? Or the mother who saves her child? So I understand that the greater honor is mine, for gaining you. But you don't need to worry, Diana. I know what we can do. I'll ask Bakhtiian to send me and my jahar to Jeds. Someone must protect his wife's possessions until she can come to claim them. Someone must act as regent. Grandmother likes the idea. It's an honor well due to our family. Then you and I can stay together, in Jeds."

She tilted her head back. He looked so damnably optimistic, like they all did, because they thought that their gods had granted them the right to rule their world. And who was to say that it wasn't true? Certainly, Tess Soerensen and her brother had come down from the heavens and now even more than before were prepared to push the balance in favor of the jaran.

"But we're not going back to Jeds. We're going far away, far across the ocean, back to Erthe, where we came from. Anatoly." Already she felt stripped to the bone with misery. It hurt to have to tell him, while he was holding her this close. He looked bewildered by her anguish. He was so sure there was some solution when there wasn't one and never could have been one. "That journey can't be taken twice, Anatoly. Once I go, I can never come back."

"But, Diana—"

"Oh, you could go with me, perhaps, if Tess Soerensen agreed, but you'd have to leave the tribes forever." Her chest was so tight, her throat so choked with emotion, that she found herself breathing hard. She could not catch her breath. But she had to make him understand how final it was, that there was no hope. That she had no choice. "You'd have to leave your jahar. You could never come back either. You're right, about the gods. They called me to be an actor. I can't turn away from that, no matter how much I might want to stay with you here." She faltered, because his expression frightened her.

Suddenly he embraced her and held her hard against him. She tightened her arms around him and just hung on, for the longest time, forever.

"You mean it," he said finally, but she could not see his face as they lay together on the carpet. "There is nothing I can say, nothing I can suggest, that will change your mind. I can't come with you. You can't stay here. There's no hope even of finding a place between your land and mine, in Jeds."

"No hope," she whispered, wanting never to let him go.

He broke free of her and gently pulled away from her grasp. Standing up, he pulled on his boots and sorted out his clothes from the chest and rolled them up in a blanket with a few odds and ends and his scraps of embroidery.

She scrambled up to stand beside him. "Anatoly—?"

"Then let it be a clean break, and a swift one." He took her by the shoulders and kissed her once on each cheek, in the formal style. "Good-bye, Diana. I will always love you. But you must do as the gods have called you to do, and so must I."

And he left.

* * *

All that night, all she did was walk from her tent to the main tent and back again; from her tent to the main tent and back again. Quinn came out and walked two circuits with her without speaking a word, and then left to go to bed. Later, in the middle of the night, Gwyn appeared and walked beside her for a time, and before dawn, Hal, from her tent to the main tent and back again.

At dawn, she took down her tent and stowed what she had brought from Earth in a single chest. Gwyn came over, and in the end he persuaded her to let him help carry the rolled-up tent and chest and pillows. They arrived at the Sakhalin encampment just in time: Mother Sakhalin was checking all the wagons. She turned, seeing Diana, and beckoned her over.

"Mother Sakhalin," said Diana. She did not want to play this scene, but she had to. She made herself play it as if she was on the stage. "Because I must leave the jaran, and your grandson, I thought it only right to return these things to you." She risked a glance around and prayed that she would not see him. If she saw him, then everything would go for nothing. If she saw him, she would break down into tears and beg him to give up everything he knew and loved and come with her to Earth.

"Anatoly and his jahar rode out last night," said Mother Sakhalin in a cold voice. "With Bakhtiian's blessing. They rode south, to join up with my nephew's army."

Ah, Goddess, he had meant what he said, that the clean, swift break was the best one. She felt sick to the very core of her heart. She did not know what to say, but Gwyn, good soul that he was, asked Mother Sakhalin in a polite voice which wagons the tent and chest and pillows ought to go in.

She pointed. "In the jaran," she said to Diana as Gwyn carried the other things away, "a woman is married to a man for as long as the mark remains on her face, or he lives. What am I to tell my grandson?"

Diana felt crushed under the weight of Mother Sakhalin's withering stare. The old woman hated her, that was clear, for breaking her favorite grandchild's heart. And why shouldn't she hate her? Mother Sakhalin had known all along that Anatoly should never have married her.

"Tell him," she said, and choked on the words, "tell him that I love him still." She meant to say more, but her voice failed.

Gwyn returned. He held in his hand a small, supple leather pouch. "Di." He faltered. "These fell out of the pillows." He opened the flap to show her the loot, the necklace, bracelet, and earrings that Anatoly had sent her.

"Those you must keep," said Mother Sakhalin. "I insist upon it. It would be rude beyond belief and forgiving to return them to him, who risked his life to gain them for you."

"But—" Diana fished in the pouch and drew out one of the earrings. "Give this to him. Please. To remember me by. So he'll have one, and I'll have one. I—" She cast an anguished glance at Gwyn, pleading for help.

But it was Mother Sakhalin who had mercy on her. "Go on, then. We're leaving now. There's no more time for this. I'll take the earring and I'll see that he gets it." She took the earring and turned away, just like that.

"Come on, Di," said Gwyn gently. "We may as well go. I'm so sorry."

And that was it. That was the end.

CHAPTER THIRTY-TWO

They laid Ursula's body, shrouded in a simple linen winding-cloth and topped by her beloved helmet and her torn, bloodied surcoat, on the pyre at the feet of the man she had followed here. It was fitting that Ursula be burned. She had died in battle, fighting for the jaran. As for the other corpse—well, Sonia hoped the gods would forgive them for the impiety.

He had, at least, been a soldier, and he had died fighting for his people—khaja though they might be; that ought to satisfy the gods. She only hoped his spirit would not take offense at the substitution. She had made sure that the necklace of gold beads he wore had been left with him, so that he might go to the heavens with something familiar and not just the shroud of the Prince of Jeds.

One of the actors sang a haunting song in farewell. David ben Unbutu spoke a long prayer. Most of them wept, even though Sonia did not think they had loved Ursula overmuch. More than anything, she thought they were simply shocked that Ursula had died. As if they thought that Ursula couldn't die, that none of them could die. Sonia made a sign against Grandmother Night, for even contemplating such a blasphemous thought. Certainly they did not weep for the prince. All of them knew, as she knew, as Ilya knew, that Charles Soerensen had not died but simply given up Jeds in order to return to his mother's homeland of Erthe.

Dry-eyed, Tess put the torch to the wood, and it caught. Farther off, ambassadors attended, and etsanas and dyans, out of respect for the dead prince, and behind them, farther still, a knot of soldiers, riders and a few Farisa auxiliaries, who attended out of respect for the woman who had led them. Karkand smoldered behind them and, in some places, still burned.

Flames leapt up the pyre and engulfed the two bodies. The scent of ulyan permeated the air. Tess moved back to stand beside Ilya, and Sonia went over to her and put an arm around her, supporting her. Tess still suffered from exhaustion; she had not yet gotten over her ride of two days past.

"Poor Ursula," said Tess to the air. "I hope it was quick."

They stood there for a while longer. The fire fanned heat over them in waves, and at last the smoke drove them back.

"We'll go home," said Sonia.

"Yes," said Tess. Together, they walked a few paces. First Sonia halted, then Tess. Beyond, others moved away as well, seeing that the formal ceremony was over. The actors walked off en masse. The golden-haired Singer wept copiously, and three of the others surrounded her as guards might, fending off the world. Ambassadors trailed away. David and the remaining members of Soerensen's party circled the pyre a final time and left without looking back.

"Are you coming?" asked Sonia, since Ilya had not moved.

"No," he said, watching the flames. "Not yet."

And it was true, Sonia reflected, that for Ilya this was a farewell to Charles Soerensen. He could hardly expect to see him again. Certainly Tess did not expect her brother to ever return, and even with the Jedan fleet, Sonia doubted that Ilya would ever have the opportunity or the means to sail across the vast oceans to a land as distant as Erthe.

"Given more time," said Tess softly, "I think they would have become friends. At least, they understood each other."

"Understanding," said Sonia, "is truly one of the most precious gifts. You look tired, Tess."

"I am."

"Well, then, leave him here to do what he must."

"It reminds me," said Tess, and her voice cracked just a little, "of the baby."

"If the gods are merciful," said Sonia, "then they will grant you many children."

"Are the gods merciful?" Tess asked, an odd note in her voice.

"The gods are just," said Sonia, "and their justice is sometimes harsh, but it is their mercy which sustains us."

Ilya still had not moved. The pyre seemed to fascinate him, or else it merely gave a focus for his thoughts—whatever they might be. Sonia drew Tess forward, and they left him there alone to say farewell.

CHAPTER THIRTY-THREE

Bakhtiian held court in the ashes of Karkand.

"An impressive show," said Laissa, drawing aside the curtain of her litter. She gazed out on the desolation that had once been the royal city of the kingdom of Habakar and at the white tent staked out and surrounded by carpets and, beyond the carpets, a flat stretch of ground that had once been a marketplace. Bakhtiian and his wife—now the Prince of Jeds—sat under the awning, elevated on a dais. One by one, they called embassies before them. One by one, embassies knelt at the base of the dais and gave gifts and were sent away with scrolls bound with gold braid, signed by the hand of Bakhtiian himself.

Six days after the final assault, the city lay stark and ruined under a clear sky. Karkand had seemed huge before, but burned and razed its endless fields of ash and shattered masonry and blackened walls and broken towers just seemed to stretch on and on and on. Yesterday it had rained, and the drizzle had chased the last pall of smoke from the air. It still smelled of smoke and ash and burnt things, here in the city, but a chilly dampness overlaid it. The cold season was sweeping down on Habakar.

"Why impressive?" asked Jiroannes, turning away from this depressing scene to look at his wife. Beneath her sheer veil she looked impossibly serene.

"Every ambassador who comes before Bakhtiian today will see this, and know that he and his people must fear Bakhtiian's wrath. You would do well, Jiroannes, to consider wisely when it comes time to accept whatever treaty Bakhtiian offers to your Great King."

"Your King as well, now that you are my wife," he snapped.

"I may place my allegiance where I please," she said, untroubled by his outburst, "since that is the right of every man or woman born into the House of the Lion and the Moon, the most noble of all royal lines of Habakar. Mother Sakhalin came to me last night and said that she and Bakhtiian had come to an agreement, that they would ask me and my cousin, who is father to the child Melatina—the girl who is to marry Prince Mitya—to act as regents in Habakar in concert with two jaran Elders until the young prince and his bride come of age."

Jiroannes had a sudden sinking feeling that there was a great deal going on in the camp that he was not privy to. He had not seen Mitya for days and days, not since before Laissa had poisoned Samae. Did Bakhtiian truly think so little of the Great King of Vidiya that he would snub the King's ambassador like this, and take this Habakar princess into his confidence and his trust? Did Bakhtiian's intelligence net spread so wide that he knew that in truth the Great King did little more than hunt and luxuriate in the women's quarters, overseeing not his lands and his army but the innumerable petty quarrels that erupted every day in the kennels and the harem? The Great King did not want to go to war. Indeed, Jiroannes doubted he was capable of leading an army, or even of presiding over one. His mother had poisoned or strangled all of his half brothers and male cousins, to leave him free of that sort of intrigue, but the Queen Mother was dead now, and upon her death he had banished all of the ministers she had so carefully chosen for him and installed his cronies, each and every one of them young princes and noblemen of similar dissipated habits to his own. His one living sibling, Her Highness the Princess Eriania, he indulged shamelessly, going so far as to let her ride out to the hunt with him and his entourage, and everyone knew she kept her own harem in imitation of the men, but for all that, she was more of a man than he was. Which man did Jiroannes respect more, Bakhtiian or the Great King? It was no contest.

"Thought becomes you," said Laissa.

He hated her at that moment, for her mocking superiority and her patronizing way of talking to him.

"Jiroannes," she said on a sigh, "you are scarcely more than a boy. It's no wonder the young prince likes you. Don't bridle up at me like that. You're intelligent. Certainly you're ambitious, or you would never have thought to marry me. Surely you and I can work together, rather than at odds, despite all the years there are between us and the difference in our stations. I must have a husband. Clearly, you need an older head than your own to guide your actions until you've grown a few years wiser than you are now."

"How dare you address me in this impertinent fashion!" he demanded, and faltered, seeing that his anger did not frighten her anymore. She was secure. Oh, she might have to endure his attentions in the bed, but that lasted but a small part of each day. The servants obeyed her; the jaran honored her; she was free of her servitude to her God, although she still prayed three times each day with apparent piety.

Maybe Laissa was right.

"I will never care for your attentions in bed," she added, as if she had read his mind, "but I will accept them as I must, and once I have borne you a healthy son, we can negotiate for secondary wives, and certainly choose a few pretty concubines for your pleasure."

He did not trust her in this placating mood. Why should he, indeed, after what she had done to Samae? She could as easily poison him, he supposed, though he had Jat tasting all his food these days, before he ate anything. Of all his entourage, he trusted only Syrannus now. Even his guards showed a partiality for Laissa, because she had busied herself about their camp in her managing way, setting it all into an order that pleased her and presumably them as well.

She leaned out a little farther. A net woven with tiny jewels and silver thread covered her hair and from it draped the veil and a shawl of fine embroidered citron silk, falling down over her shoulders to her hips. Her robes slid around her, revealing the curve of a breast and then concealing it again as the fabric shifted and she bent forward.

"Syrannus," she said. "Announce us. We will be seen now."

We will be seen now. As if she could simply dictate to Bakhtiian that he interrupt his business in order for her to come before him. As if they would not have to wait, just as the other ambasssadors had always to do, as Jiroannes had always done; as embassies did now, shivering in their robes and cloaks as a damp wind blew, shuffling their feet in the black ash that coated the ground and their shoes. They all looked nervous. Well might they be nervous. Now that Bakhtiian had so thoroughly defeated the armies of powerful Habakar—though it was rumored that in the far south the Xiriki-khai province still held out against one of his generals—no one knew where he meant to turn his eyes and his sword next.

Syrannus padded back to them, escorted by one of Bakhtiian's personal guard. "Bakhtiian sends his greetings, princess," he said, "and hopes you will honor him with your presence."

Astounded, Jiroannes could only follow silently in Laissa's wake. Syrannus walked beside him. Mercifully, the old man kept his thoughts to himself.

They stepped off ash and onto the bright carpets surrounding the court. The gold banner rode on the wind at the top of a single column, standing to the left of the tent. At the center, raised on a dais draped with cloth embroidered with birds and horses, Bakhtiian and his wife sat on silk pillows. Mitya sat next to Bakhtiian, attended by his aunt, and next to Tess Soerensen sat Bakhtiian's niece Nadine Orzhekov, looking as bad-tempered as always. A fair young man sat beside her; Jiroannes did not recognize him, but he was clearly a prince, prettily decked out in a beautifully embroidered shirt caught in at the waist with a belt of embossed gold plates, his neck wreathed in gold necklaces. Even the hilt and sheath of his saber were plated with gold.

To Jiroannes's shock, Bakhtiian rose and stepped down from the dais to come forward and greet Laissa. "Your highness," he said. A jaran woman came forward and offered Laissa a hand, to help her out of her litter. She accepted the hand gravely and climbed out gracefully enough, and thanked the woman, who then retreated.

"Where is Mother Sakhalin?" she asked. "I haven't seen her for several days."

"She has ridden south."

"Ah.

"I hope, your highness, that you will sit beside Mitya."

"I would be honored," replied Laissa.

For one wild moment, Jiroannes had the improbable idea that she actually liked and respected these barbarians. But surely not. She was no fool, he knew that well enough, and she could see where her interests lay: with the jaran, of course.

Bakhtiian escorted her back to the dais and two women helped her up. Mitya sat with his head bowed, blushing faintly. Poor boy. Was she truly to be his regent? Jiroannes hoped Bakhtiian would employ a slave to taste the boy's food. On the other hand, surely Laissa would not do anything so stupid. If she poisoned Mitya, she would have Bakhtiian's wrath to face, and she herself could see right here, around her, how ruthless Bakhtiian was willing to be.

"Ambassador."

Jiroannes started. Bakhtiian still stood there, regarding him with an amused expression on his face. On the level, Jiroannes was surprised to find that they were of equal height. Presiding over his court, riding out with his army, Bakhtiian seemed much—bigger.

"You will attend me now," finished Bakhtiian. He returned to the dais. Jiroannes followed him forward and waited. "Ah, thank you, Kirill." Bakhtiian took a scroll from one of his captains. He handed it to his wife, who unrolled it and smoothed it out. Jiroannes risked a glance at her. She was pale, but her face was set and strong, and she wore a signet ring on her middle left finger and a heavy gold chain around her neck.

"To my brother, the Great King of Vidiya," said Bakhtiian, appearing to read from the scroll, "I send this message. By the power that Mother Sun and Father Wind have invested in us throughout our own realms and through the realms of the great world, let this be known:

that we wish only to live in peace and to rejoice in the good things of life and to act for good, and that those who speak to us of war will find war, and those who speak to us of peace will find peace.

"These things, I grant between us, as long as there is peace between us: the borders as they stand now, to the full extent of the Habakar kingdom and her provinces; free trade over the pass south of the city of Targana; safe passage for merchants and envoys and couriers. To show your understanding of my decree, you may send to the jaran gifts, and ten young women and ten young men of noble birth to attend my court, so that our people and yours may come to know one another."

Hostages. Jiroannes noted that Bakhtiian said nothing about sending young jaran men or women to the Vidiyan court, though doubtless the Great King would be amused by a jaran concubine.

"For our part, as we honor our brother, we send to you—"

Bakhtiian paused, quite deliberately, and looked at Jiroannes, clearly expecting him, as ambassador, to suggest a suitable gift. Jiroannes glanced toward Laissa, and she gave him a slight nod, almost as if she was encouraging him. Well, probably it wouldn't be wise to ask for a concubine. It must be a gift that honored the Great King, and yet a gift that Bakhtiian would not interpret as tribute, going from himself to Vidiya.

"Horses," said Jiroannes abruptly, remembering the fine mare that Mitya rode. "A fine gray stallion for the Great King, and a gray mare for Her Royal Highness, his sister."

"Yes," said Bakhtiian. His wife wrote in with her own hand the decree, appending it to the letter.

Laissa nodded at Jiroannes. He even caught a glimpse of her smiling, under the gauze of her veil. Did she actually approve of his choice?

"... and a gray mare for Her Royal Highness, his sister," Bakhtiian was saying, repeating the words his wife had written down. He took in a breath and looked up at the sky, clear and blue above them. "When by the power of the heavens the whole world from the rising of the sun to the setting of the sun shall be at one in peace, then so shall we all be at peace. You may believe that your country is far away, but not so far away that we cannot ride there. You may believe that your mountains are high beyond measure, but not so high that we cannot cross them. You may believe that the seas are vast, but not so broad that our ships cannot sail them. The gods who live in the heavens will make what was difficult easy, and what was far away, near."

He fell silent. The court fell silent, waiting on him. Like a faint echo of his words, Jiroannes heard the sound of falling rock; perhaps some wall had tumbled down, out there in the wasteland that was all that remained of Karkand.

Bakhtiian took the pen from his wife and signed the letter. He rolled it up absently. "I'll send Venedikt Grekov and his jahar as envoy and escort, with the ambassador," he said.

Half the court swiveled their heads to look at the fair young man who sat beside Nadine Orzhekov, then looked away. Bakhtiian's niece smiled, but made no comment.

"Who is next?" said Bakhtiian, turning to his ministers. "Ah, the embassy from Parkilnous."

Tess Soerensen glanced up. "Good. It's the closest port. If we can manage it, I'd like to send the Company and the rest of Charles's party back to Jeds from there."

Bakhtiian regarded her for a moment, looking puzzled by her words. *If we can manage it.* How should they not manage it? Jiroannes thought. Bakhtiian was master here, and Parkilnous, however powerful and rich it might be, was simply an independent city-state, not a great kingdom like Habakar.

"Ambassador." Bakhtiian leaned forward and offered the scroll to Jiroannes. "You may leave in the morning for Vidiya. I will send Venedikt Grekov to you at dawn. Treat him with honor. His nephew is my niece's husband."

Jiroannes bowed and retreated. Laissa, the bitch, remained where she was, beside Mitya, but Jiroannes had no choice but to leave court with Syrannus. On his way out, he passed the Parkilnous embassy coming in. They were so heavily laden with tribute that it took thirty strong men to carry all the gifts.

At dusk, Jat came in to him.

"Eminence, the prince has come and hopes to see you."

Jiroannes leapt up at once. "Show him in. Bring us tea, and food, Jat. Syrannus, you will taste it for us today."

Syrannus bowed. Jat bowed and left, and a moment later he showed Mitya in.

The boy still wore his court clothes, which were rich and looked heavy to wear. Jiroannes offered him a chair, and after hesitating, Mitya sat.

"I suppose I'll have to get used to sitting in chairs," he said. "I'm sorry you're leaving."

"I must go."

"I know." He brightened. "But the journey isn't too long, is it? It won't take you above two or three years to return, will it?"

"To return?"

"But the princess said that you were coming back to be my chief minister. After all, since she is staying in Habakar, of course you will have to return—"

"She is staying in Habakar!"

Together, as if by mutual consent, they lapsed into silence.

Jat brought tea and cakes and delicately carved slices of fruit, all arranged pleasingly on a silver tray. Then he retreated to the shadowed corner.

"I thought—it isn't my right to ask—I wondered where—" Mitya broke off and stared at his hands. He murmured her name under his breath, so softly that if Jiroannes hadn't been expecting it, he wouldn't have heard it. "Samae."

Laissa, with her usual expediency, had had her servants dispose of the body. These days, there were so many, it was easy to lose one. Jiroannes felt cold all through him, and a sudden pity for Mitya, whose face betrayed clearly enough that he had cared for Samae, slave though she was.

Hesitant, Mitya went on. "I asked Princess Laissa about her, but she said that—that Samae had displeased her and that she had been forced to give her to new masters. Is it true?"

"I'm sorry, Mitya," Jiroannes said, stumbling over the words. How could he explain? He could not—especially since Laissa had managed to both lie and tell the truth at the same time. Clearly she was experienced in court intrigue. He forced himself to go on. "Once I married, the females in my house came under my wife's jurisdiction. I cannot interfere." The lie tore at his throat, he who had learned from the words of the prophets that lies were evil, who saw how terribly the words hurt Mitya. "You couldn't have married her, my prince, and her presence— since she is not a jaran woman, and bound to laws not your own ... it would only complicate your life." The poor boy fought himself, trying to keep his expression controlled; Jiroannes ached to see him suffer so. "She is a slave, Mitya, and in her land, by the laws of her gods, she can never be anything but a slave."

Mitya's hands lay in fists on his thighs. He did not move except to bow his head so that shadows covered it. In the uncertain light of the lantern, Jiroannes could no longer read his expression.

"But she cared for you, Mitya. . . ." He faltered.

Silence lay over them as heavy as sorrow.

From outside, he heard a woman laugh and a guard curse, and a goat bleat, and the ring of bridle as a troop of horsemen passed by.

Mitya stood up abruptly. "You're not coming back," he said.

"I don't—I didn't think—"

"No, I'm not accusing you. I'm not angry. Of course you want to return to your own land." He strode to the entrance, but hesitated there, facing out toward the camp, as if he did not know how to say farewell.

Jiroannes was struck by a reckless urge. Of course he would want to return to his own land: Back to the endless, cruel intrigues at the Great King's court, where his uncle lived on sufferance and he himself walked the veriest tightrope between royal favor and banishment to the provinces, where a man who did not die from swamp fever was in any case doomed to poverty, since banishment brought with it a ban on all the luxuries that made life worth living. Or he could leave Vidiya forever and come to live in Habakar, where his wife was regent and his patron and friend would be, in four short years, the reigning king.

Jiroannes rose from his chair and hurried over to the entrance. Mitya turned back, to face him, with his pale, young face and his unconsciously arrogant carriage. "I would be honored to act as your chief minister, Prince Mitya." Then, on impulse, Jiroannes knelt in front of the boy, as any man kneels in front of his sovereign lord. "When this duty is discharged, I will leave my country and return here to serve you."

CHAPTER THIRTY-FOUR

The rains brought a second flowering to Habakar, turning the grass green and encouraging late flowers to bud and open, but frost soon killed it. The army left, in its wake, pasture eaten down to dirt and villages that would have been stripped of their winter stores if Tess had not forcefully pointed out to Bakhtiian that the legacy of such an action would be a revolt by the Habakar people against Mitya.

"I don't understand," said Ilya as they sat under the awning of her tent in the late afternoon, "not truly, why your brother would leave Jeds forever, forsake his power there, to return to a place where at best he might hope by the time he dies to make some incursions against a power he claims is far greater than his own, and at worst expect to be killed for his trouble."

"Because Erthe is where his heart lies," replied Tess. The towers of Birat caught the last golden rays of the sun, gleaming against a backdrop of snow-laden mountains to the west.

"But not yours."

She sipped at her tea, cupping the ceramic mug—it was of Farisa make—in her hands and letting the steam that curled up from the depths warm her face. "Well, it is the land where I was born. But when I think of it now, I think of being ten years old with my parents dead. I think of being sent back to study there, by Charles, and being so lonely, and hating it. This is my home, here—well—" She squinted toward Birat and the mountains. "Not here, not Habakar, but Jeds, and the plains."

He leaned across and touched her on the knee. "We'll

go back to the plains, my heart, once I've set things in order here. We can have a child there, Tess, on the plains."

She bowed her head and lowered the mug to nestle in her lap. "I don't know," she whispered, not wanting to tell him that probably they could never have a child, knowing what it meant to him. Not wanting to say it aloud, knowing what it meant to her.

"It's early still." He withdrew his hand. "We won't speak of it now."

They sat in silence for a time. Birat's fields lay at peace beyond, harvested. A few bore the green sprigs of winter wheat, growing apace already. Canals glittered in a net of pathways that crisscrossed in the fields, reminding Tess of the saboteur network that she and Rajiv and the others were going to build, here, in Jeds, in Morava. The army spread out around them, but it was halved in size, now; Mother Sakhalin had gone south to her nephew, and other troops had gone in other directions, south to aid Sakhalin, north to investigate word of a revolt. Kirill Zvertkov had led a troop ahead, west, toward Parkilnous, escorting the city's embassy back and laying the ground for Bakhtiian's arrival.

"Tess," said Ilya, and stopped.

"What is it?" Then she looked at him.

He would not look at her, at first, like any modest jaran man would not, faced with a woman not of his own family, but finally he lifted his eyes to her face. "Do you think the gods know that I killed my own father? But if they do, then why would they still grant me their favor?"

"But he wasn't your father."

"Not by our laws. But by the laws you insisted I acknowledge in claiming Vasha as my son, I am certain that Khara Roskhel was my father."

"I'm sorry, then, not for Vasha's sake, but for yours. I'm sorry you killed anyone, that anyone has ever died and will ever die because of choices that other people make for them. But isn't that the nature of war? I'm not sure it ever accomplishes anything but killing, and yet we turn to it again and again, even Charles, knowing that any rebellion he leads will in the end be no different in kind than what you've done in the coastal princedoms and in Habakar."

"But once we unite the lands, and his rebellion succeeds, then there will be peace," said Ilya reasonably. "I would like to visit Erthe someday. Your philosophers are very different from ours. Do they have an elixir for long life there?"

She started and almost spilled her tea. "What makes you ask that?"

"Oh, that Habakar philosopher the old king sent us as an ambassador, he said that while he had means of protecting life, he had none to prolong it, but that he had heard that there is a country that lies along the Golden Road where the magicians brew such an elixir. I thought perhaps the philosophers of Erthe knew something of it."

"Ah. Well. Perhaps they do. I'm not a philosopher." Now it was her turn to falter. "Ilya."

He said nothing, only watched her, forcing her to speak.

"We can't send a regent to Jeds. I have to go."

At once, his expression shuttered.

"You know it's true, Ilya. You know I have to go, to establish my power there, so that they can see me and acknowledge me. I haven't been in Jeds for years and years. They'll have no way to recognize me, not truly, except by this ring and the chain. Well, Baron Santer and some of the other officials at court will probably recognize me, but I was a child when they last saw me. Tell me you see that I have to go, Ilya." Her voice broke on the last sentence.

"So your brother wins what he wanted, in the end." He stood up, that abruptly, and walked off the carpet. Twenty paces away from the tent, two guards fell in on either side of him. They vanished into the camp.

"Oh, God," said Tess, and started to cry, not just because of him but because ever since the baby had died everything made her cry easily.

Children's laughter rang through the camp.

"Tess! Tess! Come quickly."

Vasha and Katya and Galina raced into view and they halted, panting and giggling, on her carpet.

"Come *on!*" cried Katya, tugging at Tess's arm and spilling the remains of the tea on Tess's trouser leg and onto the carpet.

"Tess, why are you crying?" Vasha asked. At once the three children hushed and heaved themselves down beside Tess with such attitudes of attentive concern that Tess could not help but laugh at their grave faces.

"It's nothing," she said, wiping her eyes.

"Well, then!" exclaimed Katya, leaping up again. "You must come *now!*"

"Where is—?" Vasha faltered. He never called Ilya anything, not Uncle, not Ilya, not Bakhtiian and certainly never Father, except to leave a pause where his name went.

Tess waved vaguely in the direction Ilya had gone, not trusting her voice.

"I'll find him," said Galina, and jumped up and ran away.

Tess allowed Vasha and Katya to tug her up and drag her toward Sonia's tent. "But what's going on?" Tess demanded.

On the other side of Sonia's tent, out of sight of Tess's own awning, Josef Raevsky stood with his saber drawn and little Ivan's hand covering his own on the hilt. Ilya arrived just in time to watch with the others as Josef, with Vania's hand guiding his, marked Sonia with his saber, drawing the line of marriage down her cheek, parallel to the scar that had marked her first marriage to Mikhal Yakhov.

Tess burst into tears. A moment later she felt Ilya beside her.

"I'm sorry," he whispered, sliding an arm around her back. "I'm sorry, Tess. It isn't your brother's fault or even his victory, but my own fault, and Her victory, who has paid me back in my own coin."

"Oh, you idiot!" she said through her tears. "I just said I had to go there. I didn't say I wasn't coming back!" She broke away from him and went forward to hug Sonia.

"Well, you don't have to cry!" exclaimed Sonia, laughing at her until her tears stopped. "After all, since I must go into seclusion, you'll have to be in charge of the camp for the next ten days."

"But I don't know how to run the camp—"

"If you'd encouraged Aleksi to marry, you'd have more help, wouldn't you?"

"Oh, thank you," said Tess, laughing. "Where is Aleksi? He was just here."

"He took one of the guard's horses," said Vasha, "and rode out that way." He pointed, and Tess knew that in that direction lay the Veselov encampment.

"He isn't going to mark her if I'm not there to see, is he? We'd better go."

Sonia laid a hand on Tess's arm, restraining her. "Tess. I think if he'd wanted you there, he would have asked you to come with him. Look how dark it is already. I don't think Aleksi wants a public marking. There'll be enough celebration in ten days."

"Well," said Tess, not knowing whether to be offended or pleased. Aleksi had been her shadow for three years, a steady, reliable presence but in his own way still insecure about his place in the Orzhekov tribe. It was encouraging to see him act on his own at last, and yet it felt odd as well. "Josef." She kissed the blind rider on either cheek. Then she went to consult with Galina and Juli Danov about running the camp. Tonight it was not Aleksi, but Ilya, who shadowed her, sticking close by her, saying little but never letting her out of his sight.

Aleksi returned, alone, much later, but he had a smile on his face.

So they stayed outside Birat for ten days. There was a sudden flood of markings, many of them unmarried riders marking widowed women, and a great celebration at the end of that time, observed by the Habakar from their walls and their fields with apprehension and by the jagged western mountains with supreme indifference.

Aleksi astounded Bakhtiian by demanding his share of the treasure gained from the Habakar kingdom for his services to Bakhtiian, and he sent so much gold and jewels to the Veselov camp that when Svetlana was carried out to the fire to meet her new husband, she was almost as heavily laden in riches as was Sonia Orzhekov. Arina

Veselov had gifted Svetlana with a good tent, much larger than Aleksi's, and Svetlana herself gave wedding gifts to all the children and a beautiful carpet to Tess and Ilya that she and her sister had made, as her wedding gift to them.

"I don't know," said Cara late that evening, while dancing went on around three bonfires, "if I approve of this business of marking the women."

"Oho," said Tess, lifting a hand to touch her own cheek, where she was marked. "Do I detect the superior note of advanced civilizations in your words, Cara?"

"Probably," said Cara. "I suppose we've just found less obviously violent ways to alter our bodies. Tess, do you want to try again for a child?"

"Try again!"

"Charles suggested it, in fact. I think you and Ilya can have a child, with some help from me. A little additional lab work on you, but since you're coming to Jeds, we can do it there. And you'll need a communications implant, too, and Rajiv suggests a mini-chip demi-modeler straight into the cranium with a retinal scan trigger. Charles will send a technician down for that."

"When did Charles suggest that? About me trying again for a child?"

"The morning before he left."

"Hmm." Tess broke away from Cara to go forward and greet and kiss Arina Veselov, who was being carried by on a litter, and then came back. "What scheme is Charles hatching now?"

"Tess! Maybe Charles just acted out of pure sentiment."

Tess considered the possibility. She realized that she had a hard time imagining Charles acting out of anything but expediency. "Well," she admitted, "maybe I'm not always fair to him."

Cara snorted. "How often are we ever fair, to others and even to ourselves? Do you want to put a call in to Charles?"

"No. I know he's safe on Odys. I'll wait until we can get a safe channel from Jeds. He's a damned bastard anyway. Ilya is right. Charles accomplished what he wanted—me to leave the jaran and to accept my duties as his heir whether I wanted to or not—"

"Are you leaving the jaran?" Cara asked without a blink.

"Of course not! I mean, only to go to Jeds for as long as I have to, and I'll have to take jaran with me, a jahar, probably—but I'll come back to the plains as soon as I can."

"Then, my dear, I would advise you not to exaggerate the case. Of course, you must go to Jeds temporarily, but it's become equally important that you return to the jaran."

"Maybe Yuri was right," said Tess, musing.

"Yuri?"

"My brother Yuri. He said that the gods had brought me to the jaran to find him, to reunite us, who were brother and sister in another life. But maybe the gods had other plans. Maybe Yuri was the jaran, what they were before I came, untouched and—oh, I don't want to say innocent. Uncorrupted. And so in the end he died, because of what I brought to him and to them." She shook her head. "He would have hated this."

"The gods usually do," replied Cara, looking grave and amused at the same time.

"Do what?"

"Have other plans."

At first, Tess laughed, but as she stared out at the fires and the musicians and the dancing, the whirl of skirts, the flashing gleam of gold and bronze, the distant torches that rimmed the walls of Birat, she thought of Ilya, who had by his own lights and by the laws of his people already begun the corruption, long before she came. And yet, who was to say if that corruption hadn't begun while Ilya was in Jeds, a Jeds already deeply influenced by Charles? And yet, who was to say if it hadn't begun when a fair-haired Singer named Petre Sokolov marked an ambitious woman who didn't want him, driven by a vision that he was granted from the heavens, of the gods-touched child that he was meant to father?

* * *

It took them ten days to cross the mountains over a high pass already coated with snow. Down they rode, into a great forest that stretched endlessly out on all sides. Through this watershed they passed and in fifteen days farther on came to a great river and the fortified city of Parkilnous.

Neither Parkilnous nor its people had any of the grace and light and elegant trappings of Habakar lands. They were a somewhat lighter race in coloring, more akin to the black-haired jaran than to their darker Habakar neighbors to the east. The river streamed by, sluggish and especially filthy downstream from the great walls that rimmed its bank. There were no suburbs spread out in harmonious lines around the inner city. All the houses and markets, palaces and great merchants' mansions and hordes of poor, lay crammed in together within the confining walls. Hovels sprawled out beyond the gates, out on the dumping grounds for the city's refuse and into the marshlands that bordered a tributary stream where it fed down from the forest and into the great river itself. Farther out, fields spread, each one ringed by a rough wall of stone.

The governor of Parkilnous had already opened his gates to Zvertkov's jahar, and he came himself, barefooted and bareheaded like a penitent, to greet Bakhtiian and usher him into the city.

Parkilnous stank. Unlike the Habakar, the Parkilnese evidently had no concept of sanitation, however primitive. Tess could not bring herself to eat much of the feast laid out in her and Bakhtiian's honor in the great hall of the palace, and the entertainment—dancing girls, jugglers, and a poor emaciated bearlike creature that a burly one-eyed man wrestled—was not much better. Then the merchants came, a representative from each house, many of them elder women, and one by one they piled gifts in front of the great conqueror and the Prince of Jeds. Tess wondered if the old women really headed their families or if the Parkilnese were simply canny enough to have seen the power Mother Sakhalin had in the jaran camp and use it now to their own advantage. Obviously, they planned to

buy their way to safety. Give the barbarians enough tribute, and they would leave.

It was a relief to return to the camp at dusk, where the
air didn't reek of refuse and urine and rot, and the tents
were airy and the carpets clean.

Ilya sat down with Nadine on pillows in the outer
chamber, and they studied her maps.

"You see," Nadine was saying as Galina brought in
komis and tea and Tess paced back and forth along the inner wall of the tent, "David helped me get a fair measure-
ment of the mountain pass and the forest, and I managed
to talk to a ship's captain today and got a sense of how
far it is down this river to the sea and thence to Jeds."

"By sea," said Ilya. He drew a hand across the vast
blank reaches of the parchment, south, to where Nadine
judged that Jeds lay. "Jeds has many ships, that can sail
up and down the coast. But ships alone or land alone will
not make an empire."

"Send me to scout it, then," said Nadine, as if daring
her uncle.

"When you've given me heirs," he said calmly.

Tess almost laughed, to see Nadine's expression change
so swiftly from smugness to anger. She might as well
have had sparks flying off of her. But as quickly, Tess's
amusement turned to pity. Nadine wasn't suited to be a
brood mare. Well, no woman was, to be prized for nothing but the children she could bear. "Perhaps Nadine
could be regent, in Jeds, together with Baron Santer,"
Tess said into their silence.

"Dina?" Ilya frowned and considered his niece. He
sighed. "I wanted to install Anatoly Sakhalin as regent.
He is a prince in his own right, and it would have pleased
Mother Sakhalin, and I had thought that the Company
meant to stay in Jeds—poor boy. Mother Sakhalin said he
was heartbroken when he rode away to his uncle. That he
couldn't bear to stay, knowing his wife would leave him
soon." He cast a recriminatory glance toward Tess.

"Ilya! His sort always recovers quickly. Surely he can
marry again."

"I think," said Ilya slowly, "that women give pretty

men like Anatoly Sakhalin too little credit for intelligence and feeling. We shall see."

"What about Jeds?" demanded Nadine.

"No." Ilya shook his head. "Nowhere, my girl, until you've done your duty to me." Fuming, Nadine rolled up her parchments and jumped to her feet. "Ah," said Ilya, raising a finger. "You may leave if you wish, but I'll keep the maps here for tonight."

Nadine was too solicitous of her maps to treat them roughly. She set them gently on the table, and then stormed out of the tent.

"I don't think Feodor is a good husband for her," said Ilya mildly. "I have it in mind to send Niko and Juli as co-regents, to watch over Jeds with Baron Santer. Niko has always wanted to visit Jeds."

"Niko Sibirin is a wise choice," she agreed. She circled back to stand behind him and rested a hand on his shoulder, running her other hand through his hair. "But you could come to Jeds, Ilya. We could establish our reign, and you could strike north from Jeds. And send your armies south from here. . . ."

He rose, went over to the table, and unrolled one of the maps. "Across lands we know nothing of? No. We're not prepared for that yet. We need a greater army than the one I have now. I must consolidate here and then move forward. There is the Xiriki-khai province still to be won in the south, and the outlying desert cities beyond it. We must not just fight wars but build, a city for Mitya to rule from, armies of Farisa and Habakar soldiers as well as our own. We may not unite the lands between Parkilnous and Jeds while we yet live, Tess, but our heirs—" The sheen of the parchment glowed in the lantern light. He looked young, in the soft light, and all unbeknownst to him he would stay young, perhaps even for long enough to reach Jeds with his army, with all the lands between under his authority. She could not bring herself to regret the decision, what she had begged Cara to do to him, but she wondered if it had been wise. "Still, though," Ilya continued, so focused on the map that he was oblivious to her stare, "we must send merchants and envoys south from here, and with their intelligence we can trace the route along which we can march our armies."

"But, Ilya, if it was only for a year, why couldn't you come with me?"

For the longest time, he stared at the table, as if its swirling grain fascinated him. At first, he spoke to it, not to her. "No. I—Tess—" He took in a deep breath and turned to her. "I have to make my peace with the tribes, with the Elders, with Mother Sakhalin and my own aunt. I have to tell them the truth. I have to stand before them as I wasn't willing to or brave enough to eleven years ago, or even three years past at the great gathering of tribes at the khayan-sarmiia. I must tell them of the bargain I made with Grandmother Night. They alone can judge me, and choose whether they wish to follow me any farther."

Ilya always managed to stand so that the light lent him grace and power, as if the light itself existed on this earth in order to illuminate him. He had radiance, which quality can never be learned but only given. It was hard for Tess to imagine that the tribes might repudiate him now, but then, he had broken more than one of their holiest laws.

"Your father was right, you know, about his vision," she said. "About you." She crossed to him and laid her hands on his chest. "When I come back, we'll have a child."

"Two," he said instantly, and then embraced her and just held her. He was warm and so close that they might almost as well have been one person. "Tess," he whispered, "haven't two new moons passed since you were delivered of the baby?"

"Yes. Why?" But she laughed even as she asked the question, knowing what he meant by it. "Yes, Ilya," she said, and kissed him.

* * *

Two days later, they boarded the ship: Tess and Aleksi and his new family; the Bharentous Repertory Company; and what was left of Charles's party: Cara and Jo and

Maggie and Rajiv. Hal Bharentous and Gwyn Jones carried between them the litter on which Vasil Veselov lay, his face drawn with pain and his beauty forever mutiliated by an ugly scar. Until he got to space, of course, where it could easily enough be repaired.

Poor Karolla walked behind her husband, her face set. She was hugely pregnant. A great argument had ensued over whether Karolla could bring her tent. In the end, Tess had told Owen she would herself pay for any extra weight charges and that Karolla might bring anything she damned well pleased. The gods alone knew how difficult life was going to be for her, torn away from the tribes, without stripping her of all her worldly goods that might anchor her in the strange new world she was going to. Tess wondered if Karolla had had a choice whether to go; a real choice, that is, not just Vasil convincing her that, of course, she would go with him. But Tess was glad Vasil was leaving, for Ilya's sake. For her own peace of mind. Diana Brooke-Holt came after, holding the hands of the two children. Diana looked pallid and fragile. Tess noted how solicitous many of the other members of the Company were toward her.

On the other shallow river ship, Niko and Juli and two of their grandchildren and various of their train and one hundred riders boarded. The horses, disliking it, were led below. On the shore, David huddled over a map with Nadine. Maggie hailed him, and he started and glanced up. There was an awkward moment, one could tell by the way he stared at Nadine, and then they said good-bye without touching and he hurried up the ramp, hands clenched. He came and stood beside Tess on the deck.

On the shore, Ilya waited, he with his jahar arrayed gloriously behind him and his gold banner whipping in the breeze that skirled in off the river, rising with the dawn. What words did they need here? They had said what was in their hearts many times.

She watched him. He watched her. The captain of the ship bellowed orders. The ramps scraped up over rails. Ropes were cast free, and with poles they thrust themselves away from the dock, and then the stroke for the oars called out, a steady, pleasing pattern.

The docks receded. Beside her, David wiped a tear from his cheek and farther along, Diana clutched the railing and stared at the gap opening between her and the jaran. Karolla Arkhanov knelt beside her husband, not looking back, but her children did.

Tess turned away from the railing, finally, leaving David and Diana and the others to stare until a broad curve in the river hid Parkilnous and the jaran army from their sight. She went to help Karolla. What need had she to linger there, to mark for one final time all that was being left behind?

After all, she was coming back.

CHAPTER THIRTY-FIVE

Karolla gave birth to a healthy son the day after they sailed into Jeds. She named the child Anton. Her husband was too wracked by pain and the agony of the voyage to be aware of much beyond the fact that she had delivered the child. Diana also suspected that Dr. Hierakis had Vasil drugged, but she was not privy to the councils of the Prince of Jeds and her retinue.

They spent forty days in Jeds, and Diana had, thank the Goddess, no time to dwell on anything except work. Owen drove them through rehearsals and arranged a series of performances that included "The Jaran Diptych," as he and Ginny called the folktales. When Diana wasn't rehearsing, she took care of Valentin and Ilyana, who were not as overawed by Jeds as Diana had feared they might be. On the other hand, they had seen Hamrat and Karkand, so they knew now what a city was. Only in that small space of time between winding down from the night's performance or rehearsal and actually falling asleep did she have leisure to brood.

"Diana, my dear," said Dr. Hierakis one night, "whatever are you doing out here?"

Jeds had a mild climate, and even at midnight in winter, with the winds blowing in off the bay, Diana did not need a cloak to walk the battlements. Although a cloak might have lent more drama to her situation. "I can't sleep," she said as she turned to greet the doctor and her companion.

"Ah," said the doctor, and Diana wasn't sure whether to be annoyed or grateful for the tone of the word. "You haven't met Dr. Kinzer. She just arrived."

Dr. Kinzer was a heavyset woman with wicked blue

eyes. Diana shook her hand reflexively. "How do you do?"

"Glad to get off that choppy bay," said Dr. Kinzer with a laugh. "I don't have sea legs."

"I'm afraid I don't know your connection here...." Diana trailed off, feeling stupid.

"Owen Zerentous brought me in to look at a trauma case. Spinal injury. Quite a mess, from the preliminary imaging I've seen."

"Oh," said Diana. "Owen brought you in to look at Vasil. Can you—fix him?"

Kinzer smiled easily. "I imagine so. I can only do a preliminary operation in these conditions, though. The reconstruction work will come later, on Earth."

"Dr. Kinzer," said Dr. Hierakis dryly, "is one of our foremost experts on spinal cord trauma. Owen is spending a good deal of credit on Vasil Veselov. I hope he appreciates it."

"Who, Owen? I'm sure he does, but then, when he's in the grip of an obsession like this one ... oh, you meant Vasil."

Dr. Hierakis nodded. "Yes, I meant Vasil, who will probably never think but that he deserved it. Are you going to stay with the Company, Diana?"

"Of course!" The anger hit with the force of storm waters. "What point is there in anything if I don't stay with the Company? Oh, I know what you meant—if we tour out into Chapalii space, but as long as it's theater, what do I care? As long as I'm working, as long as we're touring, it doesn't matter where I am, and I'm used to Owen and Ginny, and we do marvelous work and—" She broke off, aware all at once of how strident her voice had become.

There was a pause.

"It's an odd view, in a way," said Dr. Kinzer kindly, walking over to the battlements. "I'm not used to the lack of lights. And it's remarkably quiet." Together, they listened.

Diana could hear the lap of the waters on the rocks below and not much else. A woman was singing in the palace, in a room that opened out onto the battlements. In a pleasant if rather thin voice, she sang the words to a jaran song, something cheerful and tender about a baby's laughter and a brand new foal.

"That's Svetlana," continued the doctor, as if aware that Diana would rather not think, much less talk. "She helps poor Karolla at night. What a pleasant, capable young woman she is. I'm so pleased, for Aleksi's sake." Then she paused and peered through the darkness at Diana. The moon gave pale light to her face, framing her dark curls against the night-gray of her skin. "I'm sorry, Diana."

Diana had taught herself to close up the instant she began to think of—anything but what was safe to think of. "Poor Karolla," Diana repeated. "What do you think of Jeds, Dr. Kinzer?"

"I really did *just* arrive. The palace is nice—what I've seen of it."

Again they lapsed into silence, and into their silence a voice called out from the darkness. "Cara? Are you out here?" It was Tess Soerensen. "Marco and Javier just got in, can you believe it? And here I thought they'd get here first!" Then, fainter, her voice floated out as she evidently turned her head and spoke in a different direction. "Yes, Marco, the Company is still here. They can't leave until Veselov is able to travel." The voice grew louder, and Diana heard footsteps as well, more than one set. "He almost died twice on the voyage here, and then there's the baby, too, now."

"You still haven't told me," said Marco Burckhardt, his voice clear and carrying on the night air, "how Baron Santer reacted when you arrived with your escort of savages."

Diana felt her blood run cold. "I don't want to see him!" she whispered, suddenly frantic.

Dr. Hierakis's hand settled fleetingly on Diana's arm and then the doctor moved away from her. "Here I am!" Dr. Hierakis called out cheerfully enough. "And Melissa Kinzer has arrived as well. But let's do go inside. I'm sure Missy has had enough sea air for the day, and if you've been on a ship, Marco, I can't imagine you want to stare at whitecaps any longer either. Was Javier horribly seasick?"

"Horribly," said Marco, and laughed. "Who's that out there?"

"Oh, one of the serving girls, frightened that she's going to lose her employment here because her father wants her to marry some old goat. She's better off in the prince's service, and she knows it. Tess, let's take some tea up to Svetlana. She's still awake with the baby."

Their voices receded. Diana stood alone again on the battlements. The sea beat on the rocks below. She buried her face in her hands and managed by sheer force of will not to cry.

The days passed, and Diana stayed busy. She did not see Marco again.

The night they premiered "The Daughter of the Sun," all the actors were aware of an additional buzz in the audience. It was annoying, as if the audience had their attention half on the stage and half somewhere else. At the Royal Court Theater, it had become the tradition that the lead actress visit the prince's box at the intermission if the prince was in attendance.

"When the first Charles commissioned and built the theater," explained Baron Santer as he escorted Diana in all her makeup and costume up the steep flight of private back stairs that led to the royal box, "he insisted on the tradition." The baron was an elderly gentleman who looked mild and had the eyes of a shark. "Some say the better to view every beautiful actress who played here. He was quite a ladies man."

"You knew him?" Diana asked politely, and then recalled with a jolt that the first Charles had been Marco.

"I was a young man, and I had the honor of counting myself his friend." He surveyed Diana in the dim light, and for an instant such a light came into his eyes that Diana hoped she wouldn't have to do anything drastic, like shove him down the stairs. "He would have approved of you," he finished, as if he thought she cared about his approval.

"I'm sure he would have," she replied glacially.

The baron bowed. Then he led her on by a private door

into the prince's box, where Tess Soerensen sat with the Baroness Santer, a woman considerably younger than her husband, and Niko and Juli. Aleksi and a young captain of the Jedan militia stood on guard.

"Diana," said Tess, but did not rise to greet her. She merely extended her hand, and Diana knew the part expected of her here. She curtsied deeply and kissed Tess's hand, on the signet ring.

"Your highness," she murmured and glanced up in time to catch a spark of humor in Tess's face.

There came a knock on the public door. "Ah," said the Prince of Jeds. Diana noted for the first time that Tess held in her other hand a folded square of paper. Perfume wafted from it, a sweet, rich scent. "Show her in."

The captain went to the door and opened it. Baron Santer raised his eyebrows, and the Baroness hid her mouth behind her fan.

A woman swept in. At once, Diana realized that she, Diana, had not done justice to her own entrance into the box. A moment later, she realized that the audience had turned its attention here, and that it must have been this woman all along with whom the actors were competing.

"Your highness," said the woman, curtsying even more deeply than Diana had and thus displaying a generous amount of white bosom from her low cut gown. She kissed the signet ring, and then promptly destroyed the illusion by lifting her head and smiling straight at Tess Soerensen, meeting her eyes.

"So you're Mayana," said Tess.

"So you're Tess," said the famous courtesan, for it was indeed she. Even Diana and the other actors had heard of her. She was a legend in Jeds, and now, this close, Diana could see that she was gorgeous, but more by self-assurance and ready laughter than from physical beauty.

"How do you know who I am?" Tess asked.

"Ilyakoria writes me letters, of course. Didn't he tell you?"

Tess laughed. "I had hoped to meet you sooner," she said, "but the affairs of state ... Still, I'm not surprised to find you here, at the performance of this particular tale."

Mayana bowed her head in acknowledgment, as if the comment was somehow a tribute to her. She had hair more bronze than gold in color, perfectly curled, and whereas the box itself was decorated in a spare Florentine style, the courtesan's gown was simply cut but floridly ornamented in a manner reminiscent of jaran embroidery, and yet the contrast was not unflattering to Mayana.

"Come to see me at the palace," said the prince.

"Is that a command, your highness?"

Tess smiled. "No, I ask it as any woman might ask another, whom she hopes will become her friend."

Baron Santer coughed into his hand. Through the sheer, painted fan, Diana saw the Baroness smirking. Or maybe not, because at that instant Mayana cast a sidewise glance at the Baroness and the two women's eyes met in some kind of communication: Diana could not be sure what.

The private door opened. "I beg your pardon," said Yomi, sticking her head through. "But I've got to call places for the second act. Diana?"

Diana curtsied again and made her exit.

Eighteen days later they made their farewells at court. Tess Soerensen sat on her throne and received them formally. She spoke with each of them, most briefly, Owen and Ginny longest, and when Diana knelt before her, she bent to take Diana's hands in her own.

"I hope, Diana, that you will keep well. I'm sorry about Anatoly."

Diana kept her gaze fixed on the pillow on which she knelt, on the sleek ship painted on the fabric and the eagle rising, wings elevated and displayed, emblazoned on the ship's sail, the heraldic device of the Jedan princely line. She could not bear to look at Tess, who had made a choice so different from her own. Who had been able to.

Tess sighed and released her hands. "Good luck, Diana." And let her go.

They boarded a sloop at the harbor and set sail out into the bay on a calm winter morning. The actors crowded the rail, waving and calling out to their admirers, to their friends and lovers from the jaran who had come this far with them, to Tess and Dr. Hierakis and Jo Singh, who were staying behind. David and Maggie and Rajiv, who had his arm around Quinn, lined the rail as well. Diana held the baby for Karolla while she helped her husband drink some water. Vasil looked strangely frail, but he had movement in his legs again. Dr. Kinzer had gone with the others to the rail to watch the city recede from their sight. Even the children had gone to look, everyone except the man too weak to move from his pallet, the baby too young to understand, and the two women who refused to look back at what they were leaving behind.

They sailed out through the islands and that evening put into the tiny fishermen's port on a windswept beach. Wagons met them, and a handful of Earth staffers, bearing torches. The mood of the actors was contagiously cheerful. They sang obscene drinking songs, and Oriana remarked that she missed Hyacinth's falsetto. Even Anahita smiled. Karolla, carrying the baby, trudged along behind the wagon on which her husband rode. Diana held onto Valentin's hand. Ilyana walked at her mother's side, staring wide-eyed around her.

The girl's eyes grew even wider when she saw the shuttle, its lean bulk gleaming silver in the little valley as the last light faded away into the chalk hills. Dr. Kinzer had Vasil deeply drugged.

"What is that?" Yana asked. Her mother looked up, and faltered.

"It's an arrow," said Valentin.

"It's a ship," said Diana, "a ship like the one we sailed to Jeds on, only this one will take us even farther away, up there, into the heavens." She pointed to the sky, where even now stars came into view as night fell.

"But only the gods live in the heavens," said Yana reasonably, "and you can't be gods, because that woman died, the one who was a soldier. And the prince died. Gods can't die."

"Well," said Diana. She did not know what else to say.

"Come on! Come on!" called Owen impatiently from up ahead. "Let's get loaded up."

Yomi hurried back down along the line. "Di! Are you having any trouble? We've only got a short window here, so we must get everyone onboard quickly."

"Karolla." Diana took hold Karolla's free hand. "This

will all seem very strange to you, but you must trust me. It's only there, up there in the heavens, that your husband can be made well again. It will be as if—he was never injured." Karolla looked down at the horrible scar disfiguring Vasil's face. He slept, unconscious of her stare, and Karolla brushed her fingers along the scar and then traced his lips, and then drew her hand away self-consciously. "You'll always be with us, Karolla. We're your tribe now."

"Yes," said Yomi, taking her cue, "and we need you, too, Karolla. We need a woman who can sew and weave and—cook and—there are many chores to be done, isn't that always so?"

"Here, I'll take Valentin on," said Gwyn, coming up. "Will you walk with me, little one?" Valentin thought about this and finally deigned to hold Gwyn's hand, although he would not stray more than ten steps from his mother.

"Your father and mother need you to be brave, little one," said Diana to Ilyana, and then Hal and Quinn trotted up.

"Here, Yana," said Hal. "I'll carry you on my shoulders, if you want."

"Can I help with anything?" Quinn asked.

Oriana and Joseph carried the litter on, bearing Vasil between them, and Karolla walked on one side and Dr. Kinzer on the other. Karolla glanced once round the passenger cabin and then sat where she was told and stared at her husband as Dr. Kinzer secured him into the larger of the two stress tanks. Valentin and Yana crept around the cabin and touched everything until at last they had to sit as well and strap in. The baby did not cry at all until the doctor took him and secured him in the smaller stress tank. Then he squawled mightily with that awful frantic infant wail through the entire lift-off and most of the trip from the surface into orbit. But at least his crying distracted his siblings and his mother from the other noises, from the pressures, and the odd sensations that surely disoriented them. At least his crying linked them to what they knew, what they were sure of—which was, that baby Anton was very very unhappy.

In orbit, the shuttle docked with a yacht sent out from Odys. Crossing the lock threshold, Diana felt as if her last physical link to Rhui had been severed. She had spent a year and a half on Rhui, and almost a year with the jaran. It seemed like a terribly long time; it seemed like no time at all. A deep sadness weighed her down, and yet, when she saw the gleaming, sterile passageway of Charles Soerensen's yacht, her spirits lifted. She was going home.

* * *

David loved the iris beds in Charles's greenhouse. He escaped from the inevitable commotion brought on by their arrival and fled to the quiet of the gardens. He sat on a bare patch of turf and just breathed in the scent of Earth. But he recalled the smell of the grass, whipped by the wind on the plains, and a whiff of smoke on the breeze wrenched him back to Karkand, that night after the siege when Nadine had come to his tent, her scent mingled with the smell of burning that had permeated the air. That night. Other nights.

David sighed. Then he heard voices, and there came Charles, leading a tour of the greenhouse for Owen and Ginny and several of the actors. Ah, well, one never could escape the world. One way or another, it always intruded. There was no point in dwelling on things that couldn't be changed. He got to his feet and went over to the others.

"Look," he said, by way of greeting. "Is that a group of Chapalli coming in? They look like protocol officers." He pointed toward the southwest entrance, beyond the vegetable flats.

"That was fast," said Charles. "If you'll excuse me," he said to his guests. "David?"

David went with him, circling the roses and the rhododendrons and crossing carefully through the neat lines of daffodils. They met the officials under the grape arbor.

"Tai Charles." The protocol officers bowed and folded their hands together. Behind them stood two Chapalii in mauve robes, three stewards, and a heavily veiled female ten steps back. Leaves curled down, framing them in green. It smelled of growing things here, heavy and rich.

"You have acted swiftly, as I ordered," said Charles, "to restore to me these members of my house."

One of the officials flushed red, the other blue. "Tai Charles." Blue faded from the official's skin, and he folded his hands into a different arrangement. "We have restored these of your retainers, as you ordered, but charges still endure on the protocol lists. As well, it is written that any ke who violates an interdiction must face the rite of extinction." Both protocol officials turned to look toward the veiled female.

David hissed softly on an exhalation.

"I will see that justice is done on the matter of the ke," said Charles. "As to the other, I order that all the charges be withdrawn."

This time, both officials flushed blue. "I beg your pardon, Tai-en, but only the Tai-en Naroshi may remove these charges from the notice of the Protocol Office, since he tendered them. If he does not wish to remove them, then they will be brought to the notice of the emperor."

"Ah," said Charles, expressionless. "I see. You may go."

They had to go, of course. Charles watched them, and when they were out of earshot, he said. "An interesting legal concept, that he can define how I choose to interdict my own planet."

David shrugged. "Come now, Charles. Be fair. They *did* break the interdiction, you know."

A smile caught on Charles's lips and vanished. He turned to regard Hon Echido and his retinue. "Hon Echido. Your presence is welcome."

Echido bowed. "You are magnanimous, Tai-en. I will dispose of this nameless one immediately, so that you need not be bothered with such a trivial matter."

Dispose of the ke. It suddenly occurred to David that since the ke had no name to lose, she must therefore lose the only other thing she possessed: her life. She did not move, and he could see nothing of her under the veil. Was she glad of the thought of death? Resigned? Rebellious?

"I have other plans for this ke," said Charles, and he paused. "If she so wishes."

There was a long silence. The female stirred and was silent. Both Echido and the other merchant flushed green, the color of mortification.

"Nameless ones have no wishes, Tai-en," said Echido, and what his colorless voice could not betray, his skin did. David wondered if they had ever before encountered a Chapalii lord who cared what a ke wished for.

"Nevertheless," said Charles, "this ke has acted to serve my house, and I will not allow her to be killed unless she herself prefers death to exile. Good Lord, Rajiv would never forgive me, for one, and for the other, she's too good at what she does for us to lose her."

"What about Duke Naroshi?" asked David, suddenly fiercely glad that Charles could save one life, at least. It was a tiny victory, but a victory nonetheless.

"Hmm." No evidence showed on Charles's face that his flying in the face of Chapalii convention bothered him one whit. David could practically see the wheels beginning to turn in his head. "The Tai-en Naroshi and I will have to have a meeting."

CHAPTER THIRTY-SIX

"On this day comes the Tai-en Mushai to Sorrowing Tower."

Tess blinked twice, but she could not get the field of vision to narrow in. A wilderness of towers grew out beyond her eyes, and like a faint tracery beneath them she could see the parquet flooring of the minor audience hall in the palace in Jeds.

"Damn," she muttered. The towers blurred and began to coalesce, and Tess chuckled and said, "Terminate." A whitish haze spread over her vision and faded, and she looked out over the audience hall, empty now except for herself, Aleksi standing guard at the far door, and Cara sitting on the steps beside her, reading a book.

"Hmm?" Cara asked, looking up.

"It's very disorienting," said Tess. "Looking at two things at once."

"Evidently that's one reason that particular technology has never become widespread. See what you can do with it. It seemed the best solution to you needing access to a modeler without any awkward physical presence."

"No, just me sitting and staring into space and muttering to myself while people wonder what I'm doing."

Cara smiled. "They'll think you're wise, or mad."

"Or both." Tess jumped to her feet suddenly and paced over to the arched windows which looked out onto the loggia which in turn opened up onto the central courtyard. Beyond the courtyard lay the greater audience hall, with its elaborate arcade fronting the great avenue that led into Jeds proper. "Ah" she said, watching as two carriages escorted by twenty Jedan militia rolled up on the paved bricks below. A swallow-tailed pennon emblazoned with a falcon rising fluttered from the first carriage. "There is the baron, finally." She practically ran back to the dais and threw herself into the prince's seat. "What *are* you reading?" she demanded of Cara, who closed her book in a leisurely fashion, stood, and came to stand beside Tess.

"The new tract by Sister Casiara. She seems to be formulating a legalistic argument against slavery, of all things, based on the principle of the spiritual equality of man."

"Good Lord," said Tess mildly. The far doors swung open and four guardsmen entered, bowed, and retreated.

"But she is a bit of an iconoclast," added Cara, "so I'm not sure if this argument will fire the church or Jedan society at large."

Tess tapped one foot impatiently on the fired tile on which the prince's throne sat; the tile lapped up against the low steps that led down to the parquet floor. It was stuffy in here, since the windows had not yet been opened for the summer, but Tess preferred the minor hall to the greater one since the huge mural celebrating the triumph of philosophy that decorated one wall of the greater hall made her feel as if Charles was watching her. Finally, a second set of guards appeared. They marched in and knelt before her, resplendent in polished breastplates embossed with the prince's eagle. Behind them walked Baron Santer in his court robes, gray hair crowned by a soft cap, and behind him, a figure veiled from head to toe. Not even its hands showed.

"Your highness," said the baron, bowing. He looked at her. Every time Tess looked in his eyes, she thought of some creature that had been dead and was now reanimated; his gaze was cold and flat, his expression bland. "I have delivered this emissary from the docks, as you desired me to do."

It was a little test. They both knew it. She ran him through hoops these days, keeping him busy, reminding him that she now held power in Jeds. He had given over his regency gracefully enough, but she did not trust him.

"You may withdraw, Baron," she said. "Attend me this evening."

He bowed again and left. Tess dismissed the guards to the loggia beyond the doors. With mounting excitement, she regarded the veiled figure. "You are safe now," she said finally, in formal Chapalii. "You may unveil."

The ke stirred but did not remove her heavy veil. "Tai-endi." Her voice had a strange sibilance, an eerie echoing quality, that sent pure thrilling shivers up and down Tess's spine. A Chapalii female, at last. "Once already has this nameless one violated an interdiction. Only before another nameless one or a female am I allowed to reveal myself."

"But I *am* a female!" said Tess, standing up.

"You are Tai-endi, heir to the Tai-en Charles," replied the ke.

Tess sighed, exasperated. "And therefore I must be male. But I'm not—" She broke off and switched to Anglais. "Oh, hell, Cara, now what? How do I convince her?"

"Maybe you let her get her bearings, Tess. Like Yevgeni Usova, she has just been exiled to strange climes, away from everything she once knew. I'll take her back to my quarters. *I'm* not burdened with a title."

"Yes, Doctor," said Tess. She turned back to the ke. "You may go with Cara Hierakis. She is a female, and in our lands, females do not go veiled in front of anyone."

"As you command, Tai-endi."

"Oh, and Cara, let her come to the audience with the baron. Perhaps if she sees the way he treats me, she'll understand that I'm female, too."

Cara paused by the small door set into the wall on the dais which led into the private apartments beyond. "What? Are you saying that you think Baron Santer treats you differently than he did Charles?"

Tess gave a short bark of laughter. "I suspect that the baron believes that if he could only bed me, he could take control of Jeds back into his own hands. It's time he and I had a little talk."

"I'll be sure to be there," said Cara, and she led the ke into the private quarters.

Aleksi sauntered up from the far door. He had changed, Tess reflected, watching him. He had grown, or refound, his confidence. To her surprise, she liked him better this way, and at times she felt a little embarrassed at the way she had treated him before, using him for her own purposes, her own needs, rather like Charles used her.

"I don't think Baron Santer likes taking orders from you, or running your errands," he said now.

"I don't either," said Tess. "Let's go find Niko and Juli. We need to plot out our tactics."

In the end, she met with the baron in her private salon, a setting intimate enough to suggest that she wished to confide in him and yet provided with a curtained gallery from which Cara and the ke might observe the scene. She kept Juli with her, like a chaperone.

Shown in by her chatelaine, the baron bowed, remarked the elderly jaran woman with his eyes but without a greeting, and seated himself in a chair opposite Tess at the only table in the room. It was cool enough this evening that Tess had built a fire in the fireplace, and candles burned on the mantelpiece, echoing the lanterns set at intervals into the whitewashed walls. "Cakes, Baron?" Tess asked, offering him the platter with her own hands. He took one, and thanked her. "You have administered Jeds wisely, Baron," she remarked casually as he nibbled at the cake. "I commend you. But it is past time that we discuss how Jeds must be administered in the future."

Coolly, he finished the cake and then regarded her with his flat gaze. "Your wish is my command, your highness."

"But surely, Baron, you must know that your understanding of the minutiae of Jedan governance far exceeds mine. I rely on you to continue to administer wisely together with the governor I have brought from my husband's empire. I, of course, have only my inheritance from my brother, may he rest in peace, what trifling knowledge I learned at the university I attended in Erthe, and my husband's army to sustain me."

Startled by this last addition, he flashed a gaze up at the two portraits hanging side by side over the mantle, the portraits David had painted: one of her, one of Ilya. Tess was inordinately fond of Ilya's portrait. "Your husband's army?"

"I have this map—" She lifted a hand, and Juli brought the map over to her, took away the platter of cakes, and brought a lantern. Tess rose. The baron rose at once. Smoothing out the map, Tess spread it over the surface of the table and placed the lantern on one corner. Its glow spread out over the parchment like the favor of God, bright nearest the flame and fading to darkness at the margins. "You see, Baron, that even with the new information I have added to my map, gleaned from Jedan merchants, I can't be sure how long it will take for Bakhtiian's army to reach Filis, given the ground he must cover and secure in between." She covered Filis, the principal city of the great princedom that lay to the north and east of Jeds, with her index finger.

"An army can meet many obstacles," said the baron cautiously.

Tess smiled and looked up to see him staring straight at her. He lowered his gaze at once, reminding her incongruously of a jaran man, although in his case modesty had nothing to do with it. "Yes," she agreed. "That is why I feel inclined to install your son as head of the Jedan force that will, slowly and cautiously, of course, push our sphere of influence northward, in order to prepare the ground for the advance of the jaran army. Better that they stable their horses in Filis than in Jeds."

He blanched. "My son? But he just turned twenty!"

So there *was* something he cared about beyond himself and his power. "It is a great honor for your son, Baron, and may he bring your house glory by his exploits. You have a daughter by your first wife as well, a bit older, I believe, than the boy and sadly enough, unwed, is she not?"

This time he went gray. "Yes," he said stiffly. A certain fire sparked in his eyes. The daughter was as old as his second wife, and while not a beauty, neither was she a horror; perhaps sentiment had kept her by her father's side all these years.

"There are few families, Baron, who will have the opportunity of marrying into the princely houses of the jaran. I know you will welcome this chance to marry her to a jaran prince. Certainly, from all I have heard, she is worthy of the honor." She rolled up the map and tied it closed with a thin strip of leather. She did not sit down. "It will mean she must travel north. I will take her with me when I return to the plains."

For a long moment, he said nothing. Juli watched in the background. The windows here looked down on the prince's private garden, a riot of buds and blossoms during the day, now that it was spring. A sliver of moon shone through the windows, and the garden lay dense and shadowed beneath, the gray walls of the farther apartments rising on the other side, locking her in. A sudden pang struck Tess. Gods, how she missed the plains. How she missed Ilya. And Sonia, and the children. The jaran.

"What if I refuse?" asked the baron softly.

"Baron, your daughter will be safe with me as long as you administer Jeds wisely in my name. Your mother was old Prince Casimund's only niece, and by such lineage you were granted the regency. And you have proven your worth to me. I would prefer to keep you as regent. That way your daughter's children may come to govern Jeds in time."

"My *daughter's* children!"

Even in the coldest fish there lurked surprising heat. She could see that the idea, shocking as it might seem, attracted him. "Your daughter's children, sired by a jaran prince."

He hesitated. But she already had him. "Do you have a prince in mind, your highness?"

"Why, yes," said the Prince of Jeds. "I do. His first wife, ah, died recently. He comes from the eldest house of the jaran."

There was a long silence. It was very quiet here, muted by walls. The wind could not move freely within the palace, and in some ways, that was what she missed the most.

"Even before you arrived," said Baron Santer suddenly, "we heard reports of a great general in the north, leading his hordes against ancient and civilized lands. It seems that every kingdom he has met has fallen before him." He paused and touched the end of the map. "But you and I both know how far away that is."

"Do not forget, Baron," she replied softly, "that a part of that army has already come to Jeds." In deference to the customs of Jeds, she wore now, as she always did in public, a gown, but in the four months since she had arrived, black and red had quickly become the most fashionable colors and the cut of the gowns had altered from a high, loose waist to a lower, more fitted one. Because she also wore her saber. "You are wise enough to make your own judgment."

He bowed. "You flatter me, your highness."

"I don't think so," said the Prince of Jeds. "I feel sure that you understand where your advantage lies." She did not add, as an important and well connected governor in a growing empire or as a minor, and threatened, prince of a small trading city. If he could even usurp the throne. He could bide his time and wait to see what happened. Doubtless he would. But meanwhile, Jeds would remain stable under his—and Niko and Juli's—guiding hands.

"I understand," he said, and bowed in the florid style that was usually reserved for the audience hall.

"Thank you, Baron. You may go. Have your daughter call on me tomorrow."

He met her eyes one last time. He had banked it all down again, concealing himself. "As you command," he replied. Juli showed him out.

"How in hell," said Tess to the air, "did Marco ever make a friend of *that?*"

"Not bad," said Cara from the balcony, drawing the curtain aside, "though perhaps a little overplayed. Baron Santer was a notorious ladies man when he was young. He and Marco got along famously. You'd never guess it now, but when Marco as the first Prince Charles instituted those odd sumptuary laws that helped reform the horrible brothels, the baron was one of his great supporters. There was even a rumor that his first wife was barren, and that the two children were actually the children of a girl off the streets, a courtesan he fell in love with who was later murdered by his wife."

"Oh, God." Tess walked back to the stairway that led up, behind an arras, to the gallery above. She laughed, just a little. "It's an endless tangled web, isn't it?" Then she stopped stock-still, holding the arras aside with one hand, because there, in the dimness at the top of the steps, stood the ke.

Unveiled.

Tess stared. Then she chuckled. The ke looked like a Chapalii, only its skin was scalier, more alienlike. Had Tess expected a revelation, like the visitation of an angel? "I am pleased," she said carefully to the ke, "that you trust me."

The ke descended the steps, and Cara followed behind her. Tess backed up to give them room to come through into the salon. The ke examined the chamber for a long while. Tess only watched.

"It is true," said the ke suddenly, "that these humans are quite primitive. Scarcely better than animals."

Tess felt her mouth drop open. She snapped it shut. The ke had addressed her in common Chapalii, without one single honorific.

"I beg your pardon," added the ke, "for addressing you in the *che-lin* tongue, but surely you cannot know the deeper tongue."

It took Tess a moment to answer because she thought her heart would burst, she was so excited. "I do not know of such a tongue—but what may I call you? And how did you come to realize that I am female?"

"*Are* you female?" asked the ke. Her voice, like that of the males, was colorless, and because of her skin, Tess could not tell at all what emotions she felt.

"Yes, I am. But then why unveil yourself? I don't understand."

"By your own testimony you are married to one of these humans. Thus you have become a nameless one, just as I am. The Tai-endi is dead, just as the Protocol Office has proclaimed." The ke wandered over to stare at the fire as if the lick and spit of flame engrossed or appalled her. "It is no wonder that the Tai-en has kept you in exile here on this planet."

Tess looked at Cara. Cara shrugged. The ke lifted a hand to the candles and held it close, as if testing their heat. Kept her in exile to spare himself the shame? Or to protect her? Or for some other, alien reason that Tess could not guess? And at the same time, Tess felt an odd exhilaration, as if the extinction of the Tai-endi—in this ke's mind, at least—granted her a sudden, reckless freedom. "You may call me Tess. Is there some—name—some *word*, that I might call you?"

The ke touched two fingers to the cherubs carved into the mantlepiece and drew her hand along the frieze, studying its heights and valleys. "By decree older than the eldest of the emperor's towers did ten of the first families lose their names because of their rashness and their pride." She turned. Tess walked closer. The ke was tall, as all Chapalii were, but layers of robes disguised her thinness. Her eyes gleamed, golden irises slit vertically by lozenge-shaped pupils. "So they became the nameless ones, and so did other names become extinct as time passed, as years turned back on themselves and followed the same course again, and again. Without a name there is no true existence, and yet, without a name, existence is boundless. So must the prince who becomes emperor lose his name. So must the ke live without names."

"But the Tai-en Mushai lost his name, and yet he is still remembered."

The ke wandered over to the table and unrolled the parchment, using her hands as much as her eyes to explore it. "So is he imprisoned in Sorrowing Tower forever," she replied.

"Well," said Tess in Anglais. "But is it possible that I might learn the—" She hesitated, shot through with hope and the fear of disappointment, riddled with it, like the very pain of the wound itself. "That I might learn the deeper tongue?"

The ke rolled up the map and tied it exactly as Tess had tied it before. "You might. But you must master *che-lin* first."

Cara raised her eyebrows. Tess had to smile. How blithely they all praised her for speaking Chapalii so well. But that did not mean that by Chapalii standards she was fluent. "With your help," said Tess humbly, "I will endeavor to do so."

The ke nodded, like master to pupil. "When do you wish to begin?" she asked.

CHAPTER THIRTY-SEVEN

Diana could not help but compare the two modes of travel: the constant jarring sway of the wagons in the army's train against the luxurious appointments of Soerensen's ducal yacht. On this yacht, the Company returned to Earth.

Vasil was in a foul temper, because every time he looked in a mirror he saw his scarred face. He even yelled at Yana one day, when she came to show him the three-dimensional picture she had drawn on a demi-modeler under Hal's supervision. Yana burst into tears and ran out of the room.

Karolla, for the first time in that long trip, came to life. "You selfish beast!" she cried, standing up. Anton lay cradled in her arms. "How dare you speak that way to her!" Diana, sitting with her, rose at once.

Vasil practically snarled. "Leave me alone," he said, and turned his face toward the wall.

At that moment, the door whisked open to reveal Yana, crying noisily in the passageway, and Dr. Kinzer. "Aha!" said Dr. Kinzer tartly, tapping her fingers on her slate. "Feeling sorry for himself again, is he? M. Veselov, you really are going to have to learn some patience. Now, I beg your pardon, M. Arkhanov, but I do need a few moments alone with my patient."

Diana took Karolla by the arm and they went out together. Anton hiccuped, stirred, and went back to sleep. Seeing her mother, Yana gulped down her tears and ran away down the corridor. Karolla looked white.

"Here," said Diana. "We'll go rest in the chapel." It was the most peaceful place she could think of. They found David praying in the chapel, but he rose when he saw them, made a final circle of grace with his right hand, and retreated to leave them alone. "I hope you don't mind," Diana continued, taking Karolla down to sit on the front row of benches that ringed the altar.

"Why should I mind?" asked Karolla in a choked voice.

"Well, it isn't a temple to jaran gods, but it's still a holy place."

"Our gods aren't jealous," murmured Karolla, and suddenly she flushed bright red. "If only I were as worthy."

"Karolla!" This was too much. "How can you be unworthy? To leave everything you knew, everyone you loved, and all for—*him*. I think you are the most selfless person I know."

Karolla stared at baby Anton's downy head, not seeming to see the soft glowing lights in the walls, the pale dome that enclosed them, the seamless benches, and the doors that opened without a touch. It was, Diana reflected, how Karolla dealt with things: She pretended she did not see them.

"If I truly loved him," Karolla said, "then I wouldn't care about—" She broke off. "But I want him to love me more. And he never will."

"Love you more than—what?" Or whom?

Karolla threw back her head. At first, Diana had wondered why a man as handsome and as vain as Vasil had married a woman who was, truly, as plain as Karolla, since she doubted Vasil cared about Karolla's finer qualities, but now she supposed he had done it because it ensured him an acolyte.

"But this place," said Karolla, seemingly at variance, "it isn't a place *he* can ever come, is it? He can't follow Vasil here. Vasil must have known that. Either Bakhtiian threatened to exile him again or else Vasil chose to leave him."

"Bakhtiian?" asked Diana haltingly. Still half asleep, Anton stuck two fingers in his mouth and sucked quietly on them.

"He wouldn't have left if it wasn't for the scar to his face. He would never have let Bakhtiian see him with that scar. Is it true that this *dokhtor* can take the scar away?"

Diana lifted a hand slowly and traced the scar of marriage on her cheek. "Yes," she said. "It's true. The doctor can make his face look as if it was never scarred in the first place."

"Then I am content," said Karolla.

They made landfall at Nairobi Port and took the train to London. Half the time Diana was thrilled to be back. The other half, she felt as if she weren't there at all. She felt as if she were someone else, watching through her eyes.

At Victoria Station, a familiar face waited on the platform to greet them.

"Hyacinth!" Oriana whooped and ran to hug him.

Hyacinth basked in their welcome. He looked wonderful, but then, Hyacinth always looked wonderful. He was aware also, of course, of the number of passersby who paused to stare at the commotion before recalling their manners and walking on. But when he had hugged them all, he turned to regard Owen.

"Well, Owen," he said in a tone that Diana had never heard from him before. "I'm sorry for the trouble I caused you. It was rash and stupid, what I did, and it caused more grief than you can ever know." He glanced to his left, and all at once Diana saw the slight, black-haired young man loitering twenty steps away.

She felt sick with envy.

And a second later, relief that she stood here unburdened of any awkward jaran presence. And then terrible guilt.

"How is Yevgeni adjusting?" asked Yomi in a low voice.

"Well." Hyacinth sighed, and he looked abruptly tired and discouraged. "It hasn't been easy. We take each day as it comes. I got your message, Ori, about *them*." He glanced toward the floating litter and the little family huddled around it, still in their alien clothing, like painted barbarians escaped from their cage. Vasil Veselov had his eyes open, and he squinted at the other man, across the distance. Diana watched as Yevgeni caught sight of the other jaran. His eyes widened and he took two steps forward and then halted, unsure of his welcome.

"Owen," Hyacinth continued, returning his focus to the director, "I'd like to audition again, for the Company, if you'll have me."

"Can't get work, huh?" said Owen.

"Owen!" scolded Ginny.

Hyacinth grinned. "Quite the contrary. I made good use of all the publicity I could get, and I have my pick of parts, by and large, though mostly in the vids." He cleared his throat. "But I miss the work. If you think there will be openings . . ." He trailed off, not bothering to hide his hope. The old Hyacinth would never have shown that kind of vulnerability so openly.

"Hmph," said Owen. "We will have openings." He glanced toward Anahita, but she had already left the group and they saw her striding purposefully down the platform toward the exit. "And more openings even than you might expect. There's something new afoot." Ginny kicked him. But she couldn't kick the light out of his eyes.

Hyacinth's face opened up. "Thank you. We need something new, Yevgeni and I." Then he made a great, exasperated sigh. "Damn it anyway, he always does this, lurking in the background. I hate it! Yevgeni! Come over here!"

Reluctantly, Yevgeni walked over. Hyacinth draped an arm around the other man. "Now. You haven't met anyone, so let me introduce you."

They made the rounds. Most of the actors even kissed him in the jaran style, formally, on each cheek. Yevgeni stopped at last beside the litter. He stared at the man lying there.

"Yevgeni?" Vasil asked in a hoarse voice. "I thought you were dead."

"We *are* dead, Veselov," said Yevgeni, low, in khush, so that Diana realized that he had been speaking Anglais to the rest of them. Then he turned away and retreated back to Hyacinth.

No," said Vasil softly. "It's we who are alive, and *they* who are dead."

"They're not dead, Father," said Yana tremulously. "Are they?" She clutched Valentin's hand and lifted her head to stare at the wild bustle of Victoria Station, which surely must seem unimaginably strange to her. "I thought they were all just—left behind."

"Dead to me," said Vasil. No one answered him. He did not seem to expect a reply.

"Diana! Di!"

The shout carried across half the station. Diana turned. There, late as usual, came her family, all pell-mell and haphazard and swarming the other travelers on the platform: her mother, her father, two sibs, one niece, darling Nana, an aunt, three uncles, and four cousins. She laughed with joy just as her father reached her and scooped her up and spun her around. At last, she was home.

CHAPTER THIRTY-EIGHT

At the tail end of summer, Tess came home. She had sent no message before her, only a courier from the coast, and she rode into camp with her escort in the late afternoon, hard on the messenger's heels, having made good time herself.

"You might have warned me," said Sonia grumpily, hugging her. "I've no celebration prepared to welcome you home."

Tess kissed her on either cheek. "You are my welcome, Sonia. Oh, gods, look how much Katya has grown. Is that *Vasha?*" She laughed. "And who are you, young man?" she said to Ivan. "I scarcely recognize you." Tess shone with happiness. Sonia felt, to be truthful, unutterably relieved to have her back. She had been gone for almost nine months, and at times, Sonia had worried that she might simply decide to stay in Jeds or even to follow her brother back to Erthe. Now, Sonia saw that she had worried needlessly. *This* was Tess's home now.

Tess caught sight of a figure wavering under an adjoining awning. "Good God, is that Nadine?" She broke away from Sonia and strode over. She could not embrace Nadine very well, since Nadine was by now so incredibly pregnant that her belly overwhelmed every other feature. "Dina! How are you?"

Nadine flushed just as Sonia hurried up to forestall the explosion. But she was too late. "I hate this!" Nadine exclaimed. "I just hate this!" She pushed Tess away and turned and waddled back into her tent.

Tess turned to Sonia. At once, her happy glow subsided. She looked guilty. "Oh. Is that the way it's been with her?"

"Let me tell you," said Sonia, drawing Tess away from Nadine's tent, "that pregnancy has made her even more foul tempered than usual."

Tess cast a glance back at the tent. The entrance flap stilled and hung there, heavy, cutting Nadine off from the rest of her family. "Can that be possible? Poor Nadine."

"Tess, my dear, you ought to save your sympathy for those of us who deserve it. And Feodor Grekov is impossible. If he's not fighting with her, then he spoils her. I can't imagine why I ever agreed with Mother Sakhalin that he would make a good husband for Dina."

"*You* agreed!"

Sonia arched an eyebrow. "Certainly Mother Sakhalin consulted me since my mother was not available. To be frank, there were other young men I preferred—a very well-mannered and clever young Raevsky son, for instance—but it might have proven difficult to persuade any of them to marry her."

Tess snorted. "Well, then, you got what you deserved." She grinned, surveyed the camp, and sighed, happy again. Kolia went up to Svetlana Tagansky's daughter and the two children circled each other like two horses getting acquainted. In her competent manner, Svetlana oversaw the unpacking and the rolling out of tents, and Aleksi took the horses out to the herd. Farther back, a young woman in a Jedan gown sat stiffly in a wagon, hands clasped in her lap and her hair covered by a loose white scarf.

"Who is that?" Sonia asked.

"She's my hostage," said Tess lightly. "A Jedan noblewoman. Baron Santer's daughter. I thought I might marry her to Anatoly Sakhalin."

"Anatoly Sakhalin!" Sonia surveyed the young woman, who seemed unremarkable except perhaps for the calm with which she regarded the jaran camp. She appeared to be an extremely self-possessed young woman. "Have you asked Anatoly about this?"

"I thought I would discuss the matter with his grandmother."

"Well," said Sonia, with deep misgivings, "I will see that a messenger goes out to them. Not that I don't think it's a good idea. Of course, I know who Baron Santer is.

But keep in mind that there are other young men—Georgi Raevsky, for instance—"

Tess gave her such a look. "You're showing a sudden partiality for the Raevsky tribe, aren't you?"

"I am giving my husband the honor he deserves. In any case, I suggest you speak with Anatoly first. He just returned from the south, from his uncle's army, two hands of days ago."

"Hmph," said Tess, and then grinned hugely and hugged Sonia again. "Oh, I missed you so much." She broke away and swept her gaze around the camp. It halted on her tent, sitting there, looking silent and alone at the heart of the camp. "But where is Ilya?" she asked, sounding rather plaintive.

"Sulking in the tent." Sonia laughed. "Or pacing, more like. The truth is, I think he's afraid he'll embarrass himself if he meets you in public."

"Wise of him, I'm sure," Tess replied, but her face had already lit. "If you'll excuse me." She had enough dignity not to run, but she vanished into her tent swiftly enough.

The next day, Mother Sakhalin and her grandson arrived from the Sakhalin encampment a half-day's ride downriver. Tess received them under the awning of her tent, and Sonia saw how unconsciously Tess carried authority with her now, as if she had grown used to wielding it in Jeds. It made her at once more formidable and yet more easygoing. Ilya sat beside her, looking remarkably subdued. Sonia reflected that it had not, on the whole, been an easy nine months, what with Nadine pregnant and Ilya's moods swinging wildly from day to day. They had traveled slowly back through Habakar, demarking territories, installing governors, and sending Kirill Zvertkov to the south to reinforce Yaroslav Sakhalin in the Xiriki-khai province. Gangana had revolted and, quite rightfully, Ilya had laid the city to waste as an example to the rest. All in all, Sonia had been relieved when they reached the plains again at the beginning of summer and Ilya had announced that he intended to remain on the plains for at least a year. For almost five years he had been fighting; it was time to rest while others consolidated and pressed forward.

"Mother Sakhalin," said Tess, "your presence honors me. Anatoly, I am pleased to see you as well."

Mother Sakhalin looked tired. Her grandson looked nothing like the expressive young man of almost two years ago who had won by his own exploits the right to command a jahar. He looked a little unkempt. He had let his hair grow, tied off in three braids, and his eyes had a hard, cold gleam to them now, echoed by the set of his mouth. There were stories—that he had covered himself in so much glory in the past year, fighting in the worst skirmishes and the fiercest battles, throwing himself always to the front of the engagement, that one could scarcely recount all of the tales in one evening. His jahar took the worst casualties, and every man who fought beside him had either been killed or badly wounded, and yet Anatoly came through every engagement without a scratch. And then, ten days ago, like a horse bolted for home, he had turned up at his grandmother's camp.

Now he regarded Tess Soerensen, his expression so masked that Sonia could not read his feelings. "I want to go to Erthe," he said without preamble.

Shocked, Sonia looked at Mother Sakhalin, and what she saw there dismayed her further. Mother Sakhalin looked not just tired but frail and old. A month ago she had not looked like this.

"But that's impossible, Anatoly," exclaimed Tess.

"It can't be impossible," said Anatoly stubbornly, "if others have gone before me."

"It *is* impossible," said Tess so coldly that Anatoly shrank back from her and, abruptly, hung his head to hide his face. "She is gone. She left you by her own choice."

"Only because I would not go with her," he said to the carpet. His hands lay perfectly still on his lap, except for his right forefinger, which twitched as he spoke.

"Tess," said Ilya in his most reasonable voice, "perhaps this is not your decision to make." Tess shot him a look filled with venom. He smiled, unruffled by her anger. "I suggest you allow Anatoly to address a letter to Diana, to ask her."

"That could take months!" Tess objected. "A year! More!"

"If Anatoly is willing to wait," said Ilya, "then I see no reason a letter should not be sent."

Anatoly's head jerked up. A light sparked in him, and Sonia realized that the coldness stemmed not from lack of feeling but from too much feeling. She had thought it the mark of a new-found cruelty. Now she thought he was just in pain. "I am willing," he said hoarsely, and Mother Sakhalin aged ten years in that moment.

Tess stewed. "Very well," she said finally. "You may tell me what words you wish to write to Diana, Anatoly. I will write them myself and I will send the letter. But if she says she does not want you, then you must agree to consider yourself a widower and abide by my wishes."

"Very well," he echoed meekly. He paused. "What are your wishes?"

She contemplated him a moment, and Sonia could see that Tess found this changed Anatoly a bit puzzling, as if he was both more, and less, than she expected. "I wish you to marry a Jedan noblewoman and together with her act as regents in Jeds under our suzerainty."

At these words, Mother Sakhalin rallied. "It would be a good marriage, Anatoly," she said firmly. "And a proper position for you. And for the tribe."

The light still burned in Anatoly's face, but it was as if it had been shuttered by glass now. "It would be a good marriage," he agreed in a soft voice. "And one due my position. But how can I know what to think of Jeds if I have never been there? Perhaps I would rather ride with the army instead."

Well! Anatoly had certainly learned something from his grandmother. He had learned how to negotiate. In time, Sonia thought, he might surpass even Yaroslav Sakhalin as a general.

Tess considered. Ilya settled his chin on a fist and watched her, a trifle bemused by a negotiation going on in which he had no real say.

"So be it, then," said Tess finally. "I will send you to Niko in Jeds. You can carry the letter that far and give it to Dr. Hierakis, who will see that it is put on a ship to Erthe. You already speak some Rhuian. Now you can see how the khaja rule there, and you can learn how to live among them and guard our interests."

Anatoly inclined his head obediently. "As you command."

Mother Sakhalin did not look happy, but she looked satisfied.

"Come back this evening," said Tess to the young man, "and I will write the letter for you."

He nodded, and he and his grandmother took their leave.

"You terrify me, my wife," said Ilya. "I am relieved that you are my ally and not my enemy."

Tess still looked angry, but she laughed curtly. "How like Charles I am," she murmured, "to push him toward an end which I have already devised."

"Anatoly is no fool," said Sonia. "He will do what is best for the Sakhalin tribe."

"No doubt," said Ilya dryly, "he will do what his grandmother wishes. But what will you do, Tess, if Diana asks him to come to her?"

But already Tess's anger had subsided into an odd ruefulness. "She won't," said Tess with such certainty that even Sonia was taken aback. Ah, well. Tess's heart might belong to the jaran, but her soul would always remain khaja.

Sonia rose and shook out her skirts. "Come, Tess. If you can manage to leave your husband for a moment, I thought we might just walk through camp for a little while, so you can see everyone again. They all want to greet you."

"I will languish here until your return," said Ilya with a smile. He looked more at ease than he had for—well, for years, really—but there was still an edge on him beyond the pure, stark vision that drove him on.

"I brought him six books," said Tess to Sonia as they walked away.

"Six!" But Tess was prince now. No wonder she possessed such riches.

"And four books for you. And three colloquies for the children."

This bounty struck Sonia to silence. They walked together through the sprawl of the camp, greeting children, women, and men, all the members of the Orzhekov camp.

"Aleksi says that a zayinu holy woman came from across the seas to Jeds," said Sonia at last. "That she wears heavy veils, since it is a grave offense to her gods if folk like us look upon her. Is that true? Why would a zayinu holy woman come to you, Tess? Especially if your brother wars against her kind?"

"Her own people sent her into exile. I wanted to bring her with me here, because there is much much more she can teach me, but—" She faltered. A fire lived in Tess as well, Sonia knew, a fire kindled out of a desire to seek and to know, a kind of discontent that wore away at her constantly as if she feared that too much contentment might kill her own seeking spirit. "But that will have to wait. I thought it better to leave her with Cara in Jeds. For now."

"You and Ilya are very like, you know," mused Sonia. "I saw that long ago, when you first came to us."

"You have a wise soul, Sonia, just as your brother did."

Sonia pressed a hand over her heart. She smiled sadly. "I am sure the gods will send him back to us, Tess." They walked a little while in silence. But Sonia had a restless, inquisitive spirit as well. "Ilya plans to call a great meeting of tribes," she said after a while. "Do you know what he is about?"

"Yes." Tess shaded a hand to stare up at the sky, toward the sun, and her mouth turned down. She was troubled.

"And you won't tell me!

"You must ask Ilya."

"I *have* asked Ilya. He is certainly no more maddening than you are!"

"I beg your pardon," said Tess with a laugh.

Sonia stopped suddenly, overwhelmed by a feeling of great contentment. Knowing, too, that because she was not afraid of contentment, she could embrace it. "I'm so glad you came back to us."

"Where else would I go?" Tess asked quietly.

Where else, indeed? Arm in arm, they walked on together.

CHAPTER THIRTY-NINE

"Winter isn't really that cold here, is it?" asked Yana on a January morning as she and Diana walked back from the greengrocer with their prize of Brussels sprouts, potatoes, and two dozen pathetic apples.

"Well, no," Diana admitted, "not compared to what you were used to, I suppose." Ilyana was the kind of girl who turned heads, her features were so perfect. She was not yet ten years old, innocent in many ways and yet a confirmed skeptic. "Will you come upstairs to have early tea with Hal and me? We have to leave for the theater in an hour."

"Can't," said Yana reluctantly. "Dr. Kinzer is coming for tea."

"But I thought you liked Dr. Kinzer."

"I do. I like her lots. But—" Then she clammed up.

Diana knew what she was going to say, anyway. It was her father's behavior that embarrassed her.

They arrived at the door to their building—an old nineteenth-century townhouse now split into five flats—at the same time as the doctor did. She had a boy of about Valentin's age with her. Yana lightened immediately. "Evan!" Yana cried, delighted. "I didn't know *you* were coming, too." She grabbed Evan's hand and tugged him after her though the door. Together, they pounded up the stairs, pushing past her father.

Even after a year, Diana had not gotten used to seeing Vasil whole and walking again, as lithe and charming as ever. He paused at the bottom of the stairs at the mirror set into the wall between the coat racks and lifted a hand to brush the flawless beauty of his face. Then he turned to Dr. Kinzer.

He bowed, took her hand, and kissed it. "*Dokhtor,* I am struck to the heart once again by the beauty of your eyes. Were they a gift to you from the gods, perhaps?"

The doctor held up pretty well under this onslaught. She smiled. "No, I got them from my grandfather." Then she winked at Diana and let Vasil escort her up the stairs to the flat in which he and his family lived. Diana did not pause to look in the mirror. She followed them up, waved to Evan through the open door of the flat, and kept going up the next flight of stairs to the flat she and Hal shared.

"Poor Karolla," she said to Hal as she dumped her bag on the tiny kitchen table. Hal was on his hands and knees in the sitting room, putting the finishing touches on a miniature stage set. "But at least it's a respectable visitor this time. Do you remember that fiasco when that producer and his friend—" She shuddered. "The kind of people who make you want to go wash after you've shaken hands with them."

Hal replied without looking up. "Valentin said it was Missy Kinzer and Evan coming over. And you know she comes more for Karolla's sake than Vasil's. What do you think?" He rocked back on his heels.

Diana studied the mockup. She sighed. Nana always said to be truthful even when you couldn't be honest. "Well, it's an improvement. I'm taking Yana and Valentin out to the farm on Monday. Do you want to come?" But he had already gone back to studying his model, and ignored her.

Two hours later, Diana propped her elbows on the counter and stared at herself in the Green Room mirror. A handsome enough face, if a little pale. She pulled her hair back tight to cover it with the wig cap, and then sighed and let it fall down around her face again. Out in the hallway, Hal was arguing with his father.

"I don't care! This is it! This is the last time I play this part, or any part, for that matter. I quit!"

"How dare you speak to me in this fashion!"

"Oh, Dad, don't start your 'ungrateful child' lecture, please. If you could see past your own nose you'd have known for years that I don't want to be an actor."

"But you *are* an actor. We made you so."

"Yes, you and Mother never did give me any choice in the matter—"

The door opened and Hyacinth slipped inside. "Goddess forgive me," he muttered, "and I beg your pardon for coming in here, but I can't get past them and I'm damned if I'm going to stand there and listen to them scream."

"What happened?"

"Oh, Prince Hal told Ginny that he wanted to go into scene design. You know what I think, Di?" He stared at himself in the mirror, smoothed the coarse hair of his black wig, and rubbed at the foundation in the hollows of his cheeks. "I *hate* that woman who designed the makeup. This always makes me look too thin."

Diana could not help but smile.

"And why shouldn't I go into scene design—!" from outside.

"What *do* you think, Hyacinth?" she asked.

Hyacinth glanced at her and then back at himself in the mirror. "I think Hal would make a damn good actor if he'd only stop thinking he can't be one because he has to rebel against his parents."

"I keep telling him he should quit the Company, but he won't."

"Well." Hyacinth sighed. "The costumes are gorgeous though, aren't they?" He straightened and admired his robes as they swayed around him. "Joseph did a wonderful job, blending styles. Look how he used the jaran embroidered patterns and the cut of their armor for *Tamburlaine,* and Habakar patterns for the robes. Did you go to his exhibit at the Globe Annex, where he's showing the models?"

"Hyacinth, did you have something you wanted to tell me?" She dipped her fingers in cold cream and smoothed it onto her face.

He sighed and sat down on the other stool. The Green Room was small but pleasant, with a carpet, the counter and mirror, a writing table and chair, and the two stools, and a modeler and theater readout built into the other wall. "Full house, my dear. And a real live Chapalii duke in attendance. Can His Royal Highness pull it off? Even with all of us covering for him?"

"Does it matter if he can't? Gwyn takes over the part next month. The audience didn't come to see how well Vasil can act. They came to see if he can act at all. You must admit his lack of accent is amazing." Then she recalled his greeting to Dr. Kinzer. Vasil put his accent on and off depending on where he thought the advantage lay.

"It's true that Veselov has a better memory even than you."

She laughed. "His memory is a hundred times better than mine."

"It's nice to see you smile, Di," said Hyacinth softly. "You've been so gloomy since the holidays." He rested a hand on her shoulder companionably.

She drew away from him, knowing what was coming next. "I've got to get ready," she said stiffly.

"Di, don't you think it's time to give it up—?"

Then he had the audacity to reach out and with one beringed finger brush her cheek where the scar ran diagonally from cheekbone to jawline, faint and white.

She rose. "I'm busy, Hyacinth."

A knock came on the door. It opened, and Yomi stuck her head in. "Sorry to bother you, Di, but—well, he says he has to leave London in two hours, and since we're doing the marathon today I said he could come see you now. I'll give him ten minutes. Hyacinth, go!"

"Your word is my command, oh bountiful Yomi," said Hyacinth, bowing extravagantly.

Yomi slapped him on the rear. "Out!" They left together.

Diana felt a sudden foreboding. She watched the doorway in the mirror. Soon enough a man appeared there. He hesitated, stepped inside, and closed the door behind him.

She gasped and whirled around. "Marco!" And took a step back, running up against the counter.

"Hello, Diana." He wore a simple thigh-length jacket over loose trousers, but even in the latest fashionable style he bore with him that air of suppressed wildness and incipient adventure that made him so attractive. "You're looking—well." His gaze darted to her cheek. He got pale all at once and then recovered. He was lying in any case. She wasn't looking particularly well and everyone knew it. When she didn't reply, he went on. "I saw the preview last night. It didn't go badly at all. I keep wondering how you actors manage to memorize all those lines. . . ." He lifted his hands up, wrung them together, and let them drop back to his side. "Goddess, that was a stupid thing to say. I'm sorry to disturb you."

"Why didn't you come backstage last night?" she asked. "This isn't a very good time for me."

"Oh. I thought I'd come tonight after the show, but I got called away unexpectedly. . . ." He trailed off and paced over to the table and laid a hand flat on it, and stared at the hand. "No. The truth is I didn't have the nerve."

The thought of Marco Burckhardt not having the nerve to do something astounded her. "How long have you been in London?" she said instead of the words she should have said, the apology she needed to make to him.

"Two days."

"A short trip."

"Yes."

Together, they lapsed into silence.

He broke it. "Charles sent me to deliver a crystal wand—that's a summons wand—to Duke Naroshi. Did you know he's in your audience tonight?"

"Yes." She didn't much care about Duke Naroshi. He had attended performances before.

There was silence again.

"I've got to get my makeup on," she said finally. She sat down and dabbed on foundation with her fingers.

"It's amazing," said Marco. She watched him watch her in the mirror. "You'd never know to see Veselov now what terrible injuries he suffered. Even that awful facial scar is gone."

With a sponge, she blended the foundation on over her cheeks. Over her scar. "Yes," she replied.

The silence was worse than the talking, and there wasn't even Hal's argument with his father to cover it.

"Diana—"

She set down the damp sponge. "Marco. I'm sorry. I

treated you horribly. I'm sorry. It wasn't deliberate, but still, that doesn't excuse it."

He lifted his hand from the table and closed it into a fist and, slowly, opened it again. Then he walked over and put his hands on her shoulders and met her eyes in the mirror. "Diana. I love you. I thought—I'm asking . . . we could handfast, just a trial, one year. . . ." He faltered.

She stared at him, only she wasn't staring at him, she was staring at his reflection, as if that was all she *had* ever seen of him, of Marco Burckhardt, the reflection she had made of him in her own mind. Not the real Marco. She had never known the real Marco. Maybe she had never really tried to know him, preferring the legend to the man.

In that moment, the dam broke.

"I wanted him to die," she whispered. "I wanted him to die a clean romantic death. Then I wouldn't have had to leave him because he would have been dead. I'm ashamed. I'm so ashamed of that. Do you know that he thought he couldn't die as long as I was with him? By leaving him, I as good as sent him to his death."

"Diana, they're at war. People expect to die."

"That doesn't absolve me. It's all I can think about, wondering if I'll ever hear."

"It's been over a year. I thought you'd have—done all your grieving by now."

"I know. I know. I thought I had. We left the jaran at Winter Solstice, did you know that? Our calendar, not theirs." She put a hand to her bracelet and twisted it, twice around. It was the bracelet *he* had given her, opulent and showy enough that Joseph had given her permission to wear it as part of Zenocrate's costume. "That was my penance, to wear the mark for a year and then let him go. And now I'm afraid to do it. I'm afraid if I erase the mark, that I'll kill him."

He took his hands off her shoulders. "Do you miss him?"

"I don't know. We had nothing in common, really, except we were both pretty and blond." She laughed at that, and heard herself how false the laugh sounded. "And I liked him. That's what I realized finally, after it was too late. After I'd already left. Maybe it was never more than infatuation. Maybe I was just in love with him being in love with me. But I liked him, too. And, Goddess, every day, there are Karolla and the children, like a constant reminder. And poor Yevgeni, struggling to make sense of it all. And Vasil, who I'd like to strangle. He's got it into his head that since I'm one of the leads that he has to sleep with me in order to consolidate his position, but at least I know it's not just me. Gwyn has been fending him off, too. They're always there, reminding me."

"Then leave the Company."

"But, Marco, I don't want to leave the Company. We're doing repertory for six months, and then there's the chance that we'll get to tour out into Imperial space. You must know about that. Owen is hoping that we'll be the first humans ever allowed to perform before the emperor himself."

Marco snorted. "Owen has grandiose dreams."

"Someone must," she said bitterly.

She saw him swallow, saw the movement of his throat. His hand slid under his jacket and he drew out a thin rectangular slab—no, she recognized it an instant later. It was paper, all folded up.

"I brought this," he said in a low voice. "I thought maybe you wouldn't want to see it, but—" He tossed it on the counter and turned and paced back to stand by the table, setting his hand flat down on the surface and staring at it. "It's a letter from Tess Soerensen."

A letter from Tess Soerensen.

There was only one thing it could be. Tess Soerensen had taken pity on her and written to tell her of Anatoly's death. She stared at the creamy, stiff parchment. She did not have the courage to open it up and read the words, because set so baldly on the page, black ink on pale paper, such words could never be erased. Yet those words would allow her to rest. And anyway, she owed it to Anatoly to use the courage she had, to honor his memory.

Tears blurred her eyes as she opened it. It crackled as she unfolded it, and the noise of it opening resounded in the room. Tess Soerensen had a neat, readable hand, but then, she had doubtless had a great deal of practice writing by hand in the last five years.

"*To Diana Brooke-Holt. From Terese Soerensen. Dear Diana, Anatoly Sakhalin is sitting with me and he asked me to write these words to you:* My beloved Diana, I have tried for months now to get myself killed in battle, but it's no use, I can't seem to manage it. The gods watch over me too well. They know I married a Singer. After all, they sent you to me. Now they're punishing me for my arrogance in thinking I could let you leave and not suffer for it. Now my grandmother and the prince want me to marry a jaran noblewoman from Jeds, to act as regent there. But I am married to you for as long as I live or the mark of marriage remains on your face, and since the mark can never be erased from a woman's face and I am still alive, then therefore I am still married. It is true that I am a prince of the Eldest Tribe of the jaran, but there are other Sakhalin princes who can ride to war or act as regents. I am the only one married to a Singer. I would ask you, that if you desire it, that I leave the tribes and journey across the seas to return to you, my angel.

"*I have explained to Anatoly what he must give up in order to go. He will not be a prince there. His name, his grandmother's name, will make no difference to anyone, and the privileges he receives here as part of a princely family, which he never thinks of because he takes them so completely for granted, will all be missing there. I hope you realize how great a sacrifice that would be for him. You must remember that the other jaran who left the tribes and are now on Earth gave up nothing, because they had nothing to give up anymore, being what the jaran call* arenabekh, *black riders, which also means, the orphaned ones.*

"*As well, he can't read or write or use a modeler. He knows nothing about the world he would be living in, and you would be his only anchor. He could never return to Rhui, not as long as the interdiction holds, and since it would be cruel to withhold from him the life extension treatments, he would live, beside you, for a long long time. I myself can't recommend that you encourage him to leave the jaran. It will be hard for him to stay here, but*

I trust that in time he'll see the wisdom of your choice, and our choice, and marry again. Anatoly has in any case agreed to abide by your decision. I hope this finds you well and flourishing. Regards, Tess.

Then, below this and written in an entirely different, almost painstakingly-precise handwriting, was another sentence, this one in Rhuian rather than Anglais. *"I beg your indulgence for addressing you in this impertinent fashion, Diana, but I hope you will at least for a moment look at this as a man would and not let that damned female practicality push aside the feelings of the heart.* This was signed simply, *Ilyakoria Bakhtiian.*

At the bottom, someone had traced onto the paper the outline of the earring Anatoly had given to her, and she back to him. It was like a signature. It was a promise.

The five minute call came up on the theater screen. "Oh, hell." Her hands shook, but she forced herself to put the letter down. She took in three breaths to steady herself and then started furiously applying makeup, eyes first. "I come on in scene two. Oh, damn."

The door burst open and Joseph charged in. "Di! Your hair! Where's your wig? You didn't give your ready call—" He jerked to a halt, seeing Marco. A look of quick sympathy passed over his face. "I will go out," he announced. "In sixty seconds I will come back in." The door shut behind him.

Diana set down her pencil and rose and turned to face Marco.

"What are you going to do?" he asked. "Tess told me what was in the letter, more or less. I agreed to deliver it because . . . well, because I was coming here, and we had to hand-deliver it. You'll have to burn it, you know. We can't leave any evidence that she's alive where the Chapalii might find it."

It was a grandiose dream she had had, two years ago, meeting him and wondering if he and she, the hardened explorer and the young adventurous actor—Goddess, it was a horrible cliché, and maybe that was why it had gone so badly. But he deserved honesty. And she had a play to perform.

"Marco, I don't know what I'm going to do. But don't

wait for me. I can't promise you anything, not yet, maybe not ever." Then she crossed over and kissed him, once, lightly.

The door opened. "Scene over," said Joseph. "So sorry. Out. Di, damn it anyway." The wig mistress charged in and stuffed Diana's hair into the wig cap and then peeled the wig on over the cap. Joseph stood over Diana while she blended on the base to cover the seam and finished with her mouth and eyes, and did the rouge. At some point during this frantic activity she saw Marco move, in the mirror, and leave, that quietly. He left a single red rose behind him, on the table.

"Stand!" ordered Joseph. He dressed her in the swathes of robes that Zenocrate, the daughter of the Soldan of Egypt, wore on her first entrance, led in by the great conqueror Tamburlaine as his captive and intended mistress.

The cue light came on above the door.

"I'll guide you up the stairs," said Joseph.

In the darkness backstage, he gave her hand into Vasil Veselov's. They entered.

It was a good, attentive audience, eager to be enthralled by the story and patient enough, with both parts of *Tamburlaine* before them, to be forgiving of Vasil's novice errors, snags in the way the energy ran, a focus thrown the wrong way, a glance held too long, although never, ever, a missed line.

To be fair to Vasil, he performed well, very well, considering how short a time he had been acting. The part was made for him, of course. She knew who he was playing. He wasn't playing Tamburlaine, he was playing Ilyakoria Bakhtiian, the way he moved, the way he turned his head, the way the sword swayed at his hips, the way he looked toward the heavens when he spoke of his destiny—Vasil had studied Bakhtiian so closely that he had internalized Bakhtiian's bearing, his tone, almost his whole being. But for his fair hair and his beautiful, flawless face, he might have been Bakhtiian, crueler, even a little comic in his excesses, but a man bent on conquering the world. It was easy enough, as Zenocrate, to fall in love with his power.

They ate dinner backstage in the two-hour break between Part One and Part Two. Yevgeni came backstage. He always did. He as good as haunted Hyacinth wherever he went, except when he worked. Yomi had found the young rider employment at a cobbler's shop, building handcrafted boots, and he seemed happy enough there and proud of his work. But then, he came from a common family. Diana tried to imagine Anatoly making boots for a living, and could not.

"Places!" Yomi announced. They went back on, for Part Two.

Zenocrate dies.

> *"Black is the beauty of the brightest day,*
> *The golden ball of heaven's eternal fire,*
> *That danced with glory on the silver waves. . . .*
> *For amorous Jove hath snatched my love from hence,*
> *Meaning to make her stately queen of heaven. . . .*
> *Behold me here, divine Zenocrate,*
> *Raving, impatient, desperate and mad. . . .*
> *Come down from heaven and live with me again!"*

In the end, Tamburlaine himself cannot triumph over his own mortality. He takes ill, he fights and wins his final battle, and when he admits at last that death is upon him, he calls on his men to bring in the hearse of Zenocrate.

From the hearse, lying still, visible to the audience and yet disguised somewhat by the frosted glastic walls, Diana watched Vasil give his final speech. She watched him cry. Not for himself. Tess Soerensen was wrong about one thing, at least: It wasn't true that Vasil hadn't given up anything. This much Diana had learned—obliquely—from Karolla. Vasil had simply given up the only thing—the only person—he had ever truly loved outside of himself.

"For Tamburlaine, the Scourge of God must die."

He died, and still tears leaked from his eyes as Hal spoke the final lines. "Let heaven and earth his timeless death deplore. For both their worths can equal him no more."

Vasil was crying for what he had lost, and for what Ilyakoria Bakhtiian would never know.

Diana cried, too, because Tess Soerensen was, after all, right. Anatoly couldn't come to Earth. It would be cruel, above all else. Anatoly belonged on Rhui, just as she belonged here. He had agreed to abide by her decision, and though so often he found some way to make the decision fall the way he wanted it to, this time she had to make the choice. She knew what her decision must be. It was time to let him go.

CHAPTER FORTY

David liked Meroe Transfer Station because he had designed it. Together with his two codesigners, he had worked in a unifying motif of huge pyramidal chambers and buttresses in the open concourses that resembled giant wings, all linked by an enclosed stream that ran through most of the station. He had managed to weasel out enough money from the design budget to commission fifty artists from varying disciplines to decorate the interior, with serpents and rams and giraffes, groves of date palms and acacia trees, sandstone statues and intricate mosaics of fused glass inlaid into gold.

Twenty years later, he still liked it, he decided as he strolled through Concourse Axum on his way to the gate from which he would take ship back to Odys, and Charles.

He wished Nadine could see it. He would have liked to share it with her, to show her how it interlocked, how the architecture and the ornamental motifs reflected each other, how the dimensionality of building in space both freed and limited the engineer. Had it really only been eighteen months since he had left her? It seemed like one month, she remained so clear in his mind. It seemed like a hundred years.

Impatient with himself and these pointless reflections, he tapped his one piece of luggage against his leg. The plastine tube thudded gently against his thigh, light but sturdy. It contained three hand-drawn maps that David and Rajiv had done together, to send on to Rhui, to Tess. They were ostensibly a map of the principality of Jeds, a detailed map of the city, and a detailed map of the palace of Morava and its grounds, based on his survey, but coded into the key was a secondary matrix on which Tess would build a secondary architecture for the saboteur network based on the architecture and layout of the palace of Jeds, the palace of Morava, and—although this wasn't mapped—the traditional spiral layout of a jaran camp, which made the arrangement of tents look haphazard until one divined the pattern by which they were set up.

Under a winged buttress, he paused to admire his second favorite sculpture, this one done in light, in three dimensions, by the famous artist Surya Neve Lao. It depicted the Meroite queen, the Candace Amanirenas, as she directed a dawn attack on the Roman garrison at Syene together with her son, Prince Akinidad. Silhouetted against the flames rising within the garrison walls, David recognized a woman as she tipped back her head and stared up at the sculpture curling back along the concourse wall.

"Diana!" he cried.

She turned and blinked at him for a moment. Behind her, the battle raged endlessly on, never to be lost, never to be won.

"David!" She smiled suddenly and it seemed that the whole concourse was brightened by her. She hurried over to him, and they embraced.

"Where are you off to?" he asked. "When I left Rajiv, he said the Repertory Company was in Bangkok. You haven't left them, have you?"

"No, I—" She hesitated and glanced behind at the sculpture, then back at him. To his surprise, she still wore the scar of marriage on her face. Right now, she looked nervous, and even a little embarrassed. "I'm meeting someone. At Scarab Gate."

"Oh, I'll walk you. I'm leaving through Antelope Gate, and it's right next door. Anyway, my favorite sculpture is at Scarab Gate."

"Your favorite sculpture? Do you go through Meroe often? You must be quite the traveler."

David grinned. Oh, well. He was proud of his work, and it was worth being proud of. "I designed it."

"This station!"

One of the things David loved about Diana was that her emotions were so wonderfully distinct. He laughed.

"But it's wonderful! Why did you make the buttresses like that, like they're wings?"

"Because they are wings. They're the wings of the Goddess." So they walked to Scarab Gate and he told her about the design and the arguments and compromises and the choices that had gone into building Meroe Transfer Station.

A beautiful bronzed arch made of huge linked scarabs bridged the concourse wall that led into the steep, four-walled chamber that was Scarab Gate and a lounge for departing and arriving passengers. A second scarab arch, smaller and less ornate, sealed off the port tube that led to the pier and the locks.

"Where are you going?" Diana asked finally.

"I'm going to Odys. Business for Charles."

Diana smiled. "His Nibs. That's what Maggie O'Neill always called him. Where is she?"

"There. On Odys."

"Ah," said Diana, and that was another thing David liked about her. She knew when he had said as much as he could say.

"Here it is. My favorite sculpture."

She stopped. "It's very simple."

It *was* simple, a simple gray sandstone statue of a young Candace, a queen, a resolute soldier bearing a sword and wearing a crown. To David, that statue was Nadine; not that it looked anything like her, but that it captured her spirit.

"I like the way the sculptor has suggested hair just by using hatching," said Diana.

"Are you coming to meet family?" David asked.

Her mouth tightened. She held in some overwhelming emotion. "Tess Soerensen told me once that it's easy to act on impulse and much harder to think about what the consequences might be. But the consequences will show up sooner or later, and then you must prepare yourself to deal with them." She looked up at him. A man could drown in the blue of her eyes. Despite himself, he found his gaze darting down to the scar. It looked oddly fresh.

"It's what we've done to Rhui, isn't it?" she asked bitterly. "We walked blithely in and watched how it changed us, but we never thought about how it might change them. They're the ones who will suffer the most."

He had thought the same thing many times. "*Who* are you meeting?" he asked, but by the expression on her face, he could guess who it was. So this was her guilt talking, that she had wanted Anatoly and had somehow managed to persuade Charles or Tess to let him come to her, and only now did she realize how hard the transition would be for her husband.

The boards lit. The familiar monotone announcement began, detailing the arriving ship and its coordinates. Diana's hands flew to her cheeks. She had gone suddenly pale.

"It was so good to see you, David," she said, lowering her hands with conscious embarrassment. "But I have to go. Please. Please, come and visit me when you come back, or if you see us, if we tour, come and see me backstage."

"I will. I wish you the best of luck, Diana."

She kissed him on each cheek, in the formal jaran style, and smiled, and left him.

Thus dismissed, he had no choice but to simply stand there and watch as she ran over toward the small gate and then jerked to a halt at the waist-high wicker fence that blocked off the egress. She shifted her weight from one foot to the other, too nervous to stand still.

Passengers streamed out. Diana waited. David watched.

The floor was sloped so that he could see farther into the port tube than Diana could, so he saw the uniformed attendant first, and her companion, a shell-shocked looking young man. Next to the attendant's dark uniform and olive skin and robust build, the young man looked almost fragile, he was so fair and so slight. But he was here.

David felt sick with envy.

It was a little scene, complete in itself. Diana wiped a tear from her face, and then she saw him. The attendant jostled his arm—what need had she to know Diana? It was apparent who was waiting for the young man—and Anatoly looked up and saw Diana.

David turned away. He could not bear to watch any more. It was too painful.

He skirted the sandstone statue and trudged back through Scarab Gate and on down the concourse to the gentler lines of Antelope Gate. Thank the Goddess, there was no delay for his flight. He boarded, found his cabin, locked the door, stowed the precious tube between his leg and the bunk wall, and plugged straight into hibersleep for the voyage.

He had no dreams.

But he did wake up with the usual horrible nausea and vertigo. Maggie was sitting on the pull-down chair, squeezed into the tiny cabin, regarding him with a frown on her face. Her freckles were prominent today for some reason, making her red hair seem all the more red. Or maybe it was just his eyes adjusting to the lights.

"You don't usually do hibersleep, do you, David? I thought it made you sick as a—Aha!" She jerked the siphon out of the wall and caught most of the phlegm that was all he had to throw up, and then wiped his face with a cool towel.

"You're a peach, Mags," he said. His mouth felt like it had a thousand-year-old growth of fungus in it. "I don't dare sit up."

"No sympathy from me," she retorted. "I hate the fumes of that stuff. Here." She bent over and extracted the tube of maps. "Do you want me to wait for you to recover, or just take this downside?"

"Maggie!"

"Oh, David." She sat down beside him and smoothed his hair with a hand. "You look rotten. Why did you do it?"

"I didn't want to think for that long, cooped up on a ship."

She regarded him thoughtfully. "Oh," she said at last. "I don't suppose you crossed paths with Diana Brooke-Holt, did you?" He didn't need to reply. Maggie knew him well enough to read his face.

"Poor Diana," she said.

"Poor Diana!"

"No, you're right. Poor Anatoly's more like it. You

know she sent him back a message saying he should stay on Rhui, didn't you?"

"What?" David felt utterly confused.

"But it was already too late. The damned scheming boy had evidently planned it all along. He got himself sent to Jeds and by one means or the other—no one is willing to take responsibility for it—he buffaloed his way onto one of the sloops by claiming he had a dispensation from Tess to go to Erthe, and by the time they realized their mistake, he'd seen a shuttle. So what could they do? They sent him to Odys. We never gave him Diana's message. So maybe it is poor Diana after all. She was wise enough to see that he ought to have stayed on Rhui." She broke off. "Oh, David," she said on a sigh. She bent and kissed him on the cheek. "David, she never could have left the planet. You know it's true."

"I know. I know." But it still hurt. "Has there ever—been any news of her?"

She opened her mouth and then shut it again. "Well. We did hear that she had a baby, a daughter, recently. Tess is pregnant again. Did you hear that?"

"No, I—I haven't been much in touch with Rhui lately," he said, and realized how stupid the comment sounded, considering the maps he carried with him. "I've tried to put it behind me, that year." But he thought of Nadine, holding a little child who probably looked like her fair-haired father. "Damn it," he murmured. "It's so stupid to dwell on something that wasn't meant to be."

"Oh, my dear friend, I didn't know you still missed her that much. Let me get you something to drink to settle that stomach of yours. Charles is waiting for you. And I'm always glad to see you. I missed you."

David felt comforted, knowing he had the solace of friendship waiting for him here on Odys.

At the palace, Charles sat in conference with Hon Echido Keinaba in the domed audience chamber that overlooked the massive greenhouse wing.

Suzanne, seated next to Charles at the ralewood table, saw David and Maggie at the door and beckoned to them to come in. Evidently Echido was by this time used to the casual way in which humans came and went, although he did stand and acknowledge the new arrivals with a pallid nod.

"... and when I officially open the female wing here on Odys, Hon Echido, I hope your family will be able to provide me with suitable females with whom I can extend my staff. Ah, hello, David. Sit down. Maggie, can you deliver—the gifts—and then go and make sure the reception room is ready? I'm expecting Tai Naroshi Toraokii anytime now."

"Naroshi?" asked David.

"In response to my summons."

"It took him long enough," said Suzanne tartly.

"Only by our standards," replied Charles. He turned back to the merchant. "So is it well with you and the Keinaba elders, Hon Echido, that I send twenty-seven apprentices into your service to learn the craft of commerce from your masters?"

"At your command, Tai-en. The proper arrangements have been made. As well, we have chosen three *chayhon*, nine *sendi-nin*, and eighty-one *ke di* to enter your female house."

Charles glanced at Suzanne, who said in a low voice, "Three of the merchant class, nine of the steward, and eighty-one ke, all female."

"I beg your pardon, Tai-en." Echido flushed blue about the cheeks.

"It is granted," said Charles impatiently. He looked at Suzanne, who looked at her slate and shook her head. Charles frowned. "He's late. Well. Now, Hon Echido, about the other matter."

"Tai-en. Neither I nor the Keinaba House have the authority to allow these disciplines you call The Arts free movement along transport lines or, indeed, access to ports of call. But if I may be allowed to take an *orchestra* back with me to Keinaba Mansion on Paladia Major, I would be triply honored by your magnanimity."

"Umm." Charles turned to look out at the greenhouse that sparkled in the pale sunlight, a swath of brightness thrust out across the curry-colored massif flats. "That will do. Perhaps once guests at your mansion hear the orchestra, they, too, will wish such human artisans to grace their homes and mansions."

"Indeed, Tai-en, if it is considered a sign of ducal pleasure, many will be eager for such a mark of distinction."

"Aha!" Suzanne jumped to her feet. "Incoming."

Hon Echido rose as well, and he bowed to the precise degree due a duke being honored by his least worthy servant. "I will withdraw, with your permission, Tai Charles."

"It is granted."

Hon Echido withdrew.

"You know what I think," said Suzanne, "I think he's beginning to read us."

"Read us?" David asked.

"I think he's beginning to get a sense of how we work, we humans. Frightening thought."

"Good thing he's on our side," said David. "If he is. If any of them can be. Why is Naroshi coming in?"

"I asked him to," said Charles. "Maggie is going to send the maps on to Rhui."

"Is she going to take them down herself?"

"No. Marco wants to go back downside."

"You're letting him?"

"We need more survey. Tess needs more intelligence, especially in Rhui's other hemisphere. He'll transfer over the maps to her and then head east, as far as he can go."

"Until he comes around back to the other side? Wait. Does this have something to do with Diana Brooke-Holt and the sudden appearance of her interdicted jaran husband on Meroe Transfer Station?"

"What do you think?" asked Suzanne sourly. "I told him he was being a fool."

"Which comment," said Charles dryly, "he appreciated greatly. In part to do with her, yes, but mostly to do with Marco. He'll be circling that globe for the rest of his life, because he's too damn restless to settle in any one place, and he always has to be testing himself."

"And seeing how close he can come to getting himself killed, without ever quite managing it." Suzanne snorted and wiped her hands together briskly, brushing them off.

"I wash my hands of trying to improve him and his miserable life."

Charles and David burst out laughing together, and Suzanne set her hands on her hips, glared at them, and then stalked out of the room. It wasn't a particularly effective exit, if only because it took so long for her to cross the tiled floor that the drama of her affronted expression had long since expired by the time she reached the far door. When she glanced back at them, David saw that she was smiling.

"Only twenty-seven apprentices? That's not very many," David said to Charles.

"David, I have three yachts in my private fleet, which are allowed to ferry on the shipping lanes between human regions and Paladia Minor and Major. Each one is manned by a crew of twenty-four, more or less. Of these twenty-four, two of each crew, the captain and the purser, are allowed to disembark at either port. As well, Tess's old friend Sojourner and her husband Rene are in residence on the Keinaba flagship. And I have one human representative who sits as my shadow in the Hall of the Nobles, in the outermost circle of the emperor's palace, just as all the other dukes have such shadow markers— well, only theirs are Chapalii, of course. Then again, that one representative changes every three months so the poor soul doesn't go stark raving mad."

Charles walked over to the field that separated the inside air from the outside air and set his hands, palms out and open, against it, and regarded the luxuriant growth within the greenhouse. David could not tell whether he was a nobleman surveying his domain, or a prisoner staring out from his cell.

"That's it. That is the entire sum of the human presence within Imperial space. Twenty-seven apprentices is a big jump, compared to that. I don't want to move too fast."

He peeled his hands away from the field and sniffed, dabbing at his nose with a handkerchief. "My hay fever is acting up again. I don't know how it carries from there into the main building."

David chuckled. "That's the thing about weeds. No matter how hard you try, you can never get rid of them."

Charles grinned. "It's good to have you back, David. I hope this time you'll stay longer. Oh. Hell. Let's go."

David had deduced one thing about the Chapalii. They loved grandeur. They loved huge, towering spaces and masses of intricate and floridly-overwhelming decoration. So Charles had built a new reception room, a small, intimate reception chamber set into one of the corner towers and furnished to his own taste.

It was David's favorite room in the entire palace.

Two walls were windows, opening out onto a balcony that looked out over the tule flats and the far green glint of the greenhouse wing. David sat on one of the two sofas while Charles went to the bureau and rummaged for drinks.

"Canadian or Martian?" Charles asked, setting out two bottles of whiskey.

"Three of those pieces are new," said David, nodding toward the white wall above the bureau, where Charles displayed his favorite art. He stood up and walked diagonally across the room, skirting the cartograph-lectern, to the opposite corner and stared at the full suit of lamellar armor that stood out on the balcony. The lacquered leather strips and polished iron segments gleamed in the long light of the setting sun. "This is new, too. That's jaran armor."

"Yes, it is." Charles handed him his whiskey.

Suzanne came in. "He's here."

Charles walked back to sit down on the other sofa, so that he could look both out the window and at the plain teak double doors that opened into the room. David remained where he was.

Suzanne opened both doors, and Tai-en Naroshi entered, followed by one of his ubiquitous stewards. The duke held a crystal wand in his right hand.

"Tai-en," said Charles.

"Tai-en," said Naroshi.

The room itself was pale, lit by the two walls of windows and by the two white walls and by the furniture, all of it a light teak. Even the accents, the throw rug and the linen cushions on the sofas, were white. Even so, Naroshi's skin was paler still.

He examined the room, and Charles allowed him silence in which to do so. He paced slowly along the wall against which the bureau stood, looking at each piece of art in turn: the tapestry of birds; the woven doormat of green and red stripes; a saber sheathed in a gold case studded with pearls and emeralds; a silk robe embroidered with the lion and the moon of the Habakar royal house; the embossed bronze teapot and the enameled vase set on the bureau; a painting of Jeds, seen from the harbor, which was in fact the only piece of art along the wall. The other things functioned, on Rhui, as utilitarian objects, however beautiful they might appear displayed here.

Naroshi circled back, paused beside the tilted podium which was Charles's cartographer's table, and crossed the room to sit on the other sofa. Suzanne and the steward stood silently on either side of the open doors.

"I received your summons," Naroshi said. He placed the wand carefully across both knees.

"I am distressed, Tai-en," said Charles, "by these charges which the Protocol Office has brought against members of my house."

"It would sadden the emperor, indeed," replied Naroshi, "to have this matter brought to his attention. If only I could be assured that such a transgression had not occurred."

Which it had, of course. David glanced at Suzanne, but she was watching the two dukes.

Charles placed a hand on each knee, echoing the placement of Naroshi's hands. "My people would never have gone down to Rhui of their own volition because they know the strength of the interdiction, and, indeed, the only reason they would ever have been forced to go down there would be because another house, other Chapalii under another lord, had violated the interdiction and thus forced these, my own people, to investigate."

Naroshi's pallor did not alter. But David waited, breathless, to see how he would respond. It was a classic gambit, of course: I know you sent your people down; yes, but I know you sent *your* people down.

"I am certain," said Naroshi finally, "that it would take

considerable provocation for any lord to break an interdiction approved by the emperor himself. I must be mistaken. I will inform the Protocol Office that they must
erase all charges on their list."

"We are agreed, then," said Charles. Now they knew
exactly where each of them stood—more or less. Did
Naroshi know that Tess was still alive? Did he guess? Did
he know that Tess had transferred to her brother the cylinder from the Mushai's banks? Did Naroshi have such a
copy himself? David hid a cough behind his hand. He decided that less had the advantage over more.

"But that is not the only reason I requested your presence here, Tai-en," added Charles.

Naroshi lifted his chin, acknowledging the comment. "I
am honored beyond measure that you would allow my
sister to design the mausoleum for your departed heir. I
have brought her design with me, for you to view."

"You are generous, Tai-en. May I hope that we can
view it now?"

The two sofas sat perpendicular to each other, one with
its back to a windowed wall, one with its back to the
bookshelves that lined the rest of the wall out from the
doors. Up from the rug that lay between them, an edifice
rose.

David caught a gasp back in his throat. It was a clever
insult. Or perhaps not an insult at all, but a tacit acknowledgment of their shared crime. It was the palace of
Morava, clearly, in its essential design, but twisted and
turned in on itself, crossed with the starker classical lines
of the Parthenon and made feminine by a profusion of
bright frescos of elegant ladies in belled skirts and fitted
jackets surrounded by flowers, and by the tiers of columns surrounding the central dome. The design was a
clear reminder of the rebel duke, the Tai-en Mushai, and
yet it was also uniquely itself. It was stunning.

Charles rose and paced once around the edifice and sat
back down again.

"What site have you procured?" he asked.

Naroshi inclined his head. "We have received a dispensation from the emperor's Chamberlain of the Avenue of

the Red Blossom to build the mausoleum along the Field of Empty Hands."

David had not a clue what or where the Field of Empty Hands was, and he wondered if Charles did, either, but Charles certainly did not show any uncertainty in his reply.

"That would be well, Tai-en. I am honored by your interest, and by your sister's skill."

"We all mourn, when a member of one of the great families dies, whether by the cessation of breath or the act of extinction, of leaving, that forever separates them from their kin."

Charles bowed his head, perhaps the better to shadow his expression. It was true that, by Chapalii law, now that Charles had acknowledged Tess's marriage to Bakhtiian, Tess did indeed lose her position as Charles's heir. So ran the Chapalii inheritance laws, and laws of marriage: a female upon marriage takes her husband's status exclusively. Presumably Naroshi's own sister was unmarried, else she would not still remain in his house. Naroshi might believe Tess was dead—Bakhtiian had told his agent that. But Cara had also told David that Tess's original marriage had taken place at Morava; did Naroshi know about that? Or was his comment not about Tess at all but simply a reference to the emperor, who severed all ties of kinship, all ties with his past, on the day he stepped up to the imperial throne? There were a hundred other possibilities, all of them too damned convoluted for David's taste.

"Tai-en," said Charles into the silence. "I have a proposition for you."

Naroshi regarded him steadily.

"Just as you have brought this to me—" He gestured toward the edifice, now curling into mist at the edges as it faded away. "—I propose to bring a human art to you. We humans create an art form that is transitory, played out each night once in a way that can never be duplicated, and yet, played out the next night in the same way that is, still, different from what it was before. It is called theater. I would bring this theater into Imperial space, if you would be willing to sponsor its travel."

"Theater," said Naroshi. The human word sounded strange and ominous on his lips. "I know what this art is." He inclined his head. "I would be pleased to sponsor a—ah, I know the word. The *tour.*"

Charles inclined his head in reply. David could not imagine how Charles could keep his face so straight as he recruited a Chapalii duke, all unknowing, to start the wheel spinning, to start the first corruption, the first step, the first wedge into the edifice of diamond and steel that was the Empire. To introduce the first tendrils of the saboteur network into the heart of Chapalii space.

Or did Naroshi know? Did he suspect? Knowing that his own agents had been in Charles's territory—knowing that Charles knew—did Naroshi then accept Charles's agents into his? Like any great dance, whirling along in brilliant colors across a ballroom floor, the movement and countermovement that flowed naturally from the interaction of the dancers seemed merely bewildering to an inexperienced bystander. On neither duke could David read the slightest expression or color.

"I will send the Bharentous Repertory Company to your palace, Tai-en," said Charles.

"I will receive it," said Naroshi.

He rose. Charles rose. The edifice dissolved into steam and vanished into air between them, where they stood at either end of their respective sofas. They made polite farewells. Naroshi left, with his steward trailing behind. David and Suzanne stared at each other. Charles sat down and drained his whiskey in one shot.

"Well," said Suzanne. "I wasn't expecting that. Getting him to sponsor the tour." She walked over and sat down where Naroshi had just been sitting.

"Neither was I," admitted Charles. "It just came to me." He grinned. "Did you see that design? It practically shouted my link to Rhui and to the Mushai and from there, I suppose, to all rebels."

"Or Tess's link," said Suzanne, "since Naroshi must know that she was last seen alive there."

"How can you risk it?" David demanded. He thought of Diana as he said it. Of Diana and her husband, who must surely end up following her wherever she went. "Putting the actors into Naroshi's hands?"

" 'I'll deliver all,' " said Charles. He leaned back into the cushions. "How can I not risk it?"

David sighed and went to lean on the lectern, but he watched the sun sink down over the horizon. The polished black surface of the table stared blankly at him.

"Earth," said Charles, and a flat map of Earth and her continents flowered into being on the table. He went on, through the planets bound together by the League covenant, by their human heritage, by the many space stations and mining colonies and frozen outposts linking them along the shipping lanes. "Ophiuchi-Sei. Sirin Five. Tau Ceti Tierce. Eridanaia. Hydra. Cassie. The unpronounceable one. Three Rings." He did not say Odys. Odys was not a human planet, only the seat of his ducal authority.

Maggie strode in, poured herself a drink at the bureau, and walked across the room to sprawl out on the sofa next to Charles. "I got rid of Marco," she said. "What a relief. He needs a vacation. But you know—" She sipped from her glass and set it down on the end table. "I almost asked him to greet Ursula from me. It's still hard to believe that she's dead. What a terrible way to die."

"She wasn't the first. She won't be the last," said Charles.

Maggie had evidently come through the greenhouse, because David could smell the perfume of newly-mown grass on her. Suzanne sighed. Under David's elbows, the screen shifted again, to show the ongoing design and work index for Concord, the great space station that housed the League offices and the League Parliament. The Chapalii Protocol Office allowed the work to continue, as long as it did not interfere with whatever quotas and taxes their human subjects must pay to the emperor. David ran a finger along a hatched grid. Nadine would have loved this, this table, with its cornucopia of maps stored within, each one available at the touch of a finger or with a single spoken word, each one a discovery, a new journey, a fresh path to explore.

"Where did you get that sword?" Maggie asked. "That saber? That's a jaran saber."

"Bakhtiian sent it to me," said Charles, "together with the armor and a beautifully embroidered red shirt."

David looked out at the armor. He hadn't noticed the shirt before, but it was there, under the cuirass, sleeves flowing out in a pattern of red interlaced with a golden road and silver eagles. And David had to smile. As if, by giving him the shirt, Bakhtiian had made Charles a member of his army.

Charles caught David's eye and smiled. Then he said, "Rhui," and the surface of the table flowed again, becoming Rhui.

Maggie got up and went over to stare more closely at the saber. She made a comment, more of a grunt, really, that meant nothing except perhaps, "Oh, how interesting." The only color in the room came from her teal shirt, and from the Rhuian artifacts arranged artfully along the wall. The display itself seemed to flow right out onto the balcony, encompassing the suit of armor and moving beyond it to the horizon. As the sun set over the quiet waters, the evening star woke and burned in the sky, so that it, too, seemed part of the room. The evening star, which was Rhui.

"I miss him," said Charles. "It's strange, knowing I'll probably never see him again."

David wiped the table clear with a sweep of his arm and went and sat down next to Suzanne. After a moment, Maggie retreated to her place. The four of them sat there in companionable silence. Night bled down over them. The bureau light snapped on, illuminating the wall, spraying a fan of soft white light up onto the saber and the robe.

" 'I long to hear the story of your life,' " said Suzanne, " 'which must take the ear strangely.' That's what comes before that line."

"What line?" demanded Maggie.

Rhui blazed in the sky, and around her, the other stars appeared, thousands upon thousands of them like the fires of the jaran army, like the torch-burdened walls of Karkand, like lights burning in the forest of towers that surrounded the emperor's palace on Chapal.

" 'I'll deliver all.' " said Charles, " 'And promise you

calm seas, auspicious gales/And sail so expeditious that shall catch Your royal fleet far off.' "

"Oh," said Maggie. "*That* line."

David felt at peace. Not for the past, not for the future, but for this moment. For now.

EPILOGUE

"We'll lead you to the stately tent of war.
Where you shall hear the Scythian Tamburlaine
Threatening the world in high astounding terms
And scourging kingdoms with his conquering sword.
View but his picture in this tragic glass,
And then applaud his fortunes as you please."

—Marlowe,
Tamburlaine the Great

The riders left the sprawl of the jaran camp at dawn, a
pack of fifty soldiers, lightly armed, and one khaja man
dressed in a drab tunic, carrying a heavy wooden tube
strapped along his back. They rode that day across grassy
plains transformed into pale gold by the summer sun.
They camped, tentless and fireless, under the cloud-
streaked sky, and stars and the full moon watched over
them.

The next day they came to a low range of hills and a
khaja village with tumbled-down walls, and through this
they rode without a passing glance, and the khaja villag-
ers trudged on about their tasks with scarcely a look in
their direction. In the afternoon they saw a great butte
looming before them.

"Goddess in Heaven," said Marco, "that's an impressive thing."

"It is the khayan-sarmiia," explained Aleksi, "Her
Crown Fallen from Heaven to Earth."

"Whose crown?"

"Mother Sun's crown. There's the camp."

Five and a half years ago, Aleksi had ridden here

bringing the news of Sergei Veselov's death to the army.
Now he delivered a messenger from a dead man. No army
camped now in the shadow of the huge rock, and yet the
camp pitched here was large, riders and archers and
women cooking and children carrying water. Set out in a
great spiral at the northeastern corner of the butte stood
the ten great tents of the ten etsanas of the Eldest Tribes.
Two tents shared the middle ground: that of Mother
Sakhalin and that of Mother Orzhekov, Bakhtiian's aunt.

"I don't see Bakhtiian's tent," said Marco as they rode
into the Orzhekov encampment.

Aleksi pointed up, toward the heavens. "His tent is
pitched up there," he said.

Marco tilted his head back and stared up at the grainy
cliffs that blocked off half the southern horizon from this
angle. The sun was already hidden behind it, and its
shadow made a cooling screen for the camp against the
summer heat. Aleksi dismounted and gave his mount to
one of his riders. Marco did the same.

"Papa!" An instant later, a small but fierce object hit
Aleksi broadside, and he grunted and laughed and
grabbed his daughter under her arms and swung her
around. "Dania, you imp," he scolded, setting her down.
She wore a little bow and quiver strapped on her back,
and a curved stick thrust in her belt. "Marco, this is my
daughter Dania."

Marco eyed the child with distrust. She folded her arms
across her chest and regarded him with disdain. "Your
daughter?" he asked, clearly puzzled.

"Yes," said Aleksi, taking pity on him, khaja that he
was, for not understanding immediately how Aleksi could
be the father of a child too old to have been born to his
wife in the nearly two years since he had seen Marco
Burckhardt last. "I married her mother, Svetlana, some
months after you left us."

"Papa," Dania announced, "Kolia got into trouble
again. He burnt his fingers because he was trying to—"

"Hush. I don't want to hear about it. Did Tess have the
baby yet?"

"No, but the doctor sent a runner down today and

called Mama and Aunt Sonia to attend, so perhaps she's having it now."

Marco gaped up at the rock. It towered up into the heavens, its flat peak seeming to scrape the pale down of clouds that streaked the sky. "Tess is up there having a baby?" he exclaimed.

"She got so huge, and the baby still hadn't come, so she decided that since she wanted to stay with Bakhtiian anyway, through the council, that she might as well walk up with him and try to start her labor that way."

A sudden gleam lit Marco's eyes. Aleksi recognized it: Nadine got the same gleam in her eyes when it came time to scout a new path. "There's a path that goes up to the top? Can we hike up there?"

"No, you can't," said Dania severely. "Only the etsanas and the dyans have walked up. They're speaking to the gods."

"Yes, you can," said Aleksi mildly, bending down to kiss the girl on either cheek. "Go on, little one. Go find your Aunt Nadine and send her to us." He straightened up to regard Marco, who still had his head thrown back, gazing up at the height. "Tess said we should come up, you and I, once we arrived. But it's true that it's a holy place, and that the gathering going on there now is not for any eyes and ears but those of the Ten Elder Tribes."

"What is going on?" demanded Marco. "Are they all overseeing the birth, or something? To make sure it's legitimate?"

"What is *legitimate?*" asked Aleksi. "Well, never mind. Let's go to Nadine's tent. She'll want to see the maps."

Nadine arrived at her tent at the same time as they did, and she greeted Marco with every show of sincerity. While he unsealed the tube and drew out the maps, she asked him a string of questions about the voyage and what the great seas were like to sail on and if it was true that there were monsters sunk in the deeps. Nadine had furnished her outer chamber in a khaja manner, with a table and chairs and a cabinet built and carved in Jeds. Marco unrolled the maps on the table and she gasped and leaned beside him, smoothing her hand out over the heavy parchment.

"David did these, didn't he?" she said in a low voice.

"David and Rajiv Caer Linn, yes," answered Marco. "David is well."

Nadine glanced up at him, at these innocuous words, and then down at the map again. "They're beautiful maps, and so detailed. How comes it, Marco, that you can sail over the far seas and back again, and yet none of the others can?"

Marco grinned. "I don't ask permission, for one, and for the other, I'm willing to take the risks onto myself." Then his face changed abruptly, and he turned to stare at the curtain that separated the outer chamber from the sleeping chamber. "I've no one waiting for me, back there, in any case."

Nadine traced a warren of chambers in a finely detailed corner of the map of the shrine of Morava, and her finger came to rest on one particular room, a tiny little chamber that bore no distinguishing mark to separate it from the rest, nothing except what lay in her memory. "Kirill Zvertkov is taking a jahar of twenty thousands and riding east along the Golden Road, to scout it," she said, sounding casual. But Aleksi knew her well enough—and had been privy to the arguments—to know how badly she had wanted to go on that expedition, and how firmly Bakhtiian had refused her request. One daughter was not enough to secure the succession.

"East from the plains?" asked Marco. "I haven't been that way. The Empire of Yarial lies on the eastern shore, they say."

"There's a country that lies athwart the Golden Road in the midst of an empty desert," said Nadine, her voice becoming rich with eagerness, "where the lands shift, where no traveler can walk without becoming lost, where the mountains move at night, and the rivers change their course between the seasons."

"But, Dina," said Aleksi, "a country like that could only exist if the khaja there were all sorcerers, or if the gods had put a curse on it."

"That may be," said Nadine tartly, "but I'd still like to see it for myself."

"When did you say that Zvertkov is riding east?" Marco asked.

"In a few days," answered Nadine. "Are you going to go with him?"

"I just might, at that," murmured Marco. "I just might." Then, to his credit, he read her expression. "I promise to send you reports by every courier who returns to the army."

Nadine sighed and placed her hands on two corners of the maps, holding them down and staring at them. The entrance flap got pushed aside. A baby announced its presence in a long musical trill, complete with a babble of meaningless but perfectly sweet syllables. "Hello, Feodor," Nadine said to the table.

Aleksi turned. It was Feodor, of course. Grekov was so proud of his fat baby daughter that the whole camp made fun of him, but then, a father was meant to spoil his daughters. Lara sat propped on his hips, riding on his belt, her chubby little hands gripping his shirt tightly. She had a smile on her face, and she gurgled happily, recognizing Aleksi and her mother. But then, she always had a smile on her face. She was the most easy-natured child that Aleksi had ever met, so sweet-tempered that everyone joked that she must not be Nadine's.

"Hello, Aleksi," said Feodor, but his gaze jumped straight to Marco. Aleksi had long since divined that Feodor did not, on the whole, like khaja of any sort, but perhaps that was only because Nadine often seemed half khaja herself. "Well met," Feodor added politely, addressing Marco.

Marco looked stunned. He stared at Feodor and then at the baby and then back at Feodor again. Finally, thank the gods, he recalled his manners. "Well met," he replied, equally polite. "I'm Marco Burckhardt."

"Yes," said Feodor, "I remember you, of course." His face softened all at once. "This is our daughter, Lara. She was born last year."

Marco took one step and then a second, and fetched up in front of the baby. He put out a hand to touch her cheek, and she batted at his hand and laughed. Feodor smiled fondly on her. Marco looked back and at that moment

Nadine lifted her head to gaze at him, and at her daughter. Their eyes met, hers and Marco's, and some message passed between them that Aleksi could not read and Feodor, tickling Lara's chin, was not even aware of. He set her down and steadied her, and she took a step, another step, a third, and more by dint of forward motion than of balance crossed the space to her mother. Nadine scooped her up in her arms. The contrast was greatest with Feodor, of course, with his fair hair and complexion, but even next to Nadine and her dark hair, Lara looked quite dusky, like twilight, with her creamy brown skin and her coarse black ringlets.

"She's hungry," said Feodor. He looked at Aleksi, and Aleksi looked at Marco, and the three men left the tent, leaving Nadine to her daughter and her maps.

Outside, Feodor excused himself and went off to mediate a dispute that had erupted between two packs of children.

"Does he know?" Marco demanded.

"Does he know what?" Aleksi asked, mystified by Marco's sudden fierce expression.

"Does David know he has a child?"

"David ben Unbutu, do you mean? How should I know? Does he have a child?"

"Aleksi, you'd have to be blind not to see that that child isn't Feodor Grekov's daughter, not with that coloring. She's David's."

The comment puzzled Aleksi. "I beg your pardon, Marco, but she *is* Feodor Grekov's daughter. Perhaps no one has told you, but there is nothing more insulting you could ever say to a man, except to insult his mother or sister, of course. I thought even the khaja knew that."

The speed with which Burckhardt backed down surprised Aleksi. "No, you're right. But—how did she—? She ought to have died."

"Who ought to have died? Oh, you mean Nadine and the child, just like Tess almost did, with the early one? It's true that she was sick for months after the birth. Everyone thought she was going to die, even Feodor. Even Bakhtiian. Tess was the only one who thought she might live. Bakhtiian sat at her bedside for twenty days straight and served her with his own hands, until he saw that she would live. He and Varia Telyegin nursed her through it. Even Dr. Hierakis says that Varia Telyegin is a great healer. But the baby was always strong. Feodor got the baby a wet nurse and then they had the worst arguments when Nadine recovered and he wanted her to nurse the child herself. I've never seen Nadine so weak and subdued. I think she only said one ill-tempered thing a day for an entire season. She's much better now."

"Of course, it's none of my business," said Marco hastily, looking uncomfortable at hearing these revelations.

"Why should Nadine have died, though?" Aleksi insisted.

Marco dragged a hand back through his hair, looking like he was reminded of something he didn't want to think about. "Because blood half of the earth and half of the heavens doesn't mix easily," he replied curtly. "May we go see Tess now?"

So they climbed the butte, winding up the steep trail as the afternoon wind tore at their shirts. At each switchback, Marco paused and stared out at the view growing beyond and beneath them. From above, the spiral along which the camp was laid out showed clearly enough, although it was hard to distinguish the pattern from the ground. The southern mountains lay in a distant blue haze, tinged with pink from the sun's long rays.

"That's where Habakar lies, that way, isn't it?" Marco looked toward the distant south.

"Yes. Mitya is still there. They're building him a new city, west of Hamrat. The Princess Melatina and her brother have lived with Mother Orzhekov for six seasons now, and she's not nearly as shy as she used to be. The princess, that is."

They climbed on. West lay the sea, hidden from their view, where the sun set, and north and east past the rolling line of hills stretched the vast golden blur of the plains.

"East," said Marco, pausing to catch his breath. Already the eastern horizon dimmed to a dusky blue, shadowed and mysterious. "East, on the Golden Road. But, Aleksi." He paused. "What about Bakhtiian's son?"

Aleksi warded off the notice of Grandmother Night
with a quick turn of his wrist. "Bakhtiian's son died."

"No. His other son. The one who's Katerina's age.
Vasha. He must be Bakhtiian's son the same way Lara
must be David's daughter."

Aleksi sighed. "Marco, you khaja always care so much
which man's seed made which child on what woman.
Vasha is Bakhtiian's son because Tess adopted him as her
son, and Bakhtiian is her husband. Just as she adopted me
as her brother."

"But—" The wind whipped at them, tearing their hair
away from their eyes, stinging and sharp and hot.

"It's true enough, I suppose, that Vasha is Bakhtiian's
son by khaja laws, too, and since his mother never married . . . well. . . ." Aleksi shrugged. "It might even be
true about David, by khaja laws, but still, Lara—"

"—is Feodor Grekov's daughter," said Marco. "I understand. I suppose it's better that David never hears
about it. It would break his heart."

"But he isn't married to Nadine—" Aleksi broke off
and trudged on after Marco, who had started on up again.
The conversation was pointless in any case. The khaja
were very strange, all except Tess, of course, and even
she— Then he grinned. Tess and her brother and the
khaja from Erthe were the strangest ones of all, because
they had come down from the heavens.

They reached the summit and the wind skirled around
them and then, as they crossed the flat ground scoured
clean by years upon years of Father Wind's rough touch,
died altogether. A single tent stood on the plateau, staked
down. The gold banner at its height hung limply, stirred
as the wind fluttered the cloth, and stilled again. Clouds
shone pale in the sky above, touched orange in the west
where they feathered the horizon.

Ilyakoria Bakhtiian knelt on the ground some twenty
paces in front of the tent. His head was bent. Before him,
in a semicircle, sat the ten etsanas and the ten dyans—
well, only nine since Venedikt Grekov was still away on
his expedition to Vidiya—listening intently. It was so
quiet, with the sun's rays bathing the plateau in a rich
golden light, that even from twenty paces away, where

they halted, they could hear Bakhtiian's voice as he spoke.

". . . and I said to Grandmother Night, 'I will give to you that which I most love if you will make me dyan of all the tribes.' And I sealed the bargain with the blood of a hawk."

Aleksi noticed, at once, that Bakhtiian wore no saber. He had disarmed himself. His horse-tail staff lay over the knees of Mother Sakhalin, and his own aunt had laid his saber on the pillow on which the dyan of her tribe—which was him, of course—would otherwise be seated. From the tent, he heard a muffled, steady drumbeat, and he heard Svetlana singing, and then laughter. Steam boiled up from two great copper pots set over a fire to one side of the tent. Vasha, who was getting all gangly and overgrown these days, sat in mute attendance on the fire.

"Afterward," Bakhtiian continued into the silence, not looking at the women and men who in their turn watched him with unnervingly intent gazes, "I thought that she had cheated me, but then I realized that she had held to her end of the bargain. Vasil was not the person whom I most loved. I was the one who tried to cheat Grandmother Night. I paid dearly enough for my presumption."

There they sat, in silence, Sakhalin, Arkhanov, Suvorin, Velinya, Raevsky, Vershinin, Grekov, Fedoseyev, and last, Veselov and Orzhekov. Arina Veselov sat on a litter, since she had never regained enough strength to be able to walk very well. Her odd cousin sat next to her. Scars had obliterated the beauty of Vera's face; her riders called her a hard dyan but a fair one, and she was known to be ruthless and aloof. Yaroslav Sakhalin had ridden two thousand miles in twenty days to come here, and the others had come long distances as well. Irena Orzhekov regarded her nephew gravely. Alone of all of them, she did not look particularly surprised by his confession.

"And what," asked Mother Sakhalin, "did you pay, Ilyakoria Bakhtiian?"

He lifted his head to look directly at her. "These lives. The life of my mother, Alyona Orzhekov. The life of my father, Petre Sokolov. The life of my sister Natalia and of her son. Of my cousin Yurinya. Of the Prince of Jeds, Charles Soerensen, my wife's brother. The life of my son."

The wind picked up again. The gold banner stirred and fluttered and spread, like a last ray of the sun, out against the vast arch of the sky. "The lives of those who followed me, and died, not knowing of the bargain I had made and then hidden." He bent his head and ran his fingers up the embroidery on his shirt. His aunt watched him, her face stern. He looked up again, for the final time. "The life of the boy I once was, Ilyakoria Orzhekov."

Katerina ducked out of the tent and ran over to the pots. She dipped a kettle into water, whispered something to Vasha, glanced toward the assembly, and then hurried back inside. Very clearly, in the silence, they all heard a woman swear forcefully and fluidly. Arina Veselov hid her mouth behind a hand. Every gaze flashed toward the tent and then away. Every one but Bakhtiian's. His gaze did not stray from Mother Sakhalin's face.

"Two more lives hang in the balance, Bakhtiian," she said quietly. "As the gods judge you today, so will our judgment be."

Aleksi shuddered. He had seen how harsh the gods' judgment could be. It wasn't fair that their judgment should be passed through Tess. And yet, Aleksi trusted in Cara Hierakis maybe even more than in the gods.

Marco crouched and settled in for a long wait, and Aleksi crouched beside him. He liked Burckhardt, really. He was an easy companion. He knew when to be silent and when to speak, when to act and when to be patient.

So they waited. The sun set and its light died and gave birth to a darkness patched with stars. Yaroslav Sakhalin and Mikhail Suvorin rose and lit torches and posted them on lances thrust into the ground at either end of the semi-circle. The wind picked up and battered at the sides of the tent. The drum beat. Inside the tent, Svetlana sang, and Aleksi closed his eyes and listened to her. She had a pleasant voice, a little thin, but it was strong and steady. Of course, compared to Raysia Grekov ... but Svetlana was not Raysia Grekov; she wasn't a Singer. She was a simple, hard-working, practical woman. She was his wife.

The thought of that, of having a sister and a wife and her siblings and a daughter and a little one on the way, warmed him through to the core of his heart.

Sakhalin and Suvorin replaced the torches with new ones. The stars wheeled around the sky, and the clouds chased away into the north to leave the black span above brilliant with light.

They waited, and out of the darkness and the silence, they heard a baby's sudden strong cry.

Bakhtiian jumped to his feet, and spun, and stopped in his tracks.

The baby cried again, and then cut off.

Silence.

Bakhtiian was shaking so hard that Aleksi could see it, even with the night and the distance between them. He was afraid. Aleksi rose then, and Marco with him, and all of them rose, the etsanas and the dyans. Vera Veselov slipped a strong arm around her cousin Arina and helped her to her feet, and Irena Orzhekov steadied Arina on her other side, and between them, Arina managed to stay upright. Aleksi felt how desperate they all were—they wanted the gods to judge in Bakhtiian's favor not just for his sake, but for the sake of the jaran.

Svetlana threw the entrance flap aside, and Katerina and Galina emerged, each girl bearing a torch. Blood streaked Galina's hands, and she grinned hugely. Sonia ducked out behind them. She held a bundle in her arms, and it hiccuped a cry as the cold air hit its face and then it began to squall.

Sonia laughed at something someone said behind her. She marched over and deposited the screaming bundle into Bakhtiian's arms. At once, the child ceased crying. Ilya stared down at it. Alert but calm now, it stared up at him.

"Tess says that her name is Natalia," said Sonia. She crossed to kiss her mother, Irena Orzhekov, and then turned and hurried back inside the tent.

"Natalia," whispered Bakhtiian. He looked stunned.

Svetlana drew aside the entrance curtains again, and Sonia and Dr. Hierakis helped Tess out of the tent. Tess moved gingerly, leaning heavily on the two women, but she smiled. Aleksi took in a breath, able to breathe again. Marco heaved his breath out abruptly in a relieved sigh.

Bakhtiian's expression blossomed into a smile that even darkness could not dim. He went to greet his wife. He kissed her on either cheek, and then he turned and regarded his audience. Aleksi had never seen him look more triumphant.

Mother Sakhalin walked over to him and offered him the horse-tail staff. "It appears, Bakhtiian," she said, "that the gods have forgiven you. Far be it from me to judge otherwise."

But, of course, with the baby in his arms—and a big, thriving child she appeared to be, too—he could not take the staff.

"Vasha," he said, and immediately the boy leapt up and ran over to him. "Hold the staff for me, if you please."

Mother Sakhalin hesitated for one instant. Then she gave Vassily Kireyevsky the horse-tail staff.

The others came forward, one by one, and greeted the new child with a blessing and Tess with a kiss on either cheek. Last, Irena Orzhekov stopped before her nephew and held up his saber.

"This is yours, I believe."

"Here," said Tess, the first time she had spoken at all. "I'll belt it on him." Sonia still supported her, but Tess took the saber from Mother Orzhekov's hands and secured it with her own hands onto her husband's belt. Irena Orzhekov embraced her, and then Tess stepped back and turned to the doctor. She looked utterly exhausted, but pleased. "I'm going to go lie down now," she announced.

And that was that. The first pale line of light, heralding dawn, limned the eastern horizon.

Smiling besottedly down at his daughter, Bakhtiian followed Tess inside. Sonia and the doctor went in behind him. Vasha placed the horse-tail staff reverently in its wooden holder, under the awning, and then Katya pushed him, and he shoved her back, and Galina huffed and rolled her eyes and they all laughed and raced away toward the trail.

"Beat you there."

"No, I will."

"I'll be first!"

The two youngest dyans took either end of Arina Veselov's litter and carried her away. Her cousin followed, and the other etsanas and dyans, with Mother Sakhalin steadying herself on her nephew's arm. The morning sun made palest parchment of the old woman's skin, and Aleksi saw clearly how very old she was, and how frail. The change had come suddenly on her, after her grandson had left.

Sonia emerged from the tent. "Marco! It *is* you! I'm so very pleased to see you. Come in. Come in."

But once inside the tent, which smelled of blood and other musky things, Aleksi had only the chance to kiss Tess on either cheek before he had to move aside so that Marco could kneel beside her.

"Marco! You arrived safely. Did you bring the maps?"

"Yes. I—"

"Oh, can't it wait until tomorrow? I really—"

He laughed. "Of course, Tess. I was just about to suggest that myself. We'll go."

They went, he and Aleksi. Aleksi paused by the entrance to look back. All the curtains within had been thrown back, making one huge chamber of the whole. Tess reclined on a couch of pillows and Bakhtiian sat up against her, one arm over her shoulders and one cradling their baby. He looked, Aleksi decided, just as stupidly ecstatic as Feodor had when he had first held Lara.

Svetlana met him outside, her belly swollen under her skirts. After he introduced her to Marco, she smiled and kissed Aleksi on the cheek. "Sonia and I are going to stay up here with the doctor. You don't mind, do you?"

He leaned his head against her hair and just breathed it in, for a moment. She always smelled of sweet things, of grass and flowers and fresh herbs and babies. "I'll see things are made ready down in camp," he said, "and send some men up with a litter for Tess."

She smiled at him and let him go.

They went down. Dawn rose in the east, and light spread out over the lands.

In the camp, a great celebration was being prepared for

the birth of the child. Aleksi left Marco with Nadine, found Galina already preparing a childbed tent for Tess, and directed four riders with a litter up to the height. Then he wandered, just wandered around the camp, observing, as he liked to do. He felt deeply content.

In the Grekov camp, Raysia Grekov was directing a rehearsal of her new telling of the "Daughter of the Sun." She had picked out musicians, each of them with a good voice, and given them tabards to wear as costumes, and built out of the old tale as told by one Singer over ten nights a new tale sung by seven singers in a single afternoon. She herself sang the Daughter's role, and Aleksi could not help but stay to watch.

The singers did not move, as they walked and sang, with the fluidity of the actors, but perhaps Raysia did not want to create the same kind of story as the actors had. Here the song itself was preeminent, supported by slow, sweeping gestures and the long frozen poses taken by the singers. The plain, bold colors and simple lines of the tabards gave each singer a distinctive look. Mother Sun wore the yellow-orange of fire. Her daughter wore the blue of the heavens, and the dyan Yuri Sakhalin wore red, which is the strength of earth and blood. One demon wore black and the other wore white. The woman who sang the sisters wore green, and the man who sang the riders of Sakhalin's jahar wore the pale gold of grass.

Raysia had used her own telling of the tale and wound it in on itself, and Aleksi found himself rooted to the spot and unable to move, listening to it, seeing it. Mother Sun exiled her daughter to the earth, and sent with her ten sisters to be her companions. These ten sisters bore the tribes of the jaran, and one day, the first dyan of the tribes fell in love with the Daughter of the Sun. She refused him, as surely any heaven-born creature must. He led his jahar into battle, and fell to a grievous blow.

Wounded unto death, he begged her for healing. Healing him, she loved him, and together they made a child. And she gave him a saber—the sword of heaven—because of which he could from then on never lose a battle.

Just as Tess and her brother had given Ilya a sword, which not even he knew the strength of.

Yuri Sakhalin never lost a battle after that, or at least, that is how the Singers sang the tale. No battle but the one every mortal being lost—that against Grandmother Night.

Aleksi strolled back to his tent, feeling thoughtful, feeling . . . curious. He knew the art of moving without being seen; it had saved his life more than once, when he was an orphan. He slipped unnoticed into Dr. Hierakis's tent, even keeping the bells from ringing, and he stood in front of her table and spoke the words he had memorized from hearing Tess say them: "Run League worlds."

Rhui he now recognized. He could recognize the broad pale expanse that marked the plains and the tiny tiny bay far to the south that marked the city of Jeds. Then the other worlds appeared, strange spheres with yet stranger names: Three Rings. Something unpronounceable. Cassie. Hydra. Eridanaia. Tau Ceti Tierce. Sirin Five. Ophiuchi-Sei. And last, *her* planet, the only one as heart-wrenchingly beautiful as Rhui, the only other one that wore as brilliant a coat of blue, symbolizing the heavens: Earth.

Aleksi sank down into a chair and watched as the program ran on, showing paler worlds and fiercer stars, showing webs of light dangling against a black void and many-eyed globes of polished metal and ships like blunt arrows docked at piers built of sparkling gossamer threads. He watched as thousands upon thousands of towers rose up from a bleak plain and became invested with lights as numerous as the stars, or as the fires of the jaran army.

No one disturbed him, hidden here in the doctor's private chambers. Outside, the celebration had already begun. Inside, in the quiet of the tent, Aleksi discovered the universe.

Kate Elliott

The Novels of the Jaran:

☐ **JARAN: Book 1**   UE2513—$4.99

Here is the poignant and powerful story of a young woman's coming of age on an alien world, a woman who is both player and pawn in an interstellar game of intrigue and politics, where the prize to be gained may be freedom for humankind from long-standing domination by their alien conquerors.

☐ **AN EARTHLY CROWN: Book 2**   UE2546—$5.99

On a low-tech planet, Ilya, a charismatic warlord, is leading the nomadic jaran tribes on a campaign of conquest, while his wife Tess—an Earth woman of whose true origins Ilya is unaware—is caught up in a deadly game of interstellar politics.

☐ **HIS CONQUERING SWORD: Book 3**   UE2551—$5.99

Even as Jaran warlord Ilya continues the conquest of his world, he faces a far more powerful power struggle with his wife's brother, Duke Charles, leader of the underground human rebellion against an interstellar alien empire.
